CATRIONA McPHERSON was born near Edinburgh in 1965 and educated at Edinburgh University. Formerly a linguistics lecturer, now a full-time writer, she is married to a scientist and lives on a farm in a beautiful valley in Galloway. Find out more about Catriona and the series on dandygilver.co.uk.

Praise for Catriona McPherson and
After the Armistice Ball

'McPherson's refreshing debut introduces the captivating Dandy Gilver . . . memorable supporting characters plus vivid descriptions enhance a compelling mystery.'
Publishers Weekly

'In this first novel from McPherson the period setting is spot on . . . [and] in Gilver we have a winning character who will hopefully find many more crimes to solve.'
Good Book Guide

'*After the Armistice Ball* superbly evokes the feel of the 1920s . . . I look forward to [the] next adventure.'
Euro Crime

'Catriona McPherson . . . has given us a novel that even Dorothy L. Sayers would have been pleased with . . . This looks set to be a series that will really take off.'
Crime Squad.com

Also by Catriona McPherson

After the Armistice Ball

THE BURRY MAN'S DAY

Catriona McPherson

ROBINSON
London

CARROLL & GRAF PUBLISHERS
New York

Constable & Robinson Ltd
3 The Lanchesters
162 Fulham Palace Road
London W6 9ER
www.constablerobinson.com

First published in the UK by Constable,
an imprint of Constable & Robinson Ltd 2006

This paperback edition published by Robinson,
an imprint of Constable & Robinson Ltd 2007

First US edition published by Carroll & Graf Publishers 2006,
this paperback edition, 2007

Carroll & Graf Publishers
An Imprint of Avalon Publishing Group, Inc.
245 W. 17th Street, 11th Floor
New York, NY 10011-5300
www.carrollandgraf.com

AVALON
publishing group incorporated

A copy of the British Library Cataloguing in Publication
Data is available from the British Library.

ISBN: 978-1-84529-592-9 (pbk)
ISBN: 978-1-84529-301-7 (hbk)

US ISBN-13: 978-0-78672-019-4
US ISBN-10: 0-7867-2019-0

Printed and bound in the EU

1 3 5 7 9 10 8 6 4 2

For Neil

with all my love

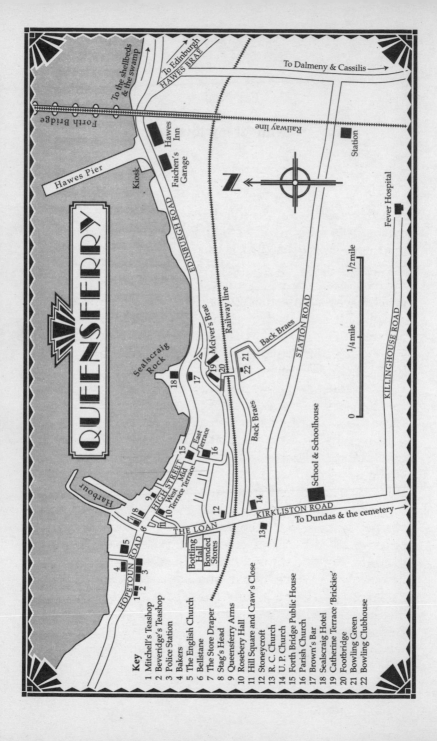

QUEENSFERRY

Key

1 Mitchell's Teashop
2 Beveridge's Teashop
3 Police Station
4 Bakers
5 The English Church
6 Bellstane
7 The Store Draper
8 Stag's Head
9 Queensferry Arms
10 Rosebery Hall
11 Hill Square and Craw's Close
12 Stoneycroft
13 R. C. Church
14 U. P. Church
15 Forth Bridge Public House
16 Parish Church
17 Brown's Bar
18 Sealscraig Hotel
19 Catherine Terrace 'Brickies'
20 Footbridge
21 Bowling Green
22 Bowling Clubhouse

To the shellbeds & the swamp

To Edinburgh

HAWES BRAE

To Dalmeny & Cassilis →

Forth Bridge

Railway line

Hawes Inn

Faichen's Garage

Station

Hawes Pier

Kiosk

EDINBURGH ROAD

Fever Hospital

Z ←

Sealscraig Rock

McIver's Brae

Railway line

Back Braes

STATION ROAD

KILLINGHOUSE ROAD

½ mile

¼ mile

0

Back Braes

Harbour

HIGH STREET

East Terrace

West Midd

Terrace Terrace

School & Schoolhouse

HOPETOUN ROAD

THE LOAN

Bottling Hall

Bonded Stores

KIRKLISTON ROAD

To Dundas & the cemetery →

Chapter One

Far above us a train hurtled past and we raised our eyes to it in longing. If we had any sense we would be up there, sitting back in a carriage, instead of down here with everything clenched as the *Bonnie Dundee* climbed each crest and smacked down again on her plucky way across the Forth. The woman beside me sucked a breath in through her bottom teeth and shut her mouth firmly as we rose on a particularly lusty swell to tremble at its peak for a moment before walloping into the hollow beyond.

With a deep breath of my own, I tried to forget about the train, now huffing and hissing its way into the station, and concentrate instead on the bridge, since here we were toiling along at its base like Lilliputians on Gulliver's beach with a better than usual chance to study it.

It is often called beautiful and it was certainly impressive from this angle but I have never cared for crochet-work and the colour is unspeakable, like the strips of dried liver one gives to dogs. Besides, I bear it grudges. For one thing, I could just remember being at its opening, four years old, and being smacked on the backs of my legs by Nanny Palmer for saying 'Ugh' in a loud voice when I saw it for the first time. Well, what colour would I have painted it, she had demanded when I – quite reasonably I thought – burst into tears.

Primrose yellow, I had said, with touches of pink, and Nanny had laughed.

I could see now, more than thirty years later, that the touches of pink were not practical but I held to my primrose yellow – because really it had to be soul-destroying to the men who spent their lives painting the thing that the paint was the colour of rust.

In addition to that long-ago slap on the legs, however, I resent it because it would not be *too* far a reach of fancy to say that the Forth Bridge had sealed my fate. I had been present at its opening, as I say, on my way to visit my grandparents who had taken a house in the Highlands for the summer but after that I had not given it a thought until, years later, staying at a house party in Derbyshire during my coming out season, I had been unable to sleep. This was not, as one might expect, because of too much Champagne and Romance but rather out of sheer boredom. (And to anyone who has never been too bored to sleep I can only say it is as unpleasant as any other kind of insomnia and not helped by being quite ridiculous.) Eventually, having planned my outfits for the following day – boring tweed for golf, boring cream voile for tea, only slightly less boring coral velvet and pearls for dinner – I gave in and turned up the gas. On my bedside table the selection of reading matter comprised Volume Two of a three-volume Victorian romance with those tissue-thin pages like a prayer book and print far too small to read at two in the morning, something initially enticing with a new and brightly coloured jacket which turned out to be a history of Nottingham and, finally, *The Flower of Scotland: Great Engineering Feats of the Century.* (I see now that the pitifulness of such a library at the bedside of a debutante doing her Season was not accidental. It was intended to send a gentle little message about getting married as quickly as possible or ending up an embittered spinster with a knowledge of Nottingham far beyond what could ever be needed.)

Anyway, thinking that at least there would be pictures I picked up the last of these, turned to the chapter on the building of the Forth Bridge for nostalgia's sake – Nanny Palmer had recently died and I missed her horribly – and read myself to sleep.

The very next evening, in my coral velvet and pearls and looking, I imagine, all the more fetching for the violet shadows with which my restless night had left me, I found myself at dinner sitting beside one of those fearfully reserved Scotchmen one tended to meet and upon asking him the usual bright questions I found that he was from Perthshire. My eyes must have blanked for he went on to explain that Perthshire was 'just across the Forth from Edinburgh'. Well! One can only assume that reading the stuff while dropping off engraved it upon my brain like the grooves on a gramophone record, because out it all poured: weights of girders, numbers of labourers, depth of foundations . . . the lot.

So I can see why this dour individual, this stern devotee of solid building and proper maintenance, this Hugh Gilver as he turned out to be, must have thought he had just met the first serious-minded woman of his life. Add to this the twinkling and simpering which had been pounded into us at finishing school until it was second nature and one can almost forgive his assuming that I had taken to him as much as he to me. Thus, you see, I can blame the Forth Bridge almost entirely for my finding myself now, *Mrs* Hugh Gilver, listener to plans of drain improvements, helpmeet in projects of pond construction, and mother to two little chips off the same dour Scottish block.

That was all a long way under the bridge now, if

9

I may be pardoned the pun, as were we: I heard a new grinding note in the ferryboat's engine and recollected myself just in time to be drenched in the backwash as the *Bonnie Dundee* drew into the pier. Shaking off the worst from my hat and hair – why cannot people shake themselves as efficiently as dogs? – I stepped up into my motor car and slammed the door. This was why I was on the ferry in the first place, this gleaming little Morris Cowley of mine, just six months old and still so much my pride and joy that I could not bear to leave it behind, and as I waited for the foot passengers to blunder off towards restorative cups of tea at the Hawes Inn, I breathed hard on the glass of the dials and rubbed them with my glove. Eventually, one of the ferrymen came to crank the starter and I roared away straight off the landing planks and up the Hawes Brae to the station where my maid, come on the train with my luggage, would be waiting.

It had hardly seemed like summer on our choppy crossing but now under the beech trees lining the road it was as warm and as richly, rankly green as August could be and Grant, sitting on my dressing case under the station canopy at the top of the ramp, clutching a pair of hatboxes, looked rather creased and cross in the heat, like a pink-faced toddler after an unsatisfactory nap. I wheeled around in the parking yard and drove backwards up the slope towards her – the ramp is terrifically steep – whereupon she stepped into the passenger side and slammed the door leaving the porter and me to deal with the small bags and arrange the delivery of the larger items in the dog-cart.

Even Grant at her most truculent, however, could not do much to dent my mood. I was on my way to visit Frederica de Cassilis, who as Frederica Pettit twenty years before had been my dearest friend in the world after Daisy; had in fact been Daisy's and my

10

chief interest whilst at finishing school in Paris – a cross between a pet and a court jester, whom we enjoyed tremendously while always believing we might tame her in the end.

After school I had thought Frederica to be lost for ever since she had contracted a dazzling marriage and disappeared into a stratum of New York society where I could not hope to follow her, but then finding herself widowed at a young age she had extricated herself from her New York connections most adroitly, remarried within a year and come with her new husband to South Queensferry, on the banks of the Forth. Here Daisy and I were now converging upon her for a visit which promised to be the most fun we had shared since we slipped our chaperone in the Louvre and went off in search of classical statuary to complete our education.

Cassilis, where Frederica and the new husband were ensconced, is one of four estates with various claims to grandeur gathered around the little Burgh of South Queensferry. Hopetoun away to the west is indisputably the most splendid – a Georgian mansion in which all three Adamses had a hand, and the seat of a marquis to boot. But then Dalmeny House squaring up to Hopetoun from the east, although it is Tudor Gothic and shelters mere earls, has a prime minister to its name, a castle in its grounds and a very pretty estate village. Dundas Castle to the south has been there since the Conqueror landed and is built on lands gifted by King David himself, all of which counts for a lot. Besides, it would have housed earls of its own had one of the Jameses not most inconsiderately died before sealing the warrant. On the other hand there is a fearful Victorian façade and the family who lives there now, whilst being perfectly respectable, are a

11

mere Lord and Lady and no connection to the ancient Dundases at all.

When set against all of this, Cassilis was very small beer indeed, or so Frederica's letter led Daisy and me to believe; neither of us knew the place. To be sure her Mr de Cassilis was a Mr de Cassilis of Cassilis which is always nice – I rather like being Mrs Gilver of Gilverton if it comes to that, although I would not call myself a snob in most ways – but he was a *Mr* de Cassilis, and a cousin come back to the old place from across the Atlantic what is more, and although Frederica reported that Cassilis Castle was a real castle and not just a house with a silly name and small windows, the estate itself she said was tiny. We had been amused and puzzled, then, to learn that shortly after arriving Frederica had found herself suddenly promoted above all her neighbours into the post of Lady Bountiful for the imminent celebration of the Ferry Fair. How this could have happened in a neighbourhood so heaving with more suitable females was beyond Daisy and me. (The Rosebery noses had to be particularly out of joint, for the family had only just built a splendid new town hall for the village and could reasonably have expected a lifetime of gratitude.) We could only surmise that no one on the committee had got to know Frederica very well yet.

I am far from being an Angel in the Home myself and am capable of mucking things up in ways that most adults of normal intelligence find incomprehensible, but Frederica made me look like an ambassador, his wife and his entire staff of diplomats rolled into one. To take just one example: at her first big party in New York where a great many of her guests were members of her husband's family, that is to say Felsteins, and most of the others were friends of theirs – various Levys, Cohens and the like – Frederica had taken it upon herself to serve a roast suckling pig as the centrepiece of the dinner. One would have come a lot further than Perth to Queensferry, then, to see what she would make of presiding over the Ferry Fair. However, one thing that must be said of Frederica is that she knows her limitations and when she invited us it was made very clear that we were there to help, not just to watch and giggle. There is a phrase in the Army, I believe – to be booted upstairs – meaning to be promoted far enough beyond one's competence to prevent one doing any actual damage and Frederica, by drafting in Daisy and me, had in effect booted herself upstairs. We were to make the speeches, fire the starting pistols and judge the competitions, leaving her to smile and look decorative, which task – unless the years had been very unkind to her – she would have no trouble carrying off at all.

Daisy and I converged indeed, almost drove into one another at the Cassilis gate lodge in fact, and she hopped out of her motor car and into mine to trundle up the drive together.

'Hello, darling,' she cooed. 'Hello, Grant. Heavenly shade of lilac, Dandy.' I blinked. My frock was white.

'The stockings, I mean,' Daisy went on.

'Ah, well, yes. Thank you,' I said. The stockings were white too, but white over sunburn *is* a peculiar colour; I had spent the previous day with the children to stop them whining about being left behind now and had lain a little too long on the riverbank in my bathing dress.

We bumped over a humpbacked bridge spanning a little burn, rounded a copse and then Cassilis Castle lay before us.

'Good God,' said Daisy. 'It's a castle. I mean, it's a *castle*.'

I knew exactly what she was getting at. Frederica

had told us it was a castle, and so we should have been surprised to see Tudor beams and horsehair plaster, but even so. What faced us now was a tower six, possibly seven, storeys high and about fifty feet square, built out of huge craggy lumps of grey stone. It sat plonked on top of a steep, grassy hill, which was utterly unadorned by trees or even the shrubs and flowers one might look for – positioned, that is, the way that castles used to be when their occupants needed a good view of approaching marauders and a clear run to pour their boiling pitch down. There was no obvious door, nor any windows on this side at least, just arrow slits and what looked suspiciously like the outlets for slop channels. We might have concluded then that this was an earlier version, kept as a garden ornament, and that the real Cassilis Castle lay somewhere beyond, but as we drew nearer the signs were against it: there was bright new timber on the roof behind the crenellations and new glass winked in the arrow slits and pistol crosses. Furthermore, on top of the roof I could see coloured cloth billowing half-heartedly in the warm air and a chance puff of stronger wind showed me just for a second a lion rampant, a Union Jack and a Stars and Stripes. No doubt about it, then, we had arrived.

I rounded the bottom of the hill and saw that on this side a track just wide enough for the motor car zigzagged up to the castle walls. Cheeringly, there were a few windows round here as well and a door, massive and heavily studded with black iron rivets, through which Frederica now burst to stand hopping up and down and waving both hands like a jazz dancer as we approached. Daisy and I stepped down, although Grant remained in her seat with her mouth hanging open.

Frederica beamed and hunched her shoulders at us

14

in the way she always did when planning some devilment or other and immediately, as though a spell had been cast, the years fell away.

'Buttercup!' Daisy and I shrieked in chorus and threw our arms around her.

'No!' Frederica shrieked back. 'Absolutely not. If Cad hears you he will never call me Freddy again. Besides, it's *much* too accurate these days, don't you think?' She patted her hips and shook her curls and, granted, both hips and curls were very buttery indeed and disconcerting when attached to the face and voice of the thin, brown-haired, most unbuttercuplike Buttercup of my memory.

'Yes, what about your hair?' said Daisy. 'A touch of the Oscar Wildes, was it?'

Buttercup chortled. One could always say anything to her and never cause offence.

'No, my darling. Not "gold from grief", I've had it this colour for years. It's called April Sunrise – isn't that killing? But thank the Lord it was gold already when the mourning came along, otherwise – shriek! Edith Sitwell. I've brought cases of it with me, if you're interested.'

She cast piercing looks at my dark head and craned to see under Daisy's hat but made no actual offer, saying only: 'Hmm. We'll talk later.' Daisy and I grimaced at each other.

'Now, come in and see the castle,' said Buttercup. 'You won't believe it.'

'I don't already,' said Daisy, but Buttercup had turned away and did not hear her.

Inside the massive door, a narrow stone passageway with a rounded ceiling and an uneven floor led to the corner of the tower and a spiral staircase. Up this we trooped, with Buttercup urging us to caution saying

15

that one got used to the bevelled steps in the end but it took a day or two.

'That's the Great Hall,' she said as we reached the next level, 'but look here first.' We stopped in the doorway to the Hall and peered down at the floor of the passage, finding under our feet an iron grille which showed us to be standing just above the front door.

'It's a murder hole,' said Buttercup. 'You hide up here with your bow and arrow and if the guests get past the doorman but they still look unappealing – peeyong! Dead.'

'Handy,' I said and walked into the Great Hall.

Great was the word. I could have driven my motor car into either of the two fireplaces and I was sure that two were needed since the room seemed so huge I could hardly believe the outside of the tower contained it. Perhaps though it was just the cold, our echoing footsteps and the fact that it was almost totally empty that made it appear so cavernous. For decoration there was only a display of swords laid out in a complicated pattern like a sunburst on one end wall and the furniture consisted of the kind of table, thirty feet long or so, in rough-hewn wood polished only by the greasy hands of centuries, that one imagines Henry VIII dining at and then sliding underneath. I wondered just how far Buttercup might be taking all of this, and how I should be able to face Grant after gnawing turkey legs and heaving flagons on to my shoulders in my new beaded chiffon.

'The chairs aren't here yet,' said Buttercup, needlessly. 'Nor the tapestries to help with the draughts. And then upstairs again . . .' She plunged off towards the spiral staircase and we followed.

Upstairs again was a little better. A drawing room and a library, each with a window, no swords and some furniture, although still with stone floors and

gargantuan fireplaces, and by the time we went up yet
further to the bedrooms it was beginning to look
almost cosy, at least one could imagine that a caveman
would think it was the Ritz and I had given up planning to offer my excuses and leave.

'There are only six bedrooms,' said Buttercup, 'but
look how clever we've been. The walls are so thick and
there are these little chambers simply all over the place,
sleeping chambers I think, or private closets or whatever, but . . .' She threw open a door in what was to be
my bedroom to reveal a dressing room just big enough
for a single bed and a tiny wardrobe. An arrow slit
above the bed gave a wink of light. Just for a moment
I wished Hugh were there so I could see his face.

'And this one,' said Buttercup, springing over to the
far side of the room and flinging open another door, 'is
the dearest little bathroom.' One could only imagine
what an architectural historian would make of the
gleaming chrome pipes and eau-de-nil bath shaped
like a shell bolted on to the stone walls, but my spirits
lifted no end. Of course Buttercup could not have spent
fifteen years with American plumbing and then come
back to dry closets and stone chutes to the garden.
Perhaps I would be all right after all.

'There's just one last thing I have to show you,' said
Buttercup. 'All the way to the bottom now.' She sped
off back down the staircase and Daisy and I descended
gingerly after her, clutching the iron rail and feeling the
way with our stockinged toes, our shoes in our hands.

'The kitchen!' Buttercup announced, entering a room
right opposite the front door. It was a vaulted cavern as
big as the hall above and fifteen feet high, with not a
single window, not even an arrow slit, and a floor criss-
crossed with channels in the stone. At the far end a
blue and white enamel stove lit by electric lamps stood
against the wall beside an ancient bread oven big

enough for all three of us to have sat in. Opposite were a pair of gleaming white china sinks and at one of these a cook was working with her back to us, her shoulders eloquent with suppressed fury.

'Don't mind us, Mrs Murdoch,' sang Buttercup, waving us over to the corner. 'Now, what about this?' We were looking through another grille in the floor to a stone-walled chamber, perfectly round and so deep we could barely make out the bottom.

'An oubliette!' Buttercup cried, eyes dancing. 'Well, a prison pit, anyway. Can you imagine anything more romantic! Just think. They would throw the poor unfortunates down there and leave them to die. And the smells of the kitchen would waft down through the grille and torture them while they starved. Only we can't think what to do with it, can we, Mrs Murdoch?'

The cook turned and gave her A Look but said nothing.

'We had thought it would make a larder,' Buttercup went on, 'but we'd have to put in a ladder and Mrs Murdoch doesn't fancy it. And anyway, there are so many other wall chambers for larders and suchlike we hardly need it.'

'Well, no,' I said. 'And do you really think you'd want to keep your food there, darling? I mean, if people died in it.'

Mrs Murdoch turned on her way from the sink to the stove and keened towards me yearningly, but Buttercup only laughed.

'Oh, we don't worry about all that, Dandy darling. It was years ago. They'd be dead now, anyway.'

I suppose this made some kind of sense.

'So I think we'll just bash through from downstairs and use it as a cupboard,' Buttercup said, sounding regretful.

'Downstairs?' said Daisy.

'The dungeons,' said Buttercup. Then: 'Damn! The basement, I mean. We haven't quite given up on the idea of persuading the servants to take up residence down there, but Cad reckons that calling it the dungeons doesn't help.'

Mrs Murdoch threw a tray of scones into the stove and slammed the door with a clang.

'Where are they now, then?' said Daisy through a mouthful of warm scone, half an hour later. 'The servants, I mean.'

'They're in the old house,' said Buttercup. 'I mean the new house. The house, you know. Where we were until the castle was ready.'

'There's a house?' Daisy asked, piningly, and I had to bite my cheeks not to giggle, but Buttercup did not see me through the gloom.

'Oh yes,' said Buttercup. 'A boring Georgian square. The de Cassilis family hadn't lived in the castle for simply aeons until Cad came back. Aren't people dull? And the servants are all still there. I keep telling them how much easier it would be for them to sleep here in the dun– . . . basement. We've fitted it up beautifully, you've no idea. But if they're silly enough to want to tramp half a mile through the park every night and morning good luck to them. They'll come around, I rather think, in the winter.'

'But what makes you imagine they'll stay?' I said. 'Servants these days just don't stay unless you treat them like the gods of Egypt.'

'Oh, I know,' said Buttercup. 'We're on the second lot of maids already. Third, maybe. And I'm in a super-inflationary wages war with Mrs Murdoch. She's up to three hundred at the last count.'

19

'Well, she's worth it,' said Daisy. 'These scones are divine. So I'd shut up about the larder if I were you.'

Buttercup chuckled, then cocked an ear. 'Oh goody,' she said. 'Here's Cad. Now drink him in and tell me what you think later.'

Cadwallader de Cassilis appeared in the doorway and strolled towards us. At once I had the fanciful notion that here was why Buttercup seemed not to notice the Stygian gloom of the castle, for he exuded light. From the top of his head, where his hair was polished and golden – real gold too, I rather thought, not April Sunrise – to the tips of his toes, in appalling patent co-respondent brogues, he shone. Part of it was the spanking new cricket jersey and cream bags – billowing acres of these – but some of it was the bursting, pulsing good health of his eyes and cheeks and teeth, the sheer Americanness of him altogether. Although one knew he was Scottish by ancestry, at least two generations' worth of buffalo steaks, corncobs and milk must have gone to produce what stood before us now.

'Sweetheart,' he cried, pronouncing it swee-durrrt. 'You should have called me. I was only up on the roof with Dudgeon. Welcome to Cassilis, girls. What do you think of the pile?' He was fearfully American, every word sounding as though he were trying to speak whilst gurgling treacle, but so affable that I took to him at once.

He threw himself into a chair and rubbed one of its arms with his jersey sleeve. 'What do you think of the library? Have we got it off?'

'Oh, Cad,' said Buttercup, blushing a little but beaming too. 'You can't say it like that, darling, really.'

Thank goodness for her intervention. The library, with its buttoned leather, portraits and brass reading-lamps, looked like the perfect stage-set of a library, just as Cadwallader's jersey and bags looked like the perfect costume for the owner of it, but one could hardly tell him.

'It's perfect,' said Daisy, and I caught her eye and smiled.

'It's good of you girls to come over and help Freddy out,' said Cadwallader, taking his teacup from Buttercup and rewarding her with a beaming smile of his own. 'Has she filled you in on the run-down?'

'Not a word,' I said. 'What are our duties, But– . . . darling? What exactly does this Ferry Fair of yours entail?'

'Oh, this and that,' said Buttercup. 'The usual, I expect. Don't you have fêtes in Perthshire, Dandy?' I shook my head. 'Odd,' Buttercup went on. 'I remember your mother fagging away at it no end that summer I stayed with you after Paris. D'you remember? I wanted to tell fortunes and she wouldn't let me, so I put red and white mushrooms in the tea-tent jam.'

'Buttercup!' said Daisy. Cad frowned in understandable puzzlement at this remark.

'Oh, don't worry,' said Buttercup. 'Boring old Dandy made me tell and I got sent home in disgrace. But I must say I thought you two would be old hands at it by now. What about you, Daisy?'

Daisy shook her head.

'The Scots don't go in much for fêtes,' she said. 'It's one of the things that makes being married to a Scotchman bearable. No Punch and Judy to speak of either, thank God. And don't take offence, Cadwallader, we don't count you.'

'You don't *count* me? As a Scotchman, you mean?'

'Well, no,' I said. 'I mean, where will you be on Saturday, for instance?'

21

'At the Ferry Fair,' said Cad. 'Saturday is the day of revelry itself.'

'Quite,' I said. 'Saturday the twelfth of August. And you'll be at the village jamboree.'

'Oh, I see!' said Buttercup. 'Yes, I see.'

'Well, I wish you'd tell me,' said Cadwallader, good-naturedly.

'The twelfth of August?' said Daisy. 'The glorious twelfth?'

Cadwallader shook his head and raised his eyebrows at her.

'Grouse,' I said, taking pity on him at last.

'Oh yes,' he said, slapping his leg. 'I did know. I just forgot.' Which was rather the point.

'That's why you two are here without the men, isn't it?' said Cadwallader. 'Silas and – uh?'

'Hugh,' said Buttercup after a difficult moment.

'Hugh, right,' said Cadwallader. 'Yes, I suppose the timing of the Fair is awkward in some respects. That's probably why it's ended up being run by that bunch of –'

'Cad,' said Buttercup, placidly enough but with a note. 'New neighbours, darling, we should give them a chance.'

'Do go on now though,' said Daisy. 'Since none of them is around to hear you.'

'Well, I don't pretend to understand what the problem is,' said Cadwallader. 'Too many cooks is one thing, but matters are . . . what would you say, Freddy? Tense? Fraught?'

'Nonsense,' said Buttercup. 'It's nothing. Lightning quick, darling,' she added as Cadwallader reached forward for more cake. 'Cocktails, remember.'

'What's nothing?' I said.

'The Ferry Fair,' said Cadwallader, after washing down his cake with a gulp of tea and looking at his watch, 'is the typical Scottish fair in most respects. I've been reading up on it, you know. It was a hiring fair to begin with, and now it's a good wholesome frolic in the sunshine. Sure, there's drinking and there are showmen and where there are showmen there are girls to flirt with them, but it's hardly a hootenanny.'

Daisy and I tried to look as though we knew what a hootenanny might be, and were fashionably un-shocked by the thought of one.

'There are games and races, fancy dress competi-tions, a children's picnic, so far so dull, right? But also there's the Burry Man.'

'The . . .?' said Daisy, blaming his accent I think.

'Wait, I've heard of the Burry Man,' I said.

'A man wearing a suit of burrs,' said Buttercup. 'You know, little fluffy things off burdock plants.'

'Hardly fluffy,' said Daisy. 'Torture I'd have thought. I fell off into some once, eventing.'

'Yes, I remember now,' I said. 'He used to walk the town.'

'Thousands of years of tradition. And they think we should just sweep it all away,' said Cadwallader.

'Good Lord,' I said. 'You don't mean to say he still does it?'

'Every year,' said Buttercup. 'The day before the Ferry Fair. Tomorrow.'

'Why?' said Daisy.

'Warding off evil spirits, wasn't it?' I said. 'Or bring-ing fertility? Something like that, anyway.'

'Yes indeed,' said Cadwallader, rather grim all of a sudden. 'It's the something like *that* that's the problem. To listen to the Parish minister – what's his name, Freddy? – you'd think the guy was used to summon the devil. And then the Presbyterian minister is caught between wanting to find fault with the Parish minister and not wanting to look like a heathen in front of him, but really he's more concerned with all the drinking and fornication.'

'The drinking which *does* go on and the fornication he imagines *must* go on,' supplied Buttercup.

'So Madam Marchioness decides to try to bring it all into line with a pageant celebrating St Margaret – who was the Queen, you know, who took the ferry at Queensferry – but of course St Margaret was a Roman Catholic, so the Parish and the Presbies are down on that like a ton of bricks, which sends the priest off into a huff, even though he couldn't care less about the Burry Man *or* the drinking.'

'Cad, you make it all sound so torrid,' said Buttercup. 'Don't listen to him, darlings.'

'So where we are now is that unless the committee either bans the Burry Man, gets up a pageant or hands out Temperance leaflets with every picnic, at least one of the ladies who usually does the honours is going to stay home and sulk.' He paused. 'Enter Freddy – which was the Provost's idea. Provost Meiklejohn is an excellent fellow, as you'll see when you meet him tomorrow.'

'Tomorrow?' said Buttercup, looking uncomfortable.

'So you're oil on troubled waters, darling?' I said. 'That's a new look for you.'

'It's all nonsense,' said Buttercup. 'And you're about to see that for yourselves. Now run along all of you and change for cocktails. Quick, quick, because they're coming at six.'

'Who's coming at six?' said Cadwallader, standing over Buttercup, hardly threatening really but tall and broad enough to be classed as looming.

'Friends and neighbours,' said Buttercup, pushing out her bottom lip. 'Lady Stewart Clark from Dundas, and Lady Dalmeny, and possibly the Marchioness although she might be away.'

24

'They've agreed to meet here?' said Cad. 'But they're at daggers drawn.'

'Well, I may not quite have said to each that the others are coming but it'll be fine. Anyway, there's them and lots of other ladies from the town and Mr Dowd and Mr McAndrew, the ministers – although I haven't told them it's cocktails, obviously. And Father Whatsisname, who didn't seem to mind the cocktails a bit. And Provost Meiklejohn, darling, whom you yourself are so keen on. And I'm sure once they've all had a little sip of something delicious and a jolly good chat everything will be as right as rain.' Cad shook his head, speechless, and I could not help thinking of the roast suckling pig.

Poor Buttercup. Cocktails were served in the Great Hall, footsteps clanging on the stone floor, swords glinting and tiny summer fires smouldering miserably in the cavernous fireplaces, and jollity was not the party's most powerful note. Daisy and I had been helpless with giggles while dressing, lying on Daisy's bed whooping and kicking our legs, but even we gulped and went quiet as we entered.

They had all got there before us and we had missed their names being announced so, although Buttercup flapped her hand at people and murmured Lady This and Mrs That – really her parents might quite reasonably have asked our finishing school for a refund – I never did get them straightened out. Besides, they had brought assorted daughters and chums so there were hordes of them in total. And the three men in dog collars, who added a surreal note, were no easier to distinguish. One would think that a Free Presbyterian, a Plain Old Presbyterian and a Catholic Priest would appear respectively as the Grim Reaper, more or less a

25

vicar, and either a fat little man with a hip flask or a dashing prince in something purple, but here were three men with grey suits and pursed mouths and although one of them must be drinking lemonade to the other two's martinis they were all drinking them out of cocktail glasses and with identical expressions of distaste.

I joined a group, taking a huge slurp from my own glass – delicious! – and began to listen. I imagine that either they thought I was one of the Dundas or Dalmeny ladies or they simply did not care, for they made no effort to tone their opinions down.

'But it's unchristian, my dear lady,' said one of the ministers or the priest.

'It's *pre*-Christian,' said a snooty-looking lady in a red dress.

'Well, then,' said another. There were puzzled looks all round. 'I mean to say,' she went on. 'So is Mrs de Cassilis.'

'What on earth do you mean?' I said.

'My dear, haven't you heard? She's a' – whisper – 'Hebrew.'

'A Hebrew?' I echoed. 'She's from Hampshire. Oh, I see what you mean. No, no, no. That was her husband.'

'Really?' said the snooty lady turning to look at Cadwallader with deep interest. A maid had just given him a whispered message and as he swept out of the Hall to go and deal with it, he looked simply too Viking for words.

'Not Cadwallader!' I said, unable not to laugh at the idea. 'I mean her first husband.'

'First!' spluttered the minister, possibly the priest, and took a restoring swallow from his glass.

'A re-enactment of the pilgrimage would shift the whole thing on to a higher plane,' said a young lady to

26

my left. At the word 'pilgrimage', the minister – probably *not* the priest? – spluttered again and I took the opportunity of the hiatus while he was being banged on the back to detach myself and join another group.

'Well, she *says* she's a widow,' someone was saying in poisonous tones, but she broke off upon seeing me. Clearly this one knew who I was. 'My dear lady,' she went on, 'if this unpleasant episode goes ahead tomorrow after all, you'll be able to see for yourself. It terrifies the children for one thing.'

'Some of them,' put in a gentle-sounding man in a pronounced Scottish rumble. This must be the Provost.

'And those it doesn't terrify are whipped up into a very unhealthy excitement by the whole proceeding.'

'And the last thing we need,' said a stout lady with a surprisingly squeaky little voice, 'is to have the children as high as kites while their parents are too intoxicated to discipline them, wouldn't you agree?' She turned on me and caught me unawares.

'Well,' I said, 'I've never seen it of course, but I believe there are games, aren't there? Races and suchlike? And nothing works off excitement like running about in the fresh air, or so we were brought up to believe. I daresay it's a fearfully old-fashioned idea these days.'

'Precisely!' said a tall man with an earnest face, marking his words with his glass and slopping a little. 'Fresh air and healthful exercise.' He looked around the gloom of the Great Hall as if ready to knock through a french window as he spoke. 'The trouble with this district goes far deeper than the Burry Man once a year.'

One of the ladies could be seen to bristle and she made a crackling sound as she did so, telling me that although her cocktail dress was bang up to the minute her undergarments were still in the Edwardian era.

'What *do* you mean?' she said.

'Ghosts and monsters, lucky charms and who knows what superstitious nonsense,' the tall man said.

'Perfectly harmless fun,' squeaked the stout lady. 'No more to do with ghosts and monsters than dancing round the maypole or bobbing for apples. Perhaps when you have been in the district a little longer, Mr Turnbull . . .' This quelled him. He smiled stiffly and walked off.

'I had heard as much,' said the crackling lady to his departing back. '*Very* peculiar ideas, I heard.'

'And no reluctance to share them,' said another.

I could not hear what was being said in all the other groups of people around the room but from the general tune of the talk – gossipy swoops over a deep hostile mutter – I saw that Buttercup's cocktail party was going exactly as swimmingly as Daisy and I had predicted, so it was with some relief that I perceived Cadwallader beckoning to me conspiratorially from the half-open door.

He drew me out and shut the door softly behind us.

'Come with me, Dandy,' he said. 'The plot thickens.' He made towards the staircase and began to ascend. 'I have a visitor,' he went on as we felt our way up the worn stone treads to the drawing-room floor. 'The Burry Man. And there's something up that he won't tell me but I'm hoping he'll tell you.'

'What about Buttercup?' I said, loath to be drawn any further into the squabble.

'What about *what*?' said Cadwallader, but we had arrived at the library door and he did not pursue it.

I was half expecting a little green man covered in burdock seeds, I suppose, for it was a slight disappointment and relief to see standing in the middle of the rug, twisting his hat in large red hands, what looked like a perfectly ordinary farm-worker of about fifty, still in his breeches and collarless shirt although with his hair slicked down for this visit to the Big House.

'Dandy, this is Robert Dudgeon. Carpenter and Burry Man. Robert: Mrs Gilver has come to help Mrs de Cassilis with the Fair and she's very much looking forward to seeing you tomorrow.'

Mr Dudgeon touched his forehead but said nothing.

'So,' said Cadwallader in a hearty patronizing voice. 'You're not really going to let Mrs Gilver down, are you? Not to mention the rest of us?'

Mr Dudgeon shifted his weight awkwardly from foot to foot. He was in his stocking soles, presumably having left his workboots at the door on his way in, and I felt a stab of pity, for his obvious discomfiture could only be deepened by having to hold this interview with no shoes on.

'I was so surprised when Mr de Cassilis told me the Burry Man still went on, Mr Dudgeon,' I said. 'I can't wait to see it.'

'Well now there, madam,' said Robert Dudgeon. 'I'm sorry about that then, but I've just been telling Mr de Cassilis here I can't do it. It's a shame, but there it is.'

'Yes, but why?' said Cadwallader, clearly very exasperated.

'I can't tell you that, I'm afraid, sir. You'll just have to take my word for it there.'

'Now look, Dudgeon,' said Cadwallader with a new note in his voice. 'Obviously someone's got to you' – Mr Dudgeon's head jerked up – 'and I want to know who it is and what he said and then I'll get to him.'

Robert Dudgeon stared at him, with his mouth stuck out in an obstinate purse making his large moustaches bristle.

'But you're being ridiculous,' said Cadwallader. 'What has he said? Is it Rev. Dowd? Is it the whisky?

Could you do it without the whisky? Is it Rev. McAndrew? Has he said that you'll bring down the wrath of God?'

'It would be a wee bit late to be worrying about that now, sir,' said Mr Dudgeon. 'I've been the Burry Man for twenty-five year.'

'Well, exactly!' said Cadwallader. 'Twenty-five years. Tradition. Not to mention the thousands of years of tradition before that.'

'Don't you think I know that? Sir,' said Mr Dudgeon, glaring at Cadwallader. 'Why do you think I've done it year in year out? It's not easy.'

'I'm well aware of that, Dudgeon,' said Cadwallader. 'And did I not say that I'd give you Monday off as a holiday? As well as Friday. And Saturday for the Fair. On top of last Monday.'

'Last Monday was the August Bank, though,' I said gently. 'One can't take credit for that.'

'Bank holidays!' said Cadwallader. 'They're a new one on me, I must say. I thought the servants were having me on. And there are dozens. All paid.'

'A handful,' I said. 'And, speaking of pay, Mr Dudgeon, what about the Burry Man? Do they pay you for that?' I am not the subtlest woman ever born and this was blunt even for me, only I was thinking that we might be witnessing a stand-off for higher wages and Cad, as an American, might not have been able to read the signs. I mean, an American who wanted more money might simply say in a loud voice: 'Give me more money, pal!' but a Scot would rather die.

'Not to speak of, madam,' said Mr Dudgeon. 'It's not the money.'

'Although there *is* money,' said Cadwallader. 'And I wouldn't have thought you could just thumb your nose at it, Robert. That's very surprising.'

Mr Dudgeon glared at him again.

'So how about it?' said Cadwallader. 'What would it take?'

Mr Dudgeon did not answer this, but just shook his head and curled his lip rather.

'Oh yes, I know what you're thinking. Coming over here, taking over, thinking he can buy anything,' said Cad.

Mr Dudgeon and I were both squirming now. Someone would have to have a word with Cad about talking to servants.

'But you mark my words,' he went on. 'They'll find a way to blame me for this. Next year when all those so-called ladies and their tame pastors have stopped playing holier-than-thou and soberer-than-thou all they'll remember – *all* they'll remember – is that the Yank came and a thousand years of history went out the window. You just watch.'

'Cad,' I said, seeing that he was working himself into a temper, but he interrupted me.

'And I'd like to know, Robert – as well as who's threatening you – just exactly what they're threatening you with. I mean you're my estate carpenter and you live in one of my cottages, so who else *can* threaten you?'

'Cad,' I said again.

'No, God damn it,' said Cadwallader. 'That's a very good point. Robert, I am ordering you to do the Burry Man routine tomorrow, as your employer and as your landlord. Do I have to make it any plainer than that?'

'Cadwallader!' I said. 'Can you give Mr Dudgeon and me a few minutes?' Cad seemed more than ready to refuse, even though this was exactly why he had roped me in, but he caught hold of himself in time and, with a last disgusted look at Robert Dudgeon, he left.

'Now then,' I said. I gestured to a chair and Dudgeon, after hesitating a moment, sat down stiffly and rested his rough, red fists on his knees. 'I am quite sure Mr de Cassilis didn't mean a word of that, and of course if you are adamant then you must have very good reasons, but let's see if we can work something out.' Robert Dudgeon looked at me stonily but seemed ready to listen. I thought for a moment or two.

'Surely someone else in the village could step in,' I said at last.

'It's hard work, madam, it takes a load of stamina and willpower to keep going all the day long. It would be a very bad thing if someone tried and failed. A very bad thing.'

'You mean bad luck?'

'It doesn't bear thinking about,' said Mr Dudgeon, and shuddered.

'But isn't it almost as bad if no one does it at all?' I said. Perhaps if I kept him focused on this aspect he would come round of his own accord. His face showed me that he was struggling, but he won himself over in the end.

'It's worse. It's the blackest bad luck you could have, but it can't be helped.'

'And can't you think of someone, *anyone*, who feels as strongly as you do about it? Who would just make himself find the stamina no matter what? Do you pass it down the generations? Do you have a boy you could play the heavy father with?' His face was clouding as I spoke, and I should have known better. One should always know better now, since the war, than gaily to ask a man of fifty if he has sons.

'He didn't come home, madam,' said Mr Dudgeon and we sat a while in silence.

'I say, what about Mr de Cassilis!' I was half joking and was delighted to get a smile out of Mr Dudgeon in spite of himself. 'He seems keen enough, judging by what we just saw, doesn't he? And he certainly has a vested interest.' The more I thought about this, the more the idea grew on me. 'There might be a bit of talk about an incomer taking over,' I said. 'But if we can swear the inner circle to secrecy, once the burry suit is on, it will be too late for anyone to do a thing about it. And no one would go as far as to rip it off again, now would they?'

He was still shaking his head but at least he seemed to be thinking, his eyes darting back and forth over the pattern in the rug.

'Are you having an idea?' I asked, eagerly. 'Is there someone?'

'Eh? Oh no, there's no one I can think of, madam. But . . . mebbes it'll be all right after all.' He was looking at me without seeing me, plotting furiously at something or other.

'You can do it?' I asked. He chewed his lip for a bit before answering.

'I think so,' he said. 'Aye, I can. I'm sure I can, madam, yes.'

We chatted on for a bit about this and that, his work on the castle roof, the determination of Cad and Buttercup to live here. I had not been used to think of myself as handling servants well – my own run rings around me – but after all, I had been mistress of my house for over fifteen years now and I must be almost exactly what Mr Dudgeon was used to, compared with Cadwallader at least.

So I fairly bounced downstairs to the Great Hall ten minutes later. On entering it, I found the guests departed and Cad, Daisy and Buttercup sitting on the table, for want of anywhere else to rest themselves, looking dejected.

'Was any blood shed?' I asked. 'I heard no klaxons.'

'All very well for you,' said Daisy. 'You escaped. I've had "fresh air and exercise" in one ear and "the demon drink" in the other for a solid half-hour, Dan.'

'So much for your sip of something delicious, darling,' I said to Buttercup. 'Expect to be damned in every pulpit come Sunday.'

'Yes,' said Buttercup. 'But even the ones who drink seem to disapprove of me anyway. Father Whatsis-name was fearfully sour.'

'They think you're divorced,' I told her.

'They're a little premature,' said Cadwallader, but at Buttercup's pout, he shoved her with his elbow and said: 'I'm only joking, Droopy,' and Buttercup cheered up and beamed.

I took pity on them at last and told my news.

'Miracle worker!' said Buttercup. 'What did you say to him?'

'Oh, I haven't told you about Dandy's new-found talent for . . . well, everything, have I?' said Daisy.

'I got chummy and then appealed to his pride,' I said. 'And I've promised him a ten-pound tip.' I had done no such thing, had only just thought of it there and then, but I felt Cadwallader needed to make some reparation for his outburst.

'We'll call it twenty,' said Cadwallader. 'Another Manhattan before dinner? I would advise it – Mrs Murdoch is a good plain cook with lots of plain.'

'Ugh,' I said, goose pimples rising at the very sugges-tion. 'Nothing with whisky for me, darling, please.'

'All right, then, a Sidecar,' said Cadwallader. 'But don't let them hear you tomorrow, Dandy. About the whisky, I mean. This town runs on the stuff.'

Chapter Two

It did indeed. One could not help thinking that the various reverends were wasting their time rather, pushing Temperance, in a town where most of the inhabitants who did not fish or farm or shop-keep worked for the whisky distiller who had an enormous bottling hall and bonded store a stone's throw up the hill from the High Street. From what I understood, moreover, since the Ferry Fair day was a holiday, many of the workers would be quite a bit *more* sober this day than most others, it being their practice not to filch the whisky in bottles or flasks but simply to glug it down during their shift, then stagger home and sleep it off.

As well as 'the bottling', of course, there was the usual, more than generous, quota of pubs. A town the size of South Queensferry in Wiltshire, say, would boast a coaching inn and perhaps a backstreet beer shop, but here there were upwards of a dozen separate establishments selling the demon drink, from the Hawes Inn at the top, drawing its respectability from History and Literature and its trade from the ferryboat trippers come to look at the bridge, all the way to the drinking shops such as 'Broon's Bar' at the bottom. The even less salubrious-sounding 'Hole i' the Wa'' had recently fallen down, suggesting that its name perhaps had referred to its architecture as much as its social standing.

Cadwallader regaled us with all of this as we motored into town the next morning, and seemed heartily in favour both of the distillery men topping themselves up as they worked and of the ratio of beer pumps to head of population.

'Because when you've just been through what we've just been through . . .' he said grimly.

'Oh, I don't know,' said Buttercup. 'I thought Prohibition was rather fun. You didn't have to worry too much at home so long as you chose your servants carefully, and the speakeasies were really quite jolly.'

Cadwallader shook his head at her as he stopped to let a crowd of tattered little children cross the road at Dalmeny village.

'For God's sake, Freddy, don't start singing the praises of speakeasies in front of anyone today, will you?' he said, waving and tooting at the children as we started up again. 'Off to see the Burry Man?' he called.

'It's hardly likely to come up in conversation,' said Buttercup. 'I must say, though, gangsters are much better value at a party than our new neighbours showed themselves to be last night, aren't they, Cad?'

Cadwallader tried to laugh this off as 'Freddy's nonsense' and although she protested – 'Well, what would you call him, darling? He always brings a case of gin and one never sees him without those two boys who look like boxers!' – Daisy and I thought it best to feign deafness.

Within minutes, we arrived at the parking yard of the garage by the Hawes and stepped down. It was a fine morning, a clear sky and just the merest flutter of a breeze from the river and Daisy, Buttercup and I debated together whether to take our little coats and our sun parasols, or both, or neither.

'Only I do hate putting on a coat and crumpling my frock sleeves then taking it off later when it's hot,' said

Daisy. 'I'd rather feel cold until this afternoon and keep my pleats crisp.'

'Come on, come on,' said Cadwallader who was holding open the gate for us. 'Good grief, think about poor Robert Dudgeon, stumping around covered in burrs all day. Stop fussing.'

'Let's leave the coats but take the –' Buttercup began, but broke off at an ostentatious sigh from the gate. She blew a kiss at Cadwallader in passing.

There were a few knots of people already on their way along the road, and there was a definite sense of anticipation about their hurry as well as high spirits. Somewhere ahead of us a clock tower sounded a single note.

'Quarter to,' said an old woman, marching along with a giggling grandchild (I guessed) held firmly by the arm, and she quickened her step.

From the Hawes around the sweep of the river there is a shingly beach on one side, separated from the road by the tidewall, and a pleasant wooded bank opposite with just a few prosperous-looking villas. The road itself is broad and even, and I began to wonder why we could not have ridden on in the car, but then all of a sudden one turns an awkward corner and finds oneself right in the middle of a rather quaint little town, with higgledy-piggledy shops and houses jutting out into one's path, as though the river had washed them up the shore a bit now and then over the years. Across the road, there were some ancient buildings, square and solid, and in between them the town had grown in the most ingenious way: above us, up smart sets of steps, broad walkways led to some really rather grand merchants' houses, while below, little shops had been tucked in underneath. I had never cared for the vertical ordering of the social classes one sees in Edinburgh, where the rich sit up-top hogging the light

37

and simply pour their potato water (and worse) down on the heads of the poor below, but South Queensferry's terraces were as pleasing to the eye in their nattiness as collectors' cabinets or dolls' houses can be, and I daresay if the plumbing were all that one could wish for, one could live and work above or below in perfect comfort.

The crowds grew thicker as we made our way along beneath another terrace, past the bank and the butchers, towards the Rosebery Hall, where quite a hundred people were gathered laughing together and humming with interest. It was mostly women, old men and children – since all others were at work – and quite a few of the elders were bent double exhorting their young charges to bravery.

'What are you to say, Isa?' asked one young woman whose daughter was wiping her grubby face against her mother's pinny and threatening to weep.

'I don't like it,' said Isa, pushing out her lip

'Och wheesht,' her mother replied. 'If you're a good girl and say it I'll give you a ha'penny to fling in his bucket and bring you luck.'

'I don't *like* it,' said Isa again stoutly.

'They're always feart the first time,' said an old man. He eased himself back against the wall between Isa's mother and me and spat expressively then, taking a closer look at my party and regretting the spitting, I suppose, he made up for it by wiping his mouth politely on his sleeve and touching his cap brim.

Just then, the clock on the town hall tower struck nine and the door swung open. Two men emerged, coats and collars off, hats on the backs of their heads. They turned back to the dark doorway holding out their hands and slowly the Burry Man emerged. Little Isa screamed, I heard Cadwallader say 'Good God!' and a cry went up from the crowd:

'Hip, hip, hooray!
Hip, hip, hooray!
Hip, hip, hooray,
It's the Burry Man's day!'

I do not know what I had been expecting, and I felt foolish for being surprised. After all, I had known that the Burry Man was a man covered in burrs and here *was* a man covered in burrs, but the effect was staggering. Perhaps I had not imagined it to be so utterly complete. Not only were his body, arms and legs encased, so that his limbs looked like prize-winning stalks of Brussels sprouts, but his whole face and head were covered too, with just the slightest shadows showing where one or two burrs had been missed to let him breathe and peer out. He must have had on some kind of very stout under-garment too, for, as Daisy had said, burdock seeds were torturous little things, and so his outline was bulbous, a huge lollipop head and the monstrously thick green body underneath, making one think of galls on tree trunks and lichen on barnacled rocks. Mouldy, encrusted, vegetative and obscene, when he walked it was the stuff of nightmares.

On the other hand, he wore a garland of flowers on his head over the burrs, and strange little nosegays sprouted from each shoulder and hip as though he were a prickly green teddy bear stuffed with flowers and they had burst out at the pressure points on his seams. Also, around his waist was a folded flag showing the head of the lion rampant, and more flowers poked out from the top of this.

His two chums guided him down the steps to the street, holding a hand each and steadying him with a grip under each arm as he swung his legs around stiffly and lumbered down, tread by tread. Isa continued to howl.

At last, arrived at street level and steadied between his helpers, he opened his hands – I saw with a shudder that his hands were bare and somehow this evidence that there really *was* a man in there was the chillingest of all – and into his grasp were thrust two huge bunches of flowers, staves of flowers really, like skiing poles. For a few minutes, as the crowd continued variously to chant or to snivel, he stood leaning on these staves waiting for his helpers to put their coats on and take up two buckets into which the gathered townspeople immediately began to throw pennies and sixpences. Then slowly, painfully slowly, the strange ensemble moved off, the Burry Man gripping the flower staves and swinging his stiff legs, the men holding him tight under one arm each and rattling the buckets in their other hands. Children broke free of their mothers and followed along, still chanting. Even Isa, brave now that she could no longer see him and not wanting to miss out on the fun, managed a tiny 'Hup, hup, hooray' and toddled off after them.

The grown-ups looked around smoothing their aprons and sniffing, seeming satisfied, as though an important task had been completed, then they began to chat to each other and drift away.

'Where is he going?' I asked the old man who had spat.

'Right roond the toon,' he said. 'But they're away to the Provost's house for a nip first.'

'Gosh, I'd have thought whisky was the last thing he'd want right at the start of the day,' I said. The old man wheezed with laughter.

'The start? He'll have a nip in every pub in the toon and plenty more,' he said. 'It's good luck and there's many can spare a tot of something a gey sight easier than a ha'penny.'

'Heavens,' I said. 'So he spends all day drinking whisky?'

'Aye,' said the old man and, winking at a couple of other worthies who were listening in, he added, 'Goan then, ask me. I ken what you're thinking.'

I flushed, for of course that was *exactly* what I was thinking. The old men roared with laughter and I joined in, helpless not to.

'Aye, it takes stamina right enough, to be the Burry Man,' said the one who stopped laughing first. 'As for they twae holding him up . . .'

'He could manage without them till dinnertime,' said another, 'But it's well seen he'll need them comin' hame.'

I was quite happy chatting away to these new chums and might have followed them to a bench and shared a pipe with them, but Buttercup's voice cut in.

'Dandy! Dandy, darling, do come on. I must get the fancy dress prizes. What do you think – ribbons for the girls and marbles for the boys or a shilling for both?'

'What about whisky?' I said. And Buttercup frowned.

'Please try to take it seriously, Dan. Her horrible Ladyship wouldn't tell me what they had last year – cat! – and Mrs Meiklejohn the Provost's wife can't remember and I don't want to ask someone else and look as though I don't know what I'm doing, even though of course I don't . . . come on, Dandy. We'll see the Burry Man again later.' For I was still gazing after him. 'He's simply all over the place all day.'

'Do you know, Buttercup,' I said, taking her arm as she made her way towards a draper's shop across from the Rosebery Hall, 'that poor man is plied with whisky all day long and he can't go to the lavatory? It's barbaric.'

'The whole thing's barbaric,' said Daisy. 'Much as one doesn't want to agree with anything those mealy-mouthed ninnies said last night, it is too paganistic for words.'

'Absolutely shivery-making,' I said. 'How they can laugh at the babies for screaming beats me. I nearly screamed myself.'

'You're not alone,' said Buttercup. 'Cad's had to go off for a stiff drink. It gave him the absolute willies.'

'I thought he was rather dashing,' said Daisy.

'If Frankenstein's monster is dashing,' I said.

'Oh, but he is,' said Daisy, quite serious. 'The untamed beast and all that.'

'For heaven's sake, Daisy,' said Buttercup. 'Shut up about fancying an untamed beast, at least while we're in the draper's. My reputation won't withstand it.'

We had a cosy time in the Co-operative choosing hair ribbons and bags of marbles, and the girl behind the desk was most obliging in the matter of letting us rootle through the contents of her till for the shiniest shillings and sixpences to hand out too. Then we turned down the lane to go to the harbour and look at the river, picking our way past several old women at the harbour head industriously gutting baskets of herring, slapping the fillets on to salt trays and flicking the noisome entrails back into the water for the gulls. As we passed, a woman in a sack apron emerged from the dark end of a lane with a bale of wet laundry done up in a sheet and began to hang it on ropes strung between poles along the harbour side. She said nothing but glared at the gulls and at the herring wives, who glared back and flicked with even less accuracy and attention than before. Between the smell, the flying innards and the flapping washing, then, the three of us decided against too long an interlude by the water's edge and retreated in search of coffee.

'I can understand her anguish,' I said. 'Gulls and laundry don't mix at all, but really one has to give Friday to the fisher folk, doesn't one? Monday's the day for washing in all of Christendom. Even I know that.'

'It's the Ferry Fair,' said Buttercup. 'Mrs Meiklejohn was telling me yesterday that everyone washes their floors and windows and changes their linen for Ferry Fair day. They clean and tidy everything in sight . . .'

We were passing the police station now, and in front of it a constable was standing in his shirtsleeves at the noticeboard, with the glass front of it propped open, and was busily removing old notices and postcards.

'Look,' said Buttercup. 'Even he's tidying for the Fair.'

The constable caught her words and smiled at us, unoffended.

'Got to, madam,' he said. 'There'll be prize notices and winners' announcements to go in tomorrow. Got to tidy out for the Fair.' He returned to his task, murmuring to himself. 'Lost property has to stay, opening hours has to stay . . .' and Buttercup rolled her eyes.

'They do it at New Year too, I believe,' she said.

'Oh yes,' agreed Daisy, 'they all do it at New Year. One can hardly hear the drunken revelry for the sound of scrubbing brushes at Hogmanay.'

'And it's a very good thing, when you consider it,' I said. 'Even the foulest sloven gives everything one good wash a year for luck – and two here in Queensferry, you say? I should think that's a strong argument right there towards keeping the Fair going.'

With this we arrived at the tearooms. There were two side-by-side, which always amuses me. If a village has two establishments on different streets then each can pretend that the ladies choose the nearer, but when they sit nestled together as did Mitchell's and

Beveridge's in Queensferry the workings of class structure and economics are laid bare. Mitchell's had blue oilcloth table covers, a sweet counter and a handwritten card in the window saying 'Cakes ½ price after four'. To Beveridge's we turned, as a man.

'Now the way I see it,' said Buttercup, talking through a cigarette clamped between her scarlet lips, a habit I suppose she must have picked up in one of those speakeasies but which was drawing startled looks and rumblings from the other tables in Beveridge's, 'we can divide the events into the straightforward sporting contests where the winner is obvious and all we have to do is smile and hand over the loot – so that's the races and the greasy pole, chiefly – and the much trickier judging competitions – the fancy dress and the bonny babies. Greasy pole and fancy dress are tonight – well, late this afternoon really, six until half past eight, such an awkward time.'

'It's after they've all had their teas,' I said.

'I suppose so,' said Buttercup. 'I must remember to tell Mrs Murdoch. Dinner at nine.'

'We can fill up on toffee apples at the Fair,' said Daisy.

'If we can fit them in around our duties,' said Buttercup. 'I don't want you trying to announce winners with your teeth glued together, Daisy darling.'

'Ah yes, our duties,' I said.

'Yes,' said Buttercup, all business. 'Now, the way I see it, I've got to live here and you two don't, so I'll take care of the races and you two can pick your way through the diplomatic minefields and then hightail back to Perthshire and leave it all behind you. Agreed?'

'Absolutely not –' I began. But Daisy interrupted.

'Done,' she said. 'Bags me the fancy dress.'

'Now hold on –' I said, beginning to splutter.

'That's that then,' said Buttercup. 'Dandy can do the bonny babies.'

'But . . .' I said, and gave up as Daisy and Buttercup melted into giggles.

'Your face, Dan!' said Daisy.

'It's easy,' said Buttercup. 'Just pick whichever one you think is prettiest.'

'I've never seen a baby I thought was pretty,' I said. 'I won't have to touch them, will I?' But Daisy and Buttercup only laughed again.

'Pick a nice big chubby one and you'll be fine,' said Buttercup. 'Bonny is just a polite word for fat, I've always found.'

'Well, all right,' I said. 'Bloated is possibly less revolting than wizened, I agree, but if we're going down such an agricultural route, why not just weigh them?'

'Think of me,' said Daisy, 'trying to choose between a pirate and a chimney sweep with doting mothers squaring up for a fight.' She fell silent with a small clearing of her throat as a tidily dressed woman came towards our table.

'Please excuse me interrupting,' she said, speaking diffidently enough, but smiling with an air of confidence from out of her healthy, rather well-scrubbed face. 'I couldn't help overhearing you discussing the fancy dress.'

Quite. The Scots as a race, that is to say the working people and the bourgeoisie, whisper and mutter away to each other when out in public so that others speaking in perfectly normal voices seem to address the room.

Daisy was looking at the woman with a nicely judged mixture of surprise and disdain, just this side of rudeness, but Buttercup, all those years in America, I suppose, was smiling encouragingly at her, eyebrows raised in invitation to say more, and to be fair I daresay if the woman had indicated some interest or expertise in the bonny baby area I should have been drawing up another chair and ordering fresh coffee.

'I'm Mrs Turnbull,' she continued, then when that achieved nothing, she went on. 'My husband is the new headmaster of the school.'

'Oh yes,' said Buttercup. 'Well, how can we help you, Mrs Turnbull?'

'Rather, how can I help you,' the woman said, earnestly. 'About the fancy dress, I wouldn't have dreamt of it, if you hadn't said yourself you were puzzled about how to decide.' She turned her beaming smile on Daisy. 'But since you did, I can venture to be bold . . . don't you agree it's best to reward the right spirit rather than anything else?' Daisy looked blank. 'From what my husband tells me, from what the children tell him, there will be a fair few ghosts and witches and monsters. And I don't think . . . that is we don't think, my husband and I . . . I mean to say I'm sure you agree that they shouldn't be encouraged in such unwholesomeness. It was bad enough at Hallowe'en, but really in the middle of summer . . .' She trailed off into silence, for Daisy was looking at her so coldly only the thickest-skinned could have continued.

'Harmless fun,' Daisy said.

'Oh, but it isn't,' said Mrs Turnbull. 'Far from it. You wouldn't believe the stories they tell the teachers. Ghosts of soldiers, grey ladies, ghosts of miners, ghost ships in the Forth, headless horsemen . . .'

'You're right there, Mrs Turnbull,' piped up a dainty-looking old lady at the next table, for of course the whole tearoom was in on it now. 'Didn't wee Mary Mott stay home from the Sunday school trip to Cramond for fear of the ghosts in the swamp.'

'Swamp?' said Mrs Turnbull, aghast to find out that the neighbourhood boasted such a thing.

'Well, they call it a swamp,' said the old lady, pink

spots appearing in her cheeks. 'The pond in the trees just past the Hawes pier.'

'The pond where the babies were drowned?' asked the waitress, pausing with a laden tray in the doorway on her way to the kitchen. 'That *is* a swamp, or quicksand anyway, because Jessie Marshall's old dog fell in and sank like a stone and he was a fine strong swimmer.'

'Babies?' mouthed Mrs Turnbull weakly and I too felt a little nonplussed at the way this had been dropped into the general chit-chat.

'The gate-lodge keeper on the estate,' said a willowy lady, wiping away cake crumbs and leaning forward to regale us, 'or it might have been the ferryman, I forget, this was away way back, Jacobite times I think, but his wife used to drown her babies in the swamp. Nine or ten of them all told. And they rested peaceful as peaceful there until the bridge was built, but now when the night train goes over you can hear them crying and screaming and the woman's voice going "ssh-ssh, ssh-ssh".'

'Ten little babies, just fancy,' said the dainty old lady. 'I've never heard about that before.' She shook her head slowly, seeming to fix her gaze upon me as though my disparagement of infant bonniness put me in the same league as the ferryman's wife.

We hurriedly settled our bill and reeled out into the street and the sunshine in relief, laughing almost.

'One begins to see what they mean,' I said.

'Oh Dandy, really,' said Daisy. 'Such nonsense. The squeal of the tracks and the swish of the pistons, darling.'

'Of course, of course,' I said. 'But the constant drip of morbidity does begin to press down.'

'Well, here's cheerfulness, then,' said Buttercup, waving towards Cadwallader who was approaching us from across the street. 'And listen!' We listened. From the distance somewhere along the street came a faint 'Hip, hip, hooray'.

'Great!' said Cadwallader, hearing it too. 'It would be a shame not to see him again, since it's only once a year, and I'm well buffered with Scotch now. Let's go find him then head for home.'

We followed the sound of the cheers along the terraced High Street and finally caught a glimpse of the crowd of children in the distance almost where the buildings ran out and the sweep of shore began. The three principals – the Burry Man and his gentlemen-in-waiting – were just disappearing into a building and the little band of followers plumped down upon the kerbstones or hopped up on to windowsills to await their re-emergence. When we caught up, I just had time to read 'Brown's Bar' above the door, before Cad swept it open and ushered us inside.

He seemed to think nothing of it and Buttercup, quite at home in the speakeasies of New York, could not be expected to demur, but Daisy and I caught each other's eyes and mimed a little mild guilt, shocked at the sawdust under our feet and the air, sharp with whisky and fuggy with beer, as startling as smelling salts after the fresh breeze outside.

There were no customers in the bar as early as this on a working day and the two guides were nowhere to be seen either so the Burry Man, standing at the counter with his pale hands splayed on its surface, and the serving maid standing behind it, her head bowed, with a whisky bottle in one hand and a glass in the other, made a kind of tableau in the shaft of light from the open door. The effect lasted only a second before she looked up at us, slightly goggle-eyed.

'Father!' she shouted over her shoulder, in the querulous tone of one who has been shouting repeatedly and getting nowhere. 'Customers!'

'Not customers, really,' said Cadwallader. 'We only came in to hand over our coins and collect our luck.' He dug in his pocket and drew out a handful of change. 'Where are your buckets, Robert?'

The Burry Man said nothing and I saw a quick frown tug at the barmaid's brow. Perhaps one was not supposed to address him or allude to his everyday identity like this. We all stood awkwardly for a moment, the girl not at all equal to the challenge of the three of us and the hulking green presence converging when she was holding the fort. She seemed to be looking anywhere but at the Burry Man.

'The whisky's for luck too,' she said at last, in a trembling voice. 'Only I'm waiting for my father.' She stamped her foot hard on the floor and shouted even louder this time: 'Father!'

Immediately there came a thumping and shuffling from below us somewhere. 'Father' was evidently in the cellar, and not alone. We heard the tread of footsteps ascending a creaking stairway behind the bar and then, like jacks in boxes, up popped the Burry Man's helpers followed by a red-faced man in a chamois leather apron, with the same russet curls and round chin as the serving maid, only rougher and thirty years older.

'Welcome, welcome, ladies and gents,' said the publican. 'Joey, have you not given the Burry Man his nip yet?'

'I was waiting for you,' said Joey, and she poured an enormous measure into the glass, added a drinking straw and set it on the counter while the two helpers picked up their buckets and stood smiling rather shiftily.

I lobbed in my half-crown and the others followed,

Cadwallader's shower of coins making a most impressive carillon. The Burry Man still stood with hands flat on the bar counter and made no move to pick up the glass before him. Although it was hard to tell, he seemed not even to be looking at it; his prickly green face with the shadows for eyes seemed pointed straight at Joey the serving maid.

'Come on, come on,' said the publican. 'A nip for luck. Help him, Joey.' Joey bit her lip and then nudged the glass towards the Burry Man's hand, flinching as she brushed his fingers with her own.

'Go on, girl, dinnae be soft,' said the publican. 'Help the man.' He sounded amiable enough but there was something disquieting about his insistence in the face of the girl's obvious reluctance, and the fidgety leering of the bucket carriers only made it worse. Joey gave her father a desperate glance then lifted the glass and guided the drinking straw towards the Burry Man's mouth, finally looking at his face, into the gaps in the mask before his eyes. For a moment they were frozen there, a tableau once again, before her face blanched, she gave a tiny cry and the glass fell. Then she spun around and bolted through the door to the back while the three men watching let their laughter go at last, whooping.

'She's always been the same,' her father said to us, chuckling and shaking his head in the direction Joey had fled. 'Petrified of him.'

'You're a bad devil, Shinie,' said one of the helpers.

'Ach, it's a bit of fun,' said the other.

We could hear Joey's voice from far away in the back: 'Father, please. Please!'

The Burry Man, silent, pushed up and away from the bar, picked up his flower staves and gripped them tightly, the knuckles showing as white as clean bone, then he lumbered round to face the door again. Not wanting to get entangled and, on my part at any rate, rather sickened by the cruelty underlying the little joke, the four of us bumbled out ahead of him.

'Hip, hip, hooray,' sang the children outside, jumping to their feet as they saw him swaying in the doorway. He slowly got to his place at the head of the crowd and the children jostled into some kind of order behind him, then the whole caravan began to move again.

We watched for a minute or two and had just turned away to set off towards the parking yard when the door of the pub behind us swung open so violently it banged back off its hinges and Shinie the publican hurried out to speed after the procession, a brimming glass of whisky in his hand.

'Ye've not had yer nip,' he said, standing square in front of the Burry Man and barring his way. The Burry Man's hands remained on his staves. Then the publican made as though to put the glass to the mouth space himself, but at that the Burry Man reared backwards away from it. For a long moment Shinie, breathing heavily, stood peering into the shadowy face, then he dashed the contents of the glass into the gutter with a contemptuous flick of his wrist and turned away.

'How simply too torrid for words,' said Buttercup once we were under way again.

'Positively operatic,' I agreed.

'He's an awkward customer, Dudgeon, isn't he?' said Cad. 'I wouldn't have dreamed it until last night and again just there . . . a very awkward customer indeed.'

'Hmm,' said Daisy. 'Village feuds, village squabbles, you'll learn to ignore it. And there are far more serious matters at hand.' She faced Buttercup sternly. 'You neglected to tell us, darling, that this shindig came in

51

two parts. Races tonight and fancy dress tomorrow, and I for one have only one suitable hat with me.'

'Gosh, me too,' I said. 'Heavens, I've only got one *frock*, I was going to wear lounging pyjamas tonight. What are we to do?'

Cadwallader tutted ostentatiously and strode ahead and we trailed after him plotting how to dole out Buttercup's fox furs and sailor collars between the two of us to cover our shame.

Promptly at five minutes to six, we were once again puttering down the Hawes Brae, in convoy this time – Cad and Buttercup ahead, Daisy and I following in the Cowley – in case some of the party should tire before the others. I slowed to turn into Faichen's parking yard, but Buttercup turned and kneeled on the seat of the car in front, waving and shouting over the sound of the engine.

'Last chance,' I heard her bellow. 'Straight on.'

'What?' shouted Daisy back at her, but Buttercup merely waggled her thumbs at us and plumped back down into her seat.

Obediently we kept going and at the Sealscraig corner, where we were forced by the crowds to stop for a moment, my high seat in the motor car afforded me a view over the café curtains of Brown's Bar. I looked in, interested to see if Miss Brown had recovered her sangfroid. By now, capped heads two and three deep at the bar spoke to a busy afternoon's trade, but behind the bar all was confusion. The shelves stood empty and the spirit bottles were crammed here and there around the till and the beer taps. Joey Brown was standing on a high stool in her stockinged feet, swabbing the painted mirror which backed the shelves, a bucket steaming at her elbow. I nudged Daisy.

'More Ferry Fair cleaning,' I said. 'Hardly timely, with all those customers.'

'Or perhaps since every last drop is going to be drunk, she might as well leave it at their elbows and get on with other things?'

As though to confirm Daisy's view, the door swung open at that moment and a figure, glassily pale, half fell out into the street beside us. Just then, thankfully, the crowds ahead of us cleared and we moved off again, so were not forced to witness whatever the sudden fresh air would add to his plight.

This time we managed to get as far as the bank before the density of the crowd and the numbers of little children whizzing around like clockwork mice all over the road persuaded us to give up and get out.

'Two minutes to six, you see,' said Cadwallader. 'We'll just catch a last glimpse of the Burry Man if we hurry.'

'Whoopee!' said Daisy sarcastically under her breath, but I was eager. Pruriently, I wanted to see for myself if he was still standing so I caught her elbow and dragged her along to the Rosebery Hall.

> 'Hip, hip, hooray!
> Hip, hip, hooray!
> Hip, hip, hooray,
> It's the Burry Man's day!'

The chanting, rather ragged now, could be heard clearly ahead of us and there he was.

'As six strikes he goes back inside – like a cuckoo,' said Buttercup. 'And once he's gone the Fair begins.'

Naturally, the protagonist himself appeared quite unchanged – stiff, green, beflowered and terrifying – but the alteration in his two attendants was extreme. They were clearly very hot, sleeves rolled up despite

53

the scratches they gathered on their forearms as a consequence, and they looked absolutely done to death. I had not taken to either fellow during the mean little trick on Miss Brown but now one felt some sympathy, as one always does for those native guides who followed intrepid Victorian botanists and what-not, carrying all the gear and getting none of the praise.

The crowd was cheering the painfully slow progress of the three, clapping in time with each step up towards the door, and I was reminded, blasphemously I suppose, of the road to Calvary; there was something moving about witnessing the end of this long day, although it was too ludicrous to be noble exactly. Then, even as I thought this, it changed. All of a sudden, the Burry Man shook off his helpers, not brutally but very firmly, and broke into a stiff trot, mounting the last of the stairs alone and disappearing into the open door-way like a terrier into a rabbit hole. The two men, exhausted and seemingly astonished, looked at each other and shrugged, then they trailed after him wiping their heads with handkerchiefs and flexing their tired arms. The crowd divided itself between laughing applause and wondering whispers.

'Does he always do that?' I inquired of my neighbours at large. 'It must be agony.'

'He's nivver done before,' said a man beside me.

'Och well,' said another. 'He must have been bursting for a – I mean, he can't have been comfy.'

There was general laughter at this, and then came the sound of a handbell and the voice of the crier demanding the under-tens for the fancy dress and announcing that the greasy pole would commence at half past six sharp. The Fair had begun.

The stalls were set up around the Bellstane, the little square at the bottom of the steep hill along from the Rosebery Hall, and although they boasted only the very ordinary staples such as coconut shies, ices and pop-gun galleries there was something rather more exciting about all of these in the evening, in a street with windows thrown up all around and people hanging over the sills cat-calling to friends below. It was a long way from the vicarage lawns of my youth and, although there was nothing to put one's finger on, it was faintly bawdy somehow.

I took a desultory look around the sideshows, then stood for a while on the terrace east of the Rosebery Hall to watch Daisy, with enormous satisfaction and a sweet smile for Mrs Turnbull, give first prize to a tot got up as Charlie Chaplin and second prize to a five-year-old Theda Bara style Cleopatra, who was practically naked. The local picture house clearly had a lot to answer for.

Presently, I began to sense another locus of noise and bustle somewhere behind me. People were funnelling into the mouth of a narrow lane giving on to the terrace and, making my way to the corner, I could see a steady trickle of others disappearing along one of the small side-streets which peeled off the steep street leading up the hill; clearly they were converging somewhere in the back lanes. Spying my expectorating chum of the morning as he passed I caught at his coat sleeve.

'It's yersel',' he cried in polite greeting and I was sure he had had a nip or two, for his old eyes were swimmier than they had been on our first meeting and his toothless grin was rather wet and shiny.

'What's going on up there?' I asked him, pointing to the crowd, growing from a trickle to a flood now.

'It's the greasy pole,' he said. 'Come on with you, you'll no want to miss that.'

'No indeed.' I had never seen a greasy pole competition before although I had often heard them described and I was sure neither Cad nor Buttercup would have seen enough to have tired of them, but I could not find either golden head amongst the crowd and since Daisy was busy on the town hall steps, trying to decide between three little pharaohs, and I was loath to miss my chance of a ringside seat, I hurried on alone.

The venue for the greasy pole seemed odd at first. Hill Square was a mean little opening between two closes with tenements all around, but it had the one redeeming feature of soft earth underfoot and, as I squinted up at the pole, I could see the point of that. It looked thirty feet high at least, a ship's mast possibly, borrowed for the occasion, for it was polished quite smooth. Slippery enough at the best of times, I should have thought, even without the liberal coating of grease I could see glinting on its surface. At its summit two bulging lumps dangled and I asked someone standing beside me what they were.

'A ham and a bag of flour, madam,' I was told, and had it not been for that 'madam' I should have suspected the man of cheek. My face must have shown my puzzlement, for he chuckled.

'The ham's the prize,' he said, 'and the flour's . . . you'll see.'

Little boys were hurling themselves up a few feet and slithering back down again, chided by the grown-ups: 'Come away now, the mess of you!' but presently the first serious contender presented himself to clapping and jeers. He was a wiry youth dressed in very stout twill trousers, and made good progress to about halfway up before, for no obvious reason, he suddenly shot straight back to earth again and landed on his bottom grinning sheepishly to the roars of laughter from all around.

The next hopeful looked even less likely; he had huge hands to be sure but also a very round stomach and short little legs. The crowd began to laugh as soon

56

as they saw him and sure enough he was hardly his own height from the ground when he let go. While yet another tried his luck, I drifted off into a daydream as I always do on these occasions. This daydream was of me, striding forward and launching myself at the pole. I tossed my head and laughed at those who would stop me, before hoisting myself effortlessly to the top and waving my hat in the air. Is it only me, I wonder, or does everyone do it? I know I have plunged (in my mind) into every circus, yacht race, steeplechase and opera I have ever seen, but imagine the shame if one ever admitted as much to a friend and got only cold uncomprehending stares in return. Besides, it was hard to decide what exactly the substance was which turned the pole greasy, but from the calls of 'yeugh' in the crowd, it seemed unlikely to be cold cream, and I shook the daydream away with a shudder.

Now there began some kind of wrangle between the officials and a wily-looking man who had fashioned a contrivance like cowboy's chaps out of sacking and attached these on top of his trousers. The head-shaking and muttering went on and on, and the crowd was beginning to grow restive, when a smart clip-clopping drew my attention to the mouth of the close, and I saw a tiny cart pulled by an equally tiny pony draw up. One is used to various makeshift equipages but this really was the sweetest and oddest-looking little outfit I had come across, a sort of cross between a bath-tub and a perambulator with one seat for a driver in front and two back-to-back, facing out to each side, for a pair of passengers behind. I was so diverted by it that I did not trouble to wonder who was climbing down from the driving seat until a voice shouted from the crowd.

'I thocht ye were away hame, Rubbert.'

Robert Dudgeon nodded vaguely, helping a woman

I took to be his wife step down from the little cart and tying the pony's rein to a gatepost.

'There's no telling him,' called this Mrs Dudgeon. 'You can try if you like, Greta, but there's no telling him.' She shook her head at her husband and seemed genuinely worried, although her words were light-hearted enough, or perhaps she was just cross with him. The woman standing at my elbow was certainly cross with *her*.

'You wouldn't believe the mess that bloomin' pony left all over the green this afternoon, and would Chrissie Dudgeon shift herself away out of it? Would she not! She had to wait for Rubbert and take him straight home, she said, and yet here he is bold as brass at the greasy pole and the filthy beastie'll be at it again.'

'Ach, Myra, it's good for yer rhubarb, you should be grateful.'

'I'll give ye rhubarb, ye wee so-and-so. The bairns have trekked it all up the stairs.'

'It's a very peculiar little cart, isn't it?' I said. 'And such a minuscule pony. One can hardly believe it could pull them along.'

'Made fae a shell hutch,' said a man nearby, in an attempt at an explanation; an attempt which failed for me at least. 'And they ponies are used wi' lugging more than that in days gone by.'

'And it's on a fine rich diet,' said Myra, still smarting. 'You should see my stair runner. Ach, it's worth it, though, I daresay, to see this.'

I was puzzled and frowned at her.

'Rubbert has a right knack for the greasy pole,' she explained. 'Pit yer paper away, Tommy,' she said to her husband. She was evidently one of those whose bad temper never quite dissolves but simply shifts to a different target as the mood takes her. 'Would ye look at this man,' she said, appealing to me. 'He comes oot tae see a spectacle and stands readin' the paper that he can see any nicht o' the year.'

'Wheesht yer moanin',' said Tommy. 'A man can dream, can he no'?' He nudged me and showed me the open page of his newspaper where there was a highly embellished advertising notice from a shipping line. 'New Zealand,' he said wistfully. 'Steerage £18. Places still available.' He sighed. 'It leaves on Tuesday. I've got three days tae pack.'

I smiled at him while his wife scowled.

'If ye're waitin' for me tae beg you tae stay,' she said, 'dinnae haud yer breath.'

'Och, give it rest the pair of you,' said a woman nearby, 'and let's enjoy this.'

Our friend with the cowboy chaps had been dismissed at last and Robert Dudgeon was walking forward. As he broke the front of the crowd a rustle of appreciative anticipation ran around the arena.

'A man of many talents,' I said, and when a small child beside me looked up and fixed me with one of those quelling stares that little children can, I explained: 'That man is the Burry Man, you know, my dear.'

The child sniffed a superior sniff, and said: 'No he's not. The Burry Man's all green. And he's away on his ghostie pony back to his swamp till next year.' The child's mother gave her a clip on the neck for cheek, but the others – me included – smiled indulgently.

'Wheesht, Molly.'

'They should hold him back a wee bit and let some o' they other clowns gie us a laugh first,' someone said, watching Robert Dudgeon taking off his coat and handing it to his wife. 'It'll all be over too soon, else.'

'I'm not so sure aboot that,' said a voice behind me. 'Rubbert doesn't look himself tonight, and he must be fu' after the day he's had.'

'Och but he's fu' every year when he climbs the pole,' said the first woman. 'I reckon it's the drink that gives him his edge.'

If Robert Dudgeon *was* drunk, I thought, it was the drunkenness of one well used to the condition. His expression, granted, was rather owlish and his movements were slow and deliberate, but he did not sway or stumble as he handed his coat to his wife and turned his cap to the side. The crowd continued to clap and cheer, but he did not play up to them, neither smiling nor grimacing as he grasped the pole high above his head and heaved himself up. He clasped his legs around the pole and twisted his feet together neatly. Thus secured, he freed first one hand and then the other, wiped them on his shirt shoulders, leaving dark marks of oil there, and took a fresh hold.

'Mair washin' fur ye, Chrissie,' shouted one of the onlookers and several people turned to smile at Mrs Dudgeon. She gave a small tight smile in return but did not take her eyes from her husband, now halfway to the top, still clamping his legs and wiping his hands, pulling himself steadily upwards. Her tense concentration seemed quite at odds with the laughs and jokes of the crowd and I wondered for a moment whence arose this trait I was beginning to recognize in Queensferry to find portents in the blameless and shadows in the sunshine. Then a louder than ever whoop from the crowd drew my attention back to Robert Dudgeon.

He was nearing the top now, and it was quite dizzy-making to look at him. One last clamp with his legs, one last heave with his arms and he was there. He tugged a string on the bag of flour and it burst out in a cloud, covering his greasy clothes and drifting down over the onlookers, who stopped their clapping to swat it away.

'Fling down the ham, Rubbert,' voices cried. 'Fling it down and I'll catch it.'

But Robert Dudgeon made no move to touch the other parcel. He clung to the pole motionless for a long half minute and then began slowly to slide.

'Ye've forgot yer –' a woman in the crowd called with a cackling laugh, but she broke off as Robert Dudgeon slithered down faster and faster. He hit the ground with a thump, fell backwards, arms spread out, legs still twined around the base of the pole, and lay quite still.

For a moment there was silence, then a few awkward giggles and then, all at once, action. People rushed forward, one of them calling for a doctor. Others began to shoo off the children, still others – women – gathered around Mrs Dudgeon and bore her away.

It was only when I found myself kneeling beside him that I realized I was one of the ones who had surged forward to help. His face was dark and perspiration still ran from his brow, mingling with smears of oil and caked-in patches of flour. I could still smell the fairground smell of his breath, the sweet toffee apples he had been eating. Heat still wafted from him. His feet were still loosening their grip on the pole, his boots creaking. His half-open eyes, though, and his wide open mouth told the same tale as his chest, still as a stone. He was dead.

Chapter Three

Buttercup and Daisy might, I am sure, have put poor Robert Dudgeon callously out of their minds and had a perfectly pleasant evening; certainly they kept lapsing out of assumed solemnity and beginning to giggle over old memories of school until a glance at Cadwallader sobered them again. For Cadwallader, awash with guilt, sat with arms on knees, hands hanging down, staring at the floor. Every so often he would raise his head, catch someone's eye and heave a great sigh before looking down again, until one began to wish he were more like the husbands one was used to, who at least would be sighing and hanging their heads all alone in their library. But then *I* should be the cold spoon in the soufflé, for I did not feel quite as unperturbed as the other two at the thought of Robert Dudgeon's death. I alone had spoken to the man for one thing and I had played my small part in persuading him to spend what transpired to be his last day in life doing something he very clearly did not want to do. So I could understand Cadwallader's feeling awkward, but he was wallowing rather.

'I'll never forgive myself,' he said for the dozenth time. Daisy broke off in the middle of a story and composed her face, hardly sighing at all. Buttercup had no such scruples, but issued a moan that I hoped was partly in jest, for one should not be able to summon such scorn for a husband of six months' standing.

'You have nothing to reproach yourself with,' I said, ignoring the memory of his heavy-handed blustering the evening before. Cadwallader rolled his eyes at me.

'He knew,' he said simply.

'Don't be a goose, darling,' said Buttercup. 'How could he have known?'

'Search me,' said Cadwallader. 'But he did. Look how hard he tried not to do it. And I made him. And now he's dead.'

'But Cad,' I said gently, 'he didn't die of being the Burry Man. We don't even know why he did die yet, do we? And he's done it for twenty-five years without coming to any harm, so –'

'Exactly!' said Cadwallader. 'All the more reason we should have taken him seriously when he put his foot down this year. He knew.'

'Knew what?' said Daisy, crossly. She was tugging at her fox fur and hungrily eyeing the drinks tray. Cadwallader had come straight into the Great Hall and we had followed him, expecting a decent little interlude of serious thought and quiet remarks – five minutes maybe – and then a leisurely bath and a large cocktail, but we had been sitting around the edges of the table for forty minutes now, marooned by Cadwallader's gloom, and it was getting rather irritating. Even when my own father died, my mother changed in time for dinner.

'Daisy does have a point,' I said. 'What could Mr Dudgeon possibly have known? If it was a heart attack or an aneurysm, which it must have been, then it came out of the blue. And if he had *known* that his heart was weak or whatever, he would have told us last night and he wouldn't have climbed that wretched pole.'

This seemed unanswerable and Cadwallader changed tack.

'*I* should have known,' he said. Daisy and Buttercup both groaned.

'Now you're just being silly,' I told him.

'At least, I should have known better,' said Cadwallader, and this was said in such a small sad voice that no one groaned or moaned or sighed at all and my heart went out to him. It was all new, I supposed, this being in charge of a staff, and although Dudgeon's death could not possibly have had anything to do with the Burry Man it was an unfortunate sequence of events to occur so early in Cad's stewardship of the estate.

He was staring at his feet again. Daisy tapped her watch and mimed eating and then below us, startlingly loud, we heard a dull clanking sound.

'Front door bell,' said Buttercup. 'Melodious, isn't it?'

'I bet that's the police,' said Cadwallader.

The scrape of the door and the rumble of voices carried quite clearly up through the murder hole towards us and then, after a pause, light footsteps came hurrying up the stone treads and a maid appeared in the doorway. She was in black with her linen cuffs and frilled table apron on and she brought with her a rich waft of cooking. A slow rolling rumble emanated from Daisy's middle.

'Please, madam, sir,' said the maid, rather breathlessly. 'The police are here.'

'Land sake's alive,' said Buttercup in a mock American drawl. 'All right, Jean, show them into the library. Cad? You'd better go up and be ready to meet them.' But Cadwallader was shaking his head.

'Bring them to the drawing room, Jean,' he said. And then to Buttercup, 'We will face them together.' The maid looked from one to the other, bobbed a curtsy and left, and then all four of us scurried out of the hall behind her and made for the stairs. At the drawing-room landing Daisy and I naturally began to carry on up but Cadwallader let out an exclamation, almost a squeak of protest.

'Don't leave us,' he said.

'Very well,' I said, glad to have my nosiness indulged, but at his look of relief I had to giggle. 'My dear Cadwallader,' I said, 'they're not coming for you.'

Of course they were not, but anxiety is terribly catching and Cad's hand-wringing trepidation, as we arranged ourselves in natural-looking poses and waited, infected all of us a little. Then the ringing tread of policemen's boots on the stone steps did have rather an ominous feel to it, and so by the time the footsteps arrived in the passage outside the drawing-room door and the two men appeared in the flesh we were all cowering a little and inclined to gulp. There was a uniformed man, young and gormless-looking, busy casting his eyes around with interest at the interior of the castle, and an older figure, dressed in a light over-coat, carrying a soft hat, and looking surprised; not as though something in particular was surprising him right at the moment, more that surprise was the look of his face when at rest; surprise or a suppressed sneeze, one or the other. Anyway, it saved him from looking at all intimidating and one would have expected Cadwallader to rally.

I waited for him or Buttercup to rise or at least to say something but nothing happened, despite Daisy kicking Buttercup's ankle quite hard, and the senior police-man spoke first.

'Inspector Cruickshank, madam, sir, madam, madam,' he said and I marvelled at the composure it must have taken to get to the end of this without faltering. Still nothing from the host or hostess.

'Good evening, Inspector,' I said at last. 'I'm Mrs Gilver, a friend of Mrs de Cassilis's, and this is Mrs Esslemont. Mr and Mrs de Cassilis are . . .' I tailed off, 'hopeless' being the only word I could think of, which was hardly apropos.

'I'm not surprised,' said Inspector Cruickshank. 'What a terrible thing to happen. Robert Dudgeon, you can scarcely credit it. Hardly fifty.'

This seemed to point very comfortingly down the heart attack or aneurysm route and Buttercup brightened visibly although Cad still hung his head like a dog expecting a kick.

'Anyway,' said Inspector Cruickshank and shifted rather awkwardly.

'Do please sit down,' said Daisy with another swift kick at Buttercup, which connected only with her chair leg and so had no effect. 'And um . . .' She glanced towards the young man hovering in the corner, but Inspector Cruickshank waved his hand and tush-tushed to say we need not worry about him.

'The police surgeon is on his way,' he said.

'On his way here?' said Buttercup, round-eyed. Inspector Cruickshank frowned and shook his head.

'The fever hospital at Killinghouse Road is empty, given the time of year,' he said. 'So the post-mortem can be done there without delay. There is a room in a wee place by the gates of the cemetery too, but it's really more for exhumed corpses and I thought Mrs Dudgeon would rather he was at the hospital.'

'That's a very kind thought,' I said.

'An autopsy?' breathed Cadwallader, paling.

'It's a sudden death, Mr de Cassilis,' said Inspector Cruickshank. 'I'd go as far as to say a suspicious death, so certainly the body must be examined. I daresay Dr

66

Rennick won't find anything, but we have to be sure. And in the meantime, I'm just asking around, to see what I can see.'

I am sure the inspector had no idea how threatening he sounded in his vagueness so while Cad continued to shrink into his seat and stare I tried to take matters into my hands and move them along a little.

'How can we help you?' I said. 'Anything that any of us can do, obviously.'

Buttercup made some kind of echoing murmur.

'Two things,' said Inspector Cruickshank. 'Mrs Dudgeon was very keen to get Robert's body home with her, and she'll need to be told there's no chance of that until tomorrow at least. She'll need to be told about the post-mortem and it will all be better coming from you, Mrs de Cassilis, than from one of my men, don't you think?'

Buttercup looked quite stricken at the thought and shook her head slightly. I felt a little irritation. After all, running a place was not all playing at castles and had it been our estate carpenter at Gilverton I should not have relished the task but I should not have shirked it.

'And the other thing?' said Daisy.

'Yes, well, as I say,' said Inspector Cruickshank. 'My guess is that Rennick will find natural causes, but just in case he doesn't, I might as well get ahead of the game while I can.' This did not quite ring true, I thought, and looking at him closely I wondered just how sure he really was. 'So,' he went on, 'I believe Robert Dudgeon came to speak to you yesterday night, Mr de Cassilis. What can you tell me about that?' A surreptitious sound from the corner drew my attention and I saw the constable flicking open a notebook and drawing out a pencil he had threaded into its spring.

'He seemed very well,' said Cadwallader. 'In good

health, you know. No signs of any illness. So it must have been terrifically sudden.'

'And how was he in himself?' said Inspector Cruickshank. 'In his spirits?' Cad shrugged as though to suggest he had nothing to add and I stared at him, shocked. The senseless guilty conscience act was one thing but he could not seriously intend to lie to a policeman. I blushed inwardly at my own moral outrage (after all, lying to policemen was not unknown to me) but this was different.

'He was troubled,' I said in a loud, clear voice. Cadwallader could say what he liked to me later; there was no point in making this any worse than it was. Inspector Cruickshank cocked an eye at me and waited for more.

'He didn't want to do the Burry Man,' I said. 'I was there too, you see, Inspector. He didn't want to do it one little bit, but he wouldn't say why.'

'And how did you persuade him in the end?' said Inspector Cruickshank. I thought about this for a moment before answering.

'I can't honestly say,' I told him. 'I can't quite remember what I said that made the difference.' I looked towards Cad, before remembering that he had left by the time it came to that. But came to what? 'I made a little joke about Mr de Cassilis taking over, but he knew I didn't mean that. Then he just seemed, all of a sudden, to change his mind.'

'Interesting,' said Inspector Cruickshank. 'Would you say he seemed frightened of the job?'

'No,' I said slowly. 'Cad, did he seem frightened to you when he first turned up?'

Cadwallader shook his head. 'He seemed exactly the same as when I was up on the roof with him earlier. Quite himself and perfectly calm, only absolutely determined not to dress as the Burry Man.'

'Until he changed his mind,' said Inspector Cruick-shank. 'And when you were with him earlier in the day, sir, he said nothing about these misgivings?'

'Not a word,' said Cad. 'That's a curious thing now that you mention it, Inspector. Why would he not?'

'Perhaps looking for an opening and not finding it?' I suggested. This would be absolutely up my street, I was sure – spending an hour with a person I had to tell something to and funking it completely so that I had to summon twice as much courage, pay a special visit and blurt it out standing on the carpet twisting my hat.

'No, that wasn't it,' said Cadwallader, 'because I was joking about it with him. We were up on the roof, as I say, and we could see some of the people still picking the burdock seeds. They're scarce this year, I believe, but there are some good big clumps of them on my land. They came to ask my permission and all that, and I was delighted to let them.' A note, not quite petulant, had crept into Cadwallader's voice. He must have felt such a rush of well-being to be up on his castle roof with his trusted servant watching peasants below picking at the bushes on his say-so. An age-old tradition carrying on thanks to *his* carpenter, *his* bushes and *his* magnanimity must have been more than many Americans ever dream of. How horridly awry it had all gone since. Poor Cad.

'Anyway, I was joking with Dudgeon about it,' he said. 'Shouting down to them to be careful to get only the prickliest ones, and Dudgeon laughed and said there wasn't much to choose between one burr and another and besides he was used to it.'

'So at that point – when would this be, sir? – at that point he was intending to go ahead.'

'Oh, definitely,' said Cadwallader. 'This was just before tea. Three o'clock or something. So whatever it was that made him change his mind happened between then and seven when he came back to tell me the thing was off.'

This was a puzzle to be sure, but who could say whether it had anything to do with what had happened at the greasy pole? Inspector Cruickshank appeared to be thinking along similar lines to me, because he rolled the thought around for a minute or two, glancing at the constable to make sure the man was getting it all down in his notebook, then he seemed to shake it out of his head and he returned to business with an expressive sniff.

'Well, we'll see, we'll see,' he said. 'Meantime, Mrs de Cassilis, would you be so kind as to pop along to Mrs Dudgeon's house and explain.' Buttercup nodded; the same hopelessness which meant she would rather die than do it also meant she had no idea how to wriggle out of it. Or so I thought.

'Of course,' she said. 'Dandy and I will go together.' I did not even bother to protest.

'We must take something,' I said ten minutes later, standing in my petticoats in Buttercup's bedroom, as we tried to divide what black clothes she had between us. 'Oh, heavenly!' I exclaimed, falling upon a figured silk tea dress in black with the merest hint of purple. Buttercup had already bagged the only black skirt in her collection that did not look like a coal sack.

'Purple roses, Dandy, be serious,' said Buttercup, rootling through dark blouses. I took the silk frock over to the window and looked at it in the light. The figuring was roses, I could see now, but I was not going to give it up without a struggle.

'Purple is perfectly funeral,' I said. 'And it's so deep as to be practically black upon black anyway, and in the twilight, and in a cottage –' There was a sharp rap at the door which made Buttercup jump and drop what she was holding, but which I recognized with long experience as Grant.

She marched in, holding over one arm a black linen frock with bottle green ribbon-threading and carrying a bottle green small-brimmed hat and black kid shoes in the other hand. I did not recognize any of them.

'Your mourning, madam,' she said, depositing them on Buttercup's bed and whisking the figured silk away from me with a pitying lift of her eyebrows.

'I bought them in the spring,' she added, by way of addressing my look of puzzlement. 'I didn't bother you with it, madam, for who likes to be reminded of the need for them?'

'And you brought them here because . . .?'

'I always pack them, madam,' said Grant, sounding astonished that I might doubt it. 'Otherwise . . .' She glanced again at the black and purple roses and her lip curled. 'Can you manage?' she went on. 'The hat will cover everything.' Grant, it will be clear, thinks little of my talents as a hairdresser. I nodded and she left.

'Well,' said Buttercup. 'Talk about the spirit of Nanny Palmer living on, Dan really.'

'Nanny Palmer was a darling,' I countered. But I knew what she meant. Nanny Palmer was a well-starched darling who stood no nonsense and it is perfectly true that a great many of my retainers since have been along the same lines.

'We have to take something,' I said again. 'Soup? Might there be a pie? Or a bottle of cordial? Flowers certainly.'

'We'll ask Mrs Murdoch on the way out,' said Buttercup. 'What a pity she's only just arrived, though. A pie is a possibility, but as for a cordial or anything in a bottle I should think the chances are slim. What about cherry brandy? We have gallons of that somehow and it's absolutely filthy.'

'So generous,' I said, as I set the bottle green hat on my head. It did indeed cover everything, and although one would think that a bottle green and all-enveloping hat would make someone of my sallow complexion look like one of the swamp creatures for which Queensferry was renowned, it suited me rather well. Grant is an angel in serge.

Mrs Murdoch, an angel in a linen pinny, was ready for us when we reached the ground floor and clearly the household tom-toms had related our mission to her for she had put together a basket with not only a pie, a bunch of lilies and a bottle of the cherry brandy, but also a fruitcake in wax paper and a bottle of tonic (her own recipe) which, she said, helped her own dear mother no end when her own dear father was taken.

I drove us, directed by Buttercup, threading through the estate on grassy tracks and glimpsing Cassilis House as we passed. (A boring Georgian box, Buttercup had called it, and it was short on the architectural furbelows and tassels which adorn many houses in the Scotch baronial style, but since her precious castle was three medieval cubes one on top of another, I could not quite see her objection.) Within minutes we had arrived at a pair of cottages sitting in some woodland about a mile away. Buttercup hesitated at the gate, clearly unsure which cottage was the one we were after, but a glance at the washing lines criss-crossing the gardens showed one teeming with little shirts and pinafores neatly arranged in order of size while the other line held only three men's vests and a tablecloth. Furthermore, a row of bright red heads – the owners of all the shirts and pinnies – popped up at a window in the left-hand cottage to watch us and so, hazarding a guess, we negotiated the path to the one on the right.

72

Buttercup squared her shoulders, heaved the basket high up in front of her like a breast shield and knocked on the door.

It was answered by a sturdy woman in her forties, with sleeves rolled past the elbow and a cloth tucked into her skirt waist as a makeshift apron. Her ruddy, mottled face was fierce and grimly set at the jaw. She glared at us and shook her head even as she stood back to let us enter.

'Chrissie's in there,' she growled and jabbed a finger at an open doorway. I was at a loss to explain our transgression, but when we entered the kitchen-livingroom of the cottage she gave just the same look to Mrs Dudgeon and then to the crockery she was busy drying and I realized that her outrage encompassed us all. It was not too hard to understand – grief and shock settle quite readily into indignation in those whose personality is predisposed that way – but one can imagine that it does not make for the most suitable atmosphere in a house of mourning. Mrs Dudgeon, sitting upright and pale with misery in a hard chair, one hand clenched around a crumpled handkerchief, looked uncomprehendingly into the fierce face then lowered her eyes.

Buttercup, predictably, boggled and shifted her feet and so it fell to me to sit down beside the woman and lay my hand over hers. The handkerchief was quite dry but as soon as I spoke – no more than saying her name – quantities of tears began at once to course down her cheeks and splash into her lap.

'There, there,' I said, thinking what an ineffectual little phrase that was, as Mrs Dudgeon spread out her handkerchief, pressed her face into it and wept with abandon.

'Where might I put these things?' said Buttercup in a panicked voice.

'Aye, come away through the scullery,' said the fierce companion. She put down the cooking pot she was drying, slammed it down actually, amongst the others still draining by the sink and led Buttercup out of the room. Mrs Dudgeon continued to sob and I continued to pat her shoulder and shush-shush uselessly.

I looked around the room as I did so, as though not to gawp at her shaking shoulders would afford her some dignity. It was a typical cottage kitchen-livingroom, more prosperous than some I had seen with its thick rug and good mahogany sideboard, but quite typical nonetheless. The range in the hearth was gleaming as was the kettle atop it, and on either side of it sat two comfortable chairs of the Windsor type, their seats adorned with cushions in knitted covers. Between them was one of the tiny wooden stools they call creepies in Perthshire, which I have always liked and long wished I could insinuate into my own sitting room somewhere. Another knitted cushion sat on this and, imagining the many evenings Mr and Mrs Dudgeon must have spent in these two chairs sharing the creepie stool between their four tired feet, I could quite see why she was perched comfortless at the table now. It would have been as unthinkable to sit in her chair and look at the emptiness opposite as it would be to sit in his chair where, if cottagers were like the rest of us, she would never have rested for a minute in her life. I withdrew my eyes from the morose tableau the armchairs made but, looking up at the mantelpiece, found no respite from the sorrow. I had forgotten what Mr Dudgeon had said last night, but there was the photograph of the young man, stiff although beaming, in a uniform so new that the sleeves and breeches' legs stuck out like the paper clothes one cuts for dolls. Beside the picture was a spray of rosebuds tied with a ribbon of Black Watch tartan and below

74

it little flat case, resting open, which I was sure would hold his medal. I looked away as a hard lump, impossible to swallow like one's twentieth walnut, formed in my throat.

At last, Mrs Dudgeon's sobs turned hoarse and dry and eventually stopped with a gulp. She raised her head and tried a small smile with trembling lips. It was not successful.

'What must you think of me?' she said, blowing her noise tremendously on the sodden handkerchief. I offered my own and she took it and wiped her eyes, which were spongy with weeping. I smiled at her.

'I think what a man your husband must have been and how you must have loved him,' I said.

I realized as soon as I had made it that this remark, honest as it might be, was hardly more helpful than grumpy housework in terms of comfort. It sent Mrs Dudgeon off into such a storm of weeping that I feared the dish-drying woman might come back and box my ears. What were she and Buttercup up to anyway? And yet, I do not know, for when Mrs Dudgeon finally raised her head from my shoulder again she did at least look cried out. She glanced at me and then looked beyond me to the window and out into the woods.

I heard movement from beyond the scullery door; Buttercup and the woman were returning.

'Is there anyone we could fetch?' I asked Mrs Dudgeon quickly, before I could be overheard. I only just managed not to say 'anyone *else*'.

'No, no,' she said, still looking out into the fading light. 'My sisters –' she began, then broke off as the door opened.

'Very well, then,' I said with one last pat on her hand, before settling back in my seat to a more normal social distance. Her sisters must be on their way,

I thought. Much the best thing. They would soon see off the stop-gap.

Buttercup seemed mysteriously emboldened when she reappeared and started by assuring Mrs Dudgeon that the next day's Ferry Fair was to be cancelled. The widow would not hear of this.

'It's not fair on the bairns,' she said. 'And Robert would never have wanted it.'

Perhaps encouraged by such doughtiness Buttercup then launched into relaying Inspector Cruickshank's message, but at the news of the post-mortem and even more so at the news that her husband's body was to be kept from her, Mrs Dudgeon's store of courage ran out.

'They can't,' she said faintly. 'They cannot do that. I must have him back with me. I must have him here.' As she spoke she looked at the picture on the mantelpiece and I wondered about her son's final resting place. If he were one of the thousands who lay somewhere in France in a row of graves, I could see why Buttercup's news could cause such anguish.

'It won't be for long,' I told her. 'He'll be brought back just as soon as can be. You'll have him here before you know it.'

'But they can't . . . I don't want them . . . interfering with –' She stopped and her face suddenly drained of colour. For a moment I thought she was about to faint but she stayed upright, rigid and still, just her eyes darting around.

'Don't dwell on it,' I said, thinking how unbearable it would be to imagine a post-mortem being carried out on a loved one. Mrs Dudgeon said nothing and did not seem to have heard me and, since Buttercup was jerking her head towards the door in a disgustingly unsubtle signal, I thought the best I could do was go. I gave a murmured goodbye, a last squeeze of her arm and quite a fierce look of my own at her friend, and we let ourselves out of the front door at last.

'Phew,' said Buttercup on the doorstep. I saw what she meant but hoped fervently that Mrs Dudgeon had not heard her.

As we made our way back to my motor car, the door of the other cottage opened and three little children – three of the redheads we had seen before – burst out and shot down the path overtaking us easily.

'Wheesht yerselves,' a voice hissed behind us, and we turned to see a girl with a baby on her hip and a toddler held firmly by the arm. She looked to be about twelve or thirteen, her own flaming red hair still loose down her back although she was well grown and strong. The toddler keened after its siblings, who were now vaulting or scaling the garden gate according to their age and agility and clustering around the Cowley.

'Get away in the woods before you make a single sound now,' their sister said, still in her stage whisper. 'Or I'll be after you and then you'll be sorry.' She turned to us and gave a sheepish half-bob. 'I ken it looks bad,' she said, 'but I cannae keep the wee so-and-sos quiet another minute, and I thought it would be worse for Auntie Chrissie to hear them whining and bickering if I tried.'

'Oh quite,' I said. 'One can't stop children playing. I shouldn't worry.'

The girl looked a little relieved as she hauled back the whimpering toddler and shut the door.

'Missus! Missus!' said the largest of the three children as we approached them. 'Can we get a hurl in your wee car, missus?' The other two joined in with the pleading; none too quietly and I could see their sister standing at the cottage window shaking her fist, although not liking to rap on the glass and cause a disturbance of her own.

'Do you know who I am?' said Buttercup, nonplussed I think by their complete lack of bashfulness, confronted by their liege lady.

'Aye,' said the smallest child, a girl whose copper-red hair and ice-blue eyes were ruined by a pink ribbon which clashed and by a runny nose. 'You're the wifie from the castle what's married to a Red Indian.'

Buttercup hooted with laughter at this and so to get her, as much as to get the red-haired terrors, out of poor Mrs Dudgeon's earshot, I opened the back door of the motor car and shooed them all inside.

They were momentarily awestruck by the wonder of its interior – as overwhelmed at finding themselves in my little Cowley as I should have been upon entering an aeroplane – and I managed to get the thing started, manoeuvre it around on the track and set off for home before they found voice again.

Around the first bend we passed a group of village women dressed in black, all ages, shapes and sizes and all carrying parcels.

'Thank goodness,' I said to Buttercup. 'These must be the sisters at last. Now then, children, where are you off to? Where shall we let you down?'

'We're goan in the woods to kill the demon,' was the startling answer from the youngest, which met with furious shushing from the others.

'Shut up, Lila,' said an elder brother. 'We're jist playing at monsters, missus, in the woods.'

'You said we were gonny catch the d–'

'Shut *up*, Lila,' said big brother again. 'Or we'll drop you doon a shell hole for the ghostie soldiers to eat you.'

'Good Lord in heaven,' said Buttercup under her breath, and I quite agreed.

Soon we passed out of the trees and into the open parkland surrounding the new house, where I drew up and parked.

'Out you get,' I said. 'Run around on the grass and play catch. Or hide and seek. And don't put your little sister down holes. Now, off with you.'

'I'm not sure I'd encourage them to rampage around the parkland,' said Buttercup mildly as we watched them roar off.

'Oh my dear, no, of course, I didn't think,' I said, ashamed of myself, for the various ragged little warriors of Gilverton do not have any such privilege. 'Well, it's a special case tonight, isn't it? But if they keep at it you can tell Cad to buy some ornamental cows. Ones with great big horns. Or stags even.'

'Who would you fancy, darling, between a poor defenceless cow and those savages?' said Buttercup. We watched the children throw themselves into the ha-ha and emerge from it again on the other side, red hair almost pulsing with light as the setting sun caught it.

'Very fair point,' I said. 'Do you think there really are shell holes? Has Cadwallader mentioned any?'

'Oh Dandy,' said Buttercup. 'I think we can class the holes with the demons and the ghosties, don't you?'

I shivered.

'I've never known a place like it,' I said. 'Did I tell you? A child watching the greasy pole this evening – quite a tiny child – declared to all around that the Burry Man lived in the swamp and got to and from it on a ghostie pony. And the grown-ups simply laughed fondly and ignored it.'

'The swamp I can see,' said Buttercup. 'I mean the

79

Burry Man *is* rather fungal, isn't he? But whence the ghost horse for him to ride on?'

'Although, if you imagine riding in a suit of burrs,' I said, 'our side-saddle torments would be as nothing.'

Buttercup giggled along with me. 'Yes, a *ghost* horse would be de rigueur, when you think about it.'

I quelled my laughter.

'Rather nasty to be making jokes about it,' I said. 'We're as bad as the children.'

'Hm,' said Buttercup. 'Come on, I need another drink.'

'An*other* drink?' I said.

Buttercup giggled again.

'Yes, Isobel and I did a bit of sampling while you were chatting to Mrs Dudgeon,' she said.

'Chatting! Buttercup, you're impossible. And I'm surprised at "Isobel" too. A taste for strong drink is hardly the norm amongst her sort.'

'Oh heavens, no,' said Buttercup. 'She stuck most resolutely to the tonic pick-me-up – apparently Mrs Murdoch's bottles of tonic are quite renowned. But actually I'd have said, from the smell of it, that it could knock the cherry brandy into a cocked hat.'

'Well, who knows,' I said. 'Friend Isobel can't have got that complexion from barley water, can she?'

'And there's to be no escape from Ferry Fair day,' said Buttercup as we reached the castle and ascended to its door, the engine whining slightly at the slope. 'I must say Cad's and my year in charge of the thing is hardly likely to go down in the annals as a classic!'

Shocking as it must sound, I too had been hoping that one faintly silver lining in the monstrous cloud of Robert Dudgeon's death would be that festivities would be suspended as a mark of respect and I would thus be able to avoid the unwanted and unwelcome duty that hung over my head. Mrs Dudgeon's stoic insistence that Robert would have wanted things to go ahead as usual, however, left me facing the bonny babies with nowhere to hide.

Chapter Four

Daisy, judicial tasks accomplished the evening before and desperate to escape the castle, where Cad still continued very sombre, was all enthusiasm the next morning at breakfast. This was taken in the Great Hall at the Great Table on the newly arrived Great Chairs, since amongst all the other matters they had neglected in their childlike embracing of castle life, Buttercup and Cadwallader did not seem to have thought of a breakfast room. It was not too bad just yet; for one thing we were all good friends and a powerful note of new plaster and varnish still hung around, but I could imagine that as time went by and the Great Hall became redolent of rich dinners and cigar smoke as all dining rooms do in the end it would become insupportable to trail in to breakfast to sit at the same table with all the same bores who had driven one off to early bed the evening before.

'We must do our very best today, Freddy,' said Cadwallader, through a huge, choking mouthful of sausage – he always loaded his fork as though pitching hay with a rainstorm threatening – 'to strike the right note. We've got to keep things perky enough to stop the whole jamboree feeling like a funeral, but at the same time we should take care not to be . . .'

'Unseemly in our merry-making?' I suggested. Cad brandished his knife at me.

'Exactly! We must respond to the mood of the crowd for one thing. We don't want to seem more morose than these good people who had known him for years. Freddy, are you listening?' Buttercup – patently not listening – nodded hastily and assumed a rapt expression. 'But at the same time we must not for one minute look as though we're careless of the fact that he died, in case some near relation or bosom pal happens to notice.'

I felt suddenly rather sorry for Cadwallader. He was in a ticklish kind of a spot and his attempts to plan a route through it only made it the more obvious how hopeless it was to have him swan in and fill the role he was filling. Hugh, I am sure, would have done more or less exactly what Cad was now outlining but he would have done it without a moment's thought and certainly without a syllable being uttered.

'At least by the end of today we should know what happened,' Cadwallader continued. 'I've asked Inspector Cruickshank and Dr Rennick to track me down at the Fair as soon as the autopsy's over and tell me the results.'

Daisy rolled her eyes. 'Mightn't that inject a bit of a note, Cad darling?' she said. 'Mightn't that tip the scales just a shade towards ghoulish?'

Cadwallader's eyes clouded with doubt, but I could not face any more strategizing and so I broke in, rather rudely, to ask Buttercup: 'What happens when? And where is it all? Please tell me the babies are first, because I won't enjoy a thing until I've got that horror out of the way.'

'Oh, I'm declaring it open at ten, I think,' said Buttercup. 'I was going to ask you what I should say in my speech, Dan.'

'Frederica, you're not even trying!' said Cadwallader, with the note of wounded exasperation I remembered hearing from mistresses and house matrons (for a while until they all gave up).

'It'll be fine, Cad darling, stop fussing,' said Buttercup, and of course, because Daisy and I spent the next hour and a half fretting over the speech for her and making notes on little cards, it was. As she delivered it, tears were wiped but there was laughter too and when she had finished, the townspeople quite seemed to regard their coconut-shying and sack-racing as marks of respect for Robert Dudgeon, so purposefully did they make their ways to the various sideshows or the table where officials were taking entrants' names. The fairmen started up their hurdy-gurdies, and a fiddler struck up a tune to which people immediately began to dance one of those terrifically complicated Scottish country dances.

By twelve a queue of children had begun to form at the town hall steps.

'Such a good idea,' said Mrs Meiklejohn, the Provost's wife. 'They queue to get a ticket, and then they take their ticket all the way along to McIver's Brae and queue again to get a bag of picnic goodies and a balloon so by the time they plump down on the grass to eat it they're nicely calmed down and well exercised to boot.'

'Do I detect Mr Turnbull's hand?' I said. 'He seems very keen on lungfuls of good fresh air and the rest of it.'

'Lord, no,' said Mrs Meiklejohn, with a laugh. 'Mr Turnbull might well have them chasing around the town to get their hands on their lunch bag, but he wouldn't approve at all of what's inside it. Mind you, Mrs Gilver, he's doing marvellous things up at the school. Drafting in lecturers from a college in Edinburgh, was the latest I heard, and the children are taking to it like so many ducks to water. In fact our doctor's wife – terribly set in her ways although a wonderful friend and neighbour really – told me almost in spite of herself that she thought Mr Turnbull's techniques were showing results already.'

The gods were smiling upon us, for it was at this fortuitous juncture that Mr Turnbull himself appeared suddenly behind Mrs Meiklejohn, with a bashful grin. Had he been half a minute earlier, it might have been awkward.

'Spare my blushes, Mrs Meiklejohn, please,' he said in self-satisfied tones. Mrs Meiklejohn looked at me with dancing eyes but managed not to giggle. 'I do my best.'

We said nothing, Mrs Meiklejohn and I, gave him no encouragement, but he was clearly one of those who did not need any.

'If I can see to it that even one child of mine stays away from the bottling hall, out of the mines and off the fishing boats,' he said, 'I shall count myself a success. Horticulture, Mrs Gilver. Horticulture, agriculture, arboriculture and husbandry. There is good wholesome work on the land for as many as want it.' He waited, preening, for some response.

'I can see why the bottling hall mightn't be to everyone's taste,' I said carefully, thinking that I for one could not spend a working day amongst whisky fumes without sickening. 'And coal mining is filthy and dangerous work to be sure. But whatever is your objection to the fishing boats? I'd have thought bobbing around on the ocean wave . . .'

'Shale mining,' Mrs Meiklejohn corrected me mildly. 'It's shale mining round here, Mrs Gilver. Not so heavy but just as beset with –' At this Mr Turnbull interrupted her.

'Coal mining or shale mining, there's very little difference in the essentials. It all encourages superstition and morbidity. And fishing is worse than either. Tall tales and talismans filling their heads with nonsense.'

'Ah,' I said, understanding him at last. 'Certainly, yes. If one puts one's life at risk every day one would naturally try to be lucky.'

'There's nothing natural about it,' said Mr Turnbull.

'And the problem with the bottling hall is . . .?' I said, although I could easily guess.

'The demon drink,' Mr Turnbull confirmed. Beside me, Mrs Meiklejohn was breathing heavily, trying to control her laughter. 'But I'll save them, Mrs Gilver. The children will pass out of my sphere as bonny and pure as they enter yours today.'

'*My* sphere?' I asked, puzzled.

'That's what I came to tell you,' said Mr Turnbull. 'Your infants await.'

'Oh golly!' I said and followed him. Ahead of us at the Bellstane I could see a gathering crowd of women, each with an armful of frilled and beribboned baby. Most of these seemed to be bawling and some of the women, dressed in black, looked so near tears themselves that one could not imagine why they had not withdrawn their entry.

'Oh well, it's only a bit of fun, Mr Turnbull, isn't it?' I said in an attempt to rally myself.

'Not really,' he said, showing no tact whatsoever, I thought. 'There is the prize.' He pointed towards a handsome wooden high chair, newly painted in a cheerful pale blue and with a motif of little ducklings across it. 'Such good practical prizes,' he went on, with immense satisfaction, nodding towards the town crier who had been parading around all the morning with a pair of boots hanging from the top of his staff.

'I had been wondering about those boots,' I said.

'They're the prize for the borough race,' said Mr Turnbull. 'The race around the town boundary. A new pair of good boots is not to be sniffed at.' I had never known a man like him for pushing wholesomeness down one's throat until it made one choke and by this time I was ready to bet that Mr Turnbull had cold shower baths every day, he and his wife taking it in turns to pour buckets of water over each other in the garden and beat themselves with eucalyptus branches. I pictured this briefly. Perhaps not.

When we arrived at the Bellstane, what looked like a couple of hundred young women stood before us, industriously primping the curls and buffing the cheeks of babies ranging from a few months old – the lolling, useless stage – to bruising great beasts of almost two who tore at their bonnets and struggled to escape the restraining grasp. These were fearsome creatures, and I quickly decided that although I should have to show some enthusiasm for each of the brats, I was determined to make the final selection from amongst the smaller, gentler specimens. The winner, I was determined, was to be one which would not bite me as I held it up for its moment of glory.

I inquired about names and ages and trotted out a little snippet of praise or appreciation for each: 'What a darling,' 'A fine strong boy,' or, when confronted by a particularly nasty one, 'Here's a character, then!' and it was easy enough to whittle out the absolutely hopeless, whose presence could only be explained by the blindness of mother-love. After that I was at a loss. I should have to shut my eyes and, so to speak, stick a pin in one, for no other option presented itself. Still, I was almost at the end of the line, my early estimate of two hundred having been panic-induced, of course: there were thirty. And only four to go. The next was quite a little one, wrapped in a gauzy shawl and held by a rather tired-looking woman in her forties.

'Who is this?' I asked, smiling sweetly towards the

bundle. I had hit upon this phrasing after coming a cropper with the more obvious, when 'What's his name?' had brought the answer 'Susan' and a scowl.

'Doreen,' said the woman, and opened the shawl a little. I peered in. Two shrewd, round blue eyes looked back at me from under a wisp of dark hair with just a glint of red in it. The baby could not have been more than six weeks old, still with the elfish look of the newborn, the look which I am sure is responsible for all those fairy tales about changelings. As her mother loosened the shawl further, a tiny fist sprang out and spread like a starfish in front of me. I bent closer and put my finger to her palm, expecting her to grasp it – my fingers had been grasped and sucked and even nibbled all along the line – but Doreen, looking past my face, sank her fingers deep into my fox fur. She was too tiny to chuckle, but she gave a small purr like a nursing cat and smiled faintly.

'A taste for the finer things in life,' I said to her mother, who gave a weary echo of the same faint smile, but said nothing. I had a cursory look at the rest of the creatures in the line, but my mind was made up.

'The prize for the bonniest baby of all these very bonny babies,' I said, 'goes to little Doreen. Congratulations.' Doreen's mother beamed and nodded but all around were rumblings.

'Wee Doreen Urquhart?'

'She's a poor wee scrap of a thing.'

'She wouldnae make half of my Andrew here.'

Too late I remembered what Daisy had said about picking the fattest one or at least the one with the rosiest cheeks.

'Yes,' I went on, rather defensively. 'Doreen Urquhart. There's an enormous personality inside that little frame and, mark my words, she will grow up to be a great beauty.' And I clapped my hands decisively, ignoring the glares.

This minor blunder of mine aside, the day seemed to be going off quite well. Cadwallader and Buttercup were circulating assiduously like a pair of diplomats at the very top of their game and from what I could tell they were managing to strike the right note. For one thing, Buttercup is such a darling close up, so chummy and unaffected, that people can't help but take to her one-to-one; it is only when she is given a large arena that she causes affront. As for Cadwallader, he shied balls at coconuts with the best of them, but when he missed he gave a rueful shrug as though respect for the Dudgeons might have put him off his stroke. Similarly, Buttercup clapped and hurrahed at the races but handed over the prizes with a pat on the arm and a smiling sigh. The townspeople themselves, too, had that natural impulse to respect the dead which meant that some of the bawdy raucousness of the previous evening was missing; this even though the precise *manner* of respecting the dead in a Scottish village meant that any man sufficiently affected to be wearing a black tie and armband was likely to be quite seriously drunk.

So, it was not exactly decorous but it was far from the Bacchanalia that Mr Turnbull feared and I stuck it out for some considerable time. By two o'clock, however, Daisy and I began to wonder when we could decently make our way back to the motor car and retire for the day. I had purchased more cheap hatpins and sewing cases than I had housemaids to give them to, and Daisy wanted only to find a suitable small child to honour with the garish teddy bear she had won by lobbing coloured balls into goldfish bowls, and she too would be ready to go.

I craned around for Cad or Buttercup, preparing my

excuses, but when I finally spotted the golden head – Cad's real gold, not Buttercup's April Sunrise – my heart rolled over. Inspector Cruickshank and a dapper little man I took to be Dr Rennick had drawn Cad aside in the doorway of a hairdresser's shop under the terrace – shut up for Fair day – and the three were talking with bowed heads and solemn faces. Daisy and I made our way over.

'Mrs Gilver, Mrs Esslemont,' said Inspector Cruickshank. 'Good news. Or rather as good news as possible under the circumstances. Death by natural causes and no need for an inquiry. We'll be able to return Dudgeon's body to Mrs Dudgeon this evening.' Cadwallader's expression was very hard to read.

'What did he die of?' I asked.

'Heart failure,' said the little doctor. There was something just slightly off about his manner. He held his head back and looked down his nose through his half-spectacles, rather ridiculously since even Daisy and I were taller than him by inches and Cad and the inspector positively loomed.

'Thank you, Doctor,' said Inspector Cruickshank. 'That's agreed then.'

This was a very odd remark and to cover it, I supposed, Cruickshank began to direct Daisy and me in rather hectoring tones to go and find Buttercup and get ready to visit Mrs Dudgeon, and when this petered out he took to bidding the doctor an elaborate farewell. Dr Rennick, with one hard-ish look at us all, melted away into the crowd. Meanwhile, I continued to stare at Inspector Cruickshank who, to his credit, after watching Dr Rennick's back for a moment or two, then looking around above my head and whistling, finally met my eye.

'You are quite right, Mrs Gilver,' he said, obviously too cryptically for Daisy who looked at him in surprise.

Before speaking again, he ushered us all out of the cramped doorway and we began to walk along the crowded street looking for Buttercup.

'A death certificate is a very serious matter,' Cruickshank went on. 'But do not be alarmed. Robert Dudgeon did die of heart failure. Only it was brought on by alcoholic poisoning.'

'Poisoning?' echoed Daisy, stopping in her tracks.

'*Alcoholic* poisoning,' said Inspector Cruickshank, putting a hand under her elbow to keep her moving, 'is the medical term. In layman's terms he drank too much and his heart gave out. At least a bottle of whisky as far as we can make out, never mind the beer, and only a wee ham sandwich to soak it up. Dr Rennick said he had never seen anything like it.'

'How on earth do you know –' began Daisy, then stopped and grimaced. 'Oh, how revolting, Inspector really.'

'And the death certificate will show . . .?' I said.

'Heart failure following on excessive consumption of alcoholic liquor,' said Inspector Cruickshank. 'We need to be scrupulous as far as the certificate goes. But let's call it heart failure plain and simple when we speak of it. I'm a great believer in taking care of the living and letting the good Lord take care of the dead.' A surprising statement to come from a policeman, I thought, unblinking zeal in the pursuit of justice being rather more usual.

'Well, I guess,' said Cadwallader, as though rolling some idea around in his head.

'Look around you,' said Inspector Cruickshank. 'Look at them all in their blacks and their armbands. Dudgeon was their friend and you can be sure near every one of them gave the Burry Man a nip yesterday. What good would it do to go using a word like poisoning and make them think they had killed him?'

I glanced around at the villagers, and felt myself beginning to agree.

'And,' he went on, 'it would awaken some very unwelcome ghosts.' I saw Daisy rolling her eyes, but when she spoke her tone was quite polite.

'Ghosts, Inspector?'

'Figurative ghosts,' he assured her. 'There was a case here before, of what might have been alcoholic poisoning. And we never got to the bottom of it.'

'Really?' I said. 'Recently?'

'Oh no, years ago,' said the inspector. 'Must have been four or five years ago now. Four more like; I remember it was about a year after the end of the war. Two young . . . gentlemen, I suppose you'd call them. Came on a sketching holiday and ended up dead.' His voice was hard. 'They went on a drinking spree along the High Street and once they were in their cups they let it slip that the pair of them had been conshies. The next morning they were found, face down and dead, down the lane behind the Sealscraig.'

'Poisoned?' asked Buttercup.

'Hard to say,' said the inspector. 'Could have been. They were certainly well pickled. Or they could have passed out and died of hypothermia, lying out all night.'

'Two of them, though?' I asked.

'That was the trouble,' said the inspector. 'Two young men in good health. The other possibility was that they were deliberately intoxicated then taken away and laid so that they'd smother in their sleep. As I say, we never got to the bottom of it and it made for a very troubled air about the place until we finally let it be. I've no wish to bring it all back to folk.'

I held no brief for conscientious objectors, and I did not want to dwell on the tale but, about the current instance, something still troubled me.

'Inspector,' I said, 'if you *did* say it was poisoning, although it would be horrid for everyone, at least it would stop the same thing happening again. I mean, I'm as loath as the next to give fodder to the Temperance gang, but in this case, just this once, don't they rather have a point?'

Inspector Cruickshank's face twisted up into a wry grin.

'Oh, don't worry, Mrs Gilver,' he said. 'They don't wait for ammunition. They'll have started already. Go to the church tomorrow morning if you don't believe me.' At that moment we passed a pair of bobbies and Cruickshank, unable to resist the chance to inspect a couple of his troops unannounced, raised his hat to us and marched towards them.

'So that's that,' said Cadwallader. 'Now, where the hell is Freddy?'

We mounted the steps to the terrace above us to scour the crowd for her and stood watching the three quite separate occasions which seemed to be taking place all at once in the street below. Children were perched on every wall, windowsill and kerbstone, licking at toffee apples and ices, or were jostling at the stalls and plucking at their mothers for more pennies, intent on winning or wheedling another sticky treat while the going was good. The women more or less ignored the stalls and sideshows, choosing instead to stand around in laughing, chattering groups, seeming not to look at the children at all until a bark of reproach or a swift cuff to a passing ear gave the lie to it. In the same way, they seemed not to be looking at one another, but I was sure that each new dress or old hat was being studied and would be discussed amongst little knots of particular friends later on, just as I was sure that Daisy and Buttercup would be ready to share with me their thoughts on Mrs Turnbull's terrible shoes and Mrs Meiklejohn's surprisingly good pearls. Finally, the men. Perhaps we had chosen an unfortunate spot as our vantage point, slap between the Stag's Head and the Queensferry Arms, but it seemed that all around working men, well-scrubbed for the day, with scraped cheeks and slicked-down hair were staggering into pubs, staggering out again, blundering along the street towards the Forth Bridge Saloon or, if they stood in gossiping groups of their own, waving like ears of wheat in a breeze and taking the occasional sudden step to the side when their balance threatened to leave them altogether. Three scenes then: the children out of Hogarth, the women from Brueghel, and the men, I fear, straight from an illustration in a Temperance pamphlet. All that was missing was Buttercup.

At last, I spied a head of bright curls disappearing around the bend towards the Hopetoun Road.

'There she is,' I said.

'She's going the wrong way,' said Daisy with a querulous note like a tired child and Cadwallader too looked at his pocket watch and threatened to glower.

'I'll catch her and you two go ahead,' I said. 'We'll meet up at home.'

With that, I plunged into the crowds again and began dodging in and out, threading my way towards my object, now and then catching just a glimpse of the glinting head. It really was the most peculiar colour. At last, after a determined effort – she was covering the ground at some speed – I called out and reached for her arm, but instead of the handful of silk georgette sleeve I had been expecting, my fingers closed on rough cotton, slightly sticky, and the head turned to reveal the face, shadowy under the eyes and blotchy with tears, of Joey Brown the barmaid.

My first thought, I am heartily ashamed to say, was that I should take great delight in telling Buttercup of my mistake in the hope of stamping out the April Sunrise for ever. Following hard upon this, though, came the proper recognition of what stood before me.

'My dear,' I said, 'whatever is the matter?'

Miss Brown took her trembling lip between her teeth, and shook her head wordlessly, while tears continued to fall.

'Come, come,' I said. 'Sit and tell me what's happened.' I drew her down on to a low wall, but she only gulped and hung her head. 'Or is there anyone I can fetch?' I said, getting desperate. She shook her head vehemently, curls bobbing. 'I say, I hope no one has hurt you?' I went on, this idea only just occurring. 'If one of these young men has made a beast of himself, Inspector Cruickshank and two of his men are just around the corner and –'

'No!' said Miss Brown at last, looking up wildly. 'Thank you, madam, it's nothing like that. It's just . . . My father wants me to go and see her and . . . I just can't. I can't go there.'

'Where?' I said. 'Where can't you go?'

She did not answer, but only continued to weep. I had been patting her arm absent-mindedly, but only at this point did it occur to me that the cotton sleeve I was patting, which had registered as sticky in the first instant, was sticky with new dye, and that more of this dye, obviously hastily and clumsily applied, had rubbed off on Joey Brown's neck. Of course, mourning.

'I see,' I said. 'Mr Dudgeon.'

Miss Brown sobbed, one hand over her mouth and the other pressed so hard against her eyes that it must be painful. I took her hands gently and drew them away, giving her a handkerchief, the thought flashing across my mind that I hoped Grant had packed plenty since this was the second I had relinquished since the same time yesterday.

'And now my father wants me to go and see her.'

'Well, that would be kind,' I said. 'But if you can't face it no one will think the worse of you. You're not a relation, are you?'

'No,' she said. 'I'm not.' And for some reason this made her howl more than ever. 'I can't go there, because it's – it's – all my fault. And I was just being silly and now he's dead.' This was delivered in a tiny whisper, hoarse with tears.

'How on earth can you think it's your fault?' I said.

'I was supposed to give him his dram and if only I hadn't looked in his face or if only I hadn't dropped it. If only I'd been braver. If only I'd known.'

'Oh, my dear,' I said, putting an arm around her. 'Oh, you silly girl. You must put this nonsense out of your pretty head at once. Why, you of all people are one of the few who shouldn't feel the slightest twinge of guilt, because you –' I stopped myself. It had been decided by those with far more say in the matter than me that this should not be touched on.

'Because I what?' said Joey, looking up at last. 'Why me of all people? What do you mean?' She looked wary and rather scared. I stared at her, spitting with exasperation that I could not tell her that if only more of Dudgeon's so-called friends had dropped the glass and run away he would be still walking around.

'Nothing,' I said at last. 'Only one can't bear to see a pretty young face spoiled by tears, and one can't bear to see a bright young head full of nonsense. You did nothing to harm Mr Dudgeon, and you know it. Your father should have known better than to play such a trick. Tell him that from me.'

Miss Brown drew herself up, and wiped her eyes.

'My father did no wrong, madam. I don't know what you mean.' She blew her nose and stood up and I must say it is a bit much to be cut dead by a slip of a girl while she blows her nose quite so lavishly into one's own handkerchief. Still, I was glad of this natural end to our tête-à-tête.

'Chin up, Miss Brown,' I said magnanimously.

'Thank you,' she said, rather more gently. 'Now, if you'll pardon me, madam, I must get back to the bar. This is a very busy day.' She set off in the direction she had come, whatever mission she had been on abandoned.

'At last!' Mrs Dudgeon half rose out of her seat as Buttercup and I entered her living room an hour later. The cottage was beset by the women we had passed the day before who sailed around her in that self-important kerfuffle which always ensues when there are more bodies desperate to help than there is help needed, but I had no great opinion of any of them as handmaidens for her grieving: if anything she seemed even more agitated than she had the previous evening, trembling and anxious, barely making sense when she spoke.

'Have they finished with him? I don't know where I had put my wits last night. I wasn't even thinking. And they've kept him all this time and all his things.'

'They have finished,' said Buttercup, 'That's what we came to tell you. He will be brought home to you tonight. A Mr Faichen?'

'The undertaker,' put in one of the women.

'Yes, Mr Faichen will be bringing Mr Dudgeon home very shortly.'

'And all his things?' said Mrs Dudgeon.

'Of course,' I said. I assumed I was correct. Why would these things – whatever it was she was so anxious to regain – be kept away from her?

'Good.' Mrs Dudgeon sat back for less than a heartbeat it seemed before she pressed forward again. 'I need . . . I want to have him here with me. And his things. I cannot bear to think of them going through his things. Did they, do you know, madam? Did they go through all his things? What did they find?' All of this was on a rising scale which brought an answering murmur of soothing noises from her companions.

'What did they find among his things?' echoed Buttercup wonderingly.

Mrs Dudgeon gazed blankly at her for a second and then spoke hurriedly.

'No – I – What I mean is, what did they find when they did the . . . What did the doctor . . .'

'Heart failure,' said Buttercup.

Mrs Dudgeon sank back into her chair.

'Heart failure,' she repeated, but even as she said it her eyes began to flit back and forward as though she was thinking furiously, and presently she added:

'So they're not going to do a post-mortem after all? There won't be any . . .' Again a rushing chorus like wind in trees began as the women tried to drown out such a bald reference to the very worst of it all.

'They've done everything necessary,' I said. 'And heart failure is what it told them. The doctor thinks it was probably down to . . . I mean, it didn't help that he had had rather a lot of whisky.'

'But he hadn't,' said Mrs Dudgeon. Her companions drew in a collective breath. 'I mean . . . he'd had a few drams but he wasn't fu'. I grant you he'd had a few nips, but he wasn't fu'.'

'These doctors,' said Buttercup. 'They would have us all on milk and water if they had their way. Of course he wasn't. I mean, he was the Burry Man for twenty years and more and the nips of whisky are as much a part of the day as the burrs and the flowers, aren't they?'

Mrs Dudgeon did not answer this although it seemed to mollify her. She chewed her lip for a moment, still casting quick glances from side to side, and then finally she raised her head and addressed me apprehensively.

'Will there be an inquiry?'

When I shook my head I saw in her face a strange mingling of expressions, growing puzzlement and something else too. She could not, quite clearly, ask whatever it was she wanted to ask, and that in some way left her helpless. I looked back at her, just as helpless, longing to ask her what was wrong, what *else* could possibly be so wrong as to supersede something as enormous and immediate as her husband's sudden death.

And did she really believe he had hardly drunk a drop all day? It was possible: people do manage to maintain such delusions. I have an aunt as wide as she is tall, fingers like sausages and calves like hams, who tells me with round-eyed sincerity, all chins a-waggle, that she lives off thin soup and grilled cutlets, actually tells me this while dipping her spoon in and out of the quivering mound of trifle with which she is cleansing her palate after the *boeuf en croute*.

Perhaps Mrs Dudgeon was not as bad as this; perhaps she knew exactly how drunk Robert Dudgeon had been and was feeling guilt that she had not prevented it with some application of wifely skill: nagging or huge helpings of milk and potatoes, but it was not guilt, that expression upon her face, nor anything like guilt. I tried to pin it down but my attention was distracted by one of the handmaidens proffering tea. The rest of them watched me almost greedily as I drank, but only for a moment did I wonder why. No fewer than three, leaning against the sideboard in a row like waitresses in a lull, had cloths in their hands and they were waiting to pounce on our used cups, desperate for even such a scrap as that to make them feel busy and helpful. Out of kindness I accepted a biscuit and a plate to put it upon, and made sure to scatter plenty of crumbs. How it must have thwarted them that the grim woman of the night before had done so much of the available housework before they got there.

'No inquiry,' said Mrs Dudgeon, just as I finished my tea and relinquished the cup and as I did so and heard her words, I remembered something and at the same time I suddenly recognized the expression on her face, but before I could put a name to either the memory or the look they cancelled each other out and the moment was gone, quite gone, like a sneeze unsneezed, or like a gun half-cocked and unfired while the pheasant flaps off into the dusk, screeching.

'So that's that,' said Mrs Dudgeon. She gazed about her as she had the day before, at the chair opposite, at the picture on the mantelpiece, and she spoke with great calmness, into the silence of the room. 'That's the end of it, then. That's that.'

'That's that?' echoed Cadwallader, later. 'She said, "That's that"?' Buttercup and I had joined him and Daisy in the library whereupon he had poured me a monstrously huge drink and demanded to be told all.

'Yes, but it wasn't the way it sounds now,' I said. 'Was it, darling?'

Buttercup only blinked.

'It was as though she were saying, I had a husband yesterday and today he's gone and there's no reason for it and no one to blame and that's that. Actually,

100

I rather thought it was her son *and* her husband, you know. She did glance towards the son's picture as she said it. She had them both and she lost them both and there's the end of it and she's on her own now. It was terribly sad and it makes perfect sense.'

'It does?' said Cad with a sly look at Daisy which I could not begin to interpret. He waited, Daisy waited, Buttercup stared into space and sipped her cocktail.

'And yet,' I said, almost reluctantly. I was tired, drained from all the giving of sympathy, not to mention the bonny babies. 'And yet . . . there was something.'

'Mrs Dudgeon said something?' asked Daisy.

'Not exactly,' I said. 'She looked . . . Oh, I don't know. It's probably nothing. Once before in my experience someone at a comparable moment behaved not as I thought she would and in that case it turned out that all was far from well. So I suppose I'm just looking for trouble and, therefore, as my nanny warned me, finding it. Ignore me.'

'So this feeling you had,' said Cadwallader, 'it was just a funny look from the widow, was it? Nothing else?' I stared at him and at Daisy too, puzzled, with a growing feeling that something was going on here I could not quite catch on to.

'What are you two up to?' I said. Cad gave back a limpid gaze, but Daisy fidgeted and would not meet my eyes. She has a dreadful habit, started goodness knows where and when, of sticking her cocktail stick, once the olive has gone, into the setting of her engagement ring, then snapping it off and sticking in the next bit, and so on and so on until her beautiful cluster of five diamonds looks like a dried porcupine. I have seen her go through an evening like this, little ragged bits of cocktail stick poking out from her finger, and I assume that her maid removes them at bedtime. Grant, I am sure, would smack my legs and put my ring in the bank if I did the like.

'One of these days, one of those stones will ping right out, darling,' I said. 'And if it goes in the fire, I shall laugh.'

Daisy raised her eyebrows in that haughty way of hers (I am immune to it) and said: 'Don't take it out on me, Dan. Just give in.'

'Give in to what?' I said.

'I knew it,' said Cad. 'Although you wouldn't listen. I knew it this morning. Robert Dudgeon knew it last night. And what you've said convinces me that Mrs Dudgeon knows it too. Now, if an autopsy had come up with something solid I was prepared to believe I was wrong but . . .'

'Not this again,' I said, almost, almost laughing. 'Robert Dudgeon died of heart failure owing to alcoholic poisoning. How can you doubt it? How can you doubt Inspector Cruickshank?'

'I don't,' said Cadwallader. 'I'm sure Dudgeon did die of heart failure, everyone does, in the end. And no one can doubt the alcohol. I'd even be willing to put quite a bet on poison.'

'A poison which the post-mortem failed to detect?' I said. 'Not an untraceable poison, Cadwallader, really! One can be drummed out of the Sherlock Holmes Society for the mere mention.' He ignored me.

'What did *you* think of the inspector, Dandy?' he said.

'What did I think of what aspect of the inspector?' I said.

'Not to mention the doctor,' he went on.

'The police surgeon?' I said. I had not thought much of the police surgeon, truth be told, but before I could properly bring him to mind and wonder why exactly, Cadwallader was speaking again.

'Did Robert Dudgeon look drunk to you last evening?' he said.

I shook my head. All of a sudden my scalp prickled.

'Well, then,' said Daisy.

Both she and Cad were looking hard at me, waiting. The ludicrous thought struck me that they thought I had had something to do with it all. Why, otherwise, were they staring like that? What did they want?

'Well then what?' I demanded.

'Will you take the job?'

'What?'

'Daisy here has filled me in as to your terms.'

'My . . .?'

'And I've told him, without a word of a lie, darling, that you're absolutely splendid, even if you do tend to store your light under the nearest bushel for safekeeping.'

'Oh, I see!' said Buttercup at last. 'Daisy did tell me about you branching out into diamond theft and murder, Dan, but I forgot.'

'I'm not sure I'd put it quite that way,' I said. 'Not on my card, at least.'

'You have cards?' said Buttercup, impressed.

'I don't,' I admitted.

'But you do have the knack,' said Cad.

I shrugged modestly.

'And you have the time, Dan,' said Daisy.

I could hardly deny that.

'All right,' I said at last. 'I'll do it.' And I thought to myself, why not? Perhaps last time was not a fluke. Perhaps I do have the knack. And I may not have a pipe, nor a deerstalker, nor a magnifying lens, nor an apparent walking cane that is really a sword and a compass, but I do have a Watson. At least I did last time and I was sure I would not have made any headway without him. Now, the question was how to get him off the grouse moor on the twelfth of August. I should have to give him the whole of my fee.

Chapter Five

Alec's face, upon first seeing the castle, was a sight not to be missed so I made sure to be standing alongside Cad and Buttercup outside the great iron-studded door as his motor car negotiated the grassy ramp. He looked up, up, up, counting arrow slits on the Hall floor, the library floor, and the first bedroom floor, then took a step back and shaded his eyes with one hand to look at the last two floors above. His head-shake as he turned his gaze back to Cad must have been meant to loosen the crick in his neck, but Cad took it as awe.

'Wonderful, isn't it?' Cad said, absolutely artless.

'Wonderful isn't the word,' said Alec.

I managed to turn my snort into a cough, but Cad was busy anyway, introducing himself and Buttercup and trying to explain to Alec's valet about the other house and the system of connecting telephones.

Buttercup could not be prevented from launching into her tour.

'We'll finish up in the library, darlings, so wait for us there,' she said, before bearing Alec away into the kitchens. I saw that she was set to turn into one of those hostesses who *process* house guests rather than entertaining them, but there are worse kinds of hostess than that since, when one has been simmered, seasoned, minced and tinned by them, one is then left pleasantly alone. Besides, the castle and Buttercup's guileless raptures over it were genuinely diverting and at least here it was rooms and fittings not dreary gardens or, worse, the drains, walls and ditches over which my own husband enthuses so mystifyingly. Hugh is always rather bewildered at his guests' blanket refusals to be shown a new kind of cattle grid or an ingenious self-filling water-trough in a far field.

While we waited in the library, I took the chance to hammer home to Cad one point I felt our earlier discussion had left rather vague.

'I do hope you realize, darling, that even though you've retained my services' – I pronounced it as I thought a real private detective might: 'a-retayned may a-suhvices', which was lost on Cad, of course, hardly Henry Higgins after all – 'I can't guarantee to find anything out. And if I do, I'm an absolutely independent agent.'

'Of course, of course,' said Cad, then spoiled it by adding, 'What do you mean?'

'I mean, I probably won't discover anything at all, but I'm setting out to discover "what" and "whether", not to confirm "that".'

'Daisy told me this would happen,' said Cad. 'She warned me that I wouldn't understand what on God's green earth you were doing, much less talking about, but that I should leave you to it and it would all come right in the end.'

'That's the thing, you see,' I told him earnestly. 'It depends what you mean by "come right".'

'And there you go again.'

'Look,' I persisted. It was quite, quite crucial to establish this, I thought, and I was most impressed with myself for my scrupulousness. After all, I wanted nothing more than to racket about in Queensferry, on expenses, with Alec, and if I ever got Cad to listen to what I was saying and take it in, I might find myself back in Perthshire instead, stuck with the children all day and nothing to look forward to but spending the evening with Hugh. 'Put it this way: if you were the peddler of a patent home Marceller – no electricity, singeing or stickiness – I would not be one of your own medical doctors saying that hair would be strengthened and rejuvenated with every application, Cad, I would be the woman who wrote to the papers saying mine had all fallen out and not grown back again. Which is not to say that you are, of course.'

Cad's face told me before I was finished that my analogy had not been helpful, so I told him straight.

'I think something strange is going on,' I said. 'Clearly Robert Dudgeon was troubled on Thursday evening, and Mrs Dudgeon is worried and perplexed as well as grief-stricken now. And Robert died. If he was murdered –'

'He was.'

'*If* he was murdered, then his fears, his widow's anxieties and his death might all be explained at one fell swoop. But it may just as easily be that he was worried about one thing, his wife is worried about another and in the middle of it all his heart gave out from alcoholic poisoning. I just want to make it very clear that although I know you feel dreadfully guilty, Cad dear, I am not a salver of your conscience in this. I'm a . . .'

'Seeker of truth.'

'Yes! Exactly.' I had, at last, got through his glowing, creamy skin. 'I'm a seeker of truth, and I'm afraid that unearthing grubby but unrelated secrets is –'

'Your speciality?' said Alec's voice. I had been so caught up, I had managed to miss their advancing tread and he and Buttercup stood framed in the doorway.

'But darling, there's your card right there!' said

Buttercup. 'Dandy Gilver: Servant of Truth. And underneath in italics: Grubby Secrets a Speciality.'

'I'll order five hundred to be going on with,' I said, drily. 'I was going to say "an unavoidable hazard". Well, Alec?'

'Quite,' said Alec, sitting.

'What did you think of the oubliette?' I went on. 'Larder? Or not?'

'Larder would be such a waste,' said Alec, turning innocent eyes on Cad and Buttercup. 'An ice house, perhaps. Or a hot bubble bath, although the plumbing would be a bit of a challenge, and off the kitchen is hardly handy. Venison smokery? Or, if one could put in a large pane of glass, it would make a tremendous fish tank. You could grow your own lobsters, de Cassilis. Or, substitute wire mesh for the glass and it could be an aviary. If I were Mrs Murdoch, I'd like nothing more than a pair of peach-cheeked lovebirds wittering away while I pounded my bread dough.'

This was going far too far and, although the pair of peach-cheeked lovebirds opposite me in armchairs seemed impervious, I frowned at him.

'Alec is teasing, Buttercup,' I said.

'Alec's doing what?' said Cad. Buttercup squealed.

'Dandelion,' she said threateningly.

'Frederica Ambrosine Rosamund Jane?' I said.

'What a memory!' she exclaimed. 'Small wonder you've turned Sherlock, darling.'

Cadwallader looked at his pocket watch with an extravagant gesture and sighed.

'I followed every word for almost three minutes then,' he said. 'But I'm lost again.'

'Give up now,' said Alec. 'Watch their teeth and smile when they smile, old man, it's the only way.'

'Oh, so it's not a transatlantic problem,' said Cad, sweet in his ingenuousness.

'God no,' said Alec. 'Now, since my cover story for being here is that I'm helping you with your stocking, what say we go up on to those splendid ramparts and you show me the lie of the land.'

'Ooh, speaking of the lie of the land, Cad,' I said, 'are there really shell holes on the Cassilis estate?'

'Shell holes?' echoed Cad. 'What do you mean?'

'I hardly know,' I said. 'Holes from shelling, I suppose. Or trenches just possibly.'

'Neither,' said Cad. 'Why would anyone shell here?'

'They wouldn't,' said Alec. He stood and turned. 'Let's go. Unless there's anything you need me for this minute, Dan?'

'No,' I said. 'I'll have to fill you in of course, but after lunch will do.' Buttercup smirked at me, adding to the ruffled and slightly foolish feelings which were whisking around me like the tails of hungry cats around one's ankles.

'Alec,' said Buttercup, 'I meant to ask you: how did Dandy persuade you off the moor in the end?'

'Oh, easily,' Alec said, looking her straight in the eye. 'I far prefer hunting to shooting, and hunting clues beats hunting foxes any day.'

'Lunch at two?' said Cad, halfway to the door.

'Mrs Murdoch looked to be boning a duck when we passed through,' said Buttercup. 'So don't be late.'

Mrs Murdoch had indeed boned a duck, and had made choux pastry and whipped rather a lot of cream, all since it was Sunday I presume, so Buttercup and Cad were happy to laze about in the library afterwards and made no protest when I commandeered Alec to walk in the park and receive his briefing. I had told him very little over the telephone the day before, only that it seemed there might be another 'case' in the offing and since I knew he had no party with him – he had only very recently come into his estate at Dunelgar and his little bit of grouse moor and fledgling staff of servants were not yet ready for a public – what did he think?

'I stopped in at Gilverton on the way,' he said now, as we set off down the slope, my summer shoes skidding slightly on the close velvet nap of the sheep-cropped grass.

'Hugh's at Wester Ross with the Wallaces until Tuesday,' I said. 'Yeek!' I slipped down another yard. 'Should have worn boots. And the children are off to the seaside with the Esslemonts. That's why Daisy had to go.'

Alec stopped dead in his tracks. 'Daisy has taken your children off to the seaside?' he said in owlish wonderment.

'Hardly, darling! I mean my boys are off to the seaside – Arbroath: brrr! – with the Esslemont boys and both nannies, and Daisy went home to wave them off. She and Silas are in Monte until September now.' I sighed, as one must when one's friend is in Monaco and oneself is in Scotland, but actually I hate gambling – having, as my boys tell me, a poker face that's not even good for snap – and with my sallow skin I cannot lie in a beach chair without turning as brown as a tinker; my pink legs from Thursday were already golder than Buttercup's hair.

'What took you to Gilverton?'

'Hedges,' said Alec. 'Your steward is an excellent chap with hedges, Dandy. I'm thinking of trying to poach him.'

'Not *my* steward,' I said. 'And he loves Hugh with a devotion you could not hope to dent.'

'Anyway, it seemed uncivil to drive right past when I might have been able to bring a message or something.'

'Damn,' I said. 'What a chump I am. You might have

collected my things. I was only meant to be here a day or so, and I'm running out badly. Practically going to be wrapped in brown paper by tomorrow.'

'Of course,' said Alec. 'What would have been easier than for me to rummage through your wardrobe and pick out a few frocks?'

'Grant is there doing the picking, idiot,' I said, severely. 'I meant you could *bring* them. Now for goodness' sake let's get on with it.'

'Yes, do stop wittering on about frocks and fish tanks, Dandy, please.'

I ignored him, gathered my thoughts briefly, and began.

'Humph,' he said, when I had finished. 'It's a bit thin, isn't it? If I've got you aright. Between teatime and dinner on Thursday, Dudgeon suddenly developed a strong disinclination to carry out his yearly duty as this green man character. I shall have to see a photograph of it, you know, because at the moment the mind rather boggles. He would not elucidate the problem, but when you tried to persuade him he promptly changed his mind back again for no obvious reason. He walked the town, drinking whisky, eating nothing, and not even – as you put it – powdering his little green nose, from nine in the morning until six in the afternoon. He was then going to go straight home with his wife – another departure from the norm – but changed his mind *again*, came back to the Fair, climbed the pole as was his wont and there, in the most theatrical way imaginable, died. The police were suspicious at first, but the post-mortem showed heart failure caused by alcohol –'

'I'm not happy about that,' I said. 'Could we say that the examination found heart failure, enough alcohol to explain the heart failure, and nothing else that would have caused him to die. Can you see how that makes a difference?'

'I can indeed, and it's a salutary point, humbly taken. Right then, his wife was upset, but not – what would you say? – not as upset as she ought to be?'

'No, it's not that. I don't think for a second she did it. She was considerably distraught. Devastated would hardly be too strong a word. But she was also worried by something, and when she heard that there was to be no investigation, that there was no question of foul play, she seemed . . .'

'Relieved? She would be.'

'Not relieved exactly. More like unwilling to believe her . . . I don't want to call it her luck for after all her husband did die and I'm sure she loved him and is heartbroken, but I think she suspects something, or maybe even *knows* something, so while she's relieved, she's also puzzled and not quite ready to trust that it won't still blow up in her face.'

'She must be cultivated, clearly.'

'Of course.'

'And not to shirk, darling, but that would rather fall to you.'

'Of course, of course. I shall have to take Buttercup along, I expect, but nothing could be more natural. Now, where you come in is to –'

'Hold on. Don't just plunge. I take it, by the way, that "Buttercup" is Frederica? Not kind. Anyway, all that – Dudgeon's ambivalence, Mrs Dudgeon's distraction and the death – that's what we know, but what do we think, Dandy? What does de Cassilis think happened? And why did the doctor miss it? Who are our suspects? What are our theories?'

I had to work hard not to let my spirits and my shoulders droop under the weight of all this. Suspects?

Theories? There were none. And yet, when I set my mind to it, various little sparks did begin to flash.

'To start with,' I said, 'I don't know about you, but I feel very wary of admitting the notion that the doctor "missed" something. I know Cad is leaping gaily on to the "untraceable poison" wagon, but it seems altogether too far-fetched to me.'

'Agreed.'

'Also Dr Rennick is practically suppressing the facts as it is, putting the heart thing centre-stage and drawing a thick veil over the whisky. He wouldn't do that if he had been less than thorough.'

'Let's hope not. But you're dismantling our case before we've even started and on the telephone you seemed to think there was something in it.'

'I do. Dudgeon was not himself. Something happened on Thursday afternoon. After his death Mrs Dudgeon was terribly worried that an inquiry was going to reveal what that something was. There is our mystery. There is our case. But I believe, I really do, that the death was exactly as Dr Rennick described it.'

'A meaningless coincidence?' Alec looked at me, inquiringly.

'I'm afraid so, unsatisfactory as it seems. Or perhaps not exactly. Perhaps the mystery contributed to the strain on Dudgeon's heart in some way.'

'And have you any idea what that mystery is?' said Alec.

'No,' I admitted. 'But have you asked yourself why Buttercup and Cad were catapulted into such a prominent role in the Fair within minutes of hanging their hats here?' Alec shook his head. 'Well, there are a clutch of interlocking little stand-offs – stands-off? – stand-offs being enacted very subtly by various parties. I haven't quite sorted the players out yet, but there's a teetotal element, which would like the Ferry Fair

113

shut down, or at least turned into a tea-party which would amount to the same thing. There's also a rather grim religious element which disapproves of the Burry Man for obvious reasons, and probably isn't too mad about the general frivolity. There's also a fearful bore of a schoolmaster who seems to straddle both camps. And I just wonder – Cad put me on to this, actually – whether Robert Dudgeon was, I believe the term is nobbled.'

'Murdered by a representative of the Temperance Movement?'

'Not murdered, Alec you goose. Haven't you been listening? Nobbled. Bribed maybe, or blackmailed.'

'I see!' said Alec. 'He undertook not to do his thing, then he double-crossed them and did it anyway and the added stress of knowing he was for it led to his heart attack and now Mrs Dudgeon is dreading the comeback. He must have been remarkably suggestible. Practically spineless.'

'Hmm, he didn't strike me that way, I'll grant you. But it's only a thought.' I stopped, since we had come to a fence, and rested my arms upon one of its posts.

'So,' said Alec. 'Worming away at Mrs Dudgeon is the first task for you. What about me? Am I to infiltrate a Temperance meeting? I doubt that the blackmail would be minuted and the sum entered into the accounts.'

'Quite the reverse,' I said. 'The first thing I'd like you to do – with Cad if it's easier or alone – is to go on what I believe is called a pub crawl. I want to get some idea of just how much whisky was involved on Friday so that we can talk Cad out of his fevered imaginings, and at the same time you can gossip away to the landlords and the bar regulars and might pick up a scent of what was on Dudgeon's mind.'

'So I'm to be quaffing beer and chatting up serving

wenches and you're to be holding the hand of the widow. That seems fair.'

'As luck would have it, though, darling, Brown's Bar where the comeliest of the local barmaids – Miss Brown – can be found is already ticked off the list. That's the one place we know he had nothing. So sucks to you.'

'Dandy, you must stop quoting those horrible children of yours.'

'Make me,' I replied. 'To which the answer is "Watch me." And then I think it's "You and whose army?" You're right, Alec. They're unspeakable. I shall have them adopted. Now where shall we go? Into the woods, over the fields, or back to the castle?'

'Not the fields. I saw them from the ramparts earlier and they're a forest of reeds, bound to be marshy. De Cassilis needs to think about some drainage if he's going to put stock on to –'

'*Et tu*? Not drainage, for God's sake, please.'

Alec laughed good-naturedly and did not pursue the topic. We looked up and down the fence for a gate into the woodland, and as we found it and clambered over – the latch being as stout as it was complicated – we began to hear distant shouts and squeals from amongst the trees ahead.

'Speaking of unspeakable brats,' I said, 'if these are the children from the next-door cottage to Mrs Dudgeon, prepare yourself. They are what enthusiasts call unspoiled and everyone else calls holy terrors.'

Sure enough, it was them. Their number had swollen to five by the addition of another two brothers smaller than little Lila, definitely brothers too with their screeching red hair. This made, I calculated, a dizzying total of eight including the work-worn eldest sister we had encountered in the doorway with her two infant charges. Today the children were swarming on and

115

around the remains of a long-dead beech tree, clearly a favoured venue for play since the earth surrounding it was bare and trodden hard and the stump itself was embellished with enough nails and pegs to allow even the smallest child to hoist himself up into its hollowed top. Here some old tin sheeting made a shelter which was currently being stoutly defended by one of the older children, waving a leafy branch in the faces of his siblings as they mounted attack.

'Lila, Lila, headless horsies!' shouted one of the boys and, with Lila's willing compliance, he scooped her up on to his shoulders, she wound her chubby legs under his arms, he clamped his hands hard over her knees, and together they charged the tree-stump again. Another pair – large brother with small brother atop – followed suit and with the little ones grabbing like lobsters whenever the big ones lunged in close, the brother in possession of the stump soon dropped his branch and, shrieking, seemed in danger of being pulled apart.

'Hey, hey, hey!' shouted Alec as we approached them. 'Steady on there.'

'The best of luck to you, darling,' I muttered under my breath.

The two tinies had let go of their prey, who was now flexing his shoulders and scowling, but they kept their seats on their brothers' shoulders so that when we drew near Alec and I were looking them straight in the face. Lila at eye-level was not a pretty sight, lavishly filthy and quite clearly not having troubled herself with a handkerchief all the day long. The boys were no more appetizing, but somehow the dust and stains on their knitted jerseys and darned flannel shorts seemed less revolting than the evidence of breakfast, lunch and hours of play on Lila's faded gingham and wretched little ribbon. Still, when one looked closely, if one could bear to, it was clear that all the dirt was today's dirt and that the hair underneath the leaves and bits of twig was shiny, the cheeks underneath the dust rosy and smooth. I had seen much worse, and even if they had only been cleaned specially for the Fair it was nice to meet them once they had been and not before.

'We're jist playin', mister,' said the oldest boy. 'And it's my shot in the castle, Tommy.' Tommy, shamed into fair play by the presence of grown-ups, scrambled out with medium-good grace: a tongue stuck out but no shoving.

'That's right, take turns like good brothers and sisters,' I found myself saying sanctimoniously. Their answering expressions, although rude, were no more than I deserved and so to raise my stock a little – why does one always suck up so shamelessly to strange children? – I said:

'So, castles today, eh? No ghosts and ghouls?'

'The ghostie's away down a hole cos Lila peed herself in the castle,' was the startling response.

'Naw-naw,' said Lila, kicking out at her accuser and causing the brother who bore her on his shoulders to stagger around in an attempt to hold his balance.

'Aye-aye,' came back the chorus from all the boys. Lila, face thunderous under her flaming hair, struggled down to the ground and set off across the woods, bawling.

'Lila pees her kni-ckers!' sang brother Tommy to her retreating back and then at Alec's cluck of disapproval: 'She does, mister.'

'That's Lila's business and no one else's,' said Alec, sounding pompous and quite ridiculous (I was smirking almost as much as the boys).

'Aye well, it got rid of the ghostie,' one of them said, philosophically.

'Hadn't you better go after her?' I suggested as Lila's howls began to fade. 'She might get lost.'

'She might get ate!' cried a small brother. 'She might get stole away and never brung back.'

'Aye, or the demon might get her.'

'Oh yes, the demon,' I said. 'You never did catch him then?'

'And make her drink blood and then she'll come back in the night when we're all in our beds and – Waarghhh!'

At this, the small brother who had started the train of thought in the first place obviously reached the limits of his courage and began to snivel. In between, we could hear the classic soaring moans of a ghost – unmistakably Lila even without the odd hiccough left over from her recent tears – and the brothers one by one cocked their ears and fell silent.

'Tommeee! Donaaald! Randaaaall!' whooped the ghost.

'She's doon by the burn,' they whispered. 'Let's fling her in.' And with that, Alec and I quite forgotten, they were off.

Listening to their shouts and laughter and with an ear cocked, in my case at least, for any sudden splashes, we made our way back to the gate.

'Cherubs all,' I said.

'Whatever happened to ring-a-roses?' said Alec.

'Ah yes. Well, along with the demon drink and the godless fertility rituals, this charming little Burgh does rather go in for bumps in the night, you'll find.'

'Perhaps I will take de Cassilis with me around the pubs then,' said Alec, 'to hold my hand.'

'At least if I'm sitting with the widow, the presence of an actual corpse as large as – Well, decency will forbid them their ghost stories for once. I might even be able to get some proper helpful gossip.'

'I must say, though,' Alec went on, 'I do approve of the practical note in their metaphysics: ghosts driven out by the simple application of a little girl with an unreliable bladder. And to think of all the chanting and potions that go into exorcism elsewhere!'

'I'm not so sure,' I said. 'They are perverse in their tales, woods full of the ghosts of soldiers even though the real soldiers all fell in the fields of France and yet not a peep about the ghosts of two young men who really did die here – and died horribly – and could easily be imagined to linger. And then the arrangement of their ontology – do I mean ontology? – seems a little random too. Why should ghosts live in holes guarded by demons and why should the Burry Man live in a swamp full of dead babies in his off-duty months?'

'Why come to that should these unfortunate infants be in the swamp?'

'Well, *there* there's an answer, but let's not pursue it or I shall have nightmares. Those red-headed angels certainly are fearless though, aren't they? I doubt that at Lila's age I would have taken off alone into a haunted wood whatever my mortification.'

'Well, they do say it's the living one need take care about,' said Alec, echoing Inspector Cruickshank, 'not the dead.'

Chapter Six

Buttercup was aghast at the notion of being dragged back to the Dudgeons' cottage that day after tea. Mrs Murdoch had done us proud – a pot of stew under a lard crust, a fruit pie and two bottles of cordial – but her mistress stuck out her bottom lip and shook her head.

'He's *there*, Dandy,' she said, shuddering. 'I simply couldn't.'

'He won't be in the living room,' I said. 'And you must. Even if it weren't for me you should have to, but I certainly can't go on my own.'

'He will be,' said Buttercup crossly. 'You wait and see. He'll be in the middle of the floor with the lid open and candles all around, and I shall faint.'

I suppose one should have felt pity; after all she had been in New York all the years of the war and had not got used to the idea, and sometimes the sight, of men dead and dying all around, but I had been no more stout of heart my first day at the hospital, indeed my knees had knocked so badly that my starched apron crackled even when I was standing still, but I had made myself face it, had got used to it in the end, and felt nothing but exasperation for Buttercup baulking at one peaceful corpse tidily in its coffin with, if we were lucky, the lid well nailed down.

'Don't people die in America?' I said, crossly. 'Go and get your hat and I'll start the motor car.'

Buttercup picked up a magazine and opened it on her lap.

'You must, Buttercup. You and Cad must both look after her now.'

She perked up at this.

'Fine. I've been twice, so it must be Cad's turn. Take him.' She pulled the bell rope before I could begin to protest at how wrong this would be and, ignoring my glares, asked the maid who answered to find Mr de Cassilis and send him to her.

I was right, of course. A bedroom window to the left of the door was thrown wide with its blind drawn down and fly netting tacked across the opening and this was the most we saw of Robert Dudgeon throughout the visit. Cadwallader moreover did not notice even this much, which was just as well since he was grumbling almost as pitifully as Buttercup.

'I was going to go for a drink with Osborne,' he said again as we knocked and waited on the doorstep. 'Several drinks, from what he seemed to be suggesting. And what on earth am I to *say*?' This in a whisper as we heard footsteps approaching. I was tempted to ask again whether people died in America, but the door opened before I had a chance and one of the women I had taken to be Mrs Dudgeon's sisters stood aside to let us enter.

'Come away in, sir, madam,' she said. 'It's that good of you to come. Chrissie'll be no end touched. Come away in.'

She ushered us into the living room, which was still full of the women we had seen the day before, and with Miss Joey Brown added to their number, her father clearly having persuaded her in the end.

Mrs Dudgeon sat as before in a hard chair, the two by the fire empty, and I caught my breath at the sight of her. Perhaps, after all, the endless daily toll of the war had coarsened us, taken us too far from Buttercup's fearful recoil, and *I* was the ghoulish one, calmly expecting that within a day the widow would rally and would be thinking of funeral invitations and refreshments. In fact, Mrs Dudgeon looked so much worse, so more stricken and agitated, than she had the previous day that I was almost sure something else must have happened. Her face was white and dry-looking, with lines which must always have been there but which I had not noticed before dividing her brow in two, more lines joining her nostrils to the down-turned ends of her mouth. Her eyes were red and pinched, their sockets deeply visible and eyelids puckered like badly laundered linen bunched at its seam. In all she looked ten years older.

'Here's Mr and Mrs de Cassilis to see you, Chris,' said the woman who had shown us in. Sorting that out took a minute or two, the more so since there was no easy way to account for its being me and not horrid selfish Buttercup who was here, but when we had cleared it up Mrs Dudgeon spoke.

'I just want, *need*, to be on my own,' she said, causing a maelstrom of shushing and clucking amongst the women, as they tried simultaneously to reprimand her, comfort her and cover their embarrassment, all without looking me or Cad in the eye. Cad, however, took a line which led us to safer waters.

'I understand,' he said. 'And you are quite right to say so – you mustn't bottle things up – but others know best. This is a time for family.'

Mrs Dudgeon frowned at him momentarily, but

122

seemed to decide not to bother pursuing it and went back to twisting her handkerchief and rocking gently in her chair, mouthing the word 'alone'.

'Aye well,' said one of the women, with a hint of bluster which I could not quite interpret, 'Izzy has her hands full with eight and wee Izzy's jist a bairn herself for all she's a rare help to her mammy.' Cad had begun by nodding along to this but was obviously mystified by the end and did not respond. I was sure he would soon become as bilingual as the rest of us but for the moment he was lost. And to be fair to him, although I understood the words and the accent and could parse it beautifully – the 'rerr hilp tae urr mammy' was as the King's English to me after all my years at Gilverton – I could not tie it to any preceding remark or fit it otherwise into the current context. I smiled vaguely and let it pass.

In doing so, of course, I was forgetting one of my hard-learned detecting maxims, which is that people always mean something when they speak. When it appears otherwise, I have missed the point. The difficulty is, of course, that to scent, track and run to ground every chance remark which puzzles one at first would not only be tiring, and not usually worth the effort, but it would put one beyond the pale in any social setting; would in fact turn every desultory chat and half-hearted passing of the time of day into a rerun of the Spanish Inquisition. Besides, it is only with hindsight that I can see how germane this would come to be. How could I have guessed it at the time?

In the excruciating silence, the sisters – could they really all be sisters? There were half a dozen including Mrs Dudgeon and, unlike the tribe next door, they were hardly a matched set – were fussing around with much muttering and sidelong glances towards us and towards the table where teacups and plates of short-bread were laid out.

'Whisky?' I heard one of them whisper, after a while.

'Sandwich, mebbes?' someone else breathed.

The difficulty was, of course, Cadwallader, for while tea and biscuits might do very well for all the females who would doubtless troop in and out to sit a while, the presence of a man, and a gentleman at that, demanded meat and drink.

'Tea, Mrs Gilver?' offered the woman who had answered the door, and then turning to Cad she inquired, 'And something for yourself?'

At that moment, Joey Brown stood up suddenly from her perch on the creepie stool and came forward. I turned to her, feeling thankful that there would be a way out of the awkwardness if she had brought a bottle from her father's establishment and was about to offer it, but she said nothing.

'Have you a bottle open, Chris?' said one of the women, rummaging in the sideboard. Mrs Dudgeon said nothing, but Miss Brown once again took a step forward. It was all getting most discomfiting, and I wished heartily that Joey Brown would overcome her gaucheness and get on with it if she did have a bottle about her somewhere, or that Cad would begin to register something, *anything*, of what was going on and defuse it. One thing to be thankful for, I thought, was that Mrs Dudgeon was oblivious and, since she was, I decided I could weigh in without causing her any embarrassment, so I murmured to the woman wielding the teapot:

'There was some cherry brandy, I believe. Perhaps in the scullery?'

At last, however, Cad solved the problem himself by saying in a maniacally hearty voice as he saw me being passed a cup: 'Ah tea! Wonderful. Tea, tea, tea. I'm getting quite British, you know, when it comes to a cup of tea.' The companions smirked and I blushed for him but at least the catering was decided. Miss Brown sank back down on to her stool.

When cups and plates were distributed and the women had resumed their seats like so many starlings resettling after a shot, Mrs Dudgeon, unclamping her jaw with almost visible effort, spoke again at last.

'I didnae mean to be rude,' she said and she swept us all up in a desperate but determined look, 'but I would do just anything for a bit of time to myself. Just tonight, maybe, and then anybody that wants to come can come back tomorrow.' The starlings were ruffled again and several of them broke out at once.

'Away, Chrissie. We'd nivver leave ye on yer own at a time like this.'

'Bet's through with him now, and when she goes hame, Tina's to stay till Izzy's got them settled and then she'll be through and Bet's wee Betty here'll be back in the morning.'

'Aye and then me the morn's nicht.'

'I'd be happy to stay awhile and let yous all away,' said Joey Brown, sounding anything but, although she spoke stoutly.

Mrs Dudgeon waited with her eyes squeezed shut until they had subsided, then she looked around wildly, at the crowd of women in her room, out into the woods, a hard stare at the sideboard and then back out of the window again. The tension crackled around her like lightning; I could almost smell it from my seat at her side, and unable to bear it any longer, I rose and took my cup and plate to the table where I laid them down on the good damask cloth. They were snatched up immediately and borne away.

Cad was talking again now, of Mr Dudgeon and the

excellent work he had done on the castle roof. Murmurs of quiet agreement came from the women:

'Aye, he was a good man richt enough.'

'We were blessed who knew him, it's true.'

Mrs Dudgeon, eyes closed again and fists tight, endured the lapping of the talk and said nothing.

'That's a thought, Chrissie,' said the woman called Tina, at last. 'You were asking, sir, if there's anything you could do?'

'Anything at all. Name it,' said Cad.

'Well, someone'll need to take thon,' she gestured to the envelope on the sideboard, 'to the toon hall.'

Cadwallader blinked at me for a translation.

'Someone has to take the doctor's certificate to the registrar's tomorrow and register Mr Dudgeon's . . .' Thankfully Cad was nodding along with me by then and I could lapse into a gentle silence before the end.

'Of course,' said Cad.

'Not tomorrow,' said Mrs Dudgeon. 'And it has to be a relative.'

'Surely there's someone,' I said. 'A male relative?'

'I'll do it,' said the widow.

'A brother-in-law?' I insisted.

I looked around the bevy of sisters, thinking that surely one of their husbands could get some time off his work.

'Donald would do it if I asked him,' said Mrs Dudgeon. 'But I just want to take care of it myself.' She was working herself up again. 'I'll do it myself, first thing Tuesday.'

'Well, it's for you to say, Chrissie,' said a voice. 'But if you ask me, you'd better get it over and then your mind'll be easy.'

Mrs Dudgeon threatened to laugh or perhaps to shriek at this, and I could not quite see how anyone looking at her now, half-mad with anguish, could fore-see ease for her any time soon.

'I can't go tomorrow because it's closed,' she said at last through gritted teeth.

'No, it's never,' said a young woman – Bet's wee Betty, I think. 'The morn's Monday, Chris.'

'Aye but the days jist run in together at a time like this,' said another, reaching out and patting Mrs Dudgeon's arm.

'It's closed this Monday for the August Bank Holiday,' said Mrs Dudgeon. 'I *ken* it was last week-end,' she almost shouted this over the voices raised in denial, 'I ken it was last weekend, but they stay open the bank holidays to let folk that's off their work get their business done and they close the next. It's closed.' She was almost shouting and had to take three or four huge, groaning breaths before her voice was back under her command. When she spoke again, she sounded exhausted. 'I'll have to go on Tuesday. Tomorrow it's closed.'

'We'll take care of everything,' said one of the sisters, laying a hand upon Mrs Dudgeon's shoulder. 'We can look out his papers and someone'll go with you.'

'What papers?' said Mrs Dudgeon, clutching at the woman's hand.

'Just his birth certificate,' I told her, 'and his marriage certificate and passport. Or no, sorry, I suppose he wouldn't have a passport, but the other two . . .'

'You never need to take all them,' said Mrs Dudgeon. 'Mr Faichen never told me you needed all them.'

'Haven't you got them?' said one of the sisters. 'Have you lost them, Chrissie?'

Mrs Dudgeon put her head in her hands and began to rock back and forward.

'We can look them out for you, Chris,' said a sooth-ing voice. 'We'll find them.' She was beginning to moan as she rocked and I glanced at Cadwallader in trepidation.

'Mrs Dudgeon,' he said, loudly. 'I shall telephone the registrar himself, at home tonight if I have to, and ask whether it matters that Robert's birth certificate is lost, and if it does, I shall take care of it all. I'll pick you up in the motor car on Tuesday, whenever you like, take you there, and bring you home.'

Mrs Dudgeon stared at him for a moment and then spoke.

'Or let me walk home by myself?'

The sisters set up a new protest at this, but Cad had the right idea.

'Or let you walk home if that's what you want,' he said, nodding.

At that, we rose to go, while the sisters rallied around Mrs Dudgeon, the starling rustle starting up again:

'. . . the doctor . . .'

'Just so's you get rest . . .'

' . . . do yourself harm if you go on like . . .'

'Goodbye, Mrs Dudgeon, ladies,' I said, but we were quite forgotten and we let ourselves out.

'Not to say I wouldn't be half mad if that lot were buzzing round me,' said Cadwallader, stopping on the doorstep, 'but . . .'

'Yes, I hope they *do* get the doctor,' I said. 'A state of nerves like that can't be sustained for long without trouble. It would only take one more thing to tip her right over the edge.'

'And not a big thing,' said Cad. 'Did you see how she took the news of having to look out a mere certificate?'

'But you were wonderful,' I told him. 'Very calming. Well done. Only, you're not really going to let her walk three miles home from the registrar's all alone, are you?'

128

'Of course not,' said Cad. 'But I thought if someone didn't stop shushing her and start agreeing with her, she was going to have a fit.'

'Still keen to be laird of the estate?' I asked him. 'Now that you see what it entails?'

'Absolutely,' he said firmly. 'You said yourself I was wonderful back there. Although, it certainly does have more to it than I could have dreamt of, when I used to sit in the lawyer's office in Manhattan signing papers and dreaming.

'It's all in such a godawful mess, Dandy. Not just the castle falling down around us, but farms running at a loss, rents unpaid for decades on the town properties, untold complications from some failed mining speculation back in the boom years. And now, just as I was beginning to get on top of it all, I've lost my carpenter.' He sighed. 'I must remember to get on to someone this evening and find out about this certificate question. Who do you think I should ask?'

That was more like it, I thought. For the first time since I had met him Cad sounded just like a husband; moaning about rents and business failures for one thing, and for another giving his word that he would attend to some matter then promptly turning to the nearest female to sort out the details for him. He was learning at last.

I regaled Alec with it all over a drink together in the drawing room later. He had been hanging around purposelessly for much of the day since, for all the beer shops and alehouses in Queensferry, there was only one establishment calling itself an hotel which could therefore offer refreshment on the Sabbath. There he had taken himself and, telling the landlord with hand on heart that he was a genuine traveller come down

129

from Perthshire that morning, he had been supplied with a pint of seventy shilling ale at the counter in the lounge bar. Only then had it struck him that the labyrinthine licensing laws ensured that none of his fellow drinkers could possibly be a local man with anything to tell him of the Burry Man's day.

'I did get a few scraps from the barman,' he told me, 'but I think we had better take it with a pinch of salt.'

'Oh?' I said. 'Why so?'

'Well, he was much too keen on muscling in to the centre of the story. Very full of this funny feeling he said he had that something was amiss. You know the kind of thing: "Soon as I saw him in the doorway, guvner, a goose walked over my grave and I knew there was trouble a-brewing." The usual nonsense.'

'A ghost,' I said. 'Isn't it a ghost that walks over one's grave?'

'Why would a ghost give you goose pimples?' Alec asked, reasonably enough. 'Anyway, I shall have better luck tomorrow, I expect. Now what of you? You say she's definitely still worried about something?'

'Worried is hardly the word,' I said. 'If you could have *seen* her, Alec. And it wasn't . . . Oh, it's so hard to explain. It wasn't the nagging kind of worry that one feels if one fears that something dreadful *might* happen. It wasn't that. And it wasn't the grind of waiting to hear something; we shall never forget what that looks like after all. This was . . . I don't know.'

'That's simply not good enough, Dandy,' said Alec. 'You must try.'

'All right,' I said, 'but don't smile at me for being fanciful. Here goes. It was . . . Imagine . . . Imagine someone you care deeply about. Your mother, say. Imagine that your mother was tied to the railway line with a train coming and no one around you spoke English or understood your frantic gestures and no one

130

would show you where the points were, or for some reason you did not dare to ask. It looked like that would. Worse, even. Horrid.'

'It sounds like a nightmare,' said Alec.

'Yes!' I yelled. 'Exactly. She looked as though she were stuck in a nightmare with no one to turn to, even though we were all there trying to help.'

'And does it fit in at all with our best guess as to what might be troubling her?' said Alec. 'Doesn't sound it. We thought perhaps Dudgeon had been nobbled and had gone back on the deal and now Mrs Dudgeon might have to carry the can. What you're describing doesn't chime with that at all.'

I shook my head in agreement. 'And the things she actually said didn't seem at all as though they could be troubling on their own account. Bank holidays, and lost documents. Trivial things really. And then this ardent desire to be alone. First she was beside herself with the need to have her husband's body back and now all she wants is for everyone to go away and leave her alone. I begin to wonder if she was quite normal before all this, because really she hardly seems sane now.'

I heard the ching! of the telephone being hung up in the library next door and then the sound of Cadwallader's footsteps crossing the floor and advancing along the corridor towards us.

'Good news,' he said, entering. 'She doesn't need the birth and marriage certificates after all. I got it straight from the horse's mouth. Well, the registrar's. As long as the contents are known and there's no doubt over identification, which there isn't, she can just walk in and do it. Even better, he *is* open for business tomorrow, so we can get the whole thing under way. I'm going to slip back round to the cottage now and spread the tidings.'

'Oh Cad, don't descend again,' I told him. 'They'll only get into another flap about feeding you. Send a footman, darling, much easier.' Cad nodded his acquiescence and pulled the bell-rope to summon the maid.

'I wonder what made Mrs Dudgeon so adamant that tomorrow was out,' I said. 'She was fierce about it, wasn't she, Cad? Can she be quite normal? Have you ever heard any rumours that she wasn't?'

Cadwallader shook his head. 'Not that I would have,' he said, which was a very good point.

'I wish I knew where to look for a good old-fashioned malicious gossip,' I said. 'You must do what you can in the pubs tomorrow, Alec, but mental trouble is not really an interest of men's.'

'Well, haul yourself around the teashops and drapers,' said Alec.

'Perhaps,' I said. 'But I daren't simply plunge in and start asking. Far too many branches of the family. Anyone I quiz is bound to be a relative.'

'Really?' said Cad. 'I haven't begun to sort the locals out yet. Well done you.'

'Oh, I haven't sorted them *out*,' I said. 'The most I could do is attach offspring to parent and only that because they seem to employ so little imagination when it comes to naming them. Bet's wee Betty, and young Tina that's Tina's lassie. Not forgetting young Izzy who's such a help to Mammy Izzy, of course.'

'Yes, there are teeming millions of nephews and nieces, certainly,' said Cad. 'You could hardly miss *them*.'

Chapter Seven

Of the three of us, Alec certainly had the best of it the next day. Cad was to take the widow to town, I was to sit with the sisters in her absence, since with Mrs Dudgeon gone their tongues would surely be loosened, and Alec was to start his round of the hostelries.

At eleven in the morning then, we scattered to our tasks, Alec taking my motor car to the first pub on his list, Cad setting off with black hat and solemn face in Buttercup's Austin to pick up Mrs Dudgeon, and I beginning my solitary tramp through the woods. Solitary, because Buttercup had once again declined to have any part in the day's adventures and had avoided being press-ganged by the simple but effective method of not getting dressed. She had still been in curling-pins and cold cream, propped up in bed when I had swept into her room half an hour before to drag her with me and her smile had been triumphant as she watched me concluding that I didn't have time to wait for her. She merely gave a happy sigh and turned the page of her *Tatler* as I glared and marched out again and worst of all, because of the luscious pile of her bedroom carpet, I could not even slam the door.

Hopeless as she was though, I began fervently to wish as I made my way into the woods that I had insisted she come with me. It was another beautiful day, getting hot as noon approached, but sweet and fresh in the trees, at least in this part of the forest where the ground was dry under birch and spruce. Elsewhere, no doubt, streams, bogs and years of broad leaves rotting would make the woodland unpleasantly rank as August sweltered on, but here was a carpet of needles and patches of sunshine. What could be more cheerful? What could be farther from mould and cobwebs? And yet, as I say, I found myself wishing heartily as I advanced that Buttercup was there, or even better that I had Bunty with me and, despite the dappling sunshine and trilling birds, my pulse was knocking by the time the edge of the wood was out of sight behind me.

Once or twice I fancied I heard footsteps, but then I was just as sure that I heard breathing, and *that* could hardly be so. Oh, for Bunty! The value of a dog, when one is walking through woods getting spooked for no reason at all, is that a dog has keener hearing but a much duller imagination than oneself and so will mooch along nose to the ground no matter what horrors one's fancy conjures, and it is only when the ears prick and the nose quivers that one can be sure there is something going on outside one's own head, and even then it is most likely a rabbit. I shook myself, firmly telling myself that there was no such thing as ghosts, that there was no one creeping along beside me breathing heavily and watching me and, although the jitters did not leave me, I at least managed to keep going and not bolt back to the castle in fright.

However, I was so thoroughly rattled by the time I arrived at the clearing that on seeing someone emerge around the corner of the Dudgeons' cottage six feet away from me as I came at the building from the side, I jumped clear off the ground and shrieked. The other person shrieked too, even louder, and it took each of us a moment to register who it was who had so alarmed the other. At last, though, I recognized Miss Joey Brown the barmaid, round-eyed and with her hand pressed to her heart, shrinking back against the cottage wall and staring, whereupon I gave a fluttering laugh to excuse myself and cover my embarrassment. Much to my surprise, however, although Miss Brown soon recovered from her initial fright, she grew no more calm; she nodded to me politely enough and murmured a greeting, but she kept making darting glances back the way she had come, and when I followed her looks with my own, she grew even more flustered, standing square before me blocking the path, as though I would want to go around to the back of the cottage and it was her duty to stop me. Then, seeming to realize how foolish she was being, she gave it up and attempted to look casual as she strolled towards the front door, only ruining it with one more fearful look over her shoulder. I stood my ground for a moment, but I knew I could not go squirrelling about the back regions of Mrs Dudgeon's house, not with the place full of mourners as it was, so I met Miss Brown's backward glance with a frank smile and followed her around the path to the front. She disappeared inside without knocking and went into the room on the left where the coffin lay, but I rapped on the open door and waited.

'Ye've missed her, madam,' said the woman I thought was called Tina, who came to admit me. 'Chrissie's away to the Rosebery Hall wi' Izzy and Mr de Cassilis.'

'Yes, so I believe,' I said, sitting and accepting the inevitable teacup. 'But to tell the truth I wanted to come while Mrs Dudgeon was out, to ask how you think she is today. Yesterday . . .' I shook my head and was met with matching head-shakes from all around. There was, as I had hoped, an air of greater ease around the place without Mrs Dudgeon there, despite the fact that the body of Dudgeon himself still lay in the next room.

'I wish I had some good news for you, madam,' said one of the older ladies. 'But if anything she's worse. Tell her, Margaret.'

'I was here last night, madam,' said Margaret. 'Donald was sitting with Rubbert, but we thought somebody should be here for Chrissie too, and were we ever right! She would not go to her bed, never mind she was fit to cowp over she was that tired. She jist sat here, telling me *I* needed to lie down, *I* needed to get my sleep. Well, of course, I did shut my eyes in the end.'

'Of course you did.'

'You're only mortal.'

I nodded my agreement with this, and loath as I was to interrupt the flow I took the chance while I had it of backtracking a little to check up on something puzzling.

'Is Donald there now?'

'Eh?'

'Next door with Joey.'

'Oh, you ken Miss Josephine Broon, do you, madam?'

There was something in her voice which hinted that if she had had her way, Joey Brown would not have been awarded her role as mourner. I decided to probe a little.

'Is she a relative?' I asked. 'Miss Brown?'

'Not exactly,' said another of the sisters.

'She should hae been.'

'It would nivver have come to nothing.'

'Och, Margaret,' said Bet. 'We're all Jock Tamson's bairns.'

'Aye, but a *barmaid*,' said Margaret.

'We can hardly turn up wur noses at her for workin' behind the taps,' said Tina and there was a little gentle laughter. I smiled along with them in a vacant kind of way, but hoped that someone would take pity on me and explain. At length, Bet volunteered.

'She was walking out with young Bobby,' she said with a nod towards the photograph on mantelpiece. 'They hadn't named the day but they were getting there.'

'Aye, only Billy – that was Joey's brother – he joined up the minute he turned eighteen and whatever Billy Broon did, Bobby Dudgeon did too. Ever since bairns this was. Bobby would never have left his mammy if he hadn't been hanging on to Billy Broon's coat-tails and here if it didnae end in heartache all round for everyone.'

'Most distressing,' I said. This snippet of news at least explained why Joey Brown's father had felt she had to be here, and perhaps if she felt some residual responsibility over young Bobby's death – since it was her brother who encouraged him to join up – that might even go some way to explain her grief and guilt when Mr Dudgeon died. I decided not to pursue it any further, but to try to get back to the main thread.

'I'm sorry, Mrs . . . Margaret,' I said. 'You were saying, before I interrupted, about having no good news of Mrs Dudgeon this morning.'

'Aye richt. Well, as I wis tellin' ye, I fell to sleep and when I woke again, it was gettin' light, near four o'clock and Chrissie was nowhere to be seen. I thocht she had gone through and lain doon at last and I jist cracked the door to have a wee keek at her, to see that she was restin' peaceful . . . but she wisnae there! I went through to Rubbert. She wisnae there either. Donald had dropped off – well, he's a long day at his work to be sittin' up the nicht – and he hadnae heard a thing. So oot we went. Quiet-like, no' wantin' to stir all they bairns, and we went lookin' for her. A good hour we looked and we were near ready to come up to the house and get Mr de Cassilis to phone to the police and start raisin' some men, when we saw her at last.'

'And?' I said.

'She was wanderin' home from wherever she had been. Cold as a dab o' ice, she must have been oot for hours. Fit to drop, she was.'

'But where had she been?' I said. 'Did she tell you?'

'She . . . well, she wisnae herself, madam, and that's the truth,' said Margaret. 'At first we thocht she had gone away to do herself harm – ye ken what I'm sayin'? – cos she had a wee bottle in her hand. "Oh Chrissie," I says, "Chrissie, hen? If you would only jist get the doctor or get the minister, or jist even lie down and rest. You'll get through, hen. Didn't I get through when Jock was taken?" Mind you, I hadnae had my only boy go off to the war and no' come hame again.'

'Dear God,' I said. 'Thank heaven you found her in time.'

'But it wisnae that after all, madam,' said Margaret. 'Thon wee bottle was nothing evil after all. It was ink.'

'Jist a bottle o' ink,' said one of the others.

'Ink?' I said, frowning around the ring of faces, puzzled. 'A bottle of ink?'

'And she hadnae drunk none o' it,' said Margaret. 'It's not like you could miss it if she had.'

'Aye well,' said Bet, 'she's no' hersel' right enough.' And she seemed content to leave it at that.

There was a time when I might have been too, but in my short detective career one of the lessons I had learned, the hard way, was never to abandon the attempt to make sense of things; random anomaly is an explanation of the very last resort. So, if Mrs Dudgeon had been wandering around in the night with a bottle of ink in her hand, it must have been for a reason.

'Did she have a pen with her?' I asked. They shook their heads.

'Did she have paper?' More shakes.

'And do you have any idea what she might have been doing?' I said. Nothing but blank looks greeted this; if the ink was not a suicide draught, it seemed, they had nothing more to offer.

'Ah well,' I said, turning the subject, determining to file away the bottle of ink and puzzle it out on my own later, 'maybe she'll be easier in herself after this morning's errand.' I got the impression from the reception this gained that the sisters had been long trying to comfort themselves with such thoughts, and failing. They nodded politely but looked unconvinced.

'Is she – Is Mrs Dudgeon –' I began. I had to tread carefully here; it was their own flesh and blood after all. Although some of them surely must be in-laws. There was no family resemblance among the set. 'I hardly know how to ask this without sounding rude,' I went on, 'and I mean no disrespect, but were Mrs Dudgeon's nerves strong before this happened? After her son's death, it would have been entirely unsurprising if she had been laid low. And if she had been at all nervous before *that*, well, by now with such tragedies heaped one upon the other . . . Might it be a good idea to see if she could get away for a rest somewhere, perhaps?' I thanked my stars for Grant and all her chatter, for without her generously shared postings from her clan I should not have been able to speak so assuredly of 'nerves' and 'rest' and might have put my foot squarely in it talking instead of sanatoria and madness. As it was, the sisters looked sceptical but not in the least affronted.

'Naw, Chrissie's never had any trouble of that kind before, madam,' said one. 'I dinnae ken if that makes it worse or better, though.'

'Even when Bobby was lost,' said another. 'They both of them took it brave. No matter there's a case to say "missing presumed" is harder to get over than anything else.'

'I quite agree,' I said. 'Torture. It must be so hard to stop hoping. Perhaps that's why Mrs Dudgeon was so very set on having her husband's body brought home as quick as it could be. That would make sense, psychologically, wouldn't it?' But I had lost them.

At that moment we heard the sound of the motor car returning. I had thought to have more of a chance with the sisters than this, but I supposed that when the walk through the woods was added there had been ample time for Cad to have driven to the village and back and for Mrs Dudgeon to have carried out her sorry little bit of business there. As it turned out, there had been time for more than that. After some murmured talk at the doorstep and the sound of the next-door cottage's front door opening and closing – perhaps some of the red-haired terrors attracted by the sound of the engine? – Cad and Mrs Dudgeon entered. She had her head bowed and greeted no one, but Cad gave me a look quivering with significance as he ushered her to a chair and he nodded a signal to me to keep my seat and wait for something worth waiting for.

'Everything well, Chrissie?' said one of the sisters.

'Aye, fine,' said Mrs Dudgeon. 'We stopped off at Faichen's after the registrar. He's comin' to get Robert. The hearse'll be here in half an hour.'

A moment of stunned silence met this remark, during which Cadwallader caught my eye and wiggled his eyebrows.

'What?' said Margaret at last.

140

Mrs Dudgeon stuck her chin up as she answered. She seemed different this morning. No more resigned, still not accepting, but less agitated and firmer in her resolve. Resolve to do what, though? I listened closely as she spoke.

'He's takin' Robert away to his place for tonight. The funeral's tomorrow,' she said. 'Donald can sit there with him tonight as easy as here.'

'But –' began Margaret, then stopped. She looked at me, willing me to think of something to say about any of this, but I was as perplexed as the rest of them.

'Do ye no' think, Chrissie,' said one of the oldest of the women, brave soul, 'do ye no' think you'd rather he stayed here the last night? Do ye no' think ye'd be sorry in the end if he lay in thon place?'

'It's my decision,' said Mrs Dudgeon, still very firmly. 'My business and mine alone.' The sister who had spoken last got two spots of colour right in the middle of her cheeks upon hearing this and I too thought it was a bit much, if I am honest. After all, this *was* her family and they had been very generous with their time in the last few days even if they had been an irritant rather than a comfort. Besides she had hardly shown steady judgement until now. 'And so I'll thank ye all and I'll take ye up on your offers. It was that kind of you all to say you'd help me out.' There were some perplexed glances at this, but she went on to elaborate. 'I cannot see myself doin' any bakin' today. I'd never have thocht to say it and I dinnae ken what folk'll say aboot me, ma ain man buried and ma kitchen cold, but Margaret, you said you'd do a big cake, and if Betty can make a good load of scones, we'll no' need soup in a' this heat. Now I've a wee bit put by so Tina, if you and Mima can get a good lot of ham from Fairlie's and do sandwiches we should manage fine.'

'Ham sandwiches,' I said under my breath, remembering.

'And I'll stay here with you, Chrissie,' said the remaining sister who had been assigned no mess duty.

'Suit yoursel',' said Mrs Dudgeon. 'There's no need and I wis going to ask you to make a big trifle, or two even if you take my bowl away with you. But I can jist as easy get Izzy to do it, or we can do without if you don't think you can manage.'

I could see the woman tussling with herself. If she was famed for her trifles the thought of letting someone else take over would be painful, and the idea that it would be published abroad that she was asked and had refused was insupportable. Mrs Dudgeon was watching her quite calmly, and eventually she succumbed.

'Aye, fine, then,' she said. 'I'll do a couple of big trifles. My custard's a sight more reliable than Izzy's. But are you sure you'll be all right here on yer own?'

Mrs Dudgeon nodded, and I found myself nodding along with her. Of course she would be all right. She had wanted to be on her own since yesterday and this was nothing short of a master stroke. The women, who one would have thought could not have been pried away from her side with a crowbar, were already fidgeting and beginning mentally to calculate what they had in their cupboards and what they would have to go to the shops and buy.

'And if ye can tie up some of your good dishes in paper the nicht,' went on Mrs Dudgeon, 'I'll send Donald in the cart to get them and I can have them all washed and ready for the morn.'

I was beginning to feel sorry for this Donald, whoever he was, doing the round on the cart to pick up everyone's best china for the funeral tea, before sitting up yet another night with the coffin.

'Wee Tina can gie 'im a hand,' said Tina senior.

'And we'll all be round the morn's morn to help you get set oot,' said Jessie. Mrs Dudgeon nodded and said she didn't know what she would do without them and it was settled.

Masterful. Before the sisters really had a chance to say a word about it they and we were being bundled out of the door, Cad offering lifts which were, of course, declined. When we were all out in the passageway, Joey Brown put her head around the door of the other room to see what the commotion was and catching sight of her Mrs Dudgeon insisted on her leaving too, insisted that she wanted a bit of time just Robert and herself before Faichen got here to take him away. Her voice broke once as she said this.

'There's no one else with him just now?' I said, glancing at Miss Brown, who had the grace to blush; it was a shocking dereliction of her duty to have sloped off and left Mr Dudgeon's body alone.

Mrs Dudgeon shut the door firmly on us all as soon as she decently could and the sisters set off down the path.

'I might go this way,' I said in a loud voice to Cad, gesturing around the side of the cottage and towards the woods, and I was rewarded with a stiff look from Miss Brown. With her jaw rigid she glanced once at me and once fleetingly towards the back of the house, then she squared her shoulders, faced front again and strode forward to meet the others.

'What for?' said Cadwallader, but I shushed him.

'It was a blind,' I said, 'and it worked. Now take me to the castle, darling. I need to make some notes before I forget all of this. Very puzzling. Very puzzling indeed.'

Alec, returning to the castle for lunch, was – there is no other word for it – drunk. He asked the butler for a glass of milk and ate slice after slice of bread, buttered and rolled up, but still his eyes were swimming.

'You have to have the milk and starch first, you goose,' I told him. 'You should have had a pint of porridge for breakfast. It's far too late now to do you any good. But what did you find out?'

'Apart from the limits of my constitution?' said Alec. 'Very little. Nothing. Only that the Burry Man had a sizeable nip at each of the pubs and that most of the "right ferry folk" also gave him either a penny or a nip, a penny if they have children most usually and a nip if they don't. Except that some of them give both, but the incomers and some of "those and such as those" do neither, or if they do it's more likely money than drink. But all in all, he could quite easily have had more than enough whisky to kill him. Just as the doctor said.'

'Is that what you were trying to prove?' said Cadwallader, looking hurt. 'Do you still not believe me that something fishy is going on here?'

'Oh certainly, we believe that,' I told him. 'More definitely all the time. Only I'm not convinced that the mystery is a *murder* mystery, that's all. Now Alec, here's a thing. I had forgotten this until Mrs Dudgeon was organizing the funeral feast this morning, and the bad news is that if you forgot too you might have to go round again and pump the publicans for more details.' Alec groaned. 'Unless,' I went on, 'on your travels did anyone own up to the ham sandwich?'

'Is that a code name?' said Buttercup.

'No,' I said. 'Don't you remember? The police sur-

144

geon said that Robert Dudgeon had nothing in his stomach except a great deal of alcohol and a ham sandwich.' There was a chorus of disgust at my choice of topic for the luncheon table, Buttercup spluttering with dainty squeamishness and Alec clearly on a knife-edge after all the beer.

'I'm sorry,' I said, 'but some of our sensibilities must be set aside. Alec and I have learned that to our cost in the past. So darling, did anyone mention a sandwich?'

Alec shook his head.

'Isn't it all part of the bravado of the Burry Man,' said Buttercup, 'that he can't eat a thing once he's in his little green suit? The ham sandwich must have been waiting for him when he disrobed at the end of the day. Mrs Dudgeon must have brought it from home.'

'I suppose so,' I said. 'After all, he must have eaten it fairly late on for it still to have been identifiable as –' Alec gulped and I stopped. 'But there's something not quite right there. Something that occurred to me on the very first night when we went round to the cottage, Buttercup.'

'Which cottage is that?' said Cad.

'Oh Lord, can't we just tell him, "Freddy"?' I said. 'I'll never remember to stop.'

'You dare,' said Buttercup. 'I know things about you I can tell as well, my dear.'

'What are you talking about?' said Cad. 'What are they talking about, Osborne?'

'No idea as usual,' said Alec. 'But the drink has made it much less annoying.'

'That very first time we went there,' I resumed, 'that awful fierce woman was banging around washing all manner of pots and pans, wasn't she?' Buttercup shrugged. 'Well, she was. I was reminded of it the next day when all the sisters were fighting over a little teacup to wipe. Now here is the question: what meal was that the washing up of?' No one responded. 'From what meal sprang those pots and pans? Do you see?' Alec gazed at me owlishly, with his mouth slightly open and Cad and Buttercup looked expectant and polite, but blank. 'If Robert was out Burry Manning all day, they couldn't be luncheon pots. And if Mrs Dudgeon packed a sandwich to take to him so that he could go straight from his rounds to the greasy pole competition then they'd hardly be supper pots, would they?'

'Well then, they must have come from the night before's supper, then,' said Buttercup. 'But I can't see that they matter.'

'The night before?' I said. 'My dear girl, Mrs Dudgeon would have you up for slander if she heard you. Dirty pots sitting overnight and all day in a decent woman's cottage kitchen? And at Ferry Fair time too. Impossible! No, the only explanation is that Dudgeon had indeed meant to go home after discarding his burrs and that Mrs Dudgeon had supper ready for him. Someone in the crowd at the greasy pole expressed surprise that he was there – I overheard it – and apparently Mrs Dudgeon had refused to shift her pony and her sweet little trundle-cart from where it stood waiting, saying that she was going to take Robert home. But . . . he doubled back. And . . . at some point he ate that pesky sandwich.'

'Which . . .' said Cad, trying to catch up, '. . . you're saying might have been poisoned?' I sighed in exasperation.

'No, Cad, for heaven's sake, which I'm *not* saying might have been poisoned. Please will you get untraceable poison out of your head once and for all. All I'm saying is that we need to find out where they got to on this aborted journey homewards; where it was that he was taken in and fed.'

'And what will that tell us?' said Buttercup. Alec showed no sign of having registered anything; his head had sunk until his chin was on his chest.

'I'm not sure,' I said. 'But it might be significant. If Dudgeon was being threatened by someone who wanted to stamp out the Burry Man, perhaps this same someone waylaid the cart on Friday evening and subjected Mr and Mrs Dudgeon to a tirade on the subject of their broken agreement.'

'With light refreshments,' said Buttercup, drily. I had to laugh.

'I admit it sounds a little odd. But look at Alec here.' We all looked at Alec, who gave a gentle snore. 'If one were determined to have a serious talk with him at the moment one might well start by shovelling in some sustenance. I'd go for strong coffee rather than sandwiches, but still.'

'I still don't see what any of that will tell us about the actual death,' said Cad, sounding rather sulky.

I refused to rise to the bait again, but I mollified him a little by saying: 'At the very least, if someone did harangue Dudgeon on his way home on Friday night, and if he thought they might follow him all the way back to his cottage to carry on haranguing him there, and because of *that* he decided to go back to the Fair instead of sleeping it all off at home, then to my mind that person has a great deal to feel guilty about. I mean, the strain of the day and the drink might be the main culprits but any upset or worry added to the mix had to have played a part. And if Dudgeon was as keyed up then as Mrs Dudgeon is now I would quite happily say that his state of mind was what tipped the scales. After all, he did the parading and the drinking every

147

other year and they didn't kill him. It was this year, with the mysterious worry, that he died.'

Cad nodded and seemed satisfied with this to be going on with.

'We'll have coffee upstairs,' said Buttercup to a maid who had come to clear the table. 'Lots of strong coffee.' She reached under the table to nudge Alec with her foot and he stirred, grunting. The maid smirked and left.

'After which,' I said, 'I'm off back to the Dudgeons' place to poke around at the back and see if I can work out what Miss Joey Brown was up to this morning.'

'Do you suspect her?' said Cad.

'I'm not sure,' I answered. 'There's something slightly off about her, but it might be quite separate from our concerns. Worth checking, though.'

'And can we do anything?' said Cad.

'You could try to come up with a reason that Mrs Dudgeon should be out wandering the woods in the middle of the night with a bottle of ink,' I said. 'Or actually, more usefully, do you have a Post Office Directory in the house?' Cad and Buttercup looked at each other and then shrugged in unison. 'If you do you could try to work out the Dudgeons' most obvious route from the Rosebery Hall towards their cottage and see who lives along the way that might be of interest.'

'Of interest in what way?' said Buttercup, screwing up her face as she used to do when asked questions in class at our finishing school. I knew exactly what I meant, but it was impossible to explain to someone who did not catch on to it automatically.

'Or,' I said, scooting down in my seat as Buttercup had done and giving Alec a sharp kick on the front of

148

the shin, 'you could see what you can do with this sorry case. Try holding him under in a water-butt perhaps and then get him to do the detecting. It's what he's here for, after all. And, finally, tell me where I can lay my hands on a dog.'

Chapter Eight

One of the stable boys, it transpired, had a dear little dog and was only too happy to loan it out for the afternoon – it was usually condemned to spend its days tied to a ring in the yard except when he could spare a few minutes. It was a typical Scottish villager's dog, about spaniel-sized, with a bit of whippet and a bit of shaggy terrier in it somewhere, no carriage to speak of, bandy in the rear legs, with an extravagantly fringed tail curving over its back. In local parlance: a wee black dug, and I felt a pang of longing for Bunty, who would have been coming back on the train with Grant and the extra clothes that very minute, except that now was not a time for her to be out in society, poor thing. I hoped fervently that Hugh was doing a good job of keeping her confined, because sweet as this little fellow was, I would not like Bunty's children to have another like him as their father.

He would serve my afternoon's purposes however, keeping my earlier shivers at bay and giving me, more importantly, an excuse to be walking through the woods. In the first of these roles, I have to say, he did not excel because far from snuffling on with his nose to the path and ignoring the phantoms which had so unnerved me on my first outing he began, as we advanced, to prick up his ears and lift his quivering nose into the still air of the forest and once or twice he looked up at me as though seeking reassurance instead of providing it, shrinking close into my legs with his tail down.

'Do you smell rabbits?' I asked him, in a hearty voice. 'Rabbits are nothing to a fine fellow like you. Or is it a fox you hear? I won't let a fox get you.'

He rolled his eyes at me and then faced to the front again as though to say: 'Well, all right then, if you promise.'

So I was forced to stride out, bravely whistling, keeping up his spirits instead of he mine and all the while trying not to think that it was ghosts that were raising his hackles as they had done to me. It might be Lila and her band of brothers, silently stalking me, except I knew in my heart that they would never do anything silently. Well then, it must be a peculiarity of the wind in the trees or some other natural oddity. It was *not* ghosts. Ghosts, for one thing, did not exist and even if they did they would hardly haunt dogs. Who ever heard of a haunted dog? Cats, certainly – cats were eerie things at the best of times – and possibly horses. But never dogs.

At last my little path fell in with the lane and I forgot all about the possible supernatural inhabitants of Cadwallader's woods as I planned the task before me. Thankfully for my purposes, all was tranquil at both houses; I was certain that if the holy terrors had been cooped up inside the walls would have pulsed with the effort of containing them. Their father was undoubtedly out at work, and there was no sign of their careworn elder sister either nor the mother, who had yet to appear. I supposed she might well be in confinement again, awaiting another addition to her brood, but I was glad that she was nowhere to be seen right now.

There were signs too that Mr Faichen had been and

gone with his hearse. A trail of fresh horse droppings led along the lane before me and there were eight rosettes printed in the dust at Mrs Dudgeon's gate showing clearly how two enormous horses had stood, shifting their hooves, waiting while the coffin was carried out. Now to my sleuthing. Luckily, there were no windows on the side wall of the cottage and so, knowing that I could not be seen by anyone inside, I bent down and untied the string from the collar of my little friend. He sat patiently while I did so and remained sitting, looking up at me, once he was free. Bunty would never have been so well behaved.

'Shoo,' I told him, in a whisper. 'Go on with you. Run along and play.'

At last, with a look over his shoulder to make sure he had understood me, he trotted off along the front of the cottages. I turned a sharp right and made my way around the back. I would 'realize' shortly that I had lost him, and then would skirt the cottages closely in my 'search' and have a good look at whatever might have been Joey Brown's object back there this morning. The stable lad had assured me that it was perfectly safe to let the dog off its leash – I was not being *that* cavalier with another's loved one – and that he would come back when called by his name, which was Nipper. 'Cos of how he was the wee-est one, mind,' the boy had assured me. 'Not cos he bites, cos he disnae.'

I strolled, whistling under my breath, along the tree-line at the back of the cottages, wishing it were autumn and I might pick up pretty-coloured leaves. (I should never actually be so soppy as to trip along in woodland picking up autumn leaves, of course, but Mrs Dudgeon or her neighbours weren't to know that and I could have dithered about quite plausibly had the season allowed.) As it was I had to make do with walking as

152

slowly as I could and shooting sideways glances towards the back of the cottages from under my hat.

There were coal bunkers and log stores along the back walls of the cottages under the scullery windows, axes and shovels hanging neatly from nails beside them. Between the cottages and the boundary of the gardens lay the washing greens, empty on one side and loaded on the other, and a pair of vegetable patches, both well-stocked and looking extremely lush in the current season. Then along the boundary closest to me were the usual little sheds and tool stores, rusting heaps of old wheelbarrows and rotten fence posts, as well as the midden heaps which I supposed had to go along with such bountiful-looking kitchen gardens. I knew rather more than I should have chosen to about midden heaps, their construction, their proper maintenance and management, and their invaluable contribution to a cropping scheme – they were another of Hugh's mystifying enthusiasms, and at the crushing end of the spectrum of boredom, even for him. These he would have heartily approved of: two pairs, one of each pair open and one covered, as all good midden heap makers know is essential. They were neatly contained inside walls of sod and utterly revolting on this hot afternoon, buzzing with flies and reeking of elderly cabbage and grass.

After these, and hardly a respite to the senses, came a rather noisome, brick-walled privy, evidently shared between the two families, and with a sudden sinking of the heart and a flush of shame it struck me that *this* might be the solution to the mystery of Joey Brown's morning excursion. Nothing more than this. If she were the dainty, easily discomfited type, she might well have been thrown into confusion upon meeting me on her way back from a visit here. But if such a visit had been her object would she not have asked one of the sisters to sit with Robert's body? Could she possibly be so ludicrously modest as all that? And her a barmaid. I could hardly believe that a girl robust enough to sit with a corpse could not summon the grit to mention a visit to a privy. If it came to that, however, I could hardly believe that the same girl who shrieked and fled Robert Dudgeon in his burry suit could calmly sit beside him in his shroud.

Since this could, I feared, be the answer to my little mystery, and since I could not skulk about here any longer without apparent purpose, I stopped, put my hands on my hips, looked about me and tutted.

'Where has he got to?' I said in what I hoped was a carrying-enough voice to reach the cottage in case anyone was watching and listening but not ludicrously stagy.

'Here, boy!' I shouted, the stable lad having assured me that he would come only to his name and nothing else. 'Here, doggy-dog! Come to heel. Oh, blast it all to heaven, what did he say the name was?'

So it went on. I strode about around the back shouting for Scamp, for Laddie, for Jock, standing still ostensibly listening for him but really looking about for anything there was to see: something hastily buried, or a hole where something had been hastily dug up, footprints – not that that dry forest floor could reasonably be expected to yield these, or anything at all. Eventually, grudgingly deciding that the privy was the answer after all, I gave up and called for Nipper. He did not appear. I called louder, but still there was no sign of him. Then with all thought of detecting forgotten, I began to shout in earnest. How awful if I should have lost him! He really was an excellent little animal and the stable lad could hardly have said no to me when I asked. If he had gone off for good, I should never forgive myself.

'Nipper? Ni-ppaaar . . . Nipper!' I shouted, trying a variety of intonations in case he was as particular as all that. I rounded the cottages on the far side, and saw him at last. Being a dog, he was of course rolling with abandon in the fresh horse droppings from Mr Faichen's hearse.

'Nipper!' I exclaimed. 'You little beast. Get up this minute!'

With a final snort, Nipper rolled over and sprang to his feet, trotting towards me with his tongue out in a happy grin.

'Shocking behaviour,' I told him, but one could not be cross with him really. For one thing Bunty would have done exactly the same, and for another I should have seen it coming. 'I must say, though,' I went on, 'even if one has to expect that sort of behaviour from you, I think it's a bit much for an undertaker to come round all solemn and respectful and then leave it behind him, don't you?' Of course, as soon as I had had this thought tongue-in-cheek, simply to make conversation with the dog, I immediately had it for real. What is more, Mrs Dudgeon might well feel the same and if the neighbours were all out then there was no chance of one of them coming to clear the mess before she could be offended by it. Only one course of action was open to me.

'What a glamorous life I do lead,' I said to myself, as I reattached the string to Nipper's collar and went around the side of the cottage to get a coal shovel.

Nipper, trotting along quite happily on a slack string as I made my way to the midden heap moments later, looked scrupulously uninterested in the contents of the brimming shovel, as though *I* might concern myself with such matters but they were far beneath *his* notice. I had almost got there, breathing through my mouth and trying not to think of what my disgusting sons said about this method of dealing with bad smells ('But if you breathe through your mouth you're eating it'), when I realized that I could have simply scraped it off the lane into the verge, and that it was the clearest sign yet of how the drip-drip-drip of Hugh's propaganda on the subject of 'compost' as he calls it was warping my brain that it never occurred to me to do anything but put it where it would do such bucolic good, even if that meant I had to carry the stuff a hundred yards at arm's length as though I was in some revolting new take on a pancake race.

I was cross, then – with Hugh for corrupting me, with my sons for their crudity, and with Nipper – by the time I got there and emptied the shovel on to the heap but my temper faded into sadness as I looked in and saw there, spread all over the top, the burrs from Robert Dudgeon's suit, some of them still with white scraps of his undergarment clinging to them. They must have been the last thing Mrs Dudgeon wanted ever to see again when she returned home a widow on Friday evening, but I supposed they had to be dealt with somehow. I even thought for a moment of digging around a bit with my shovel and trying to cover them, but there were limits. The smell and the bluebottles were not easily to be ignored, so I contented myself with scraping the shovel clean and rehanging it on its nail then setting off into the woods to take Nipper home.

We did not make very good progress. Before we were even properly under the trees Nipper gave a sudden yelp and started to the side, bumping into my legs and knocking me off balance. I dropped to my knees at once and, when I did, I saw immediately what was the problem. There was a bottle, cracked in two, lying on the rough grass. A whisky bottle no less – its label was still fresh and clearly legible: Royal High-landers single malted Scotch Whisky. I sat back on my heels and took Nipper's paws one by one in my hands squeezing gently, until I found the tender one.

'Poor old thing,' I said. 'And poor old me having to take you back to your master with a cut paw and covered in horse dung, too. My name will be mud around the stables tonight.' I sacrificed my handkerchief (another one), using it to wipe out the cut – it was not much more than a scratch really – and then turning it to the fresh side and tying up the paw to keep it clean on the way home.

'What kind of fool would throw a bottle away like that when they know there's a houseful of children nearby?' I asked Nipper, trying to keep his mind off what I was doing to him. When I stood up, however, I saw that there was a more innocent explanation at least than that. The bottle might easily have tumbled off the rubbish heap at the cottage of the red-haired children and rolled down, cracking through on its way, for there were countless other whisky bottles there; Vat 69 bottles for the most part and I wondered if the man of the house worked in the bottling hall and purloined them in the way I had heard so much about. Or no, I realized, living here, he must work for Cadwallader in some capacity and must simply spend his wages on them. My sympathy for the mother of the red terrors continued to rise, as I imagined him draining bottles, sticking the corks back in – one was still stuck in the top half of this one – and then tossing them out into the garden with never a thought for his little ones' bare feet as they scampered at play. Well, clearly I could not just leave this broken one where it was, and I was damned if I was going to rootle about in the rubbish to put it safely out of harm's way, nor dig a hole here in full view of the cottage windows, in case anyone should come back and see me, so I simply picked up the two halves, gingerly avoiding the jagged ends

157

and trying not to breathe in the fumes, and set off on my way.

'I'll get rid of it somewhere,' I told Nipper, 'but first things first. We need to get you home and have that cut cleaned out. In fact, a head-to-toe bath wouldn't do you any harm, and if I have to administer it myself as punishment for being such a poor nanny, then I'll take it on the chin.'

At times in the past, I have wondered whether there is something to that belief that we are all but pawns being moved around to make sport for the gods, and I was just about to wonder it again. If asked to pick who I would least like to encounter just at that moment, walking along carrying a broken whisky bottle, leading a dog on a string, he liberally coated in horse dung and with one paw tied up in a grubby hanky and I slightly besmirched with some of the same horse dung, at least on my hands where I had grabbed his paws to doctor him, and with dirty knees from grovelling on the ground while I did so, and with no handkerchief to remedy any of it . . . if asked who I would least like to meet in this state the people I glimpsed through the trees on course to bump right into me would certainly be amongst the top few.

Mr and Mrs Turnbull, the schoolmaster and his wife, teetotal, shining clean and with sober wholesomeness radiating from every pore, were strolling through the woods, without a broken bottle, reeking mongrel or muddy knee between them.

I could do nothing about Nipper, nor about my own dishevelment, but I hastily dug into a heap of leaf-mould with the heel of my shoe and dropped in the two pieces of glass, careful not to let them clink.

I gasped as I did so. I was no aficionado of whisky, as is well known, but this stuff must have been worse than the usual; even the empty bottle smelled powerful

enough to give one goose pimples, harsh and yet
sickly-sweet like burnt jam, reminding me of the terrible day when my cook Mrs Tilling was making
crab-apple jelly for the War Effort and got a bad
telegram just after adding the sugar to the pan. She had
been found an hour later by our butler, sitting in the
smoke as the mess boiled over on to the stove, forgotten. Odd how smell can be the most irresistible
trigger to our unbidden memories. I shook myself,
kicked some leaves back over the hole and stood
straight ready to face the Turnbulls.

'Why, Mrs Gilver,' said Mr Turnbull, when he saw
me. Mrs Turnbull nodded rather simperingly from his
elbow. 'We're on a nature walk,' he went on. My eyebrows must have risen: this was a bit too much even
for them. 'I mean to say,' he went on, 'we're preparing
possible nature-walk routes for the children, next
school year. Excellent educational aid, the nature walk.
Science, Art and PT all rolled into one. For instance,
there are seven different kinds of mushroom on this
path alone.'

'In August?' I said. 'Rather early for mushrooms,
isn't it?' He had raised my suspicions with this flood of
unnecessary information about what they were up to
here in the woods. I wondered how long they had been
skulking and whether they were the reason that my
hackles and Nipper's had been prickling. Furthermore,
I knew that *I* only babbled on to practical strangers
about what was my business and mine alone when
I had something to hide. Mr Turnbull was a match for
me, however.

'You should join us, Mrs Gilver,' he said jovially.
'I would wager you have lived in the countryside all
your life and yet you know nothing of mushrooms.
Certainly the common field variety has not come into

its own yet for the year, but there are boundless others to be found.'

'Toadstools, you mean?' I asked, trying to keep Cad's 'untraceable poison' out of my thoughts. Mr and Mrs Turnbull shared a rueful smile.

'We try to discourage such fancies,' said Mrs Turnbull. 'They are all fungi, plain and simple. Some good to eat and some not, but we try to discourage any superstitions about them.'

I had just about had enough of them already and this tipped me right over the edge. True they were perfectly free to think I was ignorant and credulous about country matters (I after all thought that they were tedious and rude about all matters we had yet conversed upon), but at least I had the manners to keep my thoughts to myself. Besides, they were on my list of suspects for Robert Dudgeon's nobblers. I decided to see if I could jolt them.

'I think you're on a hiding to nothing round here, I must say,' I told them. 'Fearfulness and superstition appear to be the norm. Look at the Burry Man, for instance.'

They frowned at me but said nothing.

'What do you think the local folklore will make of Robert Dudgeon's death?' I went on, remorselessly. 'Do you think anyone new will volunteer for next year? Or will there be stories of curses to add to all the others by then?'

'What do you mean?' said Mr Turnbull.

'Oh nothing, in particular,' I said. 'Only I wouldn't be at all surprised if in ten years' time children of Queensferry are as frightened of touching burdock seeds as they are today of touching toadstools.'

'Not if I can help it,' said Mr Turnbull, grimly determined. 'We have spoken before about the unfortunate prevalence of nonsense for those working underground or out at sea, but it irritates me beyond measure when the bounty of nature' – he spread his arms wide about him, and his voice took on an unmistakable note of sermonizing – 'the bounty of nature itself is corrupted to make their silly tales.'

'Quite right, dear,' said Mrs Turnbull. 'But we shall show them the error of their ways.' Her eyes were gleaming with unblinking zeal, like a missionary.

'You're all set to lead them into the light,' I said, fatuously and thinking I was pushing it, but they took it as a compliment and simply nodded, smugly. 'Well, good luck,' I told them. They frowned again at that. Of course, they would not believe in 'luck'. 'But your work is cut out for you. I'll lay you good odds' – this phrasing was deliberate; I was sure they would not believe in gambling either – 'that before the year is out, there will be playground skipping-rhymes about poisonous burrs and children will be daring each other to touch the Burry Man as he passes, and even the mothers and fathers will think twice before they put burdock seeds in their midden heaps to spread on their kitchen gardens. You wait and see.'

'My dear Mrs Gilver,' said Mr Turnbull, 'your imagination must be a great resource to you, but leave the horticulture to me. No gardener in his wits would put burrs on a midden heap. No goodness in them whatsoever and they'd take years to break down to a mulch. Harmless but useless, and our children know that very well.'

'But –' I began then I managed to stop myself in time. I nodded my goodbye to them, planning to sweep away with as much dignity as I could muster, but I was forced to wait for Nipper, who had chosen that very moment to make use of the facilities provided by the forest floor. Mr and Mrs Turnbull smiled stiffly at me and walked away, as though this most natural of

161

canine functions was to be classed with the nasty shale mines and fishing boats and had no place in their land of flowers.

'Thanks for nothing,' I muttered to Nipper when we were on our way at last, but he really was beginning to limp, poor little chap, and I felt too guilty to be cross with him for long. His master, however, was quite unperturbed by the news of the roll in the horse dung, and even scratched his jaw in embarrassment and said he should have warned me about it. He was no less courteous about the cut paw, saying that it could have happened at any time and I was not to 'fash' myself about it.

Thankfully, Alec had sobered up during a long nap after luncheon and was installed in the library with his pipe, looking alert if rather seedy.

'How can you?' I said, as he lit up and puffed deeply. 'At the best of times it's mysterious enough, but with a hangover? How can you?'

'I don't have a hangover, Dandy,' said Alec witheringly, but at that moment Buttercup's butler came in with a glass of something effervescent on a small tray which he proffered to Alec with an assurance that Mr de Cassilis swore by it.

'Hm,' I said, with what I thought was great restraint. 'I'm off to change.'

'Yes, please do,' said Alec. 'You stink, darling. What is it?'

'Whisky, dog's blood, horse dung and rotting leaves,' I said. 'I'll explain when I return.'

It was almost teatime before I was back with him; I had not seemed that bad while I was out in the woods, but standing on the pale carpet in my bedroom I got more and more redolent and disgusting as

I peeled off layers, and in the end I bundled up every stitch I had on and rang for a bath. Apart from anything else, a good long spell alone with no interruptions would give me a chance to digest all that I had learned, all that I had surmised on the strength of it, and what I planned to do next. No such luck. I had only just finished running over the peculiar conversation with the Turnbulls when my bedroom door was swept open and I heard Grant's voice bossing about whatever unfortunate underling had landed the job of carrying my trunk up from the hall.

'Stuffy,' I heard her say, and then, 'Worse than stuffy. What on earth has she been –'

'Grant!' I squeaked as she threw the bathroom door wide, concerned that a hallboy might still be lurking.

'Oh, you're there . . .' she said, 'madam,' with her usual pause. 'What is that smell?'

'I came a cropper with a shovelful of dung and a bleeding dog,' I told her, sure that if I made it sound revolting enough she would not ask for any details. I was right. She simply rolled her eyes.

'What were you wearing?' she demanded, her mind running naturally to laundry.

'Oh, my two-layered green and calfskin walking shoes,' I said. 'No worries there.'

'Gloves?'

'None.'

She nodded, satisfied, and squaring her shoulders went to find the washing.

Chapter Nine

'So,' I said to Alec back down in the library, 'what do you think?' Cadwallader was off on some errand but Buttercup was there, on the edge of her seat with interest, her buttery curls bouncing as she chewed her cake.

'Can they possibly be as they seem?' said Alec, meaning the Turnbulls.

'Are they for real?' said Buttercup in gurgling American. 'That's how you'd say it in New York, darling,' she said as we turned to stare. 'You'd say "Are they for real?" In the Outer Burghs anyway.'

'I don't know,' I said. 'One does meet some strange people who turn out to be exactly what they portray themselves to be. Look at Hugh. He's "for real".'

'Poor old Hugh,' said Alec. 'You are mean about him, Dan. And I'm beginning to see the other side of it, now. Gilverton is in better heart and better repair than many a grander –'

'Spare me, Alec, please,' I begged him. 'It's not the doing. It's the reporting afterwards. I spend a great deal of my time at dress-fittings. Or I used to anyway, and Hugh is often pleased with the results, but I don't bring home the paper patterns and spread them on the tea-table to explain how it's done. And to return to the subject, if they are to be relied upon, then what that means is that we need to explain why those burdock seeds ended up on the Dudgeons' midden.'

'It's not half as glamorous as I thought, being a detective,' grumbled Buttercup.

'It depends on the case,' I said. 'If I murder you now, for interrupting, there won't be any middens involved.'

Buttercup pursed her lips ostentatiously and I resumed.

'Now, what I thought was this: perhaps Mrs Dudgeon always brings them home – perhaps it's part of the mystical magical element. But this year, of course, they would have been the last thing on her mind and so one of the sisters may have dealt with them instead. Some sister who's not much of a Gertrude Jekyll and who simply thought, "Bits of dead plant: put them with all the other bits of dead plant," which is exactly what I would have done had it been me. We can easily find out – and by we I mean you, darling – from one of the Burry Man's two helpers what usually happens to the seeds at the end of the day. And you'll be killing two birds with one stone if you seek them out, Alec, because they will also be able to tell you whether they saw anyone slip Robert Dudgeon the famous sandwich.' I saw Buttercup get ready to remind me that he could not eat a thing all day – she was very proud of having spotted this before anyone else – but I quelled her. 'In a packet, I mean. For later. We certainly need to find that out.'

'The sandwich?' said Alec. 'I don't quite . . . I had a dream about a sandwich. Last night, I think.'

'It wasn't last night, darling,' I told him. 'It was luncheon today. And you weren't dreaming, you were listening to me talking through the alcoholic haze.' Alec nodded rather sheepishly.

'Now, if the Burry Man doesn't usually take his burrs

home for some ritual purpose at the end of the day, then we need to find out at whose instigation they ended up back at the cottage this year. Who gathered them up and put them in the cart. Because – and it gives me great pain to say this – I can't see any reason for them to be whisked away from the scene except the most sinister reason imaginable.'

'Oh Dandy, you can't be serious,' said Alec. Buttercup looked puzzled.

'I know, I know,' I said. 'But Mr Turnbull – or to be more exact Mrs Turnbull – with her comfortable knowledge of local fungi got me thinking. Isn't there some kind of mushroom – toadstool, really – that's completely harmless if ingested in most circumstances, but absolutely deadly if taken along with alcoholic drink?'

'Is there?' said Alec.

'I'm sure there is,' I said. 'You never met my parents, darling, but they were most . . . what's the word, Buttercup?'

'Mad?' said Buttercup. 'Not to be unkind, but I'd say they were mad.'

'Well, certainly eccentric,' I admitted. 'William Morris wasn't nearly earthy enough for them. William Cobbett, now! And they thumbed through Culpeper's Herbal as though it were Whitaker's Almanack.'

Buttercup snorted. 'D'you remember, Dan, when I came to stay with you and your mother burnt my bodice in the drawing-room fire and gave me that leaflet about consumption and healthy lungs?' We both laughed. 'Although I must say,' she went on, 'it was wonderful afterwards. No corsets for three glorious weeks until I got home again and my mother whisked me straight to the Army and Navy. She was shocked to the core.'

'I must have overheard it from them,' I said. 'I'm absolutely sure that there is such a mushroom. And –

I can't believe I'm giving air to this when Cad isn't here to enjoy it – but on the subject of untraceable poisons, there's "untraceable" and then there's "perfectly traceable if one looks for it but so unlikely that one doesn't". And I just wonder. If the burrs were poisoned, then the poison wouldn't be in the stomach at all, but only in the blood. And if the doctor didn't check the blood for that particular poison – and why would he? – then Bob's your uncle.'

'But are you saying that Mrs Dudgeon did this?' said Alec. 'Wouldn't she burn them in that case?'

'No, I don't think she did do it,' I said, 'if anyone actually did anything. It's the Turnbulls and Miss Brown who are in my sights at the moment. The Turnbulls because they have the required knowledge and their peculiar ideas almost amount to a motive and Joey Brown because she has acted rather shiftily more than once and she obviously has something on her mind. And actually, of course! That's what she might have been doing round the back this morning. Putting the burrs on the heap or checking that they had been or something. That would make perfect sense. But . . . let's consider Mrs Dudgeon for a moment.'

'If we find out that it was *not* her idea to take the burrs home, then she is in the clear,' said Alec.

'But if it *was* her idea,' I supplied, 'then perhaps the reason she was so desperate to get rid of all her sisters and have the place to herself was so that she could go out and burn them.'

'And now she *has* got the place to herself,' said Alec, sitting up suddenly.

'Yes indeed, but only by taking the extreme step of sending her husband's body to the undertakers for its last night above ground. And that obviously took a lot of resolve to carry through, Alec. She was visibly pained at the thought of doing it. And for that reason

167

I'm willing to bet that if there was a murder it wasn't anything to do with Mrs Dudgeon. I bet if you track down someone who was there you'll find that it wasn't her who put the burrs in the cart.'

'Well, who then?' said Buttercup.

'Who indeed,' said Alec. 'If we knew that we'd know everything.'

'We're getting a long way ahead of ourselves here,' I said, trying to remain the voice of reason, despite my excitement. 'We don't know yet that it wasn't par for the course. We don't know if this mushroom works through the bloodstream as well as the digestive system. We don't even know if it grows here or if it's in season. And we don't know if it's something that would stick out during the post-mortem like a sore thumb. So let's stay calm.'

'But the burrs on the midden heap?' said Alec.

'Oh yes, certainly,' I said. 'They need to be got away before Mrs Dudgeon or anyone else has a chance to start a bonfire and destroy them. But how we are to get them without being seen . . .'

'Ooh!' exclaimed Buttercup.

Alec and I waited for more, but she shook her head.

'I half remembered something,' she said. 'But I've forgotten what it was.'

'Well, do your best, Dandy,' said Alec. I was about to protest when I realized he was right. As odd as it would be for me to be spotted skulking around in the cottage garden, it would be ten times odder for Alec. Why had I put the horse droppings on top, I lamented. It would have been bad enough without them; it would be ghastly now, and Grant was going to be livid.

I was just on my way out of the door with two sacks and a pair of borrowed gardening gloves when Buttercup hallooed from above me and knelt down to talk to me through the grille of the murder hole.

'I've remembered,' she sang out. 'Don't worry about being caught, Dandy. I was supposed to tell you from Cad, that he's loaned out the Austin and a boy to take Mrs Dudgeon and "Donald's" wife whoever "Donald" is to the Co-operative draper to be fitted up with their mourning. Sorry.'

'Anything else?' I said, resisting the urge to rush upstairs and box her ears.

'Um? Yes! The children are at "their Auntie's Betty's" so you have a free run for poking about at the cottage.'

'I see,' I said. 'So there was no need to borrow the dog, which rolled in the dung, which went on the heap, which I'm about to toss like a salad with my bare hands. Well, gardening gloves. You are impossible, Buttercup.' I thought for a moment. 'This Donald has been doing all the least enticing jobs thus far and if his wife merits shop-bought mourning, then I must be right in thinking that he's Mr Dudgeon's brother. And if this wife being at the draper's gives me a clear run then they must live next door. Ah yes, that makes sense. His wife is "Izzy who has her hands full with eight". At last they all begin to fall into place. I'll bet this trip to the draper's is the most fun poor Izzy has had all year.'

If I had expected either familiarity or the scent of the chase to drive away other more fanciful notions on this third trip through the woods, then I soon found out I was mistaken: I still had the unnerving sensation of being watched as I strode along, and now when I told myself that there were no such things as ghosts I could answer myself that it need not be a ghost but might be a murderer, wondering what I was up to and just about to work it out and come up behind me to put his hands around my throat. It was Mr Turnbull's hands I imagined in this little scene and Mr Turnbull's scrubbed cheeks and shining eyes I imagined being the last thing my eyes ever saw in this life; his wife's voice murmuring 'That's right, my dear' being the last sound my ears ever heard. Despite working myself up into a muck sweat with these fantasies, however, I reached the back garden of Mrs Dudgeon's cottage unmolested, drew on my gardening gloves and set to work.

The horse dung rolled away more easily than I expected and I did not have to pick too many little seeds out of it with my gloved fingers. I deliberated fairly long, in fact, whether I had to pick any at all. Would every burr be poisoned if this was indeed what had happened? Or would only a few? If only a few, though, how ironic if it happened to be those few I left behind. At last, the spirit of Nanny Palmer came to rest on my right shoulder and I heard her voice telling me that this job was like all others in the matter of being worth doing and therefore worth doing well.

So the light was beginning to fade by the time I was finished. Actual sunset was not until eightish but the clearing was very small and the spruce trees around the back of it quite well grown, so even as early as this the gardens had seen the last of the afternoon's sunshine. Mrs Donald Dudgeon's washing would get damp again, I thought, if she was not home soon to take it in.

As I glanced at it upon this thought, my heart leapt up into my throat and I gave a cry. There was a figure standing in the Dudgeons' back doorway, standing quite still and looking towards me, and without being aware of having decided to do so I found myself running into the trees, the sacks forgotten. This was not prudence in the face of the unknown, nor even self-preservation on the off-chance that this figure might

170

mean me harm; it was blind, whickering terror, for the figure in the doorway was Robert Dudgeon.

'A ghost, a ghost, a ghost,' I snivelled under my breath, and: 'Don't look back, Dandy! Don't look back!', and I kept running until the clearing was out of sight and the trees had closed silently around me. Then I began simultaneously to tire, to slow and to gather my wits about me. When I finally stopped, panting and shaking, to lean against a trunk and catch my breath I almost – alone as I was – blushed for shame. There were two possibilities: either I had seen nothing at all, only shadows; or I had seen someone of the same build and colouring as Robert Dudgeon who just happened to be standing in his doorway. I could not, however, even be sure of *that* much, because when I thought hard I realized that it might just as easily have been the other doorway – I had only glanced. And if it was the other doorway, then it was pretty clear who the ghost was. I straightened my clothes, ruffled and untucked by my sudden sprinting, patted my beaming cheeks with my fingers in an attempt to cool them down, and set off back the way I had come.

When I reached the clearing once more, the ghost had – quite understandably – come down the garden to the midden heap where he stood, hands on hips, wondering. Of course, it was not Robert Dudgeon, although he did look rather like him. I arranged a smile on my face and prepared to meet Donald.

'Please forgive me,' I said as I neared him. He looked up at me, rather dazed. 'You must wonder what on earth . . . And please accept my sincere condolences.' Donald Dudgeon certainly looked grief-stricken enough to make this trite little phrase a necessity rather than a mere politeness. He was obviously quite a bit younger than his brother but he was drawn and tired, pinched with grief.

'You must wonder what on earth I'm up to,' I said again. 'Let me explain. One of your sisters-in-law. Or would they . . .? One of Mrs Dudgeon's sisters, that is, Mrs Robert Dudgeon. Oh well, anyway, one of the ladies seems to have put the burrs from Friday here on the midden instead of on the fire. And they won't rot down, you know. Well, you must know,' I gestured around the neatly bulging vegetable patch in his own garden, 'and I happened to notice and I thought how sad for your – for the widow when she sees them. How awful, in fact, next spring, just when she might perhaps be beginning to get on top of things and she comes out to start her garden full of hope and . . . and there they are. Do you see? None of my business, obviously, but do you see?'

He looked at me very closely, appraising me as though I were a specimen of some exotic genus and he a collector trying to decide if I was a new discovery or if he had one of this type already. It was a most unnerving examination to find oneself subjected to, and I was slightly mesmerized as I looked back innocently (I hoped), returning his stare. It is foolish, of course, to imagine that the lower orders are simple to a man (especially when one considers that some of one's own set are so very simple that to call them 'simple' at all and not something much plainer is more courtesy than accurate description). Still, it comes as a surprise sometimes, and certainly it came as a surprise to me then, to look into the face of a working man such as this and see there such a calculating intelligence, such knowing and complicated sadness, as though the world were laid bare before him and the understanding of it wearied him half to death.

The only way to interpret the *next* look that flitted over his face was as one of decision and dismissal. He seemed to conclude that I was of no interest to him and without actually saying anything he suggested that I was free to go on my way. And to be sure, it would not have taken too much wisdom and intelligence to categorize me as a harmless lunatic given the drivel I had just been spouting.

'So,' I said, gathering up my two sacks by the necks and taking a deep breath. 'I shall take these away and burn them and Mrs Dudgeon need never think about them again.'

'That is most helpful of you,' he said. 'Thank you.' His voice as much as his face was weary-sounding, but he spoke well for one of his class, the local accent still there in the clipped vowels and hissed consonants but the words articulated with care. With such care, I suddenly realized, that the most obvious explanation for all of his oddness was that he was, this very minute, profoundly drunk. I remembered the bottles on his rubbish heap and how he had fallen asleep beside the corpse the night before and had not woken when Mrs Dudgeon left the cottage to wander in the woods.

'I hope it all goes well for you tomorrow,' I said, still disposed to be sympathetic, remembering that his brother had just died, but instead of accepting my kindness in good spirit, he reared backward and stared at me. 'Sorry,' I blurted. 'I didn't mean to suggest that it could be a happy day. I mean, I know it's a funeral, but I hope it all goes smoothly and isn't too much of a strain.' This seemed to mollify him; he relaxed again and nodded and I, not wanting to try another remark after that last one had gone down so very badly, simply nodded back, turned to the woods and strode away.

This time, tramping through the trees like a fairy-tale woodcutter with my hessian sacks, I felt none of the jitters from all my earlier trips even though the sun was low enough to flash in and out between the tree

trunks in a way that could easily have suggested countless figures flitting between the trees all around me, and
perhaps it was because I was *not* peering around for
spooks that I spotted something of great actual, concrete interest that I might otherwise have missed.

I was walking with my head down, beginning to feel
the weight of the sacks in my shoulders, even though
dried burdock seeds are not particularly solid little
objects, musing on how implausible it was that a
woodcutter, even a very burly one, could carry his
slumbering children in sacks over his shoulder deep
into the woods to leave them there, and trying to
remember which fairy tale it was where a burly woodcutter did so, and thus entranced by my floating
thoughts and the steady crimp, crimp of my feet on the
needles beneath me – dreaming and dawdling, Nanny
Palmer used to call it – I saw something flash. A step
further on, the low shaft of sunlight had shifted and
the object had disappeared, but I stopped, returned to
what I thought must be the same spot and then rocked
backwards and forwards, moving my head, until it
caught the light again. I trained my eye on it and
moved closer.

'Good God above,' I whispered under my breath as
I crouched down beside it and poked it clear of the
forest litter which was just beginning to cover it up for
good. I had no idea what it meant or how it changed
things, but I was very pleased to have found it, for
it seemed to add a little measure of sense to Mrs
Dudgeon's midnight wandering. It was, of course, the
pen. I picked it up by putting a gloved finger against
each end, thinking of fingerprints, and dropped it into
my dress pocket. Alec was going to love this.

Almost home, a few minutes later, nearing the edge
of the woods at last, I did indeed catch a glimpse
between the tree trunks of countless figures bearing

down on me, but once again my heart and other innards took the sight in their stride because there was no mistaking these: the sun was burnishing their flaming tresses as the little Dudgeons from next door made their way home.

'Hello there,' I called to them, and was surprised to see some of the smaller ones clutch at each other and a couple of the medium-sized brothers falter in their steps. 'It's only me,' I said. 'You remember me.' I thought, too late, that perhaps I should have stashed the sacks behind a tree before they saw them, but with the typical lack of interest all children show in the doings of adults they barely gave these a glance. Anyway, I reasoned to myself, the way they swarmed around the woods like so many termites, the sacks of burrs were probably safer in my hands than behind any tree within swarming distance. The children were not however, I could not help but notice as I drew near them, in a swarming mood, but stood in a clump in the middle of the path and waited for me to reach them. There were six of them today, only the oldest sister 'wee Izzy' and the tiny baby missing. The littlest but one tot was being borne along in a well-worn push-chair by the biggest brother.

'On your way home from Auntie Betty's?' I asked them. A few of them nodded and little Lila's lip began to tremble. I began to tell myself that it was only to be expected that they were subdued, since their uncle had died and tomorrow was his funeral, but then I remembered that the first time I had met any of the happy band had been the day of the death itself and that they had been absolutely irrepressible then.

'What's the matter?' I asked them. 'You seem a bit glum.'

'We dinnae want to go through they woods wur-selves,' said one of the middle-sized brothers.

175

'Why ever not?' I asked, amazed.

'Cos of the demon,' said Lila. Her big brothers hung their heads and one of them nudged her to shut her up.

'But you're a match for any demon,' I assured them. 'Weren't you going to catch him a few days ago?'

'We thocht he was a pretendy one,' said Lila. 'But now we ken he's a real one.'

'I dinnae want to get put doon a hole,' whimpered one of her small brothers.

'Now look here, Miss Lila,' I said, bending down to talk to the child face to face, 'and you too, boys. You *must* stop telling each other these horror stories. You must, really. You big boys tell the little ones there's nothing to be afraid of. And you little ones don't believe a word they say.' I stopped, realizing that my advice was becoming confused.

'We didnae tell naeb'dy nothin', missus,' said the oldest boy. 'We seen 'um. In the woods, right by oor hoose. A real demon comin' to get us. Comin' to put us doon the holes with the ghosties.'

'And what made you think he was real, and coming to get you?' I said. 'Why would you think that?'

'Oor daddy told us,' said another. 'Oor daddy told us to watch out for demons and no' to let one catch us, ever.'

'And now we've tae go hame all by wurselves and it's gettin' dark and the hoose is empty til Mammy gets back with Auntie Chrissie.' They looked up at me beseechingly out of six pairs of blue eyes, and I relented. I was not, however, about to traipse back to the cottage on foot for a fourth time in one day – I was beginning to wear out a trench – but I could not withstand the trembling lips and brimming eyes a moment longer.

'Very well, then,' I said. 'Come and wait on the wall

by the castle rise and I'll fetch my motor car and run you all home. And your daddy's there, by the way, so you won't be alone once you get there.' The second half of this was lost in a chorus of cheers and whoops and they turned on their heels and raced back the way they had come towards the park. By the time I caught up and passed them, dragging my sacks, they were sitting on top of a wall in a jostling row, threatening to tip each other off and arguing about who was going to sit in the front seat.

'You gullible fool, Dandy,' I muttered to myself. 'They saw you coming.'

Chapter Ten

'So where does all of that get us?' said Alec, through toast-crumbs, the next morning. He had his breakfast napkin tucked into his stiff collar to preserve the sparkling shirt-front and the black tie. Cadwallader, surprisingly less pragmatic – perhaps wearing one's napkin in one's collar fell foul of one of those unexpected pockets of etiquette in American life, although why they bother with these odd little nods to politeness in the overall scheme of things one can hardly see – Cadwallader for whatever reason, anyway, was simply leaning over from well back with his neck stretched out and scooping egg into the bowl of his fork, rather confirming my point.

Cad and Alec were bound for Robert Dudgeon's funeral, Buttercup and I, of course, being barred from attendance along with all other females including his own widow. I had always thought this particular stricture of the Presbyterian Scotch one of the most unbending (from a very strong field) but I was glad that Mrs Dudgeon did not have a funeral to contend with; if she was no more restored to herself than she had been at my last sight of her I was sure she could not have stood it.

I had been rather wrung out myself at the end of the day before, when I had finally deposited the six little scallywags plus pushchair at their garden gate and returned home, and I had been almost thankful when Buttercup stuck out her lip and firmly vetoed any talk of the case over dinner or through our card game afterwards. Since she was breakfasting in bed this morning, however – her habitual indolence having overcome any thoughts of her role as hostess at last after five days of manful effort – I was taking the chance to bring the men up to date.

Cad had been torn between triumph and sulks when I revealed that I was coming around to the idea of poisoning after all, and seemed to think I had not been playing fair in not telling him all about my mysterious mushroom on the very first night.

'We must remain cautious,' I had told him. 'It might be something that would show up clearly in the stomach, in which case it can't have been the sandwich. Or it might be something which doesn't work through the blood, in which case it couldn't be the burrs. And we might find a perfectly innocent explanation for either the sandwich or the burrs or both, in which case we are back where we started.'

'Well?' prompted Alec. 'Remaining cautious, of course, what's next?'

'What's next,' I said, 'are some jobs suitable for the untrained enthusiast – you and me – and some for which we unfortunately need an expert. We need to find out where the cart turned around and why. I'm going to walk the obvious routes today and see what I can see. You, Cad, are going to latch on to the Burry Man's boys at the funeral – can you remember what they looked like? Good – and pin this blasted sandwich down once and for all. Then this evening, Alec, you must go to "Broon's Bar", with fingers crossed that the fair Joey is on duty, and see if you can get any further with her – I'm sure she knows something and I can't quite work out what her standing is with the Dudgeon

family. She was trusted to sit with Mr Dudgeon's body
– trust which she betrayed, by the way, in leaving him
alone – but on the other hand Mrs Dudgeon's sisters
are divided in their opinions of her. One of them
sounded very sniffy about the girl yesterday, until
another reminded her rather grudgingly that we are all
"Jock Tamson's bairns" when all's said and done –'

'All who?' said Alec.

'Jock Thompson's bairns,' I said. 'All the same
underneath I suppose is the best way to explain it. All
God's children.'

'Sounds rather a disrespectful name for God,'
said Cad.

'It wasn't a literal translation,' I said. 'Anyway, Bet –
or was it Lizzy? – said that and then Tina said that they
of all people – meaning the sisters – had no business
turning their noses up at the girl just because she
worked in a bar either. Interesting, don't you think?'

'Interesting is putting it rather mildly,' said Cad. 'It's
like a ball of wool.'

'If only it were that straightforward,' said Alec.
'It's more like a bowl of Italian noodles. Slipperier
than wool, and when it's all unravelled there are far
more than one strand and most of them are irrelevant
anyway.'

'And the irrelevant ones will look identical to the
crucial ones right until the end, knowing our luck,'
I said. Alec and I were showing off a little in front of
Cad, I suppose, but he was so easy to show off to, so
very guileless in his readiness to be impressed.

'And all the while,' I said, getting back to my pep-
talk, 'you can be thinking about what Mrs Dudgeon
would be doing with a pen and ink out in the woods
in the wee small hours. And I'll be doing the same.'

'Did you look around for paper?' said Alec.

'Why would there be paper?' I said. 'Why, if she

180

simply wanted to write something down, or write a letter, could she not have done it in her own bedroom with the key turned in the lock and a candle to work by? Why would she have stumbled out into the black night?'

'But it's just as hard to explain why she did so with only the pen and the ink,' said Alec. I agreed.

'Is this why you need an expert?' said Cad.

'No,' I told him. 'That problem only needs to be worried at until logic prevails. We need a medical doctor who knows what tests are routinely carried out during a post-mortem. And an expert – a chemist, to be precise – to augment my very slim store of memories about this alcohol-dependent poison wouldn't hurt either.'

'Mr Turnbull?' suggested Cad.

'Indeed,' I said. 'Mr Turnbull with his scientific background and extensive knowledge of plants would be ideal if he were not so in the thick of it all. What I mean is that Mr Turnbull is auditioning for the part of first murderer and doing rather well. He can't possibly understudy as expert witness too.'

'Mr *Turnbull*?' Cad was almost spluttering. 'Mr Turnbull with his rosy cheeks and "healthful exercise"?' Alec and I shared a smile, each of us thinking that Cad was a fine one to talk.

'Oh, but I'm with Dandy there,' said Alec. 'At least, I bumped into Mrs Turnbull coming out of the Queensferry Arms yesterday and she struck me as utterly ruthless. She didn't know me from Adam and yet she launched right in, sermonizing. So if she's anything like her husband . . .'

'She certainly is,' I told him. 'She's a wife in the Adam's rib style. Sickening. But I must say, darling, if this meeting was near luncheon time you must have been quite irresistible to any Temperance enthusiast for miles around.'

'Once and for all, Dandy,' said Alec sternly, whisking his napkin out of his collar and flicking away the crumbs in his lap, 'I was not drunk.' This time it was Cad and I who shared the smile.

I parked my motor car at the Bellstane and set off in the cart tracks of the Dudgeons up the steep street known as the Loan. The Burry Man had arrived back at the Rosebery Hall at bang on six o'clock, ending his day with the curious little stiff-legged sprint up the steps, as I myself had seen. Mr and Mrs Dudgeon had appeared at the greasy pole competition not long after it began at half past six. I was happy to say a quarter to seven at the latest: I remembered someone grumbling that the fun would be over too soon and that 'Rubbert' should be held back until some of the less accomplished and so much more entertaining contestants had had a bash. So, with ten minutes at least to get him out of his burry suit and into his own clothes – and considerably longer if he washed and if he rubbed his arms and legs as much as I would have liked to after such a day – and taking into consideration the numbers of townspeople still surging down the Loan towards the fun, who along with the gradient would prevent the pony from picking up any kind of pace – I did not see how they could even have got as far as the edge of the village before turning back.

Thinking it all out like this I soon realized that if they had been waylaid at all it must have been the very briefest of accostings and must have taken place in the street, the kind of encounter into which it was hard to incorporate an impromptu sandwich – Lord, how sick and tired I was of that blasted sandwich! I hoped with all my heart that Alec would manage to discover from one of the Burry Man's helpers that some whiter-than-white sister-in-law slipped it into one of the buckets for his teatime snack and we could cut it out of our considerations once and for all.

The upside to my having worked out that their little trip up the hill and down again was so short, however, was that I felt sure someone must have seen them turn. Revellers were simply flocking to the Fair and the Loan was like a funnel, pouring all comers into the bottle-neck of Craw's Close and the Bellstane Square. As I looked up the street now, I saw that one side of the Loan was unpromising for a stretch, the hulk of the bottling plant and a couple of dairies taking up most of it, but on the other side there were lanes opening off it and cottages facing on to it all the way up to the New Kirk, after which a run of villas lined one side of the road as it levelled off, these stretching past the village school to the end of Killinghouse Road and beyond. I felt sure they could not possibly have got any further than Killinghouse Road in the time. They might, of course, have turned off before that, along Station Road where a row of grander villas sat rather more anonymously behind high hedges, and if they had spotted someone they did not care to meet on Station Road and turned around in a hurry there was a chance that they might have managed it unobserved. But all in all, it looked very promising. I could but try.

Although it made me puff as I climbed it, I was glad of the steep rise of the Loan, for it gave me a reason, when I saw a pair of village women talking at the corner of Stoneycroft Lane, to stop near them and turn around, pretending to admire the view.

They lowered their voices a little and I could hear the rhythm of their chatter slow down as they took half of their attention away from the conversation to appraise me, but they kept talking and so it was the most natural thing in the world for me to turn towards them, having drunk my fill of the sight of the river, and politely exchange a few words.

'Beautiful view,' I said. They nodded, unsmiling.

'But a very sad day,' I added. I was in the black linen that Grant had provided and these two were in grey and black too, albeit under white aprons and with sleeves rolled to the elbows and hidden under white cuffs.

'We were just sayin' the Fair would nivver be the same again,' said one. 'It's a terrible thing for the Ferry.'

'Indeed it is terrible,' I agreed. 'But as to its effect on the Fair . . .' They looked at me, intrigued. 'I don't know if you heard any of the kerfuffle between the various parties.' I gestured up the hill a little to where St Andrew's UP and St Margaret's RC squared up to each other across the street. They raised their eyebrows and drew a little nearer, gossips by nature, clearly. 'I don't pretend to know who is on which side or even why,' I went on with perfect honesty, 'but there was talk about trying to stamp it out. I should have thought it would be much harder to do so now. It would look so dreadfully like disrespect to Mr Dudgeon. To my mind anyway.' This could easily have misfired, had these two women happened to straddle the sectarian divide (and I felt a little guilty about blaming the reverends quite so fair and square as all this. I was pretty sure it was the local ladies who were the ring-leaders and the ministers and priests had simply had their heads turned. Boredom, I had decided, is respon-sible for a great deal of unwarranted meddling. Look, after all, at me) but I was lucky, in this instance.

'We're both Parish,' said one of the women with a touch of pride at making up a corner of such a reason-able threesome.

'And I said as much to thon Mrs Turnbull when she

come round with her pamphlets,' said the other. 'We get all the preaching we need for the week at the Vennel on a Sunday morning, thank you *very* much.'

'Oh, she's at it already?' I said. They nodded, lips tightly pursed.

'And Rab no' even in his grave.' This was accompanied by a raising of one corner of an apron to dab at the eyes.

'What twaddle,' I said, suppressing the thought that the post-mortem had shown this to be very far from true. In fact, Mrs Turnbull with her Temperance pamphlets was suspiciously near the mark. With a feeling of thankfulness at how easily the conversation had come round to the bit, I went on: 'What a shame Mr and Mrs Dudgeon didn't go straight home on Friday night after all, though, wasn't it? Perhaps if he had gone quietly home to rest.'

'That was a thing he nivver did, madam,' said the woman who had been dabbing her eyes. 'He was Burry Man all day and then he climbed the greasy pole at nicht.'

'Aye, and won the ham most years, at that.'

'A grand man.'

'Indeed,' I said and left a respectful pause. 'But didn't you know that they set off to go home on Friday at six o'clock in their little cart and then changed their minds? I'm surprised you didn't notice them passing.'

'I was doon at the Fair well afore six.'

'Tae think we'll nivver see him again on thon daft wee shell hutch.'

'Indeed,' I said again. 'Well, that's the fact of the matter. They set off and then they turned back. I wonder why.'

'A proud man,' said the weeping woman, beginning to dissolve in earnest now. 'He must have been feelin' no' well and then his pride got the better of him and he pushed hissel' too far. Puir Rubbert.'

'But you didn't actually see them turning,' I said, making sure. Then I addressed the other, more stalwart of the pair. 'Did you happen to be about when the little cart turned around?'

'Naw, I didnae,' she said while her companion sobbed. 'I didnae see them at all on Burry Man's day. First time in my life I didnae see the Burry Man. I was that busy cleaning ready for the Fair, I jist sent the bairn to the door with a penny and I never saw him. Never gave him a nip.' She was beginning to brim too.

'Aw, Alice now,' said the other. 'Dinnae gie yersel' trouble. You couldnae have kent and like you say the bairn gave him his penny, ye've naethin' to feel bad for.'

I wondered in silence at this; it was hard to credit that one of these women, as sane and everyday-looking as one could imagine, might feel she had brought down misfortune on Dudgeon's head by neglecting to go to the door with his whisky.

'I'm as bad, if you like,' the other went on. 'I saw Chrissie the day before and I wis sure there was something no' right with her, but I wis rushin' to get done and get back hame to get the teas on and I let her go by. It's jist the way o' things. If you knew when trouble wis comin' ye'd be more careful-like.'

I listened patiently to all of it. It was just as Alec had found with his barman; everyone was now ready shamelessly to claim they had 'known something was wrong' but everyone had unaccountably done nothing about it and had somehow neglected to mention it until events proved them right. I smiled blandly, inwardly deciding that this woman at least was too full of self-important fancy to be relied upon, but then I stopped. She said she noticed something wrong with Mrs Dudgeon the day before? But as far as the world at large knew, there was nothing wrong with Mrs Dudgeon, either the day before or at any other time. Only Alec, Cad and I – and Buttercup, so far as Buttercup ever thought anything – thought that something was wrong with Mrs Dudgeon the day before.

'What happened?' I asked. 'I mean what was it that concerned you about poor Mrs Dudgeon? I mean, I'm sure you have no more to berate yourself for than your friend does.' I gave Alice's arm a friendly rub. The rub did her no good, but she perked up a little at the prospect of hearing what her neighbour had to say.

'I wis in the baker's,' said the woman, 'in the queue, and I saw Chrissie Dudgeon across the road, at the police station.'

At this, Alice gasped and I felt my pulse surge with excitement. A woman like Mrs Dudgeon would only darken the door of a police station in the very direst emergency, I was sure. Amongst her kind, frequenting police stations was on a par with popping in and out of pawnshops or having a standing account at the bookies'.

'She didnae go in. She was . . . it wis like she was minded to go in, though. She stood ootside, goin' from foot to foot, jist lookin' and then she turned, sudden-like, as if a pack of dogs was after her and away she went along the street, like nothin' on earth.'

'But why?' I said. 'What happened? Did someone say something to her? Did someone follow her?'

The woman misunderstood.

'I ken,' she said. 'I ken fine I should have gone after her, but I didnae want to lose my place. There wis only six pies left and I needed four and there was a long queue at ma back, and I hud nae time to make anything else for their teas with my Fair cleanin' needin' done, so I just watched her go. And now . . . puir Chrissie.'

'Puir, puir Chrissie,' chimed Alice. 'Wi' her man and her laddie both gone.' At this both of them gave in completely and I offered a sickly grin. I was unsure of the polite way to take leave of a person one has found chatting calmly and then reduced to tears.

'I'm so sorry,' I muttered, and left.

It was all I could do to contain my euphoria. We had been utterly stumped as to why Dudgeon suddenly changed his mind about donning the burry suit. All we had known was that whatever it was had happened on Thursday afternoon, at teatime. Now here was Mrs Dudgeon, going to the police, or rather almost going to the police, and leaving in a hurry, visibly disturbed. And on Thursday afternoon, at teatime, no less – it had to be if the cottager woman had no time to cook and could not relinquish her dibs on the shop-bought pies. Mrs Dudgeon must have seen someone, inside the police station I should guess, that she most fervently did not want to see, someone who sent her scuttling back the way she had come, to tell her husband that he had to abandon his role. It was not too much of a stretch either to imagine that she had seen this same someone on the Loan or Station Road on Friday evening, once Dudgeon had gone through with it after all, and that again she had turned and fled, this time on the little cart and with her husband beside her. Whatever hold this person had over the Dudgeons, whatever harm it was this person threatened, I did not know and could not readily guess but a picture was beginning to form in me – unimaginative as I usually am – of the two of them, harried and hunted, unable to tell anyone what was wrong, unable finally to bear the strain. In the heat of the August morning, I suddenly shivered.

There were no more villagers loitering usefully as I ascended the rest of the Loan and as I had expected there were no signs of life along Station Road, just the sweep of low walls and high hedges hiding the solid Edwardian dwellings from view. There was no way of knowing whether the cart might have turned along here on Friday evening or carried on up the hill straight ahead, but thinking that there was more chance of another encounter if I kept on, I passed the end of the road and kept climbing then, as the hill levelled off at the gates to the school playground, I heard a hearty voice hailing me.

'Good morning, Mrs Gilver.'

'Oh, God,' I groaned to myself. Of course, since I was passing the school, I was also passing the schoolhouse, and just as inevitably on this bright summer morning, Mr and Mrs Turnbull were out in their garden, engaged in healthful exercise in the fresh air. I deliberated about waving and walking on, and then decided to take the bull by the horns. For one thing, it might have been one of the Turnbulls that turned the Dudgeons round on Friday evening and sent them back down to the Craw's Close and the greasy pole. So I needed to ask what they were up to on Thursday afternoon too. And besides, I might, just possibly, be able to turn the conversation back to toadstools again – in fact, given how much they both seemed to enjoy discomfiting other people, *they* might well turn it for me – and it would be very interesting to see if they began to squirm when I veered towards the particular mushroom in question. (How I wished I could remember its name!) Even if I did not have the nerve to do this much, though, it might still be well worth my while to get them talking again: I needed to decide for myself whether I suspected them because they were actually suspicious or if I merely disliked them so much that I wanted them to be guilty. Thinking that a

189

detective's life is full of sacrifice, I organized my face into a surprised smile and called back.

'We meet again! How lovely! And what a splendid garden.' This was pure flattery. The truth was, I was very pleased to see, that their plot was not a patch on either of the Mr Dudgeons', looking straggly and rather dry, their spinach bolting for the heavens.

'You certainly do keep busy,' I added toadyingly, as I reached the garden wall. 'I'm surprised you have time for this with all your other pursuits.'

'A little each day is easily accomplished,' said Mr Turnbull.

'And it's such healthful exercise,' Mrs Turnbull chimed in. I managed to maintain my smile and suppress my groan.

'But I must leave it there for today, my dear,' said Mr Turnbull, taking a fat watch out of his waistcoat pocket, 'and get ready for the funeral.'

'Ah yes,' I said, as though only then remembering. 'Poor Robert Dudgeon. It's today, isn't it?'

Mrs Turnbull was gathering together her trowels and her basket of greenery – whether scrawny harvest bound for their luncheon table or weeds bound for the heap it was hard to tell – clearly not planning to continue her toils alone.

'I wonder if you would like to join me for a cup of coffee, Mrs Gilver,' she said. 'It's just gone eleven.'

Now, I am no snob but I was a little startled at this. The woman seemed to have not the faintest idea of her place. However, as it happened, the invitation was most welcome from a professional point of view, even if it was quite improper and without any social appeal.

'Delightful,' I gushed. 'How kind.' I unlatched the garden gate and entered, mentally looking forward with great eagerness to a day when the case would be solved and I could cut her dead.

She rang for coffee as we entered the hall and then excused herself to go and tidy the garden out of her hair and fingernails, ushering me towards a parlour. It was exactly what I should have expected. Some good late Georgian furniture, inherited no doubt, but with all its lovely gleam polished so aggressively that it looked as though it was coated in golden treacle, bare dark boards smelling strongly of household soap with not a rug in sight, and ill-fitting slub covers over the chairs and sofa in one of those prints of cabbage roses like bunches of gargoyles tied together at the neck. The same ugly print made up the curtains, the pelmet, the runner on the sideboard and even the lampshades, suggesting that Mrs Turnbull had made a bulk purchase of the stuff and run up the lot herself. Despite the warmth of the morning outside, slowly melting its way to another hot afternoon, the room was frigid, even the paper fan in the grate curling with damp, a cold not to be explained by the way that the windows were 'healthfully' open six inches at top and bottom, and I would have bet my eyes that the paper fan was kept there all year round and that Mr and Mrs Turnbull sat here in the midwinter with nothing but their own glowing selves to keep them warm. If I had been on the school board I should have taken them up about it; it takes years to warm a stone house up again once it has got properly cold, and one could imagine the next incumbent shivering through a few Januarys cursing the Turnbulls with chattering teeth.

Mrs Turnbull rejoined me just as the coffee arrived, looking rather revolting with bare legs and sleeves cut short to the shoulder. I had kept my little jacket around my shoulders and I had to try hard not to cradle the coffee cup in my hands for warmth when she passed it to me.

'Yes, poor Mr Dudgeon,' I said again, as we took our first sips.

Mrs Turnbull looked rather drawn both ways at this. She wanted nothing more than to launch into all that she felt about the death, but she did not want to start from a point of sympathizing with the departed. She pursed her mouth and made a tsk-ing sound.

'The children are terribly unnerved by it all,' she said.

'Your children?' I asked, wondering why that should be so.

'In a sense,' she answered. 'My husband and I have not been blessed with children of our own, and so we think of all his charges as our children. And, as I say, they are beginning to make up silly stories about it already to frighten themselves with.'

'It was most unfortunate,' I said. 'Dozens of them must have been right there on the spot when he fell. One can only hope that it was all over so quickly that they could be led away before they really latched on to what was happening.'

'If only that were so,' said Mrs Turnbull. 'But I'm afraid the parents, nine times out of ten, take no care at all to keep their talk away from little ears. And when they try to be discreet they simply confuse the children even more. By the very next day, there were half a dozen different versions of what had happened, all wildly fanciful, of course. I heard them regaling one another as they sat having their picnics. Quite tiny children some of them and you would not believe what they came out with.'

'Oh, I think I would,' I said, laughing. 'I've been exposed to the Dudgeons next door.'

'The who?' said Mrs Turnbull.

'Next door to Robert and Chrissie,' I said. 'The little red-headed scamps. They have some simply blood-curdling tales to tell of what goes on in those woods.'

'Well,' said Mrs Turnbull, frowning slightly, 'there we cannot blame the parents. Donald is one of our stalwarts.'

'Really?' I said, wondering to what manner of stalwart she was alluding.

'Oh yes, a tireless worker for the cause.'

I racked my brain briefly to determine which cause this might be. He did seem to have a green thumb, but could horticulture, even to such as the Turnbulls, really be called 'a cause'?

'He is quite the most charismatic speaker on our entire summer circuit,' said Mrs Turnbull. 'His success rate astonishes even me sometimes. In fact, I have suggested to him that he would make an excellent lay-preacher, but he's a religious conservative through and through. He wouldn't hear of it.'

I was having to work pretty hard by now to stop myself from gaping. Charismatic? A speaker? A lay-preacher, even?

'You seem surprised, Mrs Gilver,' said Mrs Turnbull. 'Have you and Donald met?'

'I have met him, just briefly,' I said. 'And more to the point I've seen the whisky bottles on the rubbish heap outside his cottage. I shouldn't have thought he was lay-preacher material at all.'

Mrs Turnbull threw back her head and let out a peal of laughter. Happy as I always am to provide entertainment for my fellow man, I felt the stirrings of annoyance as wave after wave of chuckles issued from her. I was glad to see that she slopped some coffee on to the lap of her dress, which was rather pale, and I hoped it left a stain.

'He speaks in our Temperance tent,' said Mrs Turnbull. 'And each time he does, men flock to the front to hand over their bottles and watch him pour them out into the ground. It's a marvellous sight, Mrs Gilver. But

I suppose it does mean that he ends up with more than a few empties!' She was laughing again, and this time I had the grace to smile a little with her.

'Well, so much for my judgement of character then,' I said with what I thought was great magnanimity. 'I thought he looked a born drinker. In fact, I thought he was drunk!'

'Appearances can be deceptive,' said Mrs Turnbull. 'It's not the first time poor Donald, with his looks what they are, has been taken for one of the lost lambs instead of the shepherd. But he is as fierce a foe of the demon drink as any man born and he is leading his children along the straight path in the most determined way.'

I thought wryly to myself that he might care to widen his scope a little. They were perhaps well drilled in the evils of drink but their minds ran far from the lessons of Sunday school when at play in the woods.

'Well, I'm glad for the sake of the children and their mother to have the source of all the bottles cleared up,' I said. I was merely making chit-chat, but to my horror Mrs Turnbull read rather more into it than I had meant.

'You're of our mind?' she said. 'I had heard that at Mrs de Cassilis's little party, you had a cocktail in your hand. But I'm delighted to hear it.'

I began to gabble. 'Well, no, that is, yes. You did. I'm not. I can't abide whisky but I'm not a teetotaller. Not that I'd say I'm a drinker, you understand. I'm – you know, a glass of sherry before lunch, a cocktail or two, wine with dinner and perhaps a little something afterwards . . .' I ground to a halt, thinking that this list sounded positively debauched when one said it out loud in one breath like that. 'Moderation in all things,' I finished, lamely.

'The doctrine of moderation in all things,' said Mrs

Turnbull, 'is as harmful as it is hypocritical.' I blinked. 'That may sound radical,' she went on. I had been thinking it sounded insufferably rude, but she was welcome to call it radical if she chose. 'But no one actually means moderation in all things. No one really advocates moderation in murder, moderation in slavery.' This was obviously a pre-prepared speech, one which had been wheeled out many a time before now and would be many more times to come. What a cheek, to make me sit through it here in her parlour where etiquette prevented me from escape!

'In short, moderation is only to be recommended where the phenomenon in question is essentially harmless.'

'I don't agree,' I said, which was a bald statement to make in any normal social intercourse, but as my sons would say 'she started it'. 'I think moderation can be safely advocated if the . . . stuff,' I had forgotten her wording, 'is harmless *in moderation.*'

'Oh, but my dear Mrs Gilver,' she said, earnestly coming to sit on the edge of her seat and leaning towards me, 'it's not. It's *poison.*'

Under the present circumstances, I felt I could say nothing in argument against that. Mr Dudgeon's intake had been far from moderate, it was true, but he was on his way to be buried that very morning and I was in no heart to champion whisky any further. One point worth noting in passing, I thought, was that this readiness on Mrs Turnbull's part to talk of whisky as 'poison' rather pointed to her innocence in the matter of Robert Dudgeon's death. She would hardly want to draw a close comparison between the two if she or her husband were the author of the crime.

'It's utter, utter poison and quite useless in the bodily economy,' Mrs Turnbull was saying. 'If my husband were only here he could tell you.'

'Your wish has been granted,' said Mr Turnbull, sweeping in the parlour door in a black tie and rather green-tinged dark suit. 'What can I tell Mrs Gilver, my dear?'

'Your wife is attempting to get my signature on the pledge,' I said, speaking with no more reverence than this silly nonsense deserved; it was long past time I staked a claim in the conversation again.

'You may scoff,' said Mr Turnbull. I inclined my head, accepting his permission graciously, then I took a hold of myself again. I must swallow all annoyance and do what was needed for the case.

'I hold no particular brief one way or the other,' I said, trying to sound lofty. 'Only I do wonder if going around saying it's poison is wise. Around here in particular.' I was speaking with forked tongue, hoping to jolt them, but if they did know anything about Robert Dudgeon they hid it remarkably well and only frowned at me in puzzlement and waited for more. 'Around here where so many depend on the stuff for their livelihood, I mean. What would become of Queensferry without the bottling hall?'

'Queensferry without the bottling hall,' said Mr Turnbull in a dreamy voice, as though he was speaking of Elysium, 'would be a better place in every way.'

'Then you would only have to close all the mines and scuttle all the fishing boats and you'd be happy,' I said, and I did not trouble with much politeness. All very well for Mr Turnbull to lay waste to any trade that was not 'healthful exercise' in another form, but we could not all be schoolmasters. 'And our young men would be off on a ship to the New World to work down their mines instead.' I remembered Tommy from the night of the greasy pole, threatening emigration to escape his wife and her nagging tongue, and I thought that I would accept a fairly long boat ride to get away from the Turnbulls right now. Mrs Turnbull, I noticed, was reddening with wifely anger to hear me speak to her husband so, but before she had managed more than a rumble, he stepped in.

'We keep our eyes raised to the heavens and our hearts follow, Mrs Gilver,' he said. 'We are not troubled by those who would pull us down.'

'Very admirable,' I replied, although thinking that there comes a point where noble idealism becomes ruthless zeal and, once beyond that point, there is no knowing what people will do in the name of a cause, 'but if you are trying to change minds, all I'm saying is that you might want to lower your sights a little. I don't see that there's any point in calling whisky "poison" in a town where so many drink the stuff every day and are manifestly alive and well. Unpoisoned, in fact,' I explained.

'But they're very far from well,' said Mr Turnbull. 'They are killing themselves, slowly and insidiously, but killing themselves nonetheless. I speak now as a student of the natural sciences, Mrs Gilver. I have studied the topic in some depth and built up quite a substantial little library on it.' He took a huge breath and I sensed the beginning of another sermon. I had to keep him out of the pulpit and try to get him to stick to particulars if I was ever to hear anything useful.

'There are many peoples of the world who lack the European's capacity to train himself to ingest this poison, Mrs Gilver. Were you aware of that?'

'I believe I've heard as much,' I said. 'Red Indians . . .?'

'And there are places in the world where the fashion is to ingest arsenic. They build up a tolerance to it, little by little.'

'Really?' I said. 'How odd.'

'And both arsenic and alcohol would kill a child. Or

kill its greatest devotee by overdose. Where is the difference between the two? And yet think of the outcry there would be if there were an arsenic factory in the middle of our little burgh. What would you say to that?'

'Um,' I said, feeling as though I were back at school being given an oral test without warning. I considered saying that the difference lay in the capacity to make a delicious punch for a party, but I refrained. 'I do see that you have a point, Mr Turnbull. I certainly do see that. Only, as I say, I wonder if the "poison" angle is your strongest lever in Queensferry of all places. People have to make a living. And I suppose one could say that if they are filching the stuff from the distillery, at least it's real whisky. I'd have thought it was a good thing in a way to have such a ready supply keeping down the urge towards "moonshine". I have a sister who married an Anglo-Irishman and the tales she has to tell . . .'

Mr and Mrs Turnbull rolled their eyes at each other, although whether to indicate that I was naive to think there were no illicit stills in the neighbourhood or simply to express horror at my readiness to find a silver lining in their personal black cloud, I could not say. One thing was now clear beyond a shadow of a doubt, however. They could not possibly have had anything to do with the death. No one in his right mind would bang on like this about the dangers of whisky-drinking if he were in the fortunate position of having his own crime tidied away on account of an excess of whisky-drinking by the corpse-to-be. So their creeping around in the woods must indeed have been a nature-walk, and the uncomfortable feeling they gave me, which I had mistaken for my detective hackles rising, must simply be the feeling one sometimes got from an innocent, everyday, monomaniacal, crashing bore.

'And another thing,' I said, free to offend them as I chose now, 'if you spout a lot of talk about poison that they don't believe and can't believe, because their livelihoods depend on it and their own eyes refute it, then they won't believe anything you *do* say. They'll simply put every word down to "teetotallers' fairy tales" and the baby will go out with the bathwater.'

'Hmph,' said Mrs Turnbull. 'There is no problem with the locals believing fairy tales, Mrs Gilver. As you yourself have found.'

'Well, they certainly enjoy them,' I answered, 'but as to believing them, who knows?' I was thinking of the artless way the little Dudgeons had insisted on their current demon being 'a real one' as they tried to orchestrate a lift in my motor car. They as good as admitted that most of their monsters were fancy.

'The children believe them and the parents give way to their silliness,' pronounced Mr Turnbull. 'So I am led to conclude that the parents themselves are taken in. No spiritual guidance whatsoever.'

'That's just what I was telling Mrs Gilver, my dear,' said Mrs Turnbull. 'About the Burry Man. The very next day! Sitting with their picnics at the Fair. And what dreadful unwholesome rubbish was in those picnic-bags. Trudie and Nellie Marshall were telling the little Quigley girl that Robert Dudgeon died because all the little spikes were poisoned and they stuck in him like a thousand darts.'

I sat up at this, trying not to look too unnaturally interested.

'And the Christie boy told me in all seriousness that his granny had told *him* that the curse of the Burry Man fell after twenty-five years and everyone knew

Robert Dudgeon shouldn't never have dared to do it this last time. I ask you!'

'Well, at least that shows that they know the Burry Man is just one of their neighbours dressed up for the day,' I said. 'Some of the other legends would have it that he's a real bogeyman who lives in a swamp.'

'Oh, there were plenty of those too,' said Mrs Turnbull. 'Netta Stoddart swears blind that she saw the Burry Man going home on his cart along the Back Braes on Friday night and that when the cart turned round the Burry Man fell off and rolled down the bank on to the railway line and was squashed by a train.'

I could not quite suppress a giggle at this. One had to admire the confidence of little Miss Stoddart to insist on her story when quite a hundred witnesses saw the Burry Man die in an entirely different way. It did occur to me, however, that although the falling, rolling and squashing were nonsense, perhaps Netta Stoddart might have seen the cart turn around.

'Was there even a train?' I said.

'None at all,' said Mr Turnbull, unsmiling.

'And was she even in a position to be a witness to this adventure?' I asked.

'Oh yes,' said Mrs Turnbull, with a disapproving note that I could not easily account for at first. 'The Back Braes run along behind Station Road down there and she was sitting at the back of the bowling green clubhouse with a bottle of ginger ale and a biscuit waiting for her father.' This sounded fairly innocent so far and so my expression did not deliver the required outrage. Mrs Turnbull went on. 'Mr Stoddart himself, of course, was in the clubhouse where they keep a jug of beer topped up on high days and holidays and let their members have glassfuls at very preferential rates. How I hate to see children sitting waiting outside for their fathers to finish drinking. And it's even worse at the bowling green. No children are allowed, which is why poor Netta was hidden around the back, sitting there among the crates of empties, telling herself stories to while away the time.'

This was admittedly rather sordid, and if Mr Stoddart had volunteered to take his daughter to the Fair then it was a bit much for him to stop off on the way and fill up with cheap beer leaving her to kick her heels, but if she had indeed seen the cart turn round and used this as the foundation for her little tale then I was rather glad that Mr Stoddart was not the upstanding father Mrs Turnbull would have him be.

'Well,' I said, rising and pulling on my gloves. 'Thank you for the delicious coffee' – it had been filthy, of course – 'and a most interesting chat. I hope the funeral goes off as one would have it do,' I said to Mr Turnbull. 'Do give my regards to Mrs Dudgeon, if you are going along afterwards.' Mr Turnbull's face puckered as though he had felt a sudden twinge of toothache. Of course he would not be going along afterwards! Watching a crowd of villagers get drunk in honour of the dead would be torture to him, and for once even he might feel that he could not hold forth on his views.

Leaving the schoolhouse by the garden gate, I turned back down the Loan and tried not to get too excited about Netta Stoddart's tuppenceworth. I told myself that although there is often a case for listening to what falls from the lips of babes and children, there was also Master Christie's 'Silver Anniversary Curse' to remind me that, just as often, what falls is gibberish.

Now, to find the 'Back Braes'. There was indeed a little lane opening off the Loan and running along the back of the Station Road villas – I could see that some of them had garden gates giving on to it – but it was terribly narrow and I could not imagine why someone would choose to drive a cart along there, with Station Road itself, broad and smooth, only a moment further up the hill. It would be impossible for any ordinary cart and a pretty tight fit even for a cart as dainty as the Dudgeons' 'shell hutch'. Still, it was worth investigating.

I started along the lane at what I was beginning to think of as my detecting pace, slow enough to take in anything there was to see but fast enough so that someone happening to look at me would believe I was strolling and not loitering. I kept my head still, as though gazing mindlessly into the middle distance, while all the time my eyes were sweeping back and forth looking at the garden gates and the walls in which they were set, the ground under my feet, the fence to my left separating the lane from the steep wooded bank which fell to the railway line below. Almost immediately, I spotted something which made my heart bump in my ribcage. The lane was tramped hard along the middle where many pairs of feet every day must flatten it and there was no chance of a pony's hoof prints showing up there, but here and there in the soft dirt towards the edges, I could see quite clearly the wheel tracks of a small cart, two sets, sometimes running along deeply on top of the other and sometimes diverging, making lozenge shapes until they fell together again. It beggared belief, I thought, that two miniature carts had recently made a one-way journey each along this tiny lane, with the brick walls looming on one side and the hawthorn and bramble grabbing at them from the other. The most obvious explanation was that one cart, for some reason – and a reason that had to be significant, I was sure – had come along and then turned back. It was almost as inconceivable

202

that it was any cart except the Dudgeons' miniature one. I blessed Mr Stoddart's neglected daughter and hurried on.

Sure enough, beyond the end of the villas, beyond the little footbridge which crossed the railway and connected to another of these 'back braes', just where the lane turned the corner at the bowling green, the tracks became confused, crossing each other and making loops. Here too, a few hoof prints showed where the pony had stepped towards the edge of the path trying to turn around in the cramped space. Most compelling of all, there were broken branches on the bushes bordering the steep siding here and some fresh-looking scrapes on the bowling club wall too.

I stood in the middle of the lane, hands on hips, and wondered. Why on earth would someone turn a cart around here? Mr and Mrs Dudgeon must have had to unhitch the pony and manoeuvre the cart around themselves; there certainly was no room to manage the thing otherwise. If they had been strangers to the town, one could understand why they might set off along the lane judging it just wide enough and then have to abandon the plan when this unexpected sharp corner was thrown upon them, but as inhabitants of long standing, it made no sense. And even if one gave little Netta Stoddart her due – she had been right about seeing the cart turning after all – and went along with the next element in her tale, it was hard to see why Robert Dudgeon falling off the cart at this corner would make him decide to go back to the Fair, when he had already made up his mind to go straight home and when Mrs Dudgeon apparently had his dinner waiting for him. Much more likely that, if he had been considering going back to the Fair, falling on to the hard ground at the end of a gruelling day would make him abandon the plan for good and go home to his hot dinner and a mustard bath. It was equally hard to see why, moreover, even if he had decided to turn back to the Fair, he would literally *turn* back, at this awkward corner, and not simply carry on to where the brae must surely rejoin Station Road and make a loop back to the top of the Loan.

So, unsure whether I had in fact discovered anything here on the Back Braes or had only added more questions to my ever-growing list, I myself turned and began to walk back the way I had come. When I got to the little bridge across the railway line, however, I decided to make a detour. There was nothing to be seen over the high garden walls the way I had come and instead I crossed the little footbridge down towards the town. From the other side there was a choice of route. I could turn right and descend on the pleasant little lane known as McIver's Brae which would give me a pleasant view of the river and the bridge, but would finally deposit me on the Edinburgh Road far beyond the end of the High Street, halfway to the Hawes almost, with a fair walk back to the Bellstane; or I could turn left and be sure somehow or other to emerge from the mouth of a close or lane or vennel somewhere on one of the terraces eventually. There were several dead ends this way, however, and at least one public house, the back yard of which one easily could end up in, and I did not want to make myself any more conspicuous than was absolutely necessary, certainly not as conspicuous as I should be lost amongst the washing lines and beer barrels. I turned for McIver's Brae. I was shortly very glad indeed that I had done so.

Chapter Eleven

The High Street, when I turned back on myself at the bottom of the brae and looked along it, was deserted. Of course, Mr Dudgeon's funeral must be due to start any minute and the shops were closed out of respect, with their shutters down. The men would all be at the Kirk by now and I could only assume that those women not closely enough connected to the Dudgeons to be already at the cottage preparing for the feast, were respectfully inside their houses, curtains drawn, and keeping the children in too. So I was glad of my mourning clothes and I hoped that if I walked sedately enough, with my head bowed, then anyone happening to glance from a window and see me would not think me too callous for being out in the sunshine strolling around.

Almost immediately upon setting off, however, negotiating the corner at the Sealscraig, I saw that not quite everyone was closed up for the funeral after all. I caught a flash of light from the corner of my eye and, turning, I saw that there was a solitary drinker in Brown's Bar and that Mr Shinie Brown was standing at the counter facing him. The light I had seen was the flare of a match as the customer lit a cigarette and when he turned to the side to blow the first smoke politely over his shoulder, I recognized him as one of the two Burry Man's boys.

This was, at the same time, both strange beyond reckoning and also too good to miss. In fact, its strangeness only made it the more irresistible for there had to be a story behind this ostentatious absence from the send-off, surely. The only question was whether I could summon the nerve to cross the threshold, alone this time, join a strange man at the bar, and strike up the conversation necessary to find out what the story was.

To excuse ducking out of it, I could tell myself that Alec would be able to grill the other helper at the funeral or afterwards. On the other hand, there was no guarantee of this; Alec after all was relying on Cad being able to pick the face out of the crowd or, failing that, being able to ask around discreetly for an introduction. Imagine his disgust if he missed the man or could not get him to talk and then he heard that I had let this other one slip through my grasp out of sheer . . . I did not even know for sure what one would call it.

I put my gloved fingers firmly around the brass handle of the door and pulled it open. Mr Brown had disappeared into the back room while I was dithering, and only the man at the bar remained. He spoke, without turning, saying:

'He's no' open.'

'Oh!' I said, flustered, and on hearing my voice the man turned around in some surprise.

'It's yoursel',' he said, obviously remembering me from our first encounter.

'Yes,' I agreed. (I have never been able to decide exactly how one should respond to this particular greeting.) 'And I'm not really looking to buy a drink. I'm just . . . Well, to tell the truth, I was out for a walk and then seeing the street so quiet and realizing *why*, I'm looking for cover. It would be pretty blatant to parade along the High Street and then roar off in my motor car.' I had joined him at the bar during this speech and he was nodding slowly in apparent understanding, but he was – I could see this now that I was close up – extremely drunk. As if to confirm the fact, he gave a huge wuthering sigh and sank his head to his chest with lips pushed out.

'What brings you here?' I asked, rather too brightly. He did not answer. 'I should have thought you'd be up at the Kirk. Mr Brown too, for that matter.'

'We've no' been introduced,' said the man, swinging to face me. I had to work hard not recoil from the beer fumes on his breath, and almost found myself offering him a peppermint. 'Pat Rearden,' he said, and held out a hand. I shook it faintly, wondering at the non sequitur, then I realized that it was not a non sequitur after all.

'I see,' I said. 'What a shame. How awful for you, I mean, if you were great friends.'

'We *were* friends,' he announced, much more belligerently than was needed since he was, after all, agreeing with me. 'Rab and me. We didnae give a – didnae care what folk said. And we aye kent that if he went first I'd be sittin' in a bar and if it wis me he'd be sittin' in a bar. Load o' bloody nonsense.'

'Hear, hear,' I answered. 'As someone else said just the other day in another context: we're all Jock Tamson's bairns.'

'We are,' said Mr Rearden, thumping the bar. 'We are that. You nivver said a truer word.'

'What about Mr Brown? Why isn't he there?' I said. He looked blank. ' Shinie?' I prompted.

'Same as me,' said Mr Rearden shaking his head morosely. 'Just the same as me. Father Cormack would have his guts for garters if he crossed the door. And it's worse for him. Fur Shinie. He's practically ane o' the family.'

'I see,' I said. 'So it wasn't another context after all.

It was exactly the same context. Ah well, Miss Brown seems to have been a staunch support to Mrs Dudgeon in the last few days nevertheless.'

'Should have been ane o' the family,' said Rearden again, threatening real tears now. 'That f– . . . bloody war.' I nodded, sympathetically. 'Left all of us old men whae'd lived wur lives and took the boys.' He gave a rough sob, and I patted his arm. 'And their boys were like brothers from they were laddies,' he said, echoing what Mrs Dudgeon's sisters had told me.

'Yes, so I believe,' I said. 'They joined up together, didn't they?'

'Aye, the Black Watch,' said Rearden. 'Rab Dudgeon's laddie was a' for the King's Own Borderers, but Billy got his way for once and the Royal Highlanders it was.'

'For once?' I said.

'The usual thing o' it was that the Dudgeon laddie said jump and Billy did the jumpin'.'

'I had heard it was the other way round,' I said.

'Oh?' said Rearden. 'Ye'd have heard that from them, right? That would be whit they were sayin'.'

I smiled, acknowledging the point.

'How impossible for Joey, in that case, then,' I said. 'Guilt as well as grief.'

'Shinie's boy was lost an' all, ye ken,' said Rearden. 'Her brother.' This I had *not* known, although it was hardly startling news. 'Missin' presumed,' he went on. 'Jist like wee Rab. And ye'd think it could have brought them closer, eh? Would ye no'? Would ye no' think that?' He glared at me until I nodded, agreeing with him on who knows what. 'They nivver talked aboot it,' said Rearden. 'Not one word a' these years, the both o' them.'

'Mr and Mrs Dudgeon didn't?' I said. 'Or Joey and Mr Brown? Didn't talk about what?'

'Shinie and Rab,' said Rearden. 'Both o' the laddies gone and they nivver once sat doon and had a dram together. We tried. Bringing him in here. Doing the old routine wi' Joey. Cannae say we nivver tried. Look up there,' he commanded suddenly, pointing a wavering finger to the row of bottles behind the bar. 'See that? Does that no' break yer heart?' I looked along the row, but saw nothing that could be called heartbreaking except to Mr Turnbull or another of his Temperance chums. 'Where is it?' Rearden was muttering to himself. 'Where is it away to?' He tried to focus, slapping a hand over one eye and slowly tracing a pointing finger along in mid-air in line with the shelf. 'That bottle there – it's up there somewhere – that bottle o' malt is fur the laddie. Eh? Kept there fur the laddie comin' hame and naeb'dy else is let lay a finger on it.' His voice was throbbing with emotion again, and as mawkish as this was in one way, it was hard not to get a little lump in one's throat at the thought of Mr Brown keeping a bottle of special whisky, saved against the homecoming of his beloved son, who lay buried under the soil somewhere in France, too horribly mutilated even to identify and send home to his father.

'Shinie!' Rearden bellowed, all of a sudden, as loud as a gun going off in my ear. I yelped. 'Here, Shinie! Where's yer laddie's drink away tae? Aye well,' he said in a quieter voice, to me. 'He's mebbes put it behind him at last. I mind once a year or two back he took it doon and had done wi' it. But then back it came. Shinie?'

I could hear Mr Brown advancing up the cellar steps, grumbling as he came.

'Whaur's yer laddie's bottle?' said Rearden, once his head came into view behind the bar. Brown frowned at me, understandably amazed to see me standing

209

there. 'Whaur is it?' said Rearden. 'I was jist tellin' this lass aboot it.'

'Hush now,' I said, mortified to let Mr Brown think that Rearden had been spouting such intimate concerns of his to a practical stranger. 'He's got a bee in his bonnet about something, Mr Brown, and no mistake. I've no idea what the matter is.'

'It's Rab Dudgeon ye should be thinkin' on the day, Paddy,' said Mr Brown. 'Not me. It's Rab's day the day. That's who we should all be thinkin' on.' His voice was strained and thick, although he seemed sure enough in his movements and his eyes were clear. Perhaps he was regretting the silly joke he had played on his daughter on the Burry Man's day, which after all needed Robert Dudgeon for a stooge and was not at all in the spirit of the Fair. Or perhaps he too was superstitious enough to think that he really had brought bad luck on Dudgeon with the dropped whisky. Certainly Brown had been keen enough to observe the ritual as to rush out into the street and try again, and Robert Dudgeon had been angry enough at the trick that he had dashed the dram to the ground. Or perhaps, in fact much more likely, it was not superstition after all. It was as Rearden said: with both their boys gone to the same fate and the union of the families never to come to pass, they should have been able to breach that wretched divide that cleaves so many Scotch towns in two, and now it was too late. Brown's repeated insistence on the respect due to Robert Dudgeon certainly pointed that way.

'It was indeed a terrible thing,' I said. 'And such a shock. He seemed so very hale and hearty just the day before.' Mr Brown simply shook his head and walked away. I heard a couple of doors open and close, dividing him from us and then, despite them, the sound of dry, hacking sobs.

Rearden gazed owlishly across the bar with his bottom lip pushed out, saying nothing, and a few slow tears began to roll down his face too.

'Well, at least you spent his last day with him,' I said, grasping at straws. 'That's something rather wonderful for you to look back on.'

'Aye but it wisnae richt,' said Rearden. 'The laughs we had on Burry Man's day over the years, I could tell you. But no' Friday. Rab Dudgeon wis in a state about somethin' that day. Awfu' strange first thing, and then goin' daft like that richt at the end. He wisnae himsel'. An' more nor me said it.'

'I saw the strange little turn at the end,' I said. 'Saw it for myself. When he suddenly broke away from you and rushed into the hall? I thought at the time that maybe it was part of the ritual, but I believe not.'

'Nivver done it before,' Mr Rearden assured me. 'And when we got in after him, he had ripped a' his suit off his heid and halfway off his back as if they burrs were red hot needles in him.' I could not help but stare at him on hearing that. Was it possible that there really *was* something off about the burrs? That Dudgeon had borne it stoically all day but had been unable at that moment to stand it a second more? Could we have hit on something with the story of poison after all?

'How odd,' I said, trying not to sound too interested. 'And usually . . . what? Usually he would just stand quietly and let them be taken off by helpers?' Pat Rearden offered nothing for another long, long moment. He was at that stage of drunkenness when the subject settles into himself like a melting jelly; almost asleep but with his eyes open.

'Aye for sure,' he said at last. 'It's a tricky job takin' them off. No' as tricky as getting' them a' on, mind, since it disnae matter whit it looks like, but they're jaggit wee buggers, they burrs. Excuse ma language, madam, Ah'm forgettin' myself. But Rab wis scratched to bits, Friday nicht, the way he'd jist hauled them off hissel' like that.'

'And first thing?' I said, speaking loudly and slowly, hoping to get through the drink which seemed to be descending over him like a blanket of fog. 'You said he was peculiar then too?'

'Wisnae himsel',' said Rearden, mumbling it into his chest. '"Leave me, boys," he says. "Leave me a minute, I need a minute jist tae myself." Nivver wanted a minute on his own afore. Should o' kent. We should o' kent.' He was beginning to work himself up again and I attempted to console him, telling him that no one could possibly have known anything and that he wasn't to berate himself now. All the time, I was thinking furiously to myself. Both he and Mrs Dudgeon, then, had been asking to be alone, begging for time alone. There was something very suspicious about it. What possible reason could there be for the Burry Man to want to be alone before his round and to want the same thing so much at the end that he broke away from his guards and made a run for it? Could it be the same reason that Mrs Dudgeon begged to be left on her own? Wandered the woods in the night to get away from others and even put her beloved husband's body away from her if that was the only way she could get rid of the mourners. I could not imagine any common purpose behind the two desires that did not smack of witchcraft, but perhaps one explanation could suffice for the Burry Man's behaviour at the start and the end of his day.

'When was this exactly?' I said, wanting to get the clearest possible picture of the thing. It was rather a stretch, but if the burrs were poisoned perhaps Robert Dudgeon knew as soon as he was dressed that something was wrong. Perhaps he felt dizzy or sick and thought he needed a moment alone to gather himself.

It was far-fetched but I thought I should press Rearden on it while I had the chance.

'When did Mr Dudgeon ask to be alone?' I persisted. 'Mr Rearden?' But Rearden only repeated to himself that it had never happened before and he should have known there was something wrong and that 'Rab' was not himself then he put his head down upon his crossed arms on the bar and was lost to me.

I watched him for a while and eventually heard doors opening again. Mr Brown returned to the bar.

'I'll ask you to forgive me, madam,' he said. 'It just . . . brought it all back.'

'Of course it did,' I said.

'I couldnae just stand here and listen to Paddy,' Brown went on. 'What's he . . . Eh, what's he been saying anyway?'

I did not wish to tell him. There was no need to mention his son and the whisky and cause him further pain for one thing, but also I was reluctant to give him any information about the case. He was, after all, Joey Brown's father and I was still very interested in Joey Brown.

'Nothing very coherent,' I settled on at last and Shinie gave his friend a rueful look.

'Just as well I'm closed,' he said, 'or I'd be in trouble for lettin' him get in thon state this early in the day.' I could well imagine what the Turnbulls would make of the scene, and I could only agree.

'He'll sleep it off soon enough, poor chap,' I said, still firmly on the side of the drinkers, thinking that the ten minutes I had spent with a maudlin drunk in this public bar had still managed to be more congenial than the turgid half-hour of lukewarm coffee and red-hot invective in the Turnbulls' parlour. Mr Brown seemed to be feeling real remorse, though; the expression on

213

his face as he looked at the top of Rearden's head was quite bleak.

'What the Temperance gang never do seem quite to understand,' I said, 'is the very real comfort of getting absolutely blind drunk when life has thrown you something unspeakably nasty.' Mr Brown looked understandably surprised at this sharp turn in the conversation, as well he might. 'I had coffee with Mrs Turnbull this morning,' I explained. He could not prevent his lip from curling and I smiled. 'And you know, even the hangover can be a comfort sometimes,' I went on. 'A real enemy to battle and a distraction from whatever caused one to get drunk in the first place. And then when the hangover clears, one is so happy to be feeling better that one's spirits can't help but lift a little. There's a great deal to be said for strong drink in response to sorrow, all in all.'

'Well, I've heard everything now!' said a voice behind me. I jumped and turned around, flushing to the roots of my hair (I could feel it from the inside, as though I had walked into a steam-bath). One of the three ministers I had met at Buttercup's cocktail party had opened the door of the bar without a sound and was standing in the threshold twinkling at me. A very useful little knack for a minister to have, I thought to myself.

'What would this be, then?' he said, advancing. 'The Ladies' Intemperance League? That's a new one.' He stopped at the bar, gave Rearden, still slumped face down on the counter, a shrewd look, then gave Brown an even shrewder one which made the landlord shuffle his feet and almost out-blush me. Ah, I thought, this must be Father Cormack. I could relax.

'He's only had beer, Father,' said Brown. 'And all on the house.' I should have thought that made it worse:

Rearden must have had to absorb simply buckets of the stuff to get this drunk on only beer.

'Well, I'm not averse to a glass of beer,' said Father Cormack, 'although it can be filling and Miss Patterson was busy making dumplings when I left.' Brown took a small glass from under the counter, polished it vigorously with a corner of his apron and poured a large tot of clear liquid from a bottle behind him.

'Can I get you anything, madam?' he said. 'On the house, since I'm closed, of course.'

'Sherry?' I said, but at Father Cormack's chuckle, I gathered my wits. 'Or lemonade?'

'I can heartily recommend the damson gin, Mrs Gilver,' said Father Cormack, lifting his glass to hold it against the gas light and swirling it gently. 'William here has his own recipe.'

'Och, Father,' said Brown. 'You're an awful man. It's hardly worth callin' it a recipe. You jist put a few damsons in a bottle o' gin and wait.'

'Of course,' said Father Cormack. 'What was I thinking? Ah, but lovely stuff it is once the wait is over.'

'Well, you've persuaded me,' I said. 'I'm very partial to sloe gin and I'd like to try a new variation.' Father Cormack chuckled again for reasons best known to himself, and Brown poured me a tot. It was, indeed, quite delicious; fragrant and spiced but with a kick like an angry donkey.

'Gosh,' I said, feeling as though flames were licking my toes. 'Hoo! Well, here's to Robert Dudgeon, gentlemen, wouldn't you say?' We raised our glasses, Brown lifting a beer tankard of his own, and drank.

'And here's to the Ladies' Intemperance League,' carried on Father Cormack. 'Power to their elbow. I'd hate to see those Turnbulls cut the heart out of our little Burgh, Mrs Gilver, and that's what it would do, make no mistake, if we lost our distilling and brewing.

Wouldn't it, William? You must know the old stories about the Hawes Inn.'

'Smuggling?' I said. 'Pirates? Surely *that* doesn't go on any more. And there's no actual distilling either, is there? It's just a bottling hall.'

'Of course, of course,' said Father Cormack again. 'What *was* I thinking?' He paused and then continued in a much more serious voice with his twinkle turned down to a peep. 'I missed you on Sunday, William,' he said, putting down his empty glass and wiping his lips with a handkerchief as Brown refilled it. 'You and Josephine. Friday too.' Then he excused this public dressing down by turning to me and saying, cheerfully: 'Aren't you glad, Mrs Gilver, not to be one of *my* flock, to be chased up and ticked off like a lost lamb when it's no one's business but your own what you do on a Sunday morning? It's a terrible burden, is it not now, William?' Mr Brown looked miserably ill at ease in the face of this bantering, but I answered the priest like for like.

'Certainly, I'm glad to be walking the broad path between such persecution and the absolute fire and brimstone on the other side. I was born in Northamptonshire, you know, where there is a happy third option.'

'Ah, the Church of England,' said Father Cormack, twinkling again, and putting his hand across his heart. 'Will I tell the lady what we call them when there's no one but us to hear, William? Will I, now.'

'Father,' said Mr Brown again. 'You're an awful man.'

I rather wanted to hear, but he was not to be persuaded – a terrible tease, it seemed – and instead he started again gently mocking me for my paean to the demon drink.

'And you're preaching to the needy, telling William here,' he said. 'Don't let all these bottles here fool you, my dear lady. He's on the slippery slope, aren't you, lad? Started out working for a distillery, moved to work for a brewery, and now he's only running a pub and selling the stuff; the poor man could end up with a lemonade stall if he's not careful.' He threw back his head and laughed and I joined in, not because any of this was particularly witty, but he was just such a dear little man with his twinkling eyes and his tuft of hair sticking out in a spout at the front with a gleaming bald head behind it. William Brown though, I noticed, did not laugh along with us, and I wondered after a moment if Father Cormack was not just a little cruel, a little cold, underneath his bonhomie; I was glad indeed not be one of his lambs.

Not long after this, a couple of heads were glimpsed bobbing along the street, just visible above the half-blinds in the windows, and we heard the clang of a shop door being opened along the terrace a-ways. The curfew, evidently, was over and Queensferry was coming back to life so I bid Father Cormack goodbye, thanked Mr Brown for the gin, causing yet another eruption of chortling, and patted Mr Rearden's shoulder in farewell. Then I opened the door a crack and looked carefully up the street and down before sidling out and beginning to walk back to my motor car trying to look as though I had just done no such thing, which was more of a challenge than one would have imagined as the fresh sea air mingled with the unaccustomed mid-morning gin and made me feel more like waltzing in circles and singing.

After the ribbing I had given Alec about his inebriation the day before I felt most concerned to be myself again before we met and so on returning to the castle I went to my room and rang for more coffee even though there was barely an hour until luncheon. I was growing rather fond of my corner of the castle keep and, although I still wished for a few more windows about the place, for some reason it made me feel extra-specially studious to sit writing at my little desk with a lamp lit. I did spend quite a bit of my free time day by day doing just that, having learned the lesson well on my first case that one cannot guarantee to remember all that one has heard unless one writes it down immediately. Furthermore, it is no good simply sifting through and deciding what one *thinks* are the nuggets because, when one is detecting, the snippets one thinks are chaff often turn out to be pure gold, and the nuggets one hugs to one's breast as treasure just as often reveal themselves to be utter clinker in the end. This, I often thought to myself, would be one of my most fiercely held detecting maxims if only I could resolve the metaphor into some respectable whole.

Accordingly, I wrote down as much as I could remember of the visit to the Turnbulls, the cart-hunt along the Back Braes and of course the drinking session in Brown's Bar, and after two cups of strong coffee and some plain biscuits, I had filled six sheets and was ready to face the others in the Great Hall. I shrugged off my dark frock and chose a pearl-grey and pink stripe which Grant is very fond of and always packs even though, to my thinking, it has a little too much of the sailor dress about it for a woman of my age; if I wore it today and tried to drop something dark down the front, it would be safely *hors de combat* for the rest of the visit (Grant never attempts complicated laundering procedures away from home if she can help it).

I doubled back at the last minute to add some notes about my encounter with the weeping village women halfway up the Loan – I had forgotten about them, which rather proved the point about needing to keep careful notes – and so I was late for luncheon. The others were already being served with tomato soup when I arrived, Alec once more tucking his napkin into his collar and Cad once more looking rather shocked to see him do so. Tomato soup, of course, was perfect for my purposes. The pink and grey stripe would be at the bottom of the trunk with a sprinkling of soda under a brown-paper patch before the afternoon was out.

'How did you enjoy your first Scotch funeral?' I asked Cad as I sat down. He considered the question for a moment, nodding sagely.

'I'm not sure that "enjoy" is the word,' he said. 'It's a damn silly idea not to let the women join in for one thing. If the women were there weeping and wailing the men could be patting their shoulders and feeling superior. With no one else there to do the blubbing it was all down to us and I've never felt so uncomfortable in all my days.'

Buttercup and I looked first at him and then at Alec – thunderstruck with his mouth open – and then collapsed into giggles.

'What?' said Cadwallader. I was not sure I could have explained 'what' exactly if I had a week to think it out, only just that he was so very unlike other men and so utterly unaware of it that it was impossible not to laugh.

'I must say, though,' Cad went on, 'I'd far prefer it if we went to the regular Sunday shindigs in that church instead of the Pisky, Freddy my love. It's much less annoying when you can't understand a word that's being said. Still not soothing exactly – the pastor doesn't have a soothing cadence – but I could learn to think of it as a kind of tone-poem, you know. Avant garde.'

'It wouldn't work,' said Alec. 'All of a sudden you'd find yourself beginning to catch the odd word and then whole phrases and then there's no turning back. It happened to me with the men working on the estate. I used to assume they were talking about the birds and the trees and the bonny heathered glens. Then when my ear tuned in at last I got a rude awakening. Clara Bow's legs, don't you know. And all points north.'

'Don't speak too soon, my darling,' I said. 'They can still catch *me* out despite the yawning eternity I've been incarcerated here. I can't, for instance, make head nor tail of what they call Robert Dudgeon's little cart.'

'I wondered about that,' said Cad. 'When I was going over the inventory. There are scores of them around, you know. We use them for all kinds of things.'

'Anyway,' said Alec, 'since I now have a passable "guid Scots tongue in ma' heid" –'

'Alec!' I said, sharply. I had spoken to him before about attempting a Scotch accent, more than once, and had told him that I would rather he scraped his finger-nails down a slate.

'Sorry!' he said. 'But you really are a bore sometimes, Dandy. It's harmless fun. Anyway, since I can now interpret the natives like a missionary's child, I did a good bit of earwigging this morning. There was a great deal of discussion about the death as you can imagine, a lot of pretty maudlin revelling in the fact that both father and son are gone and poor Mrs Dudgeon is all alone. How they rolled that around and admired it from all angles. Quite disgusting. As well as that, there was quite a bit of audible tallying of how much respect was being paid to Dudgeon, and from all that I could gather it washes out some of our suspicions about the various Ferry Fair factions. Both the Prod Padres were there and representatives of all three of the great families – four, of course, counting Cad.' Cad looked surprised but very pleased to be lumped in with the Linlithgows, Roseberys and Stuart-Clarks in this way, and certainly did not suspect for a heartbeat that Alec's tongue could be in his cheek. 'Quite an impressive turn-out for an estate carpenter, and a clear sign, I thought, that the feeling for the Burry Man goes far too deep for him to be dislodged by a gaggle of hysterical –' He caught my eye and stopped. '. . . by a few, and an unrepresentative few, ladies who have slightly lost their sense of perspective over a heartfelt difference of opinion.' He flashed me a beaming smile and I blew him a raspberry in reply. 'Now, Cad did manage to spot one of the Burry Man's boys –'

'The fat one,' said Cad. 'Not the fellow with the side-whiskers, no sign of him.'

'Yes indeed,' said Alec. 'And I did get the chance to sidle up to him and strike up a conversation.'

'And?' I said. 'Oh damn and blast. I've dropped soup in my lap. Ho-hum.'

'And I'm afraid I had to make reference to a rumour that it was the drink that did for Robert Dudgeon,' said Alec, screwing his face up in a grimace of remorse.

'Oh, Alec, you didn't!' I said. 'Please tell me you didn't. After Inspector Cruickshank and the doctor managed to keep it quiet for her. You are a stinker sometimes.'

'Well, I had to get the talk round to the sandwich and the only way I could think to do it was to start with: did he think there was anything in the rumour, and even if there was, wouldn't he say it was not enough food rather than too much drink that was at the bottom of it, and did people on the way around sometimes give the Burry Man food instead of whisky. How would you have got there starting from somewhere else, Dan?'

I thought about it for a minute or two and had to concede that there was no other obvious route to that particular destination. I took comfort in the thought that the Turnbulls and their like really had started exactly this rumour anyway and Alec had probably not done a great deal, in that particular company, to strengthen it.

'And?' said Buttercup to Alec. 'What did he say? Was there a cloaked stranger who drew up and proffered the sandwich in a gnarled claw?'

'There was not,' said Alec. 'The chap said that nobody ever gave the Burry Man food – pointed out that it would be rather cruel torture to do so since he couldn't eat it – and that nothing but whisky passed his lips between nine and six. So I said, "Oh, I suppose his wife must have brought him the sandwich, then." And he looked puzzled. And I said, "He did eat one, you know. It showed up in the post-mortem." And then he looked at me as though I had crawled out from under a stone, and since we were just then walking at sombre pace behind the coffin en route from the church to the graveyard, I can quite see that what the PM found in the way of stomach contents was hardly polite.'

'Yet the same point in respect of luncheon tables continues to elude you,' said Buttercup.

'And did you get a chance to ask any more after that gaffe or did he draw his skirts aside?' I said.

Alec waited while the butler scooped a piece of fish on to his plate and a maid following after poured some sauce over it then he resumed.

'Pray, don't spare my feelings, Dandy,' he said. 'I can take it on the chin if you care to tell me exactly what you think. Yes, I did rather lose his confidence after that, but I fell into step with . . . wait for it . . . the famous Donald.'

'Ah, Donald!' I said. 'Lay preacher, chief recruiter for the Band of Hope and all-round hero.'

'You're kidding!' said Alec. 'Donald is a Temperance Tenter?'

'I didn't think he looked the part either,' I said, 'but Mrs Turnbull assured me only this morning that he is their star turn.'

'Well, well, well,' said Alec. 'That must have made things rather awkward at times in the family circle. Anyway, Donald and I got to talking, trailing along there behind the coffin, which was quite a surprise to me at first. Since he was the chief mourner in absence of anyone closer to fill the role, I'd have thought he'd be ringed around with pals. But it seems that a funeral is like a wedding in that respect. No one ever speaks to the groom at a wedding because they always assume he should be talking to someone else.'

'I noticed that,' said Cad. 'It was one of the loneliest days of my life.'

'Ooh, I loved my wedding day,' said Buttercup. 'Both of them. I wish I could have lots more.'

'Ever the diplomat, darling,' I said, as she clapped her hand belatedly over her mouth. 'Are you going to send Cad to Brighton with a floozy or shove him off the ramparts?'

'As I was saying,' Alec resumed, sounding severe, 'Donald and I started to chat about this and that and inevitably the talk turned to Robert Dudgeon and his last day and Donald latched on to that odd little moment, when the Burry Man was almost home and dry and he slipped his leash and headed for the hills. Well, the stairs. Donald told me that Dudgeon was found inside by the dignitaries, tearing off his burry suit, only *he* didn't – Donald didn't, I mean – take this to be an indication of poison. Instead he pointed out that people who are suffering a heart attack often talk about a constricted feeling in the chest. A "tight band" or a "band of steel" are the phrases and Donald's theory is that Dudgeon felt this, took it to be sudden claustrophobia caused by being trussed up like a parcel all day and simply had to get out of the damn things with not a moment to lose.'

'Interesting,' I said. 'It certainly fits the facts. Now Alec, since you're on the subject of burrs, please tell me you remembered to –'

'I remembered,' said Alec with a great show of weary patience in his voice. 'Have some faith in me, Dandy, please.'

'Remembered what?' said Buttercup.

'Good,' I said. 'Because the other Burry Boy was out cold on the bar counter before I had a chance to ask him.'

'What?' said Cad, Alec and Buttercup together, staring at me.

'Oh yes, I've a tale of my own to tell about this morning,' I said. 'But first things first. Alec?'

'I'm rather proud of this,' said Alec. 'I asked just how bad a thing it was for Dudgeon to do that rushing and ripping off stunt. Asked – you know, very wide-eyed and eager to understand the folklore – if it was bad luck or sacrilege or anything to treat the burrs in that way.'

'Oh, good thinking,' I said. 'Excellent!'

'And Donald told me that no, not especially, although he did mention that in days gone by people used to pluck burrs from the suit as the Burry Man came around and replace them with flowers. It's died out for some reason, but Donald supposed that *that's* the origin of the few flowers still sticking out of the costume here and there.'

'What a shame it stopped,' said Buttercup. 'That must have been lovely. Cad, I think if you and I are in on this next year we should try to reinstate the flower thingummy. We can donate the blooms if our gardens are up and running in time.'

'Anyway,' said Alec, 'it was the easiest step in the world from there to asking what does happen to the things afterwards, and hearing that it's usually nothing in particular, they just go out for the dustmen once they've been picked off the inner suit. And then I asked him if he knew how they ended up back at Dudgeon's house this year, and he said he didn't know.'

'That was skating pretty close to the edge,' I said. 'Did it raise his suspicions to have you asking about them? After him finding me guddling with them yesterday, I mean?'

'It didn't seem to,' said Alec. 'He didn't mention you.'

'Hmm,' I said, stirring my spoon round and round in my syllabub. It started to collapse and then I remembered how delicious Mrs Murdoch's fruit fool had been the day before and decided just in time that this syllabub probably deserved better treatment. I licked my spoon clean and laid it down again. 'It would have been good to hear from one of the horses' mouths, just exactly what happened about those burrs,' I said. 'I can't think of any innocent reason for them to have been saved. And I can't really see how anyone except Dudgeon or Mrs Dudgeon could have organized getting them into a sack and into the cart. But then I'm absolutely convinced that Mrs Dudgeon did not kill her husband, so I can't see why she should be concerned to take the things home. And if she was then why did she let them lie for days on the midden heap for anyone to find?'

'We've already said that she was desperate to get rid of everyone from the house,' said Alec. 'To give her the chance to get the things on the fire.'

'In which case she would have been discovered wandering around in the night with a box of matches and some kindling,' I pointed out. 'Not with a bottle of ink and a pen.'

'It's terribly niggly-piggly sort of work, detecting, isn't it?' said Buttercup. 'You sound so cross with each other, bickering away like that.' She stood up and dropped her napkin on to her seat. 'I think I'll go for a nap,' she announced. 'Cad? Come and tuck me in?'

'Absolutely, my love, I'll be right there,' said Cadwallader. 'But Dandy,' he went on, 'are you really saying that the poisoned burrs theory is still on the table?' Buttercup left the room unnoticed, her shoulders in a sorrowful little slump of self-pity. Cadwallader would have to do some extra billing and cooing this afternoon to make up for the slight.

'Darling,' I told him, happy to be in the position to spread such cheer, 'I am. For one thing there is a rumour to that effect doing the rounds of the local tots and I've had independent corroboration this very morning that these little ones are to be ignored at our peril.' Cad looked at me, open-mouthed, eager for more, but I was tired of having an audience. I wanted to get Alec to myself and really thrash the thing out.

'Buttercup awaits,' I reminded him.

'Is that a secret code?' he breathed in response. Alec gave a shout of laughter, and Cad joined in with a good-natured grin.

'I think I'll leave you to it,' he said. 'It's all way, way over my head. And Freddy's expecting me.'

Chapter Twelve

An hour in the drawing room with cigarettes, pipe and sheets of paper would be enough for Alec and me to feel that we were both of one mind again, shoulder to shoulder viewing the path ahead.

'Right, then,' I said. 'These burrs, poisoned or otherwise.' For we had decided to take seriously – at least until we were proved wrong – the fantastical-seeming theory about the burrs. Alec's brainwave during our session had been to scrutinize them and, if any of them 'looked poisoned', to parcel them up and send them to a specialist for analysis.

'What specialist, though?' I said. In story books, detectives always just happen to have a very useful selection of acquaintances, chemists and locksmiths and the like, but Alec and I had no such connections to draw on and we were stumped.

'Well, no one who's anything to do with the police or the police surgeon,' said Alec. 'We must use a little discretion, at least for now.'

'And we can't just troop into Edinburgh and hawk them around the hospital corridors searching for a kind man in a white coat,' I said. 'They've been in a feed sack in a stable, for one thing. And before that, in a midden heap with horse drop–' I stopped.

'What?' said Alec.

'What about the Dick Vet?' I said. 'The Veterinary

College at the university. They're bound to have chemists and poison people there, aren't they? And one would think they'd be less sniffy about grubby samples of this and that. If we were to telephone and say . . . I don't know . . . say that a horse had come out in dreadful suppurating sores where he had been brushing against a burdock bush –'

'Plant,' said Alec. 'It's not a bush. It's a rosette with a fleshy tap root and a spike of thistle-like flowers sometimes reaching a height of up to . . .' He laughed at my expression and cut the lecture short. 'I looked it up,' he explained. 'In a horribly musty natural history of the British Isles.'

'Where?' I said. 'When? Why?'

'Here,' said Alec. 'In Cad's library, waiting for you to come home.' I always forget about the books in libraries, for some reason. Most of the books in Hugh's library at home were centuries old, pungent beyond belief and hardly ever written in English. 'As to why,' Alec went on, 'I was really looking for something else.' He waited, apparently expecting me to comprehend something.

'*Coprinus atramentarius,*' he went on when he had given up. 'The common ink cap. Your mushroom, darling.'

'Oh!' I exclaimed. 'Excellent. Well done. And?'

'In season from the early spring until November,' he said. 'Very common in any type of woodland.'

'Gosh,' I said. 'Our theory lives on.'

'For the meantime, anyway,' said Alec. 'So go on. You were saying? A horse, suppurating sores . . .'

'Yes, we could say that we suspected sabotage by an eccentric neighbour, and ask the chemist if such a thing was possible.'

'Wouldn't he ask us to bring in some of the burrs so he could check?' said Alec. 'Or even the horse.'

'At which point we could hastily backtrack,' I replied. 'Or we could say it had died. Unless that would make him even keener to see it. They have odd tastes, these vets, you know.'

'Well, it's worth a try,' Alec said. 'Where are the things, Dandy? And do you have a very stout pair of gloves? If there's the smallest chance that they killed Robert Dudgeon we can hardly go juggling them with our bare hands.'

As I had done every other time this thought had been aired, I suddenly felt rather sheepish, or at least glad that no one else was listening, and I screwed up my nose at him.

'They can't possibly be, can they?' I said. 'Not really? Not really really?' I remembered this feeling well from our first case: the feeling that one's own boring everyday life could not really be traversing these paths of murder and evil; that one must be play-acting, only doing it so well that one was more than half convinced it was true.

Alec shrugged but made no answer.

'To the stables then,' I said. (I had stuffed the bags into the empty tack room in the stable yard on my return from the woods.) 'After all,' I pointed out, 'since they had spent an hour or two cosied up with some horse droppings and they were on a bed of cabbage leaves and peapods, I could hardly lug them up to the castle and dump them in my bath.'

We made our way down the castle mound and across the park to where a stand of trees hid the stable block from view.

'I say, Dandy,' said Alec as we tramped along. 'Are you beginning to worry that they won't be there?'

The thought had not occurred to me, but as soon as Alec voiced it I was convinced. There was the fact of my dreadful feeling that someone (or something) had been watching me in the woods the previous day and, added to that, I had been caught red-handed by Donald Dudgeon while blatantly stealing the burrs. It seemed clear to me now, all of a sudden, that the most discreet way for him to foil my plans would have been simply to watch where I took the burrs and then to wait until it was quiet and steal them back. Alec and I began to walk faster and faster towards the trees.

'Although,' I said, 'there was nothing to suggest that I wasn't going to do whatever I was going to do with them right that minute. How could he – either Donald or whoever it was that was watching me if anyone *was* watching me – have known that I'd simply leave them sitting there? How on earth *could* I have simply left them sitting there if it comes to that!' We were trotting along now as we wheeled into the stable yard and we bustled straight for the unused tack room in the far corner, only slowing enough for me to sing out over one shoulder to the stable lad:

'How's Nipper?'

And to hear the response:

'He's grand, madam. Nivver you fear.'

'Now, Dan,' said Alec, barring my way with an arm flung out across the door, 'try to remember exactly where you put the sacks and how they looked when you left them. It would be good to know if anyone's been in here snooping in the meantime.' I closed my eyes and tried to bring to mind a picture of how the tack room had looked the night before, but to be honest I had been so tired with tramping to and fro through the woods all day and, what with the nervous strain of my peculiar encounters with Donald Dudgeon and the ghastly Turnbulls, not to mention the upset of poor Nipper's paw, I feared I had simply abandoned them without a glance.

'I'm sure that's roughly where I put them,' I told

Alec, on entering. 'And' – I picked up one in each hand – 'that's exactly the weight of them so far as I can remember, so I should say fairly certainly they've been left alone.'

There was no electric light in the room, but Alec lit one of the oil lamps which sat on the windowsill and hooked it over a beam above our heads. I brushed a little straw and dust from the tack table with my gloved hands, then Alec hoisted a sack, turned it upside down, and tipped out its contents. I emptied out the other and we spread the burrs out over the table top. Then we both stood looking, carefully breathing through our mouths (and so eating it).

'I feel pretty foolish,' I announced at length.

'Hm,' said Alec. 'Did you expect some of them to have little skulls and crossbones on them?' He spoke peremptorily, but he was clearly feeling much the same.

'Let's be forensic about it nevertheless,' I said. 'We've never had to do anything like this before so let's make sure our inaugural attempt is at least thorough and not a disgrace to Mr Holmes.' I buttoned the cuffs of my gloves carefully and began to poke about in the mess.

'Right. What is there to note?'

'Nothing,' said Alec. 'There are thousands of them. All identical.'

'Not really,' I said. 'Not when you look closely. Some of them are fairly fresh-looking while others are dried up and turning yellow. That supports what Cad said about the scarcity this year. The pickers could not afford to be choosy. And look, some of them have been quite carefully harvested, neat little spheres, while others have been ripped off the plant and still have bits of stalk. Lots of them have fluff stuck in the spurs.'

'Some of them are stuck together in plates,' said Alec, getting into the spirit of the thing. 'Look at this.' He held up a sheet of burrs about three feet long and ten inches wide, holding together quite firmly although ragged at the sides.

'I didn't notice that when I was bundling them off the heap,' I admitted. 'Here's a huge one.' I held up a corner, but it began to rip apart as I did so.

'Careful, Dandy,' said Alec. 'Lay it out flat. That must be the back piece or the breast piece.'

'Yes, and that long one you found first is a leg surely. Rather grisly somehow, isn't it?' But Alec was as happy as a little boy with frog-spawn now, rummaging around on the tack table for more big pieces.

'Here's some of the head, surely,' he cried, lifting a curved cap of burrs carefully over his hands. I shuddered. Alec laid the latest find at the top of the table above the large square patch and stood back.

'I'm not sure I want to reconstruct the whole thing,' I said. 'It's giving me the willies.'

'Are you afraid that when we put the last piece in place, he'll sit up and reach out towards you?' said Alec, in a whisper.

'Stop it!' I said. 'You're worse than those horrid children.' I was trying to laugh but really the idea was shivery-making. 'I'm surprised there aren't such rumours about the Burry Man,' I went on. 'Except that his bare hands would scotch it.'

'Anyway there's not much chance of our putting the whole thing together,' Alec said, fitting another short leg piece on the other side. 'Look at all these odd bits and single burrs from all the nooks and crannies. Heaps of them.'

I nodded. There were indeed undulating piles of burrs left on the table besides the large knitted-together sections. With their wisps of fluff sticking to them and their stalks jutting out they made the table top look like one of those miniature battle scenes my sons are always constructing. A wintry battle scene with patches of thin snow and lots of dead trees.

'Have you noticed,' I said, 'that all the stuck-together ones are quite clean, and all the loose ones have the white wool or whatever it is clinging to them?'

Alec took a moment to check and then nodded.

'You're right,' he said. 'That's odd. And the stuck-together ones are the best ones too, the fresh whole ones with no bits of stalk.'

'I suppose that makes sense,' I said. 'Using the cream of the crop for the places the imperfections would show and using up the dregs in the corners.' Alec was laying some more pieces on top of the body patch, trying them this way and that to make them fit.

'I wonder if this is the front or the back,' he said, half to himself.

'I'd say the back is in one piece and those are the front bits, broken up like a jigsaw,' I said. 'Remember – Dudgeon began pulling his suit off himself. He'd hardly reach round and snatch it off his back. Ooh! Here's an arm.' I handed it over to Alec who laid it in place sticking out from the shoulder.

'Can we move all these odds and ends on to the floor?' he said. 'There isn't room to make the suit up properly with all the extras in the way.'

I am not sure whether it occurred first to him or to me, but certainly by the time I had looked up to catch his eye he was already raising his head to stare back.

'And that shouldn't be, should it?' I said, with my heart thumping.

Alec looked at the table again, first at the emerging form of the burry suit and then at the battleground piles all around.

'Could these possibly be used up in the joins?' he said, talking slowly, trying to stay calm, apparently fighting excitement of his own.

'I don't think so,' I answered, 'but I'm afraid there's only one way to find out. Do you happen to have a pair of thick combinations with you, darling? I suppose not since it's August. Well, you shall just have to borrow some from Cad.'

'Steady on,' said Alec. 'We can just lay them out on the table here, surely.'

'I'd feel better if there was a three-dimensional reconstruction,' I said. 'To make sure. I know from some very unsuccessful attempts at dressmaking when I was a child that the third dimension makes quite a difference.'

'And what about the poison?' said Alec, refusing to give in without a fight.

'I think we always knew the poison was a stretch,' I reminded him. 'We only entertained the poison because we couldn't see any other reason to hang on to the burrs, but we can now. Come on, let's go and ask Cad.'

The afternoon was turning to evening by the time we had finished and the sky had blackened and was threatening rain the way it can after a hot afternoon, making the tack room horribly gloomy despite the oil lamp. Alec, out of modesty, had reconstructed his own burry trousers, working up from the ankles with loud gasps and winces, and then I had pressed the back patch to his shoulders and pieced together the other squares and strips over his front. We scrupulously avoided any burrs with white fluffy garnishing, and once I had got my eye in I found it easier and easier to tell which were the prime burrs – the fat, green, carefully picked ones – and used only these to make the joins and to fill, as Alec had put it, the nooks and crannies.

I had filched a flask of brandy from the library while the winter combinations were being hunted out and I lifted it to his lips again now, as he stood there with one hand braced against the tack room wall and the other out to the side holding a broomstick for support.

'Are you sure?' I asked, stoppering the flask. Alec nodded. 'Because I think we've fairly well proved our case as it is.'

'Heads are larger than anyone ever thinks,' Alec replied. 'I know that from drawing classes.'

'I'll go and get a flour bag from Mrs Murdoch then,' I said and made for the door. 'There should just be time before the deluge.'

'Only – Dandy . . .?' said Alec. I turned. It was hard not to smile seeing him standing there, until – that is – I looked into his eyes. 'Hurry back, won't you?' he said. I nodded, sober again, and sped off.

Once the flour bag was thoroughly banged against the wall to dislodge the dust I lowered it over Alec's head and felt with a piece of coal for his eyes and mouth. Then I took it off and set about the coal marks with my nail scissors. When it went back on again it no doubt felt better to him but it looked even worse to me and I remembered how it was the eyes and dark hole of a mouth that were the worst of it all on the Burry Man's day; that and the white hands grasping the staves. I shuddered. Alec must have felt it because he said:

'Try this end of the stick, darling,' and I apologized.

When the back of his head was covered I began on the face, ringing his eyes and putting a strip down his nose, partly to lighten the mood and partly to give myself a pattern to work to. I was engrossed in the task of getting the things on in some kind of order, and had almost forgotten Alec in spite of the closeness of his steady breathing when suddenly I felt him begin to shake under my fingers.

'No!' he shouted. 'Take it off. Take the bag off. Now!'

I grabbed the top of the flour bag despite the barbs piercing the palms of my hands and tore it off, ignoring the rip as the joining layer of burrs along his shoulders protested.

'Sorry,' he said. 'Can't really account for that, I'm afraid, but I just couldn't stand it a minute longer.'

'It doesn't matter,' I told him. 'The bag itself is more than half covered whether you wear it or not. And look.'

He craned round stiffly and looked at the table, where the snowy battleground lay undisturbed, easily as many burrs as Alec was wearing, all lying there, left over.

'Right,' he said. 'I think I can stand this long enough for you to get Inspector Cruickshank, Dandy. So long as he's available now and willing to come along. But God knows how Robert Dudgeon did it for hours on end.'

'Well, that's the point, isn't it?' I said. 'He didn't. Paddy Rearden told me as much. "He wasn't himself that day." He told me over and over again, if I'd only had the wits to hear it. The Burry Man wasn't himself at all.'

Inspector Cruickshank was at his tea when I banged on the door of his house ten minutes later, but he covered his plate with a pan lid and set it to the side of the stove to keep warm, all without a murmur, even though it was fried fish and potatoes and bound to be soggy when he returned.

'It may seem terribly theatrical when you see what we've done, Inspector,' I said to him as we drove back

236

up the Dalmeny road for the Cassilis stable yard through the beginning of the rain, 'but we felt we had to convince you because without the evidence of your own eyes it all sounds so very nebulous and strained. And we have to convince you because although we've made an important discovery we have no earthly idea what it means or where to go next.'

'And this is to do with Robert Dudgeon, is it?' said Inspector Cruickshank. 'I thought as much. You weren't happy that day at the Fair, were you, madam? With the doctor's report? I've not had a look like that since I scuffed my new boots first day on and had to come in and tell my mammy.' He spoke affably enough, but even so I blushed. I had not realized that my disapproval had been quite so obvious as all that.

'Well, I think I owe the doctor and you an apology,' I said. 'I have no reason to doubt the report. What we've found isn't about how Mr Dudgeon died, but it's a strange thing that needs some explanation all the same. As you'll soon see.'

I swung the motor car into the east gate of the park and took the back lane to the stable, going very slowly around the corners since it was just after five and the stable lads were all making their way home, heads bent against the downpour which had begun in earnest now.

'I found the burrs from Mr Dudgeon's suit on the midden heap behind the cottages,' I explained as we drew up and got down. 'And I – well, I suppose I stole them.' I could see the oil lamp in the tack room and could just make out the figure of Alec standing at the back of the room like a scarecrow. 'We've been doing a bit of reconstruction,' I said, beckoning the inspector towards the door, 'and we've made a rather startling discovery.'

Alec's neck must have been getting terribly stiff and it was no doubt this that caused the slow creaking turn of his head as we came in, but if he had spent the whole of his time alone thinking it out he could not have come up with a more eerie finishing touch to the whole tableau.

'Bloody hell!' yelped Inspector Cruickshank, and took a step backwards on to my foot.

'Alec Osborne, sir,' Alec said. 'We haven't met.'

I began to laugh at that as much as at the inspector's outburst, hopping about shaking my crushed foot, and Alec grinned too. Even the inspector gave a rueful smile along with his apology to me, then his eye was caught by the contents of the tack table and the smile switched instantly off.

'There were two quite separate garments underneath,' I explained a moment later. 'You can tell from all this white stuff. We think the ones we've used here were the real Burry Man's burrs, the ones gathered officially and put together by people who knew what they were doing. They're still hanging together in patches, many of them. These ones are terribly second rate.' I stirred the heaps with my finger. 'Hastily collected, inexpertly picked, and stuck to ordinary combinations, from which they gathered a great deal of stray fabric. I daresay when we take Alec's suit off it will be covered in little bits of the same.'

'Yes indeed,' said Inspector Cruickshank.

'Well, if you're convinced,' said Alec, 'might I trouble someone to help me disrobe? I've had enough of this.'

'Certainly, sir,' said Inspector Cruickshank. 'Now the easiest thing for you and quite handy for me too for I'd like to keep a hold of this suit all made up like that, the easiest thing would be if I just cut you out of it with my army knife here. Slit the combinations down the back and pull them off your front.'

He turned and looked at me. Alec too was smiling at me, waiting.

'Oh!' I said. 'Yes, of course. I'll step outside.' I pondered whether to go and tell Cad the bad news about the fate of his combinations but, inspector or no, the man was standing behind Alec with an army knife at the ready and, since the case was still wide open and we did not know who we suspected and who therefore we did not, I decided to stick very close by. Besides, the rain had turned to hail stones now, one of those astonishing, but short-lived, hail storms which had always seemed so unseasonal to me when I had first come north but which I now knew very well. Across the yard, Nipper's master was sheltering in a doorway, Nipper himself tucked pitifully at his heels and looking up at the sky with the whites of his eyes showing.

'This is a surprise, isn't it?' I called over.

'Naw. I kent it would come to hell,' the lad called back, making me blink.

'Sorry?' I said.

'I could tell fae the sky. I kent it would come tae hell stones afore it was done.'

'Oh, I see,' I said. 'Hail stones. Yes, I see.' What had I been saying to Alec, about the impossibility of ever really getting a 'guid Scots tongue' into an English head?

'Now then, Mrs Gilver,' said Inspector Cruickshank, sweeping open the tack room door. Inside, Alec was knotting his tie with arms which still looked rather stiff and fumbling. 'We can go down to the station or I can come up to the castle, whichever suits you the best. I know you're a guest there and if you'd rather not –'

'Oh no, no, no. It will be absolutely fine,' I assured him, thinking that Cad would hate to miss this. 'In fact, it was Cad – Mr de Cassilis, you know – who was first convinced that something was up and persuaded me to take the c– . . . to look into it.' I felt rather bashful about

239

revealing my status in the matter now that a real professional was about to enter the arena.

'All well and good,' said the inspector. 'To the castle it is.'

'So then,' said Inspector Cruickshank, settling into an armchair in the library with a large whisky and soda, the half-eaten plate of fish and chips and the pot of tea apparently put well behind him. Alec and I, the principals, were facing him on two further armchairs while Cad and Buttercup sat perched on a bench under the window, keeping quiet and hoping not to be sent out, like two children past their bedtimes. 'We had an extra Burry Man running around the place on Friday, did we?' went on the inspector. 'And up to no good, I imagine. Tell me what first roused your suspicions, and we'll take it from there.'

'I'll let Dandy tell you, Inspector,' said Alec, whom Cruickshank seemed to be addressing. 'She was here first after all.'

'All right,' I said, attempting to order my thoughts. 'The first thing to say is that even though we're not sure about much, I don't think it was exactly what you say: a rogue Burry Man duplicating the real one. What would be the point for one thing?'

'Money?' said the inspector. 'In the buckets? Or whisky? I think I'll put a couple of men on just to check that the Burry Man didn't come round twice to the same place with different helpers.'

'Wouldn't everyone know that it should be Pat Rearden and . . . the other one?' I said.

'Not these days,' said Mr Cruickshank. 'The Ferry's getting bigger every year with incomers. It's not the place it used to be. And as for the helpers: people would hardly question whether it was genuine as long as the Burry Man was there in the middle of it all. Maybe it was a burglary scheme. Everyone outside cheering the Burry Man and one of the gang in the houses looking for anything worth lifting.'

I was finding this rather flustering, truth be told, unused to someone else confidently barging in with his own theories, and such dull little theories at that. It revealed to me as nothing else would have just how very collaborative Alec was in comparison.

'You know best, Inspector,' I said, I hoped placatingly. 'But we were thinking more along these lines: that the real Burry Man – Robert Dudgeon, that is – was elsewhere on Friday and was using let's call him the duplicate Burry Man as an . . . well, as an alibi. If I explain where our suspicions arose, you'll see why that is.

'First of all, there was Dudgeon's sudden and extreme reluctance to do the job. It came over him out of nowhere on Thursday afternoon, making him try with some considerable determination to wriggle out of the commitment. Then just as suddenly he seemed to change his mind back again and think that it could be managed. And now that I come to think of it, I did joke a little about Mr de Cassilis stepping into the breach – it *was* only a joke, Cad – and I think I did say that even though he was a newcomer and it would not be popular with those in the know, I expected that once he was in costume no one would be any the wiser.

'That's one suspicious circumstance. Then, of course, it was clear right away on Friday night that there was something wrong with *Mrs* Dudgeon. Something extra wrong, I mean, over and above the grief and shock. Only now does that begin to make sense. She knew, you see, and she dreaded anyone else finding out. Also, there was the blasted ham sandwich which Robert Dudgeon ate sometime before his death. We

241

simply could not track down the origin of that ham sandwich, Inspector. Obviously, he could consume nothing during his round and we knew that Mrs Dudgeon did not intend him to dine off a sandwich because she was all set to take him straight home and she had made a meal for him to eat when he got there. The dishes were still being washed up later that evening when Mrs de Cassilis and I visited her.'

'Now as to the switch itself,' said Alec. 'That was very neatly handled indeed. Tell him, Dan.'

'This is conjecture, you understand,' I said to the inspector, 'but it all fits. Pat Rearden told me that in the morning, for the first time in all his Burry Mann-ing years, Robert Dudgeon asked to be left quite alone. I need to check with Mr Rearden – or I suppose it will be you who checks now, Inspector – but I'll bet that this moment alone was requested once Dudgeon was completely in costume. He would then withdraw into a cupboard or something and be replaced by the other Burry Man who'd been waiting in the same cupboard to be handed the baton.' Inspector Cruickshank looked rather sceptical, but said nothing. 'At the end of the day, as we all know, the Burry Man – not Mr Dudgeon, so let's call him X for the moment – X dashed off up the stairs away from his guards and when they caught up with him, somewhere in the bowels of the Rosebery Hall, they found Robert Dudgeon ostensibly having ripped off the headpiece and some of the body suit. In fact of course he had shrugged most of it back *on*, and only just left a bit undone. X, the Burry Man that Rearden and his pal had been steering around all day, was once again tucked away out of view.

'Now, here is another very significant piece of evidence, Inspector, and one that we are very lucky to have got our hands on. Mrs Dudgeon had her pony and cart parked in Craw's Close on Friday as she waited for her

242

husband's return. She refused to move it even though the pony – as ponies will – left droppings all over the Craw's Close washing green and the women of the Close were not best pleased. You know the layout of the town better than me, of course, but I'm sure we'll find that the spot where the cart stood is handily situated for a back exit from the Rosebery Hall. There are back doors giving on to that general area, aren't there?' The inspector nodded. 'I thought so. Very well then, the decoy Burry Man scurries into the cart – there's an opening at the back under the seats, you know – and Mrs Dudgeon, again for the first time in all her years of connection with the event, bundles up the burrs from Robert's costume and shoves them in there too. Next they set off for home, up the Loan and – most unaccountably, it seemed to me at first – along the Back Braes just below Station Road.'

'There's never room for a pony and cart along there,' said Inspector Cruickshank.

'Well, the Dudgeons' little cart really is tiny,' I said.

'Of course,' said the inspector. 'Robert made himself a wee bogie from one of the hutches when the works here closed, I was forgetting.'

'So there is room, just,' I said. 'But there's certainly no room to turn it. And yet that is exactly what happened. At the bowling green corner, with much toing and froing and with the pony and cart uncoupled while it was carried out, they turned the cart, went *back* along the brae and rejoined the Fair in time for the greasy pole.'

'And how do you know this?' said the inspector.

'They were seen,' Alec told him. 'What was her name, Dan?'

'Netta Stoddart,' I supplied. 'Sitting at the back of the bowling green clubhouse waiting for her daddy, Netta Stoddart saw them turn the cart. This much

I believed right from the start. I now believe the next section of her evidence too. That the Burry Man fell off the cart and rolled down the hill to the railway line. I had that down as a taradiddle. For one thing, why would Dudgeon come back to the Fair if he had just had a tumble? But I now see that little Netta was not talking about "Robert Dudgeon"; she was talking about a "Burry Man". That is, a man covered in a suit of burrs, and she saw him rolling out of the cart and down the slope to make his getaway. Of course, the next bit – that a train came along and squashed him – is just Netta making life more interesting for herself and can be filed away with the ghost pony and the swamp. Not to mention the holes with the ghostie soldiers down them, the demon in the woods and the dead babies who cry in the night.'

Inspector Cruickshank gave all of this very careful consideration, but when he began to speak, the opening sniff said it all.

'A very clever tale, madam,' he said, 'but a bit too fanciful for my taste, I'm afraid, even if you have managed to convince Mr Osborne here.'

Alec looked rather startled at this take on things, but said nothing.

'I mean to say,' the inspector continued, in a patient tone, 'you say yourself that the Stoddart girl made things up –'

'Yes but –' said Alec, but Inspector Cruickshank sailed on.

'And I still don't think there's room for the cart along that lane,' he said. 'Never mind space to turn it.'

'There are clear tracks,' I said, but then we both looked out of the castle window where the hail storm had given way once more to hammering rain.

'And why was it that Mrs Dudgeon took the burrs, you're saying?' he asked.

244

'Ah, this was a nice touch,' said Alec. 'What better place to hide a lot of burrs than with another lot of burrs after all.'

'And if the tragedy of Friday night had not occurred,' I chipped in, 'no doubt Dudgeon would soon have burnt the lot.'

'And why didn't Mrs Dudgeon do the same?'

'I'm not sure,' I said. 'Perhaps she forgot about them in all the horror of what happened. She was absolutely beside herself, Inspector. Or perhaps – if Mr Dudgeon was the gardener in the family – she did not know that they wouldn't just dissolve harmlessly there on the heap.' This was rather feeble and I could see that I was in danger of losing him completely.

'Meanwhile this other one, this X, went all the way from the bowling green corner along the edge of the railway line up to the Dudgeons' cottage to put his burrs on the heap there too? Why would he do that now? Whoever he was.'

I looked to Alec, hoping that he had an answer for this, but he was looking back at me, hoping the same.

'Maybe,' I said slowly, thinking as I spoke, 'if we knew who it was, that would become clear.'

'And what's more, you're saying he went there in the burrs. Actually wearing all the burrs? Why would he do that?' I had no answer this time.

'So that he wouldn't be recognized?' suggested Alec.

'And why should he care about being recognized?' the inspector said.

'Again,' I insisted, 'we might be able to answer that if we knew who he was. I can easily believe that he would make his way to his destination still wearing the burrs, though, even if it *was* torture, because he would have been beautifully camouflaged amongst the trees and anyone who saw him was likely to doubt his own eyes or be doubted if he tried to pass the news on. And

245

actually,' I said, finding my stride now, 'he would have been pretty safe. There were no trains just then and there was not likely to be anyone in the woods. No children playing there for once, since everyone was at the Fair. Once he was beyond the footbridge over the line – and he went past that still on the cart – there was a clear run all the way back to Cassilis.'

'But why?' said the inspector. 'I'm not saying I agree with anything you've said, mind, but just for the sake of argument if any of that did happen, *why*? Why did Robert and Chrissie Dudgeon not go all the way home with this mystery man hidden under the back of the cart? That would have been much safer than leaving him to flit through the woods on his own no matter how empty they were. It would only take one sober, respectable adult to see him and the game would be up.'

I could see the sense in this.

'Perhaps,' I said, making a last attempt, 'perhaps they were concerned to make everything look as near normal as possible, and normal on that particular evening meant staying at the Fair and climbing the greasy pole.'

The inspector was shaking his head again.

'You've put together a wondrous tale,' he said, 'but it's all smoke and mirrors when you get right down to it. Still, good work with the burrs, Mr Osborne. I'll certainly have to look into that. It could be that there's a lot of folk have things missing from the house and they haven't put two and two together. Or maybe they have and they're hanging back not wanting to point the finger at Robert Dudgeon when he's not here any more to defend himself.' I could not believe that he was brushing off all our lovely evidence and our beautifully knitted-together explanations and sticking to this boring account of petty thievery, but there did not seem to be anything else to say that would convince him he

246

was wrong, so Alec and I simply bade him farewell with as much good grace as we could muster.

'If I can have the use of your telephone, Mr de Cassilis,' he said, 'I'll ring the sergeant and get him to pick me up and take the evidence away at the same time. No, no, no,' he brushed off Buttercup's mutterings of hospitality, 'I'll wait in the stable yard, if it's all the same, Mrs de Cassilis. He'll only be a minute up from the Ferry to get me.' He bowed slightly to me and I inclined my head in return but when he turned his back to leave, I stuck my tongue out at him and crossed my eyes.

Chapter Thirteen

'Do you think he's right?' I asked Alec as soon as I thought the inspector would be out of earshot.

'No,' Alec replied. 'Not a chance of it. He has no explanation for how all the burrs ended up on the Dudgeons' midden for one thing. I expect he's just one of those people who needs to make his own way to an idea. Not everyone relishes being told what to think.'

'Hm,' I said. 'Especially by some silly chit of a woman, you mean. Didn't you notice how you got all the glory for the burrs and I got all the scorn for the rest of it? You should have told him when he asked you, and not left it to me.'

'And what would you have said to that?' said Alec, laughing. 'If I had and he'd *still* not believed a word, you would have told me I'd barged in and mucked it up, wouldn't you?'

'Probably,' I conceded, laughing with him.

'Well, one thing's clear,' said Cad, speaking for the first time since the inspector had entered the room. 'You two must certainly carry on. There's no question of handing the whole thing over to the police and sitting back if they're going to show such staggering lack of imagination. He didn't even mention the question of why Dudgeon actually died. But then – I couldn't help noticing – neither did you.'

'You're quite right,' said Alec. 'We've been so excited

about the burrs and working out how that bit was managed that we've barely thought about the death all day.'

'And now the burrs have been carted off into police custody and we have no chance of running any of them past our toxicologist,' I wailed.

'You said . . . You said . . .' spluttered Alec. 'Dandy, you germ. You let me lacerate myself from head to toe and you still thought they were poisoned?'

'You have a toxicologist?' said Cad, sounding impressed and Alec laughed in spite of himself.

'I was joking,' I told Alec. 'And no, Cad, we don't. Nor, I fear, are we going to need one. Our mushroom theory was only needed if Dudgeon had spent his day with two babysitters hanging on his arms. And anyway, I'm still sure it's as I said, I'm afraid. Remember? Right at the start. I said that there was something going on that was worrying the Dudgeons and in the middle of it all Dudgeon died, but there was no reason to think the worry and the death were connected. I don't see any reason to abandon that now. All that's happened is that we've found out what it was that the Dudgeons were up to.'

'But not why,' Alec pointed out. 'We've not even begun to wonder why. Have we, Dan? Dan?'

'Sorry, darling, I was just thinking,' I said. 'That there might be a connection after all. Far too twisty for Inspector Cruickshank, but see what you think. Only don't get excited, Cad, I fear it's not nearly twisty *enough* for you. It's as I was saying to the inspector – one possible reason for the Dudgeons to stay at the Fair on Friday evening was to make everything look as near normal as it possibly could. A guilty conscience seriously disrupts the judgement on these matters; one doesn't dare to do anything the least bit odd if one has something to hide and one begins to imagine that any

249

little thing one *does* do is going to stick out like a red banner and draw the crowds. So although we can imagine that people would just have shrugged and thought nothing of it had Robert not climbed the pole that evening, Dudgeon himself might have thought it was an indispensable part of his "I've just been the Burry Man as usual and I'm having the Burry Man's usual day" routine. So if he was trying to get every detail just so . . . what was the other striking feature of the Burry Man's day? Apart from the burrs.'

'Whisky,' said Buttercup.

I clapped my hands. 'Have a gold star, darling, and go to the top of the class. Whisky, exactly. Do you see?'

'I think so,' said Alec, as I would have expected.

'No,' said Cad, just as predictably.

'Dr Rennick the police surgeon thought there was enough alcohol in Dudgeon's system to have poisoned him even if he'd sipped it over the course of a long day and done a good bit of walking in between times. Imagine if Dudgeon – after getting back to the Rosebery Hall – tried to catch up all at once. Wouldn't that make the poisoning much more likely?'

'If he glugged down a bottle of the stuff?' said Alec. 'I suppose it could do, although I'm happy to say I've no personal experience on which to draw.'

'It stands to reason, though, doesn't it?' I said. 'Oh God, you do realize that the obvious way for us to find out is to go cap in hand to Mr Turnbull and ask for borrower's privileges for his "substantial library" on the demon drink.'

'Needs must,' said Alec rather complacently.

'I'm glad you agree,' I told him. 'I certainly can't suddenly feign an interest after making my thoughts on the matter so very plain. No, that delightful little task is going to fall to you.' I bared my teeth at him in an innocent smile. 'Meanwhile . . .'

'Meanwhile?' echoed Cad.

'Meanwhile we must find out what Robert Dudgeon was up to. We must discover how the Burry Man spent his day. It would also be helpful to discover who the stand-in was, although I suppose that's the kind of task the police are better placed to handle. They can go around questioning everyone's whereabouts without getting a "mind your own business" and a bop on the nose.'

'Who do you think it might have been?' said Alec. 'Any ideas?'

'Well, it would have to be a man roughly the same height and weight . . . my initial hunch would be to investigate the ever-obliging Donald.'

'It wasn't Donald,' said Cad. 'He's my dyker – my wall-mender, you know – and my men didn't have the day off.'

'As far as you know they didn't,' I said. 'But did you see Donald with your own eyes on Friday? If not, I think it's worth checking.'

'What about the whisky?' said Buttercup. 'I thought Donald was dead set against it.'

'Oh damn, you're right,' I said. 'It depends on the circumstances, though, surely. I daresay family feeling could overcome his scruples in a sufficiently tight pinch. It *was* only a hunch, mind you. It needn't be someone bound to the Dudgeons by brotherly loyalty. It could be an accomplice, plain and simple, bound by common cause.'

'Yes, but what cause?' Alec said. 'What tight pinch? What the hell was going on? Something very peculiar when you consider all the details. It had to be premeditated since he knew in advance that it was coming off, and yet not too premeditated because he didn't seem to know very *far* in advance, did he? Thursday teatime. What could it have been?'

'Mail train robbery?' said Buttercup. 'And he only found out from the rest of the gang on Thursday afternoon when the train with all the loot was going to be on the tracks?'

'Welcome home, darling,' I said. 'You are not in the Wild West any more and Robert Dudgeon was neither a cattle rustler nor a robber of mail trains.'

'New York isn't the Wild West,' said Buttercup. 'But I see what you mean, sorry.'

'Freddy's got a point, though,' said Cad. 'Not a train robbery, but a robbery of some kind perhaps. Because Dudgeon was in difficulty with money. He came to me a week or two ago asking about an advance on his wages and offering to do extra work for extra pay. D'you remember, Dandy, when he was trying to wriggle out of the Burry Man's day, and you asked him if he was paid for it and I hinted that if so he surely couldn't pass it up? I did it quite subtly so as not to embarrass him but you might have picked up on it.'

'Yes, I think I did just manage to catch a whiff of something,' I said, keeping a straight face but not daring to look at Alec. 'I don't suppose he told you what the emergency was?' Cad shook his head. 'And did you give him the advance?'

'Not exactly,' said Cadwallader. 'But I looked through the wages books with the steward and when I saw what he was being paid I gave him a raise. Back-dated it to when I arrived. Old Uncle Cad really was the most god-awful skinflint.'

'So in effect, he got the money he was after,' said Alec. 'Doesn't that thicken the plot? Wouldn't he have been able to get out of his commitment – whatever it was – if he didn't need the money?"

'Perhaps,' I said. 'But say there was a gang, with a plan to do something nefarious, and say Dudgeon bought his way out with the cash from Cad. That doesn't mean they couldn't renege at the last minute on Thursday afternoon and put pressure on him to come in with them after all.'

'No honour among thieves?' said Alec.

'But I don't like that explanation,' I said. 'For one thing it doesn't fit with what I saw of Robert Dudgeon. He simply didn't seem the type to be mixed up in anything criminal. And he certainly didn't seem the type to mix his wife up in it with him. And mark my words, she was in it with him. Up to her neck.'

'But Dandy, that's quite run of the mill, you know,' said Buttercup. 'Gangsters' molls are ten a penny in some places and lots of them are every bit as fierce as their boyfriends.'

'In some places,' I said. 'But do you think Queensferry is one of them? And do many gangsters have estate carpentering as a sideline?' I did not wait for a response. 'We must be thorough, of course. We can't rule it out of hand right now. So . . .?'

'We can look in the newspapers, see if any likely crime was committed on Friday,' said Alec. 'And we should certainly share our thoughts with Inspector Cruickshank. Whether he agrees or not, it's better that he should know, so that if he comes across something odd he'll be able to put the bits together.'

'And I shall continue to cultivate Mrs Dudgeon,' I said, 'in hopes that I can persuade her to trust me and tell me what's going on. Only I need to get to her before the police.'

'What if your hunch about her were wrong, though?' said Alec. 'What if you got her to tell all, assuring her that she could trust you, and then she told you something you simply *had* to pass on to the inspector?'

I shook my head, unwilling to countenance the notion. 'How could she? How could those people – Dudgeon and Mrs Dudgeon, I mean, with their neat vegetable patch and their knitted cushions on the footstool – be mixed up in anything truly bad?'

'You hardly know the woman,' said Alec. 'And you only met him once.'

'It does not always take extensive acquaintance to get the measure of a man,' I said. 'The moment I set eyes on Mr Dudgeon – standing in this very room in his stocking soles – I could see that he was as honest as the day is long.'

'Oh yes?' said Alec. 'And what about some of your other first impressions? Rearden, say? Or Shinie Brown? What about the inspector, or that stable lad you seem to have struck up a friendship with? When was the last time you met someone whom you *didn't* immediately decide was a good egg?'

'He's right, you know, Dandy,' said Buttercup. 'You were just as bad at school.'

'Donald,' I said, stoutly. 'I didn't take to Brother Donald at all. And I can't stick the Turnbulls.'

'Oh well, the Turnbulls!' said Alec. 'There are limits even for you.'

At that moment, the telephone on Cadwallader's desk began ringing and he went to answer it, laughing along with the others; I suppose it must have made a nice change for him to have someone else be the butt of the jokes for a while.

'It's for you, Dandy,' he said. 'One of your conquests, no doubt. Ringing to ask you out for a walk in the moonlight,' I gave a good-natured smile and took the receiver.

'Dandy?' said Hugh's voice down the line. 'Who in the world was that?' I sobered immediately. Hugh was not likely to have rung me up just to hear the sweet sound of my voice, and I feared a summons home. What he said next only confirmed it.

'Look, this can't go on. It's been days on end now and it's getting a bit much.'

'How's the shoot?' I asked him. I felt I knew the answer. Hugh would only ever decide he needed me at home if things were going very badly on the grouse moor and he needed a recipient for his grumbles. Indeed he can get testy enough, if driven to it by recalcitrant birds and clumsy beaters, to hold me and the other wives in the party responsible; for keeping the guns late at breakfast and distracting them after dinner with cards and silly gossip. Obviously, if I were away from home and his party was one of bachelors and widowers only, as this year, and yet the bag was still disappointing it was much harder to lay the blame at my door. Hence, my essential return. His next words, however, suggested that these assumptions were wrong.

'What?' he said. 'The shoot? Oh, fine, fine, fine. If I could get a minute's peace to enjoy it. It's that bloody mutt of yours, Dandy. It's well out of season now, has been for days, and it's upsetting the whole household' – by 'household', I knew that Hugh meant his smelly pack of hounds, terriers and accidents – 'so I'm sending it to you.'

I had a vision of Bunty with a brown label around her neck being carried up the castle drive in the basket of a bicycling postman.

'Drysdale put it on the 5.28. You're to meet the train at Dalmeny at 7.40. It's in the guard's van.'

'Hugh!' I squeaked.

'Too late to argue,' said Hugh. Of course it was. He deliberately had not rung me until it was too late to argue; that was him through and through, but his machinations were redundant in this case.

'I'm not arguing,' I said. 'What a sweet thing to have thought of. Thank you.'

255

There was a puzzled silence from the other end of the line. Hugh does not and cannot believe that I actually like Bunty, *love* Bunty, and do not simply pretend to love her to annoy him. I was sure it had given him a thrill of guilty pleasure to pack her off to me like this, but it had backfired.

'Have you sent her things?' I asked.

Hugh rumbled.

'Oh, Hugh, please! You have sent her things along with her, haven't you?'

'It's a dog, Dandy,' said Hugh. 'It doesn't have things.'

With this he had the upper hand again and there was no regaining it so I thanked him and rang off.

'Bunty?' said Alec. I nodded. 'And dastardly Hugh has sent her out into the harsh world without so much as a flask of tea and a change of underwear?'

'You don't mind, Buttercup, do you?' I asked. 'My dog coming? Too bad if you do, really, because she's arriving off the 7.40. She's no trouble. Beautifully trained and . . .' I trailed off, aware that there was no point in building her up when they were just about to meet her face to face and learn the truth. 'Well, she's still a puppy, really,' I said.

'She's seven,' said Alec. 'If she were a person she would be older than you.'

'No, we don't mind if Buttercup comes, do we, Freddy?' said Cad.

Buttercup did not answer, but only shook her fist at me and growled.

I walked to the station – there was just time – thinking that Bunty might be a bit overwrought by the excitement of the journey and a ride in a motor car on top of it would not put her in the best light when she met her hosts. Besides, the rain and hail had spent themselves and the evening was sparkling again as the sinking sun caught the droplets on leaves, grass and fence wire. I tramped along, sniffing the damped-dust smell that summer rain leaves behind it, and feeling very content with my lot. We were making headway with the case – and we now had the strong arm of the law to take on the nosy-parkering jobs that give the amateur detective so much trouble – Bunty was coming, Alec was here and Hugh, now that he had got rid of my darling from under his feet, was apparently quite happy to let me do as I chose for as long as I chose to do it. Added to all of this, because either the afternoon's storm or Robert Dudgeon's funeral in the morning had brought an interruption to the work of the day, there were men and children amongst the hay, there were women out in front of the Dalmeny cottages, putting their washing back up to catch the last warmth of the sun and there were labourers at work in a far corner of a road-side field, the steady tock-tock of their hammers against the stones sounding like a metronome to keep the gurgling songbirds in time. In short, bucolic bliss.

I slowed, stopped and retraced my steps until I could see the glint off the bare shoulders of the labourers again. If they were at work in a corner of a field, bashing hammers against rock, they could only be wall-menders, which meant that one of them was more than likely Donald Dudgeon.

Obviously, I could not scale the nearest gate and make straight for them, but if I were to go back to the corner by the village green and start from there, making for the station, I would pass through them as though on a plumb-line. So, with my feet already beginning to squelch in my light shoes, I set off. There were no meadow flowers to pick as late in the season as this, which was a shame since that would have explained very nicely why I should splash through a

257

field instead of walking sensibly down the road and along the bottom, but the straight path across the field was the shortest route, so I began to walk very fast and looked at my watch with an extravagant gesture every few seconds or so. If they saw me coming they would naturally think I was late and making a beeline. Actually, when I focused on my watch-face during one of these ostentatious checks I saw that I really was rather late, and I redoubled my pace.

'Phew!' I said loudly, nearing the group of men a minute or two later. 'Who would have thought it could get so warm again after that downpour?' I said this partly to put them at their ease about being discovered with their shirts off, partly just in greeting, and by the time I'd delivered my little speech I had had time to look around the group and see that I recognized none of them. They all touched their caps and then stood staring at me, wondering what I was doing suddenly in their midst. 'Still it must be much more pleasant work now than at noon, I daresay.'

One of the men, the oldest and so probably the boss, answered.

'It is that, madam. That it is.' Again he looked inquiringly at me.

'I'm making for the station,' I said, to nods of dawning comprehension. Most helpfully at that moment we all heard the sound of the train beginning the crossing of the Forth towards us, the metal of the bridge setting up a rumble like distant thunder.

'I doubt ye've missed it,' said the foreman, looking over his shoulder at the field I still had to cross to get there, but I assured him that I was only going to collect a parcel and I leaned companionably against the mended bit of wall while one of his underlings set about untying the string holding the gate shut to allow me passage.

'I suppose you're behindhand, what with the rain and the funeral?' I said. 'And you're short of men too, without Donald Dudgeon.' This was rather clunking but I could think of no better way to lead up to it before the gate was opened and I was forced to leave them.

'Donald whae?' said the foreman, looking around his team as though to check that all were present and correct.

'Wasn't he off all day in mourning?' I said. 'And Friday too? Am I right in thinking he was off on Friday?'

'Mourning?' said the foreman. His expression, as plain as could be, was asking what on earth I was wittering on about, but he was too polite to follow it up in voice.

'Rab Dudgeon was buried today,' said one of the lads. 'Is that what ye're meaning? But whae's Donald?'

'Oh!' said the foreman. 'Flamin' Donald, you mean. Naw, Flamin' Donald's no' one o' ma men. He's wi' that Yank over Cassilis.' He spoke as though Cassilis was in the next but one county, not just a stroll in summer shoes up the nearest road.

'I thought you *were* Cassilis men,' I said. There was a ripple of low laughter at that and the foreman shook his head.

'Naw, that's a tinpot wee caper,' he said. 'Jist Flamin' Donald and one laddie. We're Rosebery.' So I had splashed through the field and made myself late for nothing. 'Here,' went on the foreman, 'has the Yank been goin' about sayin' this is his land?'

'Here, Addie,' said another. 'He's maybe got battle plans. If yous hear musket fire, get ready to lay doon yer life.'

'Aye, ken whit thon pilgrims are like,' said the foreman, showing a rather shaky grasp, I thought, of colonial history. The boy had got the gate untied by now and I passed through with a nod of thanks, considering briefly whether to reveal that I was a guest of thon pilgrim Yankee but deciding against it.

I scurried across the fields towards the station, racing the train even while I told myself I had not a hope of beating it. Poor Donald Dudgeon! One could understand why he had attracted such a nickname if he really were the star-turn of the hellfire and damnation preaching world in these parts, but it was bound to be a grievance to him if he were as strait-laced linguistically as these types usually seemed to be. I remembered one particular nursemaid of my youth, terribly purse-mouthed and unyielding, who smacked my hand with a pudding spoon just for saying 'Heavens!' Her name had been Florence Poste and we children had called her Fencepost which was an absolutely accurate description of her outline and general demeanour, but she had not seen it in that light when she overheard it. I had always been immune from nicknames myself, friends and enemies alike agreeing that they could not improve on Dandelion Dahlia, but I had sympathy for those saddled with real burdens. Buttercup, for instance, had my pity although it would never be possible for me to think of her as anything else, and to be fair when she was dubbed Buttercup it was not intended to be descriptive. I wondered briefly about Shinie Brown as I jumped down from the final gate and trotted between the two rows of railwaymen's cottages while the train drew into the station above me. He was not bald, nor particularly red-faced, and there was no obvious source of boyhood shininess that I could think of. If his surname had been White or even Gold . . . The engine gathered steam and began to haul away and as it did so I could hear, loud and clear, a stream of excited barks and whines and the sound of the station-master swearing.

Buttercup once again vetoed discussion of the case around the dinner table and the talk veered chaotically amongst Bessie Smith's New York debut, which Buttercup was desolate to have missed, the Royal Family, whom Cad seemed cheerfully optimistic of meeting sometime soon, and the Klu Klux Klan of whom Alec kept demanding to know what they were *for* exactly and Cad kept insisting that he had no idea. I have never been able to keep up with those conversations where each of the participants sticks to his own personal topic and barely seems to notice that the others are doing just the same, and so to save myself from developing the inevitable headache if I tried, I retreated into my thoughts and left them to it.

'You can't!' said Alec, when I told him afterwards what plans for the evening I had been hatching. I was determined that Inspector Cruickshank would not beat me to the widow. 'She buried her husband today, Dandy, and you absolutely quite simply can't. You must wait until tomorrow at the very least.'

'That's exactly what the inspector will be thinking,' I said. 'He'll be there tomorrow with a constable and a little notebook, and he doesn't have to wait until a decent time for making social calls. Imagine if he got there before me. Or worse, if I were sitting there and he marched in. And anyway, I'm going there as a friend, to warn her and to offer an ear and a shoulder. And to prove it, I'm taking her pen back.'

'Have you even told Inspector Cruickshank about the pen?' Alec asked.

'No,' I admitted. 'I forgot about it. But it was the merest chance that I found it or that she dropped it, and the bottle of ink is common knowledge. He can intuit the pen for himself. As he and I would both have had to if I hadn't happened to spot it there.'

'But if the police start a real investigation they might decide to search the woods, Dandy, and if they find out afterwards that there was something there to find but you'd removed it before they got the chance . . . Well, I'm not sure that isn't one of those spoilsporty sounding things one can go to jail for.'

'What do you mean?' I asked, laughing. 'What spoilsporty sounding things are these?'

'Oh, interfering with a criminal investigation or obstructing the police in the execution of their duty or whatever they're called. They've always seemed to me to be a bit much.' I was laughing in earnest now at the sincerity of his outrage. 'No, really,' he went on. 'It doesn't seem fair to let the police decide what they think is annoying and then make up a pompous name for it and call it a crime. Wouldn't we all like to do that?'

'It would make a splendid parlour game.' I said. 'I'd have "Obstructing me in the execution of my pleasure by sitting me next to a bore at dinner". Ten months' hard labour for that, and Daisy Esslemont would be breaking stones in a chain-gang as we speak.'

'Or how about "Wilful and malicious amateur drama"?' said Alec. 'I could have shut down a good few house parties over the years with that on the statute books.'

'Be all of that as it may,' I said, seemingly unable to stop talking like a member of the legal professions now that I had started, 'I'm off to Mrs Dudgeon's. Come and lounge in my bedroom doorway while I get my hat and coat. Stop Grant from ticking me off about the state of my afternoon shoes.' Alec heaved himself to his feet, leaving his pipe politely in the ashtray, and accompanied me, shuffling up the stone steps to the bedroom floor, holding tight to the banister rope. I, as Buttercup had predicted, had got used to the bevelled stone and the inky blackness and was now tripping up and down the spiral steps like a Gaiety Girl in her tap shoes.

Grant was indeed frowning and muttering over my sodden shoes, and ripping up sheets of today's newspaper – which I had not had a chance to read yet – in order to stuff them. She always makes a point of doing a great deal of her maidly chores right there in my bedroom instead of behind the baize door, but I supposed one had to forgive her in this instance, since the servants' wing was half a mile of parkland away.

'Ah, Grant,' I said. 'I'm off out with Bunty before bedtime.' Grant shot a poisonous look towards Bunty who had been fast asleep on the middle of my bed, recovering from the excitements of the day but, at the sound of my voice, had opened her eyes, given a great creaking yawn and begun rolling and twisting on her back with all four legs pedalling in the air and her tail sweeping the counterpane.

I tore off the feathered band I had been wearing at dinner and pulled on the little mourning hat in its place. Grant and I reached the wardrobe door neck and neck, I to withdraw my grey linen coat – it was long and wide and would cover my beaded dress perfectly – and Grant to take out the skirt and coat she clearly thought were essential for even the shortest country walk.

'I'm not changing, Grant,' I told her. 'I'm only going down the lane and back.'

Grant replaced the skirt and coat and took out a devoré wrap with a huge fur collar instead, the very wrap I usually wore with this little dress if dining out.

I ignored her and shrugged into my linen coat, buttoning it up to the neck to hide all trace of what lay underneath, then I kicked off my evening slippers and sat down on the edge of the bed to pull on my short boots. Wet feet once a day was more than enough for me. Grant closed the wardrobe door and left with meekly downturned face although boiling with rage inside I could tell.

'Grant would have got on very well with Leviticus,' I said once she was out of range, 'at least in the matter of wearing cloth of mixed thread. Come on, Bunty.'

Chapter Fourteen

Alec saw us off and watched as we picked our way carefully down the slope on grass even more slippery for the afternoon's rain then he shut the door with a clang and went back, I presumed, to his pipe. It was almost full darkness now but Bunty was gleaming in the moonlight and I was getting to know the twists of the lane very well so I was content to strike out into the night like a cat. As ever, my eyes adjusted within minutes anyway, and very shortly I had gained the familiar clearing without mishap.

It was hard to say whether there was a material difference on this trip which could be held responsible for my sanguinity, but there was no return of the dread I had felt on my sorties the day before, even with Nipper in tow, and one would have expected the woods to be creepier at night if anything. Perhaps it was the presence of Bunty, plodding along in front of me, the shifting muscles on her back making her spotty coat wink and ripple. My children always fancied that they could see in Bunty's coat a picture of a circus clown juggling five balls. In fact, when they were small they had got into the biggest trouble of their young lives by finishing off this vague illustration using oil paints and a fine brush. I looked for the juggler again now, walking up the path to Mrs Dudgeon's front door, but not with much success although the five balls themselves were indisputable.

Pausing on the doorstep with my breath held, I listened to hear if there was still the murmur of visitors sitting with the widow, or worse the hubbub of a wake in full swing, but even though the living-room window was open at the bottom and a light was shining out from the crack in the curtains I heard nothing. Mrs Dudgeon it seemed was alone. I knocked and the steps that came in response were surprisingly fleet, the voice which called out from behind the door wavering with anxiety.

'Is that – Who is it?'

'It's Mrs Gilver, Mrs Dudgeon,' I called back. 'Can I come in?'

The door opened and Mrs Dudgeon stared out at me, searching my face.

'Just you?' she said, glancing behind me. I spread my hands in a gesture of openness. Just me, I tried to show her, and I mean you no harm.

'Have you come with a message?' she asked me.

'No,' I said, wondering what she could mean by this. 'I just came to see how you were.'

At last, she stepped aside and gestured for me to enter and I went into the living room with Bunty at my heels, to find the remains of the funeral feast still spread on the table, although the extra cups and plates were all washed and stacked tidily on the sideboard waiting to be returned.

'Actually,' I said, sitting at the table, shoving Bunty under it and keeping her penned there by bracing my leg against the pedestal, 'I wanted to return something of yours. I found it in the woods quite by chance and I thought it best to give it back into your safe-keeping.' Mrs Dudgeon's face had drained as I spoke, turning a blue-ish yellow, and she looked around wildly, at the door, up above the mantelpiece behind my head, and then back at me.

I unclasped my bag and fished around in it, while Mrs Dudgeon again threw a terrified glance towards the wall behind me and then towards the door. My hand closed round the pen finally and I drew it out and held it towards her.

'You dropped it, I believe.'

She stared at the pen for a good three or four of her panting breaths before she seemed to be able to understand what it was, then she put her hand out and took it from me.

'What made ye think it wis mine?' she said.

'One of your sisters told me you were out in the woods with a bottle of ink,' I said. 'So when I found this naturally I assumed . . .'

'One o' my sisters?' she echoed. I realized that I had very likely just dropped someone in it. 'Whae?'

'Tina, I think it was,' I said.

'Ahh,' she said. 'Aye, they are that. They are that.' Then she shook herself. 'I had forgotten. I've no' been myself,' and then with a heart-rending attempt at levity she gave a little laugh. 'I dinnae ken whit wis up wi' me that nicht, traipsin' around the woods like a daftie.'

'It's been a very difficult time for you,' I said. 'And I'm afraid it's far from over.'

Again the three-cornered look, up at the wall, over at the door and back to my face.

'What do ye mean?' she whispered. 'What's happened?'

'The burrs,' I said. 'All the burrs that you brought home?'

'Where are they?' she said, her eyes widening until I could see the whites all around. 'I cannae believe it! I forgot a' about them. We were suppose tae burn them and I forgot.' Then she did something I had never seen before and hope never to see again. She clamped both fists against the sides of her head and looking up at the wall behind my head she drummed her knuckles fast and hard on her scalp, her face stark with terror. Unable to bear the sight or the sound of this, I reached forward and caught her wrists in my hands. I had to let go the barrier keeping Bunty under the table top, but she stayed where she was, cowering further back into the shadows if anything.

'Someone put them on the midden heap out the back,' I said.

'We've got tae burn them,' she said. 'Quick.' Again the eyes darted to the door and up to the wall.

'We can't do that, Mrs Dudgeon,' I told her. 'I'm afraid that the police have them now. And they know there are twice as many as there should be. It's too late.'

'When?' she said. 'When did they get them? How long have they known?'

'Since this afternoon,' I told her. 'But I wouldn't say they "know" anything much. They're certainly going to try to find out though.' To the wall, to the door, back to my face again.

'Since this afternoon, you say? They've never been near me. They'd never . . . They'd never work it a' out without comin' to me. No' in time.' The glance flicked around twice, to the wall, to the door, to my face, as she spoke.

I craned around awkwardly, hurting my neck, still holding her hands. Above me and behind me on the wall was their kitchen clock; when I turned back she was looking up at it once more.

'In time for what?' I asked her.

She shook her head and said nothing.

'Inspector Cruickshank thinks that someone was impersonating your husband,' I said, 'going around with two helpers of his own getting money and whisky or robbing people's houses while they all came out to greet him.' Again it took her a moment or two longer to understand this than it should have, but when the message did get through, she looked at me alert, intrigued.

'*That's* whit they're thinkin'?' Her voice was almost scornful.

'And – this is only my guess – but I think they'll be round here tomorrow first thing, so you need to get ready and decide what you're going to tell them.'

'Tomorrow?' she said. 'No' tonight?' To the door, to the clock and back to my face again. I shook my head.

'I don't think so,' I told her. 'If they were coming they would be here by now. It's almost ten o'clock after all.' I felt a shiver go through her body as I said this, and this time both she and I looked up at the clock together.

'Are you expecting someone?' I asked as her eyes made their route around the room once more. She shook her head.

'They can come if they like tomorrow,' she said. 'I'm no' carin' what happens tomorrow.'

'Would you like me to go? If you're expecting a visitor.'

'No!' she said and she wrested one of her wrists from mine only to clasp my arm in return. Bunty gave a tremulous little yelp at the sudden movement. 'Don't leave me, I'm beggin' you, madam. I'm fit to go mad wi' it, if I'm on ma' own. Don't leave me alone.'

I would have preferred a less ambiguous answer to my question before I told her yes or no: the only sense I could make of her fevered glances to the clock and the living-room door was that someone was on his way here to arrive at an appointed hour not long hence and if that person could reduce Mrs Dudgeon to the shambles of nerves before me I was not at all sure I was

269

equal to being one of the welcome party. My only consolation was that Bunty, thoroughly rattled by the tension in the air and huddled quite out of sight under the table, would not stand for any harm coming to me, but would launch herself on any assailant and, while Dalmatians are the least intimidating of all dogs – threat and polka-dots being mutually exclusive – they are really quite large, especially when they have paws on one's shoulders and are barking right into one's face. Hugh once found this out when Bunty, happening into a room where he was trying to take a splinter out of my hand and I was being a coward about it, made an understandable mistake and went for him like a wolverine.

'Of course I won't leave you,' I said in what I hoped was a staunch yet soothing voice, 'but won't you please tell me what it is that's wrong? Maybe I can help.'

Mrs Dudgeon shook her head and spoke in a soft, bleak voice.

'Naeb'dy but the good Lord can help me now,' she said. 'And I cannae even bring myself tae ask him.'

So we sat on like that, my hand on her wrist and her hand on mine, without talking, hardly moving, not even looking at each other. Every few seconds I felt a slight shift as she raised her head to look at the clock and turned it to look at the door and I could see the face of my watch on my stretched-out arm as it ticked round, five minutes to ten, three minutes to ten. I was getting a knot between my shoulders and a dull ache lower down from my awkward pose, leaning forward with both arms in front, but I dared not move, lest I miss the sound of feet approaching or the latch lifting on the front door. I could just see Bunty out of the corner of my eye, her eyes gleaming dully in the shadows and her nose quivering with anxious interest at the strangeness of all this.

Then, all of a sudden, I felt Mrs Dudgeon give way like a sandcastle breached by the tide. I thought I must have missed a sound and I looked wildly around at the doors and windows, heart hammering, but there was nothing to be seen, no one there. Mrs Dudgeon lay back in her chair with eyes closed.

'Are you –' I began, suddenly convinced that what I had felt was the life escaping her.

She opened her eyes and smiled at me.

'Thank you,' she said. 'That wis a great kindness, madam. To sit wi' me like that. I thank ye. Now!' She rose to her feet, slowly and with all the marks of extreme tiredness, but with a calm determination which I could not begin to interpret. 'Will ye take a cup o' tea?' she said. 'For yer pains. Or a wee nip o' somethin' maybe?'

'I don't understand,' I said. 'I don't know what just happened.' As far as I could tell, *nothing* had happened, and yet suddenly she was released from the prison of worry she had been in for the last four days. Was she mad after all, then? Was she communing with spirits here? Or imagining herself to be?

'Thank ye for tellin' me aboot the police comin',' she said as she filled her kettle from a jug and drew it forward on to the grate. 'I'll need tae make sure and be ready fur them. No' that I'm carin' whit happens now. No' really.'

'Mrs Dudgeon, I do wish you would tell me what it's all about,' I said. 'I'll find out, one way or another in the end, I'm sure I will, but if you told me we could put our heads together and keep the police out of it.'

'And why would you do that for me, madam,' she said, 'when ye dinnae even ken whit it is ye're asking me to tell ye?'

'Because I trust you,' I said. 'Because I'm sure that whatever it is that's wrong, I'd be on your side.'

'Mebbes if you were standin' where I am,' she said, her face hardening. 'But ye're not.'

'I don't have to be,' I told her. 'It's no more than common humanity to feel compassion for your suffering. Sorrow for your losses.'

She frowned at me when I said that and her body sagged, just a little, as though someone had let the tiniest peep of air out of a balloon.

'My losses,' she said, and she turned away from me, burying her face into the teacloth she had taken to wipe out the cups. 'Oh, Robert. Oh, God help me. I'm all alone now.'

'For all the world as though she had only just remembered that he'd died,' I told Alec, half an hour later, sitting in the firelight in the library once more. Cad and Buttercup had retired for the night but Alec had waited up for me and was now listening raptly, sucking on yet another pipe and scratching Bunty between the ears as she rested her chin on his thigh. She had gone straight to him as soon as I let her off her leash, craving some solid, masculine calm after the hysteria of the little scene in the cottage, the turncoat.

'And what on earth could have put the thought of her husband's death out of her head, on the day of his funeral no less, with all the plates of drying sandwiches still littered around?'

'The more I hear about this the less sense any of it makes,' Alec said. 'Are you sure she's not just insane?'

'Absolutely not,' I said. 'There was something definite and – if I'm not mistaken – something rather horrid due to happen at ten o'clock and when it didn't materialize, Mrs Dudgeon felt her first moment's peace since Friday.'

'Just as well for her that it didn't happen,' said Alec,

rather grimly. 'You don't seem to feel any of the anger you'd be perfectly justified in feeling, that she was apparently ready to let you sit there and get swept up in it, whatever it was.'

'It wasn't like that, Alec,' I said. 'I'm still absolutely convinced that she's innocent of any real wrongdoing in this. She said I would understand and sympathize if I were standing in her shoes. She'd hardly say that if it were something shabby.'

'Perhaps she just meant you'd understand if you were a poor woman like her instead of a rich woman like you, then you'd understand the lengths someone might go to.'

I shook my head with impatience. 'She's not a poor woman, Alec. She's a perfectly snug, secure, working man's wife. Or at least she was. And I can't foresee that she'll be turned out of her cottage just because her husband is gone.'

'By Cad and Buttercup?' said Alec, eyebrows raised. 'Hardly.'

'Anyway, it wasn't like that, I keep trying to tell you. I was talking to her about fellow feeling and the brotherhood of man – that kind of sympathy. I said I was on her side out of sorrow for her losses. That's what reminded her that her husband had just died in fact.'

'Losses?' said Alec. 'Plural?'

'Her son died in the war,' I said.

'And what was his name?' said Alec. I screwed up my face trying to remember.

'Young Bobby, I think,' I said. 'At least I wouldn't be at all surprised if it were, with Donald and wee Donald and Isobel and wee Isobel next door. Not forgetting Bel's wee Bella, and young Tina, Tina's lassie. They are a family of little imagination, either that or monstrous egos.'

'Well, there you are then,' said Alec. 'She hadn't forgotten about her husband at all, but when you said losses plural it reminded her about her son too. And that cry of "Robert" was for him.'

'Well, I feel an absolute heel now,' I said, convinced that he was right. 'I'm going to go to bed and pick away at that like a sore all night, darling. Thank you.'

'You'll do no such thing,' said Alec. 'Look.' He reached down beside his armchair, dislodging Bunty who had fallen asleep sitting up with her head in his lap. She gave a long two-note moan from deep in her throat and after circling twice curled up to sleep in earnest. With an equally heartfelt groan, Alec heaved an armload of newspapers on to his lap and patted them.

'*Scotsmans* and *Evening Newses* for Saturday, yesterday and today,' he said. 'I've scoured the household for them while you were out. We're looking for anything that Dudgeon might have been mixed up in. Anything that happened on Friday.'

'Oh, not tonight,' I pleaded. 'I'm absolutely all in.'

'Certainly tonight,' said Alec. 'There's not much else that we can do until the sun is up and the world is open for business again. So let's get started and with luck, before the morning comes, we'll have something to lay before the inspector.'

'Such as what?' I asked.

'Any odd happenings, any other unexplained deaths, anything at all.'

'Dudgeon's death isn't unexplained,' I said. 'Damn!'

'What?'

'Oh, just that I wish I'd remembered to ask Mrs Dudgeon tonight if Robert did indeed take a great draught of whisky at the end of the day. She might have told me straight out if I'd asked her tonight. But she's dedicating herself to getting a story all ready for the police even as we speak – I myself suggested that

274

she should, no less! – so if I ask her tomorrow there's no reason to think she'll tell the truth.'

'Time to make up for that blunder with a bit of solid detective work, then,' said Alec. It was quite sickening the way he was plugging this task, just because he had been the one to find the newspapers.

'Well, pour me a drink,' I said. 'And bags me the *Evening News*. Not so many long words.'

Stiff-necked from hunching over the tiny print and streaked with ink from rubbing our weary faces, after scrutinizing Saturday's and Monday's editions we had nothing to show for our efforts beyond a burglary at a manor house outside Linlithgow where a collection of Italian drawings had gone missing.

'What a very law-abiding bunch these Lothianites are,' said Alec. 'Very slim pickings.'

'And even that can't really be worth considering,' I said. 'There would be no earthly reason not to do it some other time instead. The place was shut up under dust sheets and one day was as easy as the next. Besides, why would the gang need a carpenter?'

'To get them out of their frames?' said Alec, but he was wincing even as he spoke at how feeble this sounded.

'Ludicrous,' I said.

'Well, let's keep at it anyway,' said Alec, shoving today's *Evening News* towards me, and opening the last of the *Scotsmans*. I sighed and followed suit.

'Tommy has missed his chance,' I said, finding the advertisement for steerage to New Zealand again. 'I'm so bored I could have joined him.'

'What?' said Alec.

'Oh, nothing,' I said. 'Just a joke. Ignore me.'

He did and all was peaceful except for the occasional turning over of a page and the sounds of Bunty's dreams until Alec exclaimed in a loud voice: 'Dandy!'

'Wha– . . . have you found something?'

'You're reading an advertisement for dress patterns. Really!'

'I know,' I said. 'I'm sorry, Alec, but this is a complete waste of time. I'm sure of it. It's all wrong for the character of Robert Dudgeon to imagine that he'd commit a crime and even if it weren't it doesn't make sense of the last minute turn-around on Thursday evening. You can't suddenly find out with only twelve hours to spare that you're going to need an alibi. You don't "find out" something like that, do you see? And that's very much how it seemed to me when I spoke to Dudgeon. Something had come up, something had unexpectedly moved forwards, or backwards, making an unforeseen clash. It happens to me all the time.'

'What do you mean?'

'Oh, you know,' I said. 'You say to yourself I'll spend next week on Christmas shopping and then the week before Christmas on writing letters and going round the tenants and I'll just be able to fit it all in, and then you look at your diary and you realize that next week *is* the week before Christmas which means there's exactly half as much time as you thought there was and you haven't a hope in hell.'

'Well, if it were a diary clash of some sort – and I can't really see what sort, I must tell you – why wouldn't Dudgeon just tell Cad about it?'

'Any number of reasons,' I said. 'It could have been very personal or something he didn't feel particularly proud of. But it needn't be the kind of thing that gets into the papers. We've scoured every inch of them barring the Births, Marriages and Deaths!'

'I'm not willing to settle at "any number of reasons", Dandy,' said Alec. 'Name some; name at least one thing that must suddenly be done and can't be left undone and is worth all the rigmarole of the stand-in Burry Man to get it done, because I can't think of any.'

'Nor can I,' I admitted, 'except speaking of births, marriages and deaths . . .'

'What?' said Alec.

'Just that,' I said. 'One has to register them by a certain date and when the date comes round it can't be put off any further.'

'But anyone can register a death,' said Alec. 'Within reason. And I suppose the same goes for a birth too. It's only a marriage that needs the principals to – What is it?'

'Listen!' I said. 'Don't look at me like that. On Saturday – no, Sunday – one of the times I was at the Dudgeons' cottage anyway, do you remember? Mrs Dudgeon was holding forth about not being able to register Robert's death the next day, because the registry office was shut. Her sisters tried to shout her down but she held to it adamantly, maintaining that it had been open the week before on the August Bank Holiday to let everyone who had business then get it done while they were off their work, and that it was shut this Monday – i.e. yesterday – to let the staff have their holiday too. Alec, I think that's it! Why would Mrs Dudgeon know all the ins and outs of the registry office holiday times unless she had just found out with a terrible jolt that it was shut when she thought it would be open? That's it. Dudgeon found out on Thursday afternoon that the office was closed on Monday and that Friday was the only chance to go, but he couldn't tell anyone why he had to go there.'

Alec blinked.

'But she was wrong,' he said. 'And even if she wasn't, why *did* he have to go there? We've already said it couldn't be to register a birth or death.'

'Well, it must have been to register a marriage, then,' I said.

'Whose?' said Alec. He sounded terribly irritated and I supposed I was looking rather smug, but for one thing it had been his idea to sit up until we were both tired beyond the point of politeness and for another I had just thought of something. An explanation both plausible and easily checked.

'His,' I answered. 'It had to be. Because if anyone can register a birth or a death the same goes for witnessing a marriage. It's only the principals in each who aren't interchangeable. He was getting married.'

'But . . . if you're right – although I am sure you're not – who was he going to marry?'

'Mrs Dudgeon?' I suggested. 'Or the woman we've been calling Mrs Dudgeon.'

'If he was going to legitimize his marriage to his wife,' said Alec, 'she would have to know that they weren't actually married already.'

'Why not?' I said. 'In fact, I think she did know. When I blurted out to her – during that same conversation – that she would have to look out his certificates, meaning his birth and marriage certificates and his passport – she flew into a complete panic. And her sisters twittering round asking if she had lost the certificates and offering to look for them only made her worse. And – Oh my, Alec! This must be right – do you remember? She was beside herself when the body wasn't brought home. She kept asking about his *things*, asking if they had gone through his pockets and looked at all his *things*. I couldn't work out for my life what it was that she could be so very worried about being seen, but imagine if he had some document to do with the marriage and someone read it. What a scandal that would be.'

'Indeed it would,' said Alec. 'Which raises the question: how could they possibly not be married? They've lived here all their lives, surrounded by brother and sisters all of whom were probably *at* their wedding. And it will be recorded large as life in the parish register for all to see. Also, if it was such a dark secret, who did they let into the plan?'

'Why need they let anyone in?' I said.

'X?' said Alec. 'Remember X? Someone was in on it. Someone who was willing to step into Robert Dudgeon's shoes. And anyway if he were going to marry Mrs Dudgeon she'd need to be there. And she wasn't, she was sitting in Craw's Close in her little cart.'

'So maybe he was going to marry someone else,' I said.

'Who?' said Alec. 'Why? And if he was going to marry someone else, Mrs Dudgeon would hardly help him.' He stretched luxuriously in his armchair and dumped the lapful of newspapers off his lap. 'I think this is one of those ingenious explanations which occur in the small hours and seem quite hopeful until one looks at them again in the light of day. And it doesn't explain anything about Dudgeon's death.'

'Neither does anything else we've come up with,' I pointed out. 'At least this adds enough stress and strain to explain why his heart might give out.'

Alec merely stared at me.

'You're right,' I said. 'I'm talking drivel. It's time for bed. But in the morning I'm going to go and look in the parish register at least.'

Chapter Fifteen

I made another attempt to convince Alec the next day as he, Bunty and I walked down to the Rosebery Hall where the parish registers were stored. We had cooked up a tale about him discovering that he had forebears from this area and wanting to squint through the parish books to see if he could find them and we were hoping that the clerk in charge would let us go through the things in peace and not ask a lot of questions and try to help us.

'If he does, we can give up and go to Register House in Edinburgh,' I said, 'and be sure to pick a name that isn't actually going to appear. Now, here, in the cold light of day, are my reasons for thinking this is it: one, Mrs Dudgeon knew quite a bit more than we can otherwise explain her knowing about registry office opening hours – or rather thought she did. Two, Mrs Dudgeon was beside herself about the police surgeon going through Robert's things. Three, Mrs Dudgeon was frightened at the thought of having to produce a marriage certificate in order to register the death. These incontrovertible facts are all neatly handled by the solution that Dudgeon was off to get married that day.'

'Nonsense,' said Alec. 'For one thing, Mrs Dudgeon was wrong about the office being shut on Monday. It was open. Two, she might have any number of other reasons for not wanting the police to go through her husband's belongings; a natural reticence and desire for privacy would be enough. Three, you don't know it was the marriage licence that was troubling her. You said you mentioned birth, marriage and passport. It could have been any of them.'

'Well, I wasn't really thinking when I said passport,' I said. 'I would doubt very much whether he had one. And it doesn't really matter that she was wrong about the office shutting, does it? It's the fact that she had an opinion on the matter at all that's interesting.'

We had arrived at the town hall steps where three little boys playing marbles on the memorial garden to the side were easily persuaded to look after Bunty for a penny each.

'Only don't try to ride on her back,' I said, not liking the way one of them was eyeing her up. His crestfallen look told me I had divined his intention correctly and I followed up my warning with a stern look before following Alec inside.

The records clerk was delighted to oblige us, happily lugging volumes of the old parish registers from some back premises and laying them reverently on the large table in the public consulting room.

'We have them all here,' he said. 'Much better really when you think of the damp in those church vestries. Some of the earlier ones are terribly spotted and foxed as it is, the years they mouldered there. Much better safe here with me.' There certainly was no chance of them growing damp now, I thought, unwinding my scarf and unbuttoning my cardigan even though they were only silk chiffon, for on this August morning the windows were clamped shut top and bottom and there was a roaring coal fire in the grate. The clerk himself seemed perfectly comfortable, though, in a suit and with a woollen jersey in lieu of a waistcoat. In fact his hand – slightly foxed and spotted itself – was cold when it brushed against mine. Alec shrugged off his own coat and loosened his tie as soon as the old man had left us.

'Phewf!' he said. 'I hope this isn't going to take too long, Dan. Where should we start? Any point looking at Friday?'

'No, of course not,' I told him. 'If I'm right about what Dudgeon was up to, he certainly wouldn't have done it here. He'd be away in Edinburgh somewhere where no one knew him. Now, I'd say he was about fifty, and let's say he would have married at about twenty, after the end of his apprenticeship, but certainly in time to have had a son who was old enough to go off to the war, more's the pity for them all. So let's start in '88 to be on the safe side.'

It was terribly slow going at first, partly because of the crabbed handwriting of the old parish minister and partly, in my case, because I kept being distracted by all the other entries. I found the death of several female de Cassilises – the records of the line dying out which led to Cad, Buttercup and hence me being here in the first place – and some of the names were highly diverting.

'Pantaloupe?' I said. 'Can anyone possibly have called their baby girl Pantaloupe? Isn't that a fruit of some exotic kind?'

'Cantaloupe, you're thinking of,' said Alec. 'And I rather think the child was Penelope. The loop of the f above is mixed up in it.'

'Of course,' I said. 'Well, that's good – they would have been bound to call her Panties at school, poor thing. Where are we now, darling?'

'1895,' said Alec. 'And there they are. 17th April 1895. Robert George Dudgeon born 1st June 1873, Carpenter, 2 New Cottages, Cassilis, Dalmeny to

Christina McLelland, spinster of this parish, born 8th May 1875, 17 Clark Place.'

'Hmph,' I said, staring at the entry. 'Well, then. Bang goes my brilliant idea.' I continued to turn the pages, searching the columns.

'What now?' said Alec.

'Nothing,' I said. 'Just looking. There he is. 21st June 1899. Robert George Dudgeon.'

'Doing what?' said Alec, looking over my shoulder.

'Being born,' I said. 'This is young Bobby.' I sighed and shut the book, just as the clerk came back to check on our progress.

'Can I get you anything else?' he asked, surprised to see us sitting back from the table with the volumes before us closed.

'Not today,' said Alec. 'But you've been most helpful.'

'There is one thing,' I said. I could hear barking and shrieks of laughter from outside and I knew I had better not leave Bunty much longer but I was still troubled.

The clerk was looking at me, eagerly helpful, with his hands pressed together.

'You were open for business yesterday, weren't you?' I said.

He gave a tight little sigh, almost a tut, of irritation.

'Yes, of course,' he said. 'I can't imagine where everyone is getting the idea that we weren't. You're the second person to ask, you know. Some foreign gentleman telephoned to the registrar himself and asked the same thing only days ago. I must make a sign for the window, but really I can't see how it came to be in question.'

I suppose one must have an orderly mind to be a good registrar's clerk and this wild rumour about odd days of holiday here and there was clearly upsetting him.

'The notion was that you'd stay open on the bank holiday to give people a chance to conduct their business and then you'd close the week after so that you could have a day off yourself,' I said. It did not go down at all well.

'I?' said the clerk. 'I? I've never agitated for "bank holidays". I can't imagine where you would have heard that.' He spoke as though I had accused him of joining the Workers' Union as a marching member, and I had to struggle to keep my mouth from curling up at the corners. 'And besides,' he went on, 'our business is not the kind that can be saved up for a holiday. What an idea!'

This made perfect sense, of course, and should have occurred to us earlier. We left him rather despondently and turned down towards the promenade to walk up and down and reconsider, while Bunty rushed at seagulls and chased after stray pieces of picnic litter left over from the weekend and the Fair.

'We're not getting anywhere very much, are we?' I said, leaning against the sea wall and watching the waves lap the rocks below. 'We still don't know who X is, or why he was necessary, or how Dudgeon died if it wasn't a heart attack. How I wish I'd asked Mrs Dudgeon about a flask, Alec.'

'A flask?'

'When Robert got back to the Rosebery Hall, you know. Whether he topped himself up with whisky.'

'It would take more than a flask,' said Alec. 'I'm no drinker, but even I could down a hip flask and come to no harm. If we're talking about enough to make the doctor believe that he'd been at it all day, we'd need to be looking at a bottle. A half-bottle at the very least. And don't be too hard on yourself, Dan. It was only yesterday we cracked the puzzle of the burrs after all.'

'But I know we're missing something about the

registry and the documents,' I said. 'I was sure we wouldn't find that marriage entry.'

'Well, there was no mistaking it,' said Alec. 'And it was right in the middle of the page, not even at the bottom where we could say it had been squeezed in by a master forger.'

'I know you're joking,' I said. 'But Mrs Dudgeon *was* out wandering in the night with a pen and ink, and we *did* ask ourselves what one could need to write that one couldn't write in the comfort of one's own bedroom.'

'Are you suggesting that she tramped all the way down here, and broke into the registry to tamper with an entry?' said Alec. 'I agree the pen and ink need to be explained, but I don't think that particular explanation is going to do the job.'

I was worrying at a piece of moss growing in the crack between two copestones on top of the wall, picking at it with the hard point at the tip of my glove where the seams met and then blowing the pieces away.

'Grant will scold you,' said Alec, mildly. I said nothing. 'Oh, come on, Dandy,' he went on. 'Give it up. It's not like you to hold on so obstinately to an idea just because it's your own.' I thought back to the newspapers of the evening before but forbore to mention them.

'Let's think about X instead,' I said.

The sea breeze was beginning to make my eyes water and I turned my back on the view and leaned against the wall facing McIver's Brae instead. A brewer's cart had drawn up at the awkward corner by Brown's Bar and the draymen, having thrown a stuffed sack to the ground, were expertly letting barrels fall on to it then bounce off towards the open hatch to the cellar. A sudden prickle ran down the back of my neck, more than could be explained by the wind ruffling my collar.

'Joey Brown!' I exclaimed. 'Alec, remember what I told you about when Joey Brown gave the Burry Man his dram? That was before we knew about X and we believed that she was just being a ninny. But now, thinking about it now, I don't think she *was* just spooked by the costume. I think she knew it wasn't him.'

'But if she noticed, wouldn't lots of other people?'

'No, darling. She was a close friend of the family. Her brother was the Dudgeon boy's lifelong chum and she was practically their daughter-in-law. And add to that the fact that she was frozen with terror and so probably looking much more closely at him than anyone else – you know the way your eyes are drawn to sights that terrify you. I was there. I saw her look at his hands and then look into his eyes and then shriek.'

'And then she told her father?' said Alec. He looked just as excited as I felt. 'And when Willie Brown came rushing out into the street with the glass of whisky it was to check the story out, or to see if he recognized who it was. Would that fit with how the scene played?'

I thought back to the curious little drama on the cobbles just along the road from where we now stood, and nodded.

'Yes, and what's more, I think that was why the Burry Man refused the glass and the proffered whisky was dashed to the ground. Shinie didn't really want to give the "cup o' kindness" to someone who had tricked him and X wasn't about to take it from someone who wasn't playing along. Oh, Shinie Brown and his whisky. It's all very torrid and heaving with significance, isn't it?'

'How d'you mean?' said Alec.

'I mean the bottle of Royal Highlander for his son really, I suppose,' I said. 'Haven't I told you about that?

I thought it was touching at first – he keeps a bottle of special malt in case of his son's miraculous return from the war – but now I'm beginning to find it a little strained, a little mawkish. There are things in life too solemn to be played out with whisky after all.'

'Spoken like a true cocktail drinker,' said Alec. 'And there's no such thing as Royal Highlander whisky, I'm sure.'

This was going a step too far.

'I may not like the stuff, Alec, but I do pay attention to details when I'm on a case and I tell you I saw it with my own eyes. Royal Highlander whisky, with a picture of a regimental piper on the label.'

'Are you sure you're not thinking of porridge oats?' said Alec, and then stepped smartly out of the way of my toe as I went to kick him.

'Positive,' I said. 'Pat Rearden told me all about it that day in Brown's Bar. Apparently it sits on the top shelf. Come on, I'll show you while we quiz Miss Brown.'

It was just on eleven and since today was a working day there was only one pair of old men to be scandalized by my entering the pub. Not even that, because when they turned to look as the door opened I recognized one of them as a neighbour from the crowd at Craw's Close on the night of the greasy pole.

'Grand day,' he said in greeting as we reached the bar and Alec rapped on the counter for service.

'A grand day to be bringing yer wife into a public bar at eleven o'clock in the forenoon,' said the other witheringly, which was a bit much since he was sitting there himself with a small glass of beer and an enormous whisky before him.

'I'm not his wife,' I said which, on reflection, was hardly helpful to my bid for respectability. My chum from Friday evening only laughed his wheezy laugh and told us to 'never mind Sandy'.

'Good morning, Miss Brown,' I said as that young lady appeared in response to Alec's knock.

'Madam,' said Joey Brown. 'Sir. What can I get you?'

'I'll have a large whisky,' said Alec. 'And the same for you, Dandy?'

'Is there any of the damson gin still on the go?' I asked. Joey Brown shook her head with her eyes wide and staring and the two old men at the end of the bar broke off their conversation and craned to look at me. I could feel two spots of colour begin on my cheeks and start to spread out across my neck in blotches. Was it really so shocking?

'Lemonade, then,' I muttered.

'Somebody's settled intae the Ferry awfy quick,' said the sour one of the old men half under his breath. Joey Brown poured some whisky for Alec and then reached a bottle of lemonade from under the counter, shook it violently and unstoppered it. I watched her as she poured it expertly into a glass, but I was aware of the tilt of Alec's chin out of the corner of my eye as he looked up and along the row of bottles on the top shelf.

'As I thought,' he said softly, 'no such thing.' I sighed extravagantly and looked up for myself, ready to enjoy the moment when I pointed out to him that there it was in plain view all the time. Macallan, Glenmorangie, Glenfiddich, Jura, Highland Park . . . I could not see it.

'Highland Park?' I said doubtfully.

'And the piper?' asked Alec. He was right, the picture on the Highland Park bottle was the usual one of an anonymous glen done in garish daubs.

'Miss Brown,' I said, taking a sip of the lemonade, which was delicious; sweet-tart and very cold, 'I hope you won't mind my mentioning it, but your father and I and Mr Rearden were chatting the other day – and

288

then I happened to tell Mr Osborne here – about the bottle of Royal Highlander.'

There was a sucking in of breath from one or both of the worthies at the end of the bar, and I supposed it was rather clod-hopping of me simply to launch in like that. Joey Brown said nothing but only stared at me with her customary terrified rabbit stare. One wondered how such a nervous, flustered type ever coped when the men were three deep at the counter and baying in slurred voices. (I remembered that when I had passed on Ferry Fair's Eve she had coped by turning her back on the crowds and cleaning behind the bar.)

'Your brother's whisky?' I said, trying to speak as gently as I could. 'The special bottle your father keeps for your brother? Only I can't see it now. Was it drunk? Please don't tell me someone stole it – I understand it was rather a special one. I do hope no one was so disrespectful as to . . .'

Joey Brown had been blinking faster and faster and rocking on her heels as I spoke, and at this point she broke away and fled into the back shop bumping hard off the door lintel and stumbling. I bit my lip and looked at Alec, horrified. The two old-timers were looking most uncomfortable.

'Ye're right enough, though, missus,' said the friendly one, after an awkward pause. 'Take a look, Sandy. It's away again.'

Sandy screwed up his face and squinted at the top shelf, then nodded.

'Ye're right,' he said. 'It used to sit in the middle there between the . . . Och, but they're a' jumbled up from Joey cleanin'.'

'Aye well,' said his friend. 'It's for the best, doubtless, don't you think?'

'I do indeed,' I said to him. 'Although one can hardly

imagine how much it must hurt his father to give up after all this time.'

'He tried before, ye ken,' said Sandy. 'Took the bottle away without a word. This was years back. Four or five years now.'

'Four, it'll be, Sandy,' said the other. 'I mind it was just about a year after the end o' it all. The bottle was gone and then it was back again. Mebbes this time, though, eh?'

'Perhaps,' said Alec. 'Although Miss Joey still seems considerably upset.' There was still neither sight nor sound of Joey Brown returning.

'I'd better go after her,' I said. 'Since it was me who put my foot in it. I can't just leave her to weep.'

Alec gave me a shrewd look and I knew what he was thinking. Part of me wanted to comfort Joey, it was true, but there was another part of me which knew if I comforted her into a proper lull I could then ask some questions with a hope of a plain answer. Hardly something to be proud of but there it was. Alec lifted the wooden flap of the bar and I stepped behind and through the doorway to the passage.

There was no sign of the girl in the back kitchen or in the passageway where I threaded my way along beside crates of empties and boxes tied shut with twine, but a door at the end was ajar. I knocked softly and pushed it open a little more.

'Miss Brown?' I called. There was no answer. I was at the head of a set of stairs leading down and although the steps themselves were in darkness there was a suggestion of a light on somewhere below. I began to feel my way down carefully. Five days at Cassilis Castle had fitted me well to tackle strange stairways in the dark and these were wooden and straight; I reached the bottom without mishap and set off towards the light, passing various dungeons where barrels rested and pipes gurgled. I knocked again on the door with the light behind it and then went in.

It was a large, square cellar with a door open to the back yard. Shinie Brown was in there, standing in the middle of the floor with a polishing cloth in one hand and an empty bottle in the other looking between me and the corner of the room, frozen in astonishment. I followed his gaze and there sat Joey huddled on a brick ledge in the wall, half-hidden by the wash copper, as though trying to stay warm.

'I'm so sorry to be barging about like this,' I said, dividing the apology between the father and daughter, 'but I've upset you, Miss Brown, and I wanted to come to apologize.'

'I broke it,' said Joey Brown. It took me a couple of minutes to understand her meaning.

'I broke it when I was cleaning, Burry Man's night,' she said. She threw a terrified glance towards her father as she said this, and I looked too, hoping that he was not going to fly into a rage with her and force me to leap in to her defence. He was still staring at me, however, an amused glint beginning to mingle with the amazement in his eyes. Eventually he turned towards the girl and spoke.

'That's right, lass,' he said. He went over towards Joey and drew her away from the corner, tidying up as he did so, shifting the lid of the copper into place and tucking the hose pipes in neatly underneath it out of the way. If Joey was halfway through a wash she seemed to have forgotten it, and she followed her father meekly out into the centre of the room.

'It's time to put that behind us,' he said. 'I could never have taken it doon myself and got rid o' it, madam, but when Joey here said tae me she'd broke it, I found I wisnae angered nor sad, I was jist relieved. It's time tae put a' that ahint us.'

Joey Brown seemed to take no comfort from any of this, however, but searched her father's face as though he spoke in some code she could not decipher.

'I'll take you back upstairs,' I said. I was sure being down here among the fumes of this noxious chamber could not be good for her, upset as she was. 'I'm sorry to have disturbed you, Mr Brown,' I said. 'I can see you're busy.'

Shinie Brown shrugged with a gesture of great magnanimity and again the look of amusement danced in his eyes. I could see that I must be a ridiculous figure to him, bumbling around, no sense at all of how to behave, and I was glad to draw Joey Brown's arm into mine and lead her away.

'I found out about Bobby Dudgeon and you,' I told her as we mounted the dark stairs again, 'since we spoke last, and I wanted to say how sorry I was. I understand now why you were so very upset at Mr Dudgeon's death.' We edged our way back along the passageway and into the kitchen, where Joey Brown turned to face me.

'I don't know what you mean, madam,' she said.

'I mean I know you were engaged,' I said, thinking how very childlike she seemed with her blanket denials, like a toddler standing over the bits of a broken vase insisting she never touched it.

'I never said that,' she whispered, glancing back the way we had come as though frightened her father would hear.

'Mrs Dudgeon's sisters told me,' I said to her. 'I know it wasn't universally welcomed. I'm so sorry.'

'I don't know who you're talking about, madam,' said Joey, the toddler and the broken vase going strong.

'But you've obviously been a great comfort to his parents,' I said. 'And now to his mother alone. You've been a good girl.'

'I don't . . . I don't . . .' said Joey, but her voice quavered and failed.

I hated myself for it, but we were right here, just the two of us, face to face, and I might never get another chance to ask. Alec and I were getting nowhere with the case, I thought, and surely if someone was in a position to help I had to swallow my scruples and plunge in.

'I know you must have spent some considerable time with the Dudgeons, Joey,' I said. 'Long enough to know that it wasn't Robert Dudgeon in the burry suit on Friday, when you looked at his hands, was it? Or when you looked into his eyes?'

She was shaking her head, quickly enough to make herself dizzy I thought, and I put out a hand to try to calm her.

'Inspector Cruickshank knows,' I said. 'But he doesn't know who it was in there or why they swapped.'

'I don't know what you're talking about,' said Joey.

'So if you recognized who it was as well as who it wasn't,' I said, 'it's your duty to tell the police.'

'I don't know what you mean,' she said again and I gave up.

'It's absolutely infuriating,' I said to Alec as we left the bar minutes later. 'Just saying: I don't know what you mean, I don't understand, I don't know who that is. I mean – I said, "Mrs Dudgeon's sisters" and she said, "I don't know who you're talking about." Ridiculous girl. She didn't quite have the gall to claim no knowledge of the Dudgeons themselves and she let a reference to Inspector Cruickshank go past without wondering aloud who *he* was, but apart from that it was a perfect festival of denial.'

'It seems a remarkably effective strategy,' said Alec. 'It got rid of you.'

'Hmph,' I said, almost jollied out of my temper by his tone. 'Well, I'm glad she has to live in a smelly pub and do her laundry in a beer cellar full of fumes. I've no patience with the girl, Alec, none.'

'And does your impatience extend to going along to the police station and telling tales on her?' asked Alec.

'Absolutely it does,' I said. 'At least, I'll ask whether they've got anywhere themselves with the identity of X, but if not then certainly I'll tell them I think Joey Brown has an idea, and possibly Shinie Brown too. Or you tell them, Alec. After our experiences with the inspector I think perhaps the information would carry more weight coming from you. And I'll wait outside and make daisy chains.'

It was just as well that he had teased me back into humour in this way and that we had elected to play by the inspector's rules and let Alec do all the talking; if I had stood outside the police station boiling with impotent rage or if Alec had stood there fussing with his pipe while I went in to report or if we had both gone in and bearded the sergeant together, we might never have solved the case at all.

As it was, Alec entered the inner sanctum alone and I sat placidly outside on the wall, perusing the notice-boards. There was one official one with close-typed signs regarding licensing hours and motor car lights, names and telephone numbers and office hours for all the officials one could ever need in a long lifetime, notices regarding customs and excise, immigration and emigration, emergency procedures for fire, flood and power failure; all very dull. As well as this, though, there was another much more interesting noticeboard where the less official, more home-made signs could be found: a lost cat with a red collar and a bounty of two shillings on its head; a found headscarf 'real silk, pattern of horseshoes, rather stained and mended' which I doubted, after that description, anyone would have the courage to claim, real silk or no. There also were the new Fair notices, one proclaiming the grand total of the police station's collection in aid of the Ferry Fair fund – £7 10s 3d – and a list of winners of the Fair events, including, I was proud to note, the name of Doreen Urquhart opposite the new high chair and the towel bale donated by the Co-operative Store Drapers.

Alec was taking his time and soon I had enjoyed all that there was to enjoy of the human side of the noticeboard and was back with the regulations and procedures. I noticed that the library hours seemed especially designed to prevent anyone from ever being able to borrow a book without taking a day off work or school to do so, and that the rules about how long a catch could stay harbour-side and in what kind of container at what times on what days seemed to be a signal to the fishermen to have a taxi waiting as they moored so that they could throw each fish into the back seat without its scales ever touching the ground.

And then I saw it.

Almost as soon as my eyes had registered what I was seeing, or my brain had heard what the voice in my head was reading, the door of the station opened and Alec was at my side.

'What is it?' he said. Goodness only knows what expression I must have had on my face.

'Look,' I said, putting a finger on the notice. He bent close to read the small and rather smudged black type.

'". . . will remain open on all bank holidays between the hours of ten o'clock and three, and on all local holidays between the hours of nine o'clock and five, and will close in lieu upon the following Monday except where . . ."' He shifted my finger off the paper where it was hiding the print underneath, and said: 'Passports.'

'Passports,' I said. 'Edinburgh and Leith Emigration Agents. Passports, ticketing, travel documents prepared.' My mind was racing, or not so much racing, nothing so linear as racing, more as though my thoughts were schoolchildren who had been inside all morning while the snow fell and were now released to gather it up, roll it together and throw it all around. 'He was getting a passport. He was going to run away.'

'From what?' said Alec.

'Or not run away,' I corrected. 'But he was going to leave. They both were, on the quiet, for some reason, and on Thursday afternoon Mrs Dudgeon saw this sign, read that the office was closed on Monday and – look here – it's closed every Saturday and on Sunday, obviously, and so Friday – the Burry Man's day – was the only chance.'

'Why not Tuesday?' said Alec. 'Or some other day? And where were they going? And why?'

'I have no idea why,' I said. 'But where, I think I can hazard a guess. At least there's a possibility that also explains why a later day was no good. There was a ship leaving Leith on Tuesday bound for New Zealand. I read about it when we were going through the papers last night. He would need to get the passport before the ticket and the tickets were on sale on Friday. Alec, this must be right. Remember I said Chrissie Dudgeon was so very keyed up, looking at the clock, looking at the door and then suddenly she just seemed to relax for no reason? It was around ten o'clock last night and I'll bet my eyes that she was sitting there watching the clock tick round to the moment of sailing, thinking about the plan and about how if she had the nerve she could still go, alone, if she dared. Then all of a sudden it was too late; she hadn't gone. The chance had passed and it was almost like a relief to her. Terribly sad, but a relief.'

'That doesn't make any sense,' said Alec. 'She couldn't have got there in time without a magic carpet and she would have had to go through customs and everything.'

'I didn't mean literally,' I said. 'You can be very prosaic sometimes, darling. I meant that she sat there while the other path of her life was being bricked up – Oh, don't look at me like that, you know I'm right. And it also explains why she was so worried about the police going through Robert's things. She was frightened they would find the passport and the tickets and begin to wonder what was going on.'

'As am I,' said Alec. 'What on earth would make them suddenly up sticks to New Zealand without telling anyone?'

'Once again we come up against my conviction of the Dudgeons' basic honesty. The only likely reasons in general don't seem at all likely for them.'

'No matter,' said Alec. 'We don't have to offer a motive. We can check the facts with the greatest of ease.'

'The passport office would never let us trawl through the records,' I told him. 'And aren't these emigration agents a rather shady bunch? Oughtn't we to hand it over to the police?'

'Not the passport office, Dandy,' said Alec and, seeing my puzzled glance, he rolled his eyes. 'There really should be a basic training course,' he said, 'for all budding detectives. We can go to Leith to the shipping line and look at the passenger lists. Or rather look at the ticket-booking receipts. They won't be on the passenger lists, of course, since they didn't go. Some pair of lucky adventurers waiting on the quayside on the chance of a space will have got a windfall on Tuesday night, Dan.'

'Just imagine,' I said. 'Imagine bundling up all one's belongings and going to wait, not knowing whether one is off to the other side of the world for ever or whether one will be trailing the same bundle back through the dark streets to more of the same.'

'Yes, said Alec. 'Just imagine. But walk quickly while you're at it, won't you? And you drive, darling. I've never been to Leith.'

I had never been to Leith either, or at least as I pointed out to Alec not to the docks, but I knew where it was and I navigated us there safely along the coast roads through Cramond and Granton and Trinity, braking and surging around the narrow twists and doglegs of the village streets, weaving through crowds of herring wives and, as we drew near the port, rather wobbly sailors newly released on leave. I remembered the name of the shipping company from my daydreaming over the steerage notice in the library last night and we were helpfully directed to their offices by a nautical-looking chap standing on fairly steady legs on the corner of Great Junction Street, whose accent was so much gibberish to me but in which Alec recognized the music of Dorset and of home. We wasted a good few minutes while the two of them reminisced about 'The Bay', but at last Alec dragged himself away again.

'I miss these old Dorset boys,' he said. 'And the sea. Perthshire is delightful, of course, but when one has been brought up in sound of the sea it is a wrench to leave it. It must have been something fairly cataclysmic, I imagine, to drag Chrissie and Robert Dudgeon so far from the many bosoms of their families.'

'Although New Zealand is not short of sea at least,'

298

I pointed out. 'On maps it looks as though the tide might wash right over it at the height of springs, although I daresay that's scale. Number fifteen, you said? Here we are.'

Brunwick, Allanson, the shipping line, had offices which struck a balance between the sepulchral dignity of a private bank and the rather more rakish atmosphere of a merchantman's bridge during a party. There were a good many clerks flitting about in shades of grey but the panelled rooms were festooned with outdated nautical equipment of a semi-decorative sort and a few rather salty characters could be seen here and there through open doors. Above everything a mixture of lemon wax and pipe smoke gave a spice to the air that no bank ever had.

The desk clerk could not have been more helpful, but it soon became apparent that we were asking the most awkward of questions possible, inquiring about the passengers on a ship which had only left port the day before; in fact, the staff of the office were still referring to the departure time in hours of the nautical clock and would not, we were informed, begin to use the calendar date until the following morning when twenty-four hours had passed and the ship itself had docked and de-docked from the next port of call which was Plymouth.

'If you wanted to see the passenger lists from last year, now,' said the clerk, gesturing behind him at a wall of bound volumes with dates stamped in gold on their spines, 'or ten years ago or even fifty, that would be the work of a moment with the help of a strong lad to lift down the book for you. But yesterday?' He blew out his breath in a tootling little tune and shook his head. 'And you're not asking in an official capacity?'

'We're not,' I told him, 'but depending on what we find, someone soon might be. It's best to be honest,'

I said, turning to where I could see Alec squirming beside me; clearly thinking we should have played our cards a little closer to our chests than this, fearful that the clerk would shut like an oyster at the hint of trouble.

The man merely shrugged and scratched at his chin, however.

'We've nothing to worry about here at Brunwick, Allanson,' he said. 'We don't have much to do with agents, and it's not like the old days when we were our own excise men and our own policemen too. I've been forty years with the firm, you know, madam, and it's changed.' He settled his elbows on his counter and seemed disposed to launch into a tale. Perhaps even a clerk picks up the habits of sailors after forty years. 'It was like the Wild West in the old Queen's day,' he went on, 'before these picture passports and all the regulations. Well, that was the war, was that. There had to be some kind of a clampdown for wartime. Then it never really changed back and I don't suppose it ever will now. So it's up to the passport office these days to verify identities and make sure that all's in order. At the quayside, as long as they turn up with a ticket and passport and are sober enough to say their names and walk aboard, we check them off on our boarding list and wave them through.'

'Well, we don't think these particular passengers did turn up, sober or not,' said Alec, 'but they certainly got a passport and we would make a large bet with our own money that they bought tickets too. Steerage tickets. On Friday.'

'Steerage?' said the clerk. 'On Friday?' I suspected that he might ring to have us removed on finding out that our interest was in something so lowly as a steerage ticket, but I could not have been more wrong. 'In that case . . . and if you only want to see the ticket

300

receipts themselves . . . that does help a little. They're in date order – roughly – until we can cross-check the final lists and then we keep them all until the year end and send them to the bindery. But if you know it's Friday and you don't mind looking yourselves . . .'

We assured him that we did not, and although he huffed a little more about the slight irregularity and had to talk himself into it, telling us (as if we did not know) that these were public documents after all and that we were doing no harm, then he muttered for a moment about the Empire and the war and asked himself what the point was of fighting it if we were not now able to live free lives under His Majesty and, eventually, he left to fetch them.

The current records might be what passed for an unholy mess in the clerk's opinion – he said as much with a great many apologies as he returned – but when one has recently gone through two sacks of burdock seeds with a garnish of horse-dung a box file full of papers can hold no fears and they were, as he said, in roughly date order. I untied the tape holding the file shut and the side dropped down. The early-booked, first class and cabin class tickets on the bottom were stacked in a neat-edged pile but as we got nearer the top towards the last-minute steerage bookings the receipts took on the dishevelled and scraped-together look one could imagine of the passengers themselves. I wriggled a finger into the stack just where the neatness stopped and the crumple began and heaved the top lot out.

'Last Tuesday,' I said, reading off the bottom chit, and I began to flick through them until I had isolated the fat bundle for Friday. I halved these and pushed Alec's portion towards him.

Starting at a steady pace, I worked through my bundle, distraction always threatening – it was of some interest to see how many single men, how many young couples, and how surprisingly many huge families of children had set out on this trip – but as I pondered them I became aware of Alec whipping through his pile, snapping each receipt off the top, no more than glancing at it, and smacking it face-down on the growing stack at his other side. Almost automatically, I began to speed up too; I knew what he was up to. He wanted to be the one who found the prize and, in case he did not have it in front of him, he was ripping through his portion planning to take what was left of mine too. Having two sons for whom small daily bouts of competition were as necessary and as much relished as their four square meals, I recognized this immediately, ludicrous as it might appear, and being only human myself I did feel a pang of irritation when he spoke up.

'Got it,' he said. 'Robert George Dudgeon, Cassilis, South Queensferry. One-way, steerage class, paid cash in full.'

'And?' I said.

'And nothing,' said Alec. 'What do you mean?'

'Just him?' I said. 'No Mrs Dudgeon? Let me see that.' I snatched the receipt from him and looked for myself.

'Would she be mentioned separately if she was on his passport?' said Alec.

'Absolutely she would be,' I said. 'Look at this: Bernard Lessom, Mrs Lessom, and all the little Lessoms down to Margaret Ann 15th May 1923 – imagine setting off with a babe in arms. Alec, if Chrissie Dudgeon was ever planning to go her name would be here.'

We sat for a minute drilling looks at the scrap of paper as though it could possibly have more to tell us, then Alec spoke at last.

'So he was going to leave her, then.'

'And she murdered him?' I said. 'Impossible. And

anyway, she was in on the whole thing. Driving the cart, hiding the burrs. She wouldn't collaborate in her own abandonment.'

'Well, perhaps the plan was that they were both going and he double-crossed her. She found out and she murdered him for that.'

'I don't like the way this murder keeps blinking on and off like a faulty lamp whenever it suits us,' I said. 'We've been very remiss about tracking down these loose ends, you know. *If* Robert didn't drink enough whisky to explain his death, but he *did* drink some at least, *and* he took some poison such as the mushroom, which *wouldn't* show up on a post-mortem examination . . . those are a great many things to assume.'

'Let's start at the beginning,' said Alec. 'We need to find out whether he downed a whole bottle in the changing room at the Rosebery Hall. If he didn't then we know at least that there's a case to answer.'

'Unless it was a heart attack,' I said, dispirited even though I knew it was wicked to be dispirited at the idea of a natural death instead of murder.

'Which would be a monstrous coincidence,' said Alec. 'Now, who do we ask about the whisky?'

'Pat Rearden, I suppose,' I said. 'He was there in the disrobing room at the end of the day. But I'd like to start by asking Mrs Dudgeon. I don't expect she'll tell us straight but I want to see her reaction to the question. Let's go.'

Chapter Sixteen

'Oh Lord,' I said, as I swung the motor car into the mouth of the lane and saw the swarm of red bobbing around against the tree trunks. 'We could have done without them.'

I honked my horn and the red disappeared as five of the little Dudgeons turned to see where the noise had come from. They misinterpreted the signal though and came whooping and galloping towards us, thinking they had been summoned. The first to arrive clambered up on to the running board and hung their arms over the open windows with not a thought to my paintwork and the others jostling from the back and shoving against their siblings hardly helped.

'Now, now, be careful,' I said, but my voice was drowned in the hubbub.

'. . . another hurl in yer car, missus.'

'. . . huvnae been in the front seat yet and Lila's been twice.'

'. . . on a picnic and take us wi' ye, missus.'

This last request was so bold and so untempting that I could not help but laugh.

'It's good to see you all out playing in the sunshine again,' I said. 'No more demons and ghosties?'

'Naw,' said the boy I thought was Randall. 'They're away somewhere else.'

'Aye, and Auntie Chrissie did her exercises,' said Lila. 'And they cannae come back.'

'Well, isn't that splendid,' said Alec, after rolling his eyes at me. 'You're free to roam in perfect safety then. Excellent.'

'Aye, as long as we stay oot o' they shell holes,' said a small boy.

'Of course,' I agreed. 'It's never a good idea to go falling down holes, nor to shove your little sister down there, boys. Remember that.'

'Well, we wouldnae fa' cos there's ladders,' said Randall. 'But we're no goin' doon the ladders cos there's ghosties *there* for sure.'

My shoulders sank but Alec only threw back his head and laughed, telling them to get off the boards and let us proceed or there would be the ghosts of five squashed children in the woods. They were obviously rather taken with this idea and they fell away writhing on the ground as though shot and beginning already to emit their ghostly moans.

'Unspeakable, aren't they?' Alec said as we rolled forward. 'Do you think Chrissie Dudgeon really performed an exorcism?'

'Hardly,' I said. 'Perhaps she went out with a broom and shouted "Shoo!" to humour them, but the "exercises" must have got into their heads from elsewhere. Rather nasty when it gets as serious as that.'

Mrs Dudgeon was alone when we reached the cottage, and the relief on her face when she opened the door and saw it was us told me that she had not yet had her visit from Inspector Cruickshank.

'It's only me,' I assured her and she smiled before glancing at Alec.

'I'll wait out here,' he said tactfully, patting his pockets in search of his pipe. This had not been agreed but I saw immediately that it was best and I followed Mrs Dudgeon inside.

'How are you?' I asked her as we sat, although I winced as I said it. How could she be anything but utterly wretched after all? When I looked closely, however, I was surprised to see that she looked rather better than I had ever seen her before, calmer and more rested, although admittedly with the unmistakable tug of bottomless sadness behind her eyes.

'I'm no' so bad,' she said, perfectly summing up in these few words what showed in her face. 'Thank ye kindly, madam, for comin' and askin'.'

I squirmed a little at that. Not to say that I should not have visited again with simple condolences – it was obvious that Buttercup did not count these attentions among her duties – but my purpose was far from kind, however one viewed it. Even justice, if I dared cast my current pursuit in that light, was far from compassionate and tended to dole out its rewards and punishments more ruthlessly than I could, if it were ever left to me.

'I need to ask you a question,' I said. 'Two questions actually.' For I had thought of another; even less likely to get a straight answer but worthy of the airing nonetheless.

'I wish to goodness ye'd –' she said, but she bit it off.

'On Friday evening,' I went on as though she had not spoken, 'when your husband returned to the Rosebery Hall, did he drink anything? Any whisky?'

She studied me for a moment before answering. I could practically hear the thoughts whirring, engaging and disengaging, as she decided how best to answer. Eventually she lifted her hands and let them fall into her lap with a soft clap.

'A tate fae his flask,' she said, and the defeat in her voice told me that she had given up trying to work out what I was up to and had simply answered me.

'A slug of whisky from his hip flask?' I said.

She nodded. 'More than a slug, really. A good swallow, like. It wis full and he more or less drained it. Does that tell ye what ye want tae ken?' She spoke as though I had beaten this out of her.

'And is the flask of the usual sort of size?' I asked.

She stood and went to the sideboard drawer, where she found it instantly. Of course she did, since it must have been in her husband's pocket until the last few days and she must only just have decided where to keep it now, or where to store it while she decided whether to keep it at all. She passed it to me and I felt the weight of it in my hand, an everyday little flask, made of pewter, the size of my palm. There was no way the contents of this could kill a drinking man. I unscrewed the cap and sniffed it, jerking my head back sharply at the hated, half-familiar, fruity stink. Then I locked eyes again with Mrs Dudgeon. I was sure she was telling me the truth about this, and that sealed her innocence as far as I was concerned

'I think your husband was murdered,' I said, not even trying to dress it up or soften it in any way.

She shook her head, vehemently, blood instantly draining. 'The doctor said himself it wis his heart. You were the one that told me.'

'But that's when he thought that Robert had been drinking whisky all the day long,' I told her. 'He knew – or thought he did – about the Burry Man's day, he found some whisky still to be absorbed and he put the two together and concluded that there was enough whisky there to put a strain on Robert's heart. But there wasn't, was there, Mrs Dudgeon? And he didn't have a weak heart, did he?' She was shaking her head, looking defeated again, and numb with sorrow.

'Don't you want to find out who killed him?' I asked her. Again she shook her head.

'Yer a wummin yersel', are ye no'?' she said, looking at me searchingly. 'A wife and a mither o' bairns?' I nodded. 'Can ye no' jist leave it be?' she asked. 'Can ye no' for the love of God jist leave it?'

I was more puzzled than ever. What woman would not want the murder of her husband to be investigated? What woman in the world would not want her husband's killer to be caught? What did she mean?

'I can't leave it, Mrs Dudgeon,' I said. 'But I promise that I'll do my best to keep your private business private.'

She looked at me very shrewdly, almost amused, and said to me: 'I'd doubt that, madam. If ye kent whit it wis. I doubt you'd do that.'

'Two more questions,' I told her. 'You don't have to answer but I need to ask. First, what were you doing that night, with the pen and ink?' She shook her head and gave a short, bleak laugh.

'Nothin',' she said. 'Runnin' roun' the woods like a daftie.'

'Very well,' I said. 'I'm not going to press you. And now this is my last question, I promise. Do you know why, can you tell me why, Robert was going to leave you?' Her look of incomprehension was quite genuine, I was sure. 'I know about the ticket,' I told her, 'I know it was for your husband alone.' It took a moment or two for her to understand what I meant and then there was no flush of annoyance or shame, only a tired shake of the head to brush the silliness out of her way.

'I will find out in the end,' I said. 'I must.'

'Well, if you must you must,' she said, her tone almost mocking. 'But it's no matter to me, madam. It's no matter at all now.'

I recounted all of this to Alec as we made our way home, trying to give him a flavour of her mood, her strange serenity, even though there was nothing very concrete to which I could pin it.

'It could just be grief,' he said, showing me that I had failed. 'Or maybe she finally got the doctor to prescribe a little something as her sisters were pressing her to do. Very frustrating for us, obviously, but the police will be able to make her talk. So it will come out in the end even if we don't have the satisfaction of getting our questions answered.'

'It was just one question she wouldn't answer,' I said. 'About the pen and the ink. She was perfectly honest about the hip flask, I'm sure, and her face answered me more plainly than any words could have on the point of Robert leaving her. Whatever he was up to it wasn't that.'

'It must have been,' said Alec. 'Nothing else makes sense. Her face must just be better suited for poker than you're giving it credit for. What about X?'

'X?' I said. 'X leaving her? I'm not with you, darling.'

'I mean did you ask Mrs Dudgeon about X? Did you ask her who he was? If anyone's in a position to verify his identity, it must be her. He was in the cart with her.'

I groaned. Somehow, unbelievably, I had forgotten to ask a single thing about that. So there was another question we needed to hand over to Inspector Cruickshank. Unless . . . I took my foot off the accelerator pedal and the car began to slow gently in the soft dirt of the lane. It was not possible, surely, for all of these

309

questions to be unrelated. X, the ticket to New Zealand, and the pen and ink all had to be connected somehow, and thanks to something that Alec had just that moment said, something which found an echo in my memory, I began to see what it was.

'In a position to verify his identity,' I said.

'Oh Lord,' said Alec. 'Did I really just say that? Forgive me. Detecting is one thing, Dan, but please stop me if I start to speak like a newly promoted sergeant with his own bicycle and bell.'

'It was the chap at Brunwick, Allanson you were quoting,' I told him. 'Not that he's much of a role model either.' The motor car had ground to a complete halt now and I disengaged the gear and turned to face him.

'Listen to this,' I said. 'What if the ticket wasn't for Robert Dudgeon at all. What if it was for X. X needed to get away – not the Dudgeons, not Robert – they were just the go-betweens. Perhaps X had a criminal record and would set off alarms if he bought a ticket with his own passport. So Robert planned to do it for him, only when the news broke about the passport office being closed and they realized the clash with the Burry Man it looked as though they were scuppered. Then they had the idea that while Robert was standing in for X, X could stand in for him.

'Afterwards they were supposed to give him the ticket, in plenty of time for the departure on Tuesday evening, but Robert Dudgeon died and all the paperwork he had on him was stuck in the mortuary. Absolute panic stations. And even when the body and all his belongings were returned, the house was overrun with sisters and X couldn't get near.'

'And the pen and ink?' said Alec.

'Was to doctor the ticket,' I said feeling triumphant. 'To change it from one name – Dudgeon's – to another

– X's. Only once again, Donald was sitting with the body and one or another of the sisters was sitting with the widow and the day was approaching ever closer. Hence Mrs Dudgeon out wandering in the woods trying to furnish X with what he needed to do the job himself. And hence also her extreme agitation as ten o'clock rolled around on Tuesday night. If X was caught, she would be tried for fraud, or for something anyway, but once he was off British soil and away she was safe.'

'There's something in that,' said Alec. 'It's not perfect but . . .'

'In what way isn't it?' I demanded. 'It could even explain how Dudgeon died. X killed him. X didn't trust Dudgeon not to go to the police and confess before X had a chance to get away, and so he killed him. In what way is this not the perfect solution?'

'Well, doctoring the ticket, for one thing,' said Alec.

'The clerk said that as long as they turn up sober –'

'As long as they turn up with a passport and ticket and sober,' Alec said. 'But I'm sure that if the name on the ticket were scratched out and another one scrawled underneath they would have something to say about it.'

'Well, then, maybe there aren't names on the ticket,' I said.

'Then what would X need the ink for?' said Alec, which was a very good point. 'And why would the Dudgeons do this? It must be illegal in some way although I don't know the name of the crime. Why would they take the risk?'

'For money?' I said. 'If X were paying them? Or threatening them. They might do it out of fear, under duress.'

'Also,' said Alec, 'I don't really see why Mrs Dudgeon would be in a state about registering Robert's death if what you're saying now is the answer to the riddle. By Sunday night she had all of his papers back, didn't she? What was the difficulty?'

I rubbed my nose, trying to think of an answer. There was none as far as I could see, but I was still sure I had hit on something.

'Perhaps just my saying "birth certificate and passport" together like that when they were so very much in the front of her mind? I don't know.' I looked at my watch. 'But I wonder if there's time to telephone to Brunwick, Allanson and offer that clerk enormous bribes to let us go in and look through the passenger lists, try to match them up. If we find a name on the passenger list that doesn't appear on the ticket receipts, that, my darling, will be X.'

'So it will,' said Alec. 'Well, get a move on then, it's nearly five.'

The clerk did us even better than that, though. When we had been put through to his office by the girl on the main switchboard, far from having to bribe him with favours, he sounded tremendously pleased to hear from us and launched in right away.

'I took to heart what you said, sir,' he began. Alec was talking and we were sharing the earpiece, huddled with heads together making what Nanny Palmer used to call, with a shudder, nit bridges. 'About there being official persons coming to sniff around after you had gone. I didn't want Brunwick's to look bad in their eyes, so I've spent the entire afternoon since you left making up the final lists. Lord, you want to hear those lady clerks grumbling about being put to the trouble, as though they're not paid a perfectly good wage for *taking* the trouble. It's not like the old days. Anyway,

312

sir, I'm happy to report that there were no irregularities, none at all, so there's a load off your mind.'

'Ask him –' I began in a whisper, but Alec was ahead of me this time.

'Did you happen, I mean is it possible – do you cross-reference the last-minute stand-ins in any way? Is it possible to lay one's hands on them without cross-checking the whole list?'

'The last-minute stand-ins, sir?' said the clerk. 'I'm sure I don't know what you mean.'

'Well, no,' said Alec. 'I daresay that's not what you call them. I mean people who come along having bought a ticket at second-hand or who come along and wait in hopes of a berth becoming available. If it were the theatre we'd call them returns.'

The clerk spluttered, scandalized.

'There would never, never be anything like that on a Brunwick's ship. Stowaways, sir? Not nowadays, anyway. Different in the old days before the war, of course. Then you would have whole families turning up on the off-chance, to be sure, but not now. Every ticket has the name of the passport holder on it and both are checked at boarding and that's what I'm saying. There were no irregularities at all.'

Alec, for all his quibbling earlier, looked quite as disappointed as I felt to have our latest theory scuppered in this way.

'So,' he said, 'how many vacant places were there? In total? How many no-shows?'

'None,' cried the clerk. 'As I'm saying to you, no irregularities at all. A perfectly orderly, smooth departure. We don't send lady clerks to the boarding desk, you know.'

Alec and I pulled faces at each other and tried not to laugh. Despite our personal setback it was rather entertaining to hear this poor man talking himself into such

313

a hole. It was beginning to look likely that there was the most glaring irregularity possible right there under his nose.

'I wonder,' said Alec, 'since you've worked so hard to get the lists ready, is it possible to double-check on a particular entry? Are they accessible? Would it take long?'

'They're right here in front of me,' said the clerk and we could hear the thump of him patting something with the flat of his hand. 'What is the name of the passenger you're interested in?'

'Robert George Dudgeon,' said Alec, and immediately we could hear a furious fluttering and snapping of pages at the other end of the line.

'Robert George Dudgeon,' said the clerk. 'He'll be rounding the Cape to Portugal now, sir, and his ears will be burning. Robert George Dudgeon. Here he is. Robert George Dudgeon, 1st June 1899, Cassilis, Dalmeny. Boarded the ship at nine-oh-five pip emma, rather late but we won't hold that against him. Anything else I can help you with, sir?'

Alec assured him that there was not and rang off.

'So much for their marvellous system,' he said. 'I wonder if they'll ever find out that he's not there.'

'I blame the lady clerks, naturally,' I said. 'Odd though, that they should have a time of boarding and everything, wasn't it?'

'Remind me never to sail with Brunwick, Allanson,' said Alec and he dropped into a cruelly accurate approximation of the clerk's voice. '"Lifeboats, sir? Oh plenty. I have the list right here. No irregularities at all with the lifeboats, sir."'

'Well, shall we call the inspector now, or leave it until tomorrow?' I said. 'I'm for leaving it, I must say, sleep on it all and see if we can make something a bit more consistent out of it tomorrow morning. At the moment it's a dreadful lot of scraps and rags. X planned to leave but the plan fell through and we don't know who he is or why he had to flee or why the Dudgeons helped him. And Robert died in the middle of it all for no particular reason.'

At that moment, as though to stop us worrying away at it any longer, we heard Cad hailing us from the bottom of the stairs – 'Dandee? Alec? Tea!' – and we both burst into fits of uncontrollable giggles.

'Poor Cad!' I managed to say finally. 'Can't you take him aside and tell him man-to-man, Alec?'

'Tell him what, though?' said Alec.

'Well, for a start, not to halloo up the stairs like a nursery governess to tell guests that it's teatime,' I said.

'But that would only teach him that one thing,' said Alec, 'and there's no knowing what he'll do next. If there were some general rule from which all behaviours could be deduced, I'd happily tell him what it was.'

'Well, it's getting desperate,' I said. 'Even Buttercup was laughing at him yesterday. He came through the yard at the other house and some of the laundry had blown out of its pegs in the breeze, so he picked it up and began to rehang it, then realizing that it was dry he took it all down instead and set off into the kitchens with the basket looking for someone to give it to. He is a love, actually,' I concluded. 'Even if you do work out the general rule don't tell him, Alec. I've changed my mind.'

'Not much chance of it,' said Alec, glumly. 'At least, I don't seem in danger of stumbling over any organizing principles as a detective's assistant, so I don't suppose I'm suddenly going to see the light as a . . .'

'Husband-trainer?' I suggested. 'But I think you can give yourself the title of detective, don't you? Under-detective, anyway. I don't think of you as an assistant.'

It gave me pause, if I am honest, to hear that he did. Or rather, to extrapolate from that point to the fact that as far as Alec was concerned I was the boss. I was in charge. I was not altogether sure that I liked the idea either. I had certainly had one or two flashes of inspiration in the last few days and if I were being kind to myself I should say I was bumbling a little less than I had on my first adventure, but still there were a great many trailing threads and no chance in sight of their being knotted and snipped any time soon. It was terribly deflating to be forced to hand it all over to the police in this ragged state.

We reached the ground floor and went out of the massive front door to join Cad and Buttercup who were sitting at tea in those peculiar American deck chairs with the very short legs, basking in the sunshine against the west wall.

'Well?' said Cad, rather breathlessly as we plumped down into the low seats and waited for our cups and scones. Cad himself, I was enchanted to notice, had given up on that particular little bit of authenticity and was holding a tall glass of milk in one hand and a cigarette in the other.

'Well, we've found out what Dudgeon was up to,' I said. 'To a point, although not why. And we've found out enough to be able to conclude that it was either murder or a straight heart attack, one of the two; it *wasn't* the drink. But we still don't know who X is.'

'Well, do tell all, Dandy,' said Buttercup. 'And don't sound so jaded. It's only been days. How are you getting on with the ham sandwich, for instance, if you can manage it without any gory details.'

'Lunch in a pub, more than likely,' I said and Buttercup's face fell.

'That's hardly thrilling,' she said. 'What about the pen and ink?'

'No idea,' said Alec. 'One of the many things that Inspector Cruickshank will have to get to the bottom of. Even if he needs to arrest Mrs Dudgeon to do so.'

There was a spluttering sound from beside me and Cad sat up straight, wiping his mouth.

'Dandy,' he said, 'are you resigning?'

'Resigning?' I echoed.

'I'm not sure you can, you know. I entered this business arrangement in good faith and now you say that you're fed up and you're simply going to tell the inspector all he needs to know to arrest one of my estate tenants who has had enough trouble to last her a lifetime? Well, all I'm saying is I'm not sure that's on. Not sure at all.'

This was, I think, the sternest speech I had ever heard Cadwallader make and I was about to appeal to Buttercup and Alec for support, to remind Cad that I had taken pains right from the start to explain to him about the unkindness of justice and the impossibility of telling where the ball would roll once one had let go of it, but before I could gather my wits to speak it struck me that he was right. I could not possibly hand over what I knew to Inspector Cruickshank and just leave Mrs Dudgeon to his mercy; not because she was under Cad's wing and Cad had employed me – I was firm on that point and always would be – but because I knew in my very bones that Cad was right: she *had* had enough trouble to last her a lifetime. And if cruel blind justice would only make her suffer more, then cruel blind justice would have to do it without my help.

· I did not quite know what to make of this revelation as it struck me; I should far rather have thought of myself as 'Dandy Gilver: servant of truth' than as 'Dandy Gilver: woman, wife and mither o' bairns' and

I knew that taking cases and meddling in police business was only justified so long as I marched in step with them, doing what they also would do. Once I began to plough my own furrow, I was in danger of committing one of those 'spoilsporty' crimes Alec so despised and I would be had up for it if they caught me. Not that I would be in a position to obstruct much police business in the future unless I could harden my heart: for if I did ever have business cards made, then 'sentimental fudging of the facts a speciality' would not bring me many plum jobs. In the present case, though, neither my future as a sleuth nor my fear of prosecution could sway me, for if sentiment, compassion, love for my fellow man – whatever I chose to call it – if it trumped justice then it certainly trumped money too and it should, if I was any kind of 'wummin' at all, trump fear of the police and what they might do to me. It certainly seemed to for Chrissie Dudgeon.

The sun beat steadily against my face and limbs and yet, upon this thought, goose pimples began to start out on my skin. The stone wall behind me radiated the warmth of a whole summer and yet my neck prickled with cold.

'What is it?' whispered Buttercup in an awe-struck voice.

'What's what?' said Cad, also whispering.

'Ssh!' hissed Alec.

'I've thought of something,' I said in a steady voice.

'Yes, dear, we noticed,' said Alec. 'Really, Dandy, if you ever get sick of detecting you could make a fortune running seances. Most theatrical. What is it?'

'It ties in the passport, the birth certificate, the passenger lists and above all – *above all* – the reason they did it.'

'Go on,' said Alec. He took the teacup out of my hand and put it down for me on the table.

'Not money,' I said. 'And not fear of threats. And not because it was "right" in some abstract sense, because they knew that it wasn't. They did it for love. They gave X Robert Dudgeon's birth certificate and passport and the ticket and X got on the ship and went away to a new life in New Zealand.'

'But that couldn't possibly work,' said Alec. 'The new passports have photographs on them. You can't simply hand them over to any Tom, Dick or Harry.'

'I'm not suggesting that you can,' I said. 'I'm suggesting that one could hand one's passport over to one's brother, or cousin or nephew, and that somewhere amongst the labyrinthine relations and connections of the Dudgeons there is a bad egg, a black sheep, whom the Dudgeons could not – for love – refuse.'

'Must be a relation, not a connection,' said Alec. 'And one with quite a family resemblance, come to that, to get past the officials on a borrowed passport.'

'Well, these photographs are not works of art, darling,' I said. 'And they're tiny. A family resemblance would do it, or one striking feature. I daresay, for example, that any of the little ones next door would be able to pass for another in years to come with their mother's red hair.'

Alec nodded, rather grudgingly.

'Father's,' he said. 'But yes, you could be right. We need to find out if any of the Dudgeon clan is missing.'

'Father's what?' I asked him.

'Nothing,' he said. 'Cad, are there any more Dudgeons around on the estate here? Before we go searching further afield.'

'Father's red hair,' said Buttercup, two steps behind as usual.

'Whose father has red hair?' I said, and all three of them turned to look at me.

'What on earth do you mean?' said Buttercup. 'The savages' father, of course. Donald.'

'Donald doesn't have red hair,' I said. 'They must get it from their mother.'

Cad, Buttercup and Alec were now exchanging looks of utter bewilderment.

'Flaming Donald?' said Cad. 'Are you colour blind, Dandy? Flaming Donald has the reddest hair I've ever seen. Freddy couldn't *buy* a bottle of redder hair than Flaming Donald's.'

'But I met him,' I said. 'He's . . . He's called Flaming Donald because of his beliefs, isn't he? And he's Robert Dudgeon's brother.'

'No,' said Cad. 'His name is Lamont and he's married to Chrissie Dudgeon's brown-haired sister. Isobel.'

'So . . . that man that I met . . .' I said, speaking slowly although thinking very fast. 'He was most definitely a relative and he could have been – yes! – he *must* have been X. He must have, mustn't he, Alec? Hanging around at the cottage that afternoon when everyone else was away. My God, it must have given him a shock to see me grubbing around in amongst the burrs.'

'I'm surprised he didn't cosh you on the back of the neck,' Alec said.

I thought back to the fevered stream of apologies and explanations I had spouted to the man and remembered how he seemed to sum me up as a harmless idiot. I blushed.

'So,' I said, trying to bluster my way out of my feeling of shame even as the flush spread to the roots of my hair, 'who is he? A brother?'

'I don't think so,' said Cad. 'Dudgeon was the son of the old estate carpenter, the *only* son.'

'X could be the son of one of his sisters, I suppose,' I said. 'Chrissie's sister-in-law, that is. I never really believed that Tina and Bet and Lizzie and Margaret could all be Chrissie Dudgeon's actual blood sisters. Some of them at least must be in-laws, and one of them could be the mother of X.'

'Well, of course they couldn't be sisters,' said Alec. 'When you think about it. Tina *and* Chrissie? Lizzie *and* Bet?'

'Anyway,' said Buttercup suddenly, 'the charmless Isobel is Mrs Dudgeon's only sister. She told me that the very first night when we were in the scullery. '

I put my head into my hands and groaned. Time and again over the days, I had seen my listener frown and puzzle and never stopped to wonder why. Joey Brown had said she did not know who I was talking about; the men working at the wall didn't know who Donald Dudgeon was; even Mrs Dudgeon herself had asked me what I meant when I talked of 'one of her sisters' and when I had told her I meant Tina she had smiled and said she supposed they were.

'But Mrs Dudgeon said it herself that night,' I said, clutching at straws now. 'She clearly said "my sisters".'

'"My sisters" what?' said Alec.

'Nothing,' I told him. 'It was when we were alone, she said "my sisters" and then she heard Isobel coming back and stopped.'

'Well, there you are then,' said Alec. 'She was saying "my sister's coming back" probably.'

I nodded, defeated.

'So who were those women?' I said. 'Who are they? And what were they all doing there all the time?'

'They were Mrs Dudgeon's workmates from the bottling,' said Buttercup. 'You should have heard Isobel talking about them. Very sour.'

'And you never said a word of this?' Alec

321

demanded, turning to her. 'You must have heard us talking about Mrs Dudgeon's sisters over and over again! Weren't you *ever* listening?'

Buttercup shrugged.

'Why did it matter anyway?' she said.

'Because,' I explained, very patiently, 'if I had known everyone's name and who they were I would have known that the man in the cottage garden that day wasn't Donald, and I might have been able to work out that he was X, before the ship sailed.'

'Ah well,' said Buttercup, comfortably. 'What's in a name?'

So, you see, she really was asking for it.

'Cad,' I said, 'Freddy's nickname at school was Buttercup.' Then I shouted over the top of the resulting laughter and cursing: 'But never mind that now. The question remains. If X wasn't a brother or a nephew, then who was he that he could unite both Mr and Mrs Dudgeon in such a risky . . .'

'It does seem a bit extravagant for a cousin,' Cad began, but Alec shushed him.

The goose pimples were back, and the neck prickles and I heard Mrs Dudgeon's voice once more, telling me exactly who he was. At least telling me who I was and who she was and what that meant.

'She's off again,' said Alec.

'Dandy, what is it?' said Buttercup. 'You look very peculiar.'

'He looked exactly like Robert Dudgeon,' I said. 'Like a younger and sadder version of Robert Dudgeon. And he's the only one who – even if he *had* killed Robert and got away – Mrs Dudgeon would not want anyone to find out and bring him back. Not her. Not any "mither o' bairns".'

'Who was it?' said Cad.

'Young Bobby,' said Alec and I nodded.

'But he died in the war,' said Cad.

'No,' I said. 'He went missing in the war. Missing presumed dead. And it took him years but he finally made it back here to where people would help him even if they knew it was wrong. Goodness knows how long it took to hatch the plan. He was living in the woods – the ghost of a soldier like the children told us – counting on his parents to help him.'

'A deserter?' said Cad. 'I can't believe it of them.'

'She told me as much,' I said. 'Mrs Dudgeon. I assured her that I would keep her private business private and she said if I knew what her private business was I would soon change my mind.'

'And you don't think the ship's people would be able to tell the difference?' said Alec. 'Between a young man and his father?'

I shook my head. 'For one thing, Bobby Dudgeon doesn't look like a young man,' I said. 'I thought he was Donald, father of all those rascals. And for another . . .' I laughed. 'I thought the clerk had made a mistake when he read from the passenger list. Robert George Dudgeon. 1st June 1899.'

'The pen and ink!' said Alec, sitting up straight and slapping his hands on his thighs.

'The pen and ink,' I agreed. 'Dudgeon was born in 1873 and his son certainly couldn't pass for fifty.' I traced the digits on the tea-table cloth with my finger. 'It could be done. A seven into a nine. A three into a nine. It could easily be done.'

'Of course, Robert Dudgeon getting a passport at fifty years would be safe from any checks against military lists,' Alec said.

'So as easily as that,' I went on, 'Bobby could have got a passport and ticket which matched his birth certificate. The passport would show a photograph which possibly did not do him justice but, these days, who would point out to a young man that he looks rather haggard for his years and ask him what on earth he had been up to to get that way?'

'And the clerk himself told us that they do no checks at boarding,' said Alec. 'It was a perfect plan. Inspired.'

I looked intently at him, not quite straight-on so that he would not see me looking. He was not a woman, wife and mother of sons like me and I could not decipher from his face or his words what he made of this, whether or not he was about to leap to his feet and storm away to Inspector Cruickshank demanding that the ship be met at Lisbon and the traitor brought home.

'Perfect until the shock news of the day's holiday in lieu,' I said. 'But in the end they weathered even that.'

'And then,' said Cad, 'he killed his father?'

There was a gasp from Buttercup.

'That's what Chrissie Dudgeon believes,' I said.

'But why?' Buttercup asked.

I shrugged.

'Perhaps Robert Dudgeon was changing his mind,' I suggested. 'Perhaps he suddenly said to Bobby that he couldn't let him go through with it. We never did explain to ourselves why Chrissie was standing outside the police station that day when she saw the holiday notice. Perhaps she was loitering there, considering whether or not to turn him in.'

'Can't have been that,' said Alec. 'Can't have been. Bobby can't just have conjured an untraceable poison out of his hat on the spur of the moment because his father surprised him with bad news. Robert Dudgeon must simply have died, as we've been saying all along. And now that we know what he was doing, the notion of his heart giving out under strain only becomes more plausible than ever.'

We sat quietly in our ring of chairs for a while then. I supposed each of us was waiting for someone else to decide what to do. It was my case, it was at Cad's behest that I had taken it, but Alec alone amongst us was in the position to call for mercy. He was the only one who had faced what Bobby Dudgeon had faced and had resisted the escape route that Bobby had taken. The rest of us had no right to cast any stones.

Surprisingly, it was Buttercup who spoke up, at last. Unsurprisingly, when she did, it was to plant both her feet on the sore spot with all the grace of a bison.

'Well, Alec?' she said. 'Obviously it's up to you.'

But Alec's mind was working away at other things, it appeared.

'Joey Brown,' he said, and I could not help a little cry of enlightenment escaping me.

'Of course! Joey Brown. She didn't only recognize who the Burry Man wasn't. She recognized who it was.'

'Yes, yes of course,' said Alec. 'But what I meant was, I think we should put it to Joey Brown. I've always been interested to know . . . how could one not be? But usually there's no balance to the thing. Chrissie Dudgeon is all one way. Shinie Brown all the other. This is a rare opportunity indeed. Will Joey Brown choose to save her brother's honour or her sweetheart's neck, if we put it to her, if she's to decide?'

There was a high hardness in his voice that did not quite manage to cover every trace of the tremor beneath it and I ached to be able to comfort him. One thing I had learned though, in that ghastly uniform in that living nightmare of a nursing home, was that punching someone in the eye, raging at blameless little maids, getting roaring drunk with the other soldiers, or

325

taking nurses away to hotels on overnight passes, all these could bring some kind of comfort. Actual comfort, delivered by volunteer ladies two afternoons a week, was absolutely bloody useless and only made the punching worse.

Chapter Seventeen

This time there was no pussy-footing around ordering drinks and starting up apparently innocent conversations. I was hurrying along at Alec's heels when he marched into Brown's Bar like the wrath of God, and so I could not see his face, but both Joey and Shinie looked up at the sound of the door and did not need to ask what he was there for: they knew. What is more, they had quite clearly been waiting for this moment to arrive.

'Joey,' said Mr Brown, jerking his head towards the back.

His daughter lifted the flap of the bar counter to let us pass.

'I'll give ye five, ten minutes,' said Brown, 'then I'll come up and let Joey down again. Somebody needs to stay here.' There were indeed several customers in the pub tonight and so this seemed reasonable, although I had noticed in earlier visits that the Browns did not usually take pains to man the counter. I wondered if perhaps it was more that each felt disinclined to talk to us in the presence of the other.

Joey led Alec and me through the kitchen and along the passageway, clear today, all the boxes vanished.

'Upstairs, Miss Brown,' I said, 'if it's all the same to you.' I did not want another interview in the noxious wash-house in the basement. Joey nodded without turning her head and opened a door concealing a box staircase to the upper floor. A few moments later we were facing one another, a little too close, in what seemed to be a spare bedroom at the back of the house. There was nowhere to sit except the narrow bed and so we remained standing, awkwardly, waiting for someone to speak.

Perhaps we can blame the compulsion to make sure one's guests are always having fun at one's parties, deeply ingrained at finishing school where we were taught how to handle any social encounter with aplomb, or perhaps the even earlier training of being scrubbed and primped and brought down after tea to bore Mummy's guests with endless verses of 'The Blessed Damezel'. Of course, it is only now that one can see how bored they must have been. At the time, well-schooled themselves, they seemed enchanted. For whatever reason, it was me who cracked first and broke the silence.

'You recognized him,' I said, making not quite a question but more than a statement of it. Joey Brown heaved an enormous guttering sigh and turned away from us. In the silence we could hear voices from the bar below.

'I thocht I did,' she said.

'And are you saying that he didn't make any attempt to contact you?' said Alec. 'That the only time you saw him was here, on the Burry Man's day?' She turned back at that, looking at him quizzically.

'I *thocht* I recognized him,' she said with more emphasis, 'but I wis wrong. He wis that like his daddy. And wi' the face all covered up and jist the eyes and the hands, I wis sure fur a minute, but I wis wrong.'

I could not quite see where this certainty came from but I could understand the sadness in her voice: even if she had concluded that the vision of her sweetheart

328

was a haunting, she would rather have had that than nothing. I could not think what to say to her to bring comfort. Would it be better for her to keep believing that her eyes had played tricks or would she want to know that he had indeed been here and was still alive, but had left her without a word? I wished the clamouring voices downstairs would hush and let me concentrate.

'Did you tell your father?' Alec asked her. 'Is that why he rushed outside to challenge him?'

She nodded.

'And was it your father who told you you were wrong?'

Joey seemed to consider this carefully before she spoke.

'Aye,' she said at last. 'Father telt me it wis Rab Dudgeon right enough. Telt me I wis bein' daft – I've always been feart o' the Burry Man.'

I tried to catch Alec's eye to see if he knew where to go from here. It was possible, I suppose, that she had recognized Bobby Dudgeon but had been persuaded out of it by her father, but there was more going on here than Miss Brown was telling. Alec was studying her intently, frowning a little, as distracted as I was by the cries from below.

'Shop!' came a particularly lusty yell, followed by laughter.

'Shinie! Joey! We're dyin' o' thirst here,' came another.

'You had better go down,' I said to her. 'Your father is obviously on his way to find us and your customers seem to be getting restless.' Joey bobbed a curtsy without looking us in the eye and hurriedly left.

'Do you believe her?' I asked Alec once she had gone. 'Do you believe that it was only a passing notion – one

329

that happened to be spot on – or do you think she knew full well that it was Bobby Dudgeon in the suit?'

'I'm not sure,' said Alec. 'There's something not right here. Lord, I wish those men would shut up. She should be there by now. What's taking her?' Indeed, the shouts for service from the bar customers had, if anything, got louder and more sustained.

'I'm trying to cast my mind back to that day,' I said. 'There was always something odd about the way Shinie Brown went crashing out into the street to confront him. The way he held out the glass, the way they locked eyes. There was something so urgent about it all. So I can believe easily that Shinie rushed out to see if it was true – to see if it really was Bobby – and that he recognized that it was, and Bobby knew he'd been recognized, and Shinie knew that he knew and so on and so on. And they didn't bumble the glass and spill the whisky, you know. The Burry Man reared back like a stag at bay and Shinie quite deliberately, contemptuously, dashed it away on to the ground. So that fits too.'

'Yes,' said Alec. 'The father of a lost soldier wouldn't want to welcome home a deserter with a glass of cheer.' He was having to talk loudly now to be heard above the chanting from below.

'Hardly,' I said. 'He'd sooner . . .'

'What?' said Alec.

'I was going to say he'd sooner poison him.'

'If he happened to have poison lying around.'

'And not just the Turnbulls' idea of poison,' I said. 'Good God, what a noise from down there. Where are they, do you suppose? Shinie was supposed to come to us when Joey went back.' We waited a moment or two longer, and then it seemed to dawn on us both together: the shouts for service had begun even while

330

Joey was here. She had led us upstairs out of the way and, like lambs, we had followed.

We practically fell over each other trying to get out of the door and down the narrow stairway. There was no one behind the bar counter or in the back kitchen, only the customers shouting for their beer and joking about search parties. Then we wasted precious moments searching for a back door into the yard before realizing that the only exit must be from the basement. We clattered down the steps, banged open the door to the cellar room and ran in.

A sharp cry stopped me dead. Joey was there, huddled once more into the same corner behind the copper, shaking. Alec, beside me, still panting, looked around and his mouth fell open.

'Good God,' he said.

'Where is he?' I demanded, going up to Joey and taking her chin in my hand. 'Where did he go?'

She bit her lip and shook her head, tears beginning to gather in her eyes.

'I wis wrong,' she said again. 'I telt him it wis Bobby and I wis wrong. It's all my fault.'

'Listen to me,' I said, grabbing hold of her arms but managing not to shake her. 'You were right. It *was* Bobby.'

'But it was his father who . . .' she said.

'It was his father who what?' I asked. I could sense that we were getting to it now.

'It was his father . . . afterwards.'

'Yes,' I said. 'It was his father again afterwards.'

'And he never went home. He stayed and went to the greasy pole and – and – he died. So I must have been wrong.'

Suddenly I could see what she meant. She had been inside somewhere, probably right here, that day when

Brown had followed the Burry Man outside. She had not seen a thing.

'He didn't drink it,' I said. 'Do you hear me? He didn't drink from the glass out there in the street. I saw it all.'

'But he must have,' said Joey. 'He died.'

'So it *was* poison?' said Alec.

Joey nodded in a tiny voice, and said something that sounded like 'believe'.

I tightened my grip on her arms and spoke to her as though she were a very young child.

'Where is your father?' I asked her. 'Where has he gone?'

'Cassilis,' said Joey in the faintest whisper.

Alec and I were upstairs, through the bar and out on to the pavement before I was aware of having decided to move, then I caught myself short, staring up and down the empty street.

'He's taken my car,' I said. 'Quick, run to the police station, Alec. I'll catch up.' But Alec had had a better idea. Following Brown's example, he strode across the street to where an Austin car, ancient but very well-kept and shining, was parked outside Sealscraig House. The motor was running before I was in my seat, then he turned in three expert darts in the narrow space and roared away along the road to the Hawes.

'Shinie Brown,' he said. '*Shinie* Brown. Why did none of us ask what that meant?'

'I don't understand you,' I told him.

'Moonshine, Dandy,' said Alec. 'You saw it for yourself.'

'Where?' I said.

Alec glared at me, the car swerving as he took his attention from the road. 'Right there. In the cellar. That, my dear, was a still.'

I boggled for a second or two but soon caught up.

'The damson gin,' I said. 'Of course. Father Cormack was absolutely tickled pink to see me drinking the damson gin and he joked with Brown about giving me the recipe. He even told me Brown used to work for a distiller. What a brainless idiot I am! But I still don't see how it would have helped us. Not really.'

'It would have helped us,' said Alec, grimly, 'because when it comes to moonshine, the Turnbulls are right. Anyone who can distil alcohol that's fit to drink can just as readily distil lethal poison.'

'But why would he?' I said. 'Why would it *be* there? I mean, chemists can make poison too, but if the average chemist flies into a murderous rage, he doesn't just reach out his hand and close it around a bottle of the stuff.'

'Perhaps he kept it for the very purpose he ended up using it for,' said Alec. 'For deserters. He's not exactly balanced when it comes to his lost son after all. Perhaps he kept the poison in the name of his boy as well as the special whisky.'

'And *how* did he do it?' I said. 'When did Dudgeon drink it?'

We had just entered the Cassilis estate on the back lane and were rushing so fast along such a narrow space between the trees that I bit my lip and squeezed my eyes shut, sure that at any moment we were going to hit one of the trunks and burst into flames. When we came to the first fork in the road, Alec slewed to a stop.

'Where will I go?' he asked me. 'Where will *he* have gone?'

It was not until that moment that I realized I did not know. Joey Brown had said 'Cassilis' and off we had shot, but there was no way of telling whether that meant the castle, one of the cottages or some secret place in the woods.

'Let's quickly check the castle,' I said, 'then warn Mrs Dudgeon. Then, if we haven't seen him, we'll start searching the estate.'

It felt to me as though aeons had passed but when we crossed the ha-ha and approached the castle mound, there Cad and Buttercup still were in their wooden deck chairs by the west wall, only with cocktails in their hands instead of tea. Alec began a fanfare on the horn as we neared them and I leaned out of the Austin's window beckoning them down the slope.

'Whose motor car is th–' began Buttercup, until I shushed her.

'Go inside and stay there,' I said. 'And call the police. It was Shinie Brown. He poisoned Robert Dudgeon and he's somewhere here right now, doing God knows what. Quick, Buttercup!' I screamed as she blinked slowly, trying to take in my news through a fug of tea, cocktails and warm afternoon.

'I knew it!' Cad was saying as I hopped back in. 'Murder! I knew it all along.'

There was no sign of my motor car at Mrs Dudgeon's cottage. We skidded to a halt and jumped down as both front doors opened to reveal Mrs Dudgeon in one doorway and a man who had to be Flaming Donald in the other.

'Mrs Dudgeon,' I said, rushing up the path. 'Has Mr Brown – Shinie Brown – Willie Brown – is he here? Has he been here?'

Mrs Dudgeon dithered from foot to foot on her doorstep and gobbled, looking at me and at Alec's grim face, bewildered. I took this to be a no.

'Where is he, then?' I asked Alec. 'Was Joey lying to us?'

'He must be somewhere out on the estate,' said Alec. 'In the woods. But if he's still in your car we'll find him.' He made as though to go off down the path, but Mrs Dudgeon put out a hand and stopped him.

'Whit d'you want wi' him?' she said.

Alec and I glanced at each other and nodded.

'Let's go inside,' I suggested, mindful of Donald standing so close and watching the scene with eyes wide and mouth hanging open.

'He killed your husband,' Alec told her once the door was shut behind us and we were standing in the narrow hall.

'Willie Brown?' she said. 'Willie Brown? Not –' but she could not even say the thing which had been haunting her.

'No,' I said. 'Willie Brown.'

'But why?' she wailed.

Alec and I flicked a glance at each other again.

'He thought,' I began carefully, 'he thought he recognized the Burry Man.' She looked at me for a moment until what I had said sank in, then she lowered her head.

'Aye, that would be reason enough,' she said. 'He never did get over his laddie.' Then a fresh thought struck her. 'But how did he dae it? When?'

'We don't know,' Alec said. 'He might have had poison in his cellar.'

'But Rab never went near Broon's Bar that day,' said Mrs Dudgeon.

'Well, then Brown must have come to him,' I said.

'I'd have seen him,' she insisted. 'Rab wisnae oot o' my sicht fae the minute he come oot the toon hall to the minute he . . . fell. You're wrong aboot this, madam, ye must be.'

Alec looked half convinced by her. He was chewing his lip and frowning at me, waiting for me to speak.

'When we came along the street at the end of the Burry Man's day,' I said slowly, trying to remember,

'Joey Brown was alone in the bar. I could see in, you know, and I remember thinking how odd it was because the place was thronging and she was all on her own and was even doing her Ferry Fair cleaning, had all the bottles off the shelves behind the counter.'

'What's that got to do with anything?' said Alec.

'Just that Shinie Brown could have been out of the bar,' I said. 'He could have been along at the Rosebery Hall, lying in wait.'

'And how would he have persuaded Mr Dudgeon to swallow poison?' said Alec.

Mrs Dudgeon gasped and I put an arm around her shoulders. She was shaking and felt unsteady, tottering slightly as I touched her. My mind, despite everything, ran instantly to the need for a little something medicinal to calm her nerves.

Suddenly I had it.

'Mrs Dudgeon,' I said. 'Do you still have the flask?'

She nodded wordlessly.

'And have you rinsed it out?'

She looked at me, confused, for a moment then her eyes flared as she got it too. She turned on her heel and disappeared into the living room, returning a second later with the small pewter flask, pressing it into my hand. I began to pick at the stopper but Alec took it, wrenched it open, and sniffed warily.

'Good grief,' he said. 'We don't need a chemist. *I* could write the report on that.'

'Whit is it?' said Mrs Dudgeon.

'Methanol,' said Alec. 'Absolutely lethal, but close enough to alcohol to pass for it if no one had reason to check. Good Lord, a flask of this stuff? Your poor husband didn't stand a chance.'

'It makes sense, I know,' I said. 'But I can hardly believe that he just marched into the Rosebery Hall in broad daylight and put it in the flask. What if someone had seen him?'

'He cannae have been in his senses,' said Mrs Dudgeon. 'He's no' been the man he wis since he lost his laddie. Nivver been the same.' I began to lead her towards the living room hoping to comfort her, but Alec stopped me.

'No time,' he said. 'Mrs Dudgeon, I'm sorry, but we have to go. Stay here and lock your door.'

Back in the Austin, we crept forward through the gathering gloom of the woods; I sent a prayer of thanks for the careful owner of the little motor car with its smooth, quiet running.

'Why didn't you take the top off and sniff it yourself, Dandy?' said Alec. 'When she first showed it to you.'

'I did,' I told him. 'I just thought it was that particularly dreadful whisky one comes across that smells of apples.'

'No whisky in the world smells of apples,' he said.

Aware that my ignorance had let us down again, I should have hung my head in shame but I was still stubbornly sure that I had smelled exactly that sickly apple smell before.

'God,' I groaned, remembering. 'When I knelt at his side at the bottom of the greasy pole, I remember thinking that he couldn't be dead because he smelled so alive. Of sweat, you know, and flour dust and of the fairground itself. I thought he had eaten a toffee apple – that sweet fruity smell. And then how many times did we tell ourselves afterwards – a ham sandwich and too much whisky. A ham sandwich and too much whisky . . . and I never made the connection, or rather noticed that there wasn't one. If I had mentioned the apply smell right there and then . . .'

'Yes,' said Alec, not even trying to comfort me.

'But I was *sure* that whisky could smell like that too.'

337

'Look!' said Alec. 'What's that?' He paused, the little motor car trembling as his foot attempted to hold the balance of the clutch. 'No,' he said at last, 'I thought I saw a light shining, but it's the tin roof on the den, I think.'

'Yes, it could be,' I said. 'We're near the rascals' stamping grounds here.'

'And don't berate yourself about the whisky, Dan,' said Alec. 'We both know it's not your strong point.'

'Wait though,' I said, for thoughts were stirring in me, of glinting things in the woods and the smell of apples from a bottle of whisky, and then it fell into place with a click.

'Oh, *bloody* hell,' I said. 'Alec, you're going to kill me. Turn round. We need to go back.'

Alec did so and drove in silence, waiting for me to explain.

'I know how Brown happened to have poison to hand,' I said. 'And I know why I thought that whisky could smell that way. I even know what Joey Brown was doing hanging round here after the death.'

Again he waited and at last I plucked up the courage to lay out how blind I had been.

'It was the bottle of Royal Highlander,' I said. 'The special bottle of whisky for Billy Brown's return.'

'Of course,' said Alec. 'The Royal Highlanders.'

'Otherwise known as the Black Watch. Billy's regiment. Bobby's too.'

'So the special bottle wasn't whisky at all,' said Alec. 'It was methanol. It was poison.'

'And so it wasn't exactly *for* Billy. But it was in his honour. To be used exactly as Brown tried to use it. And when Joey told her father that it was Bobby Dudgeon in the burry suit he didn't hesitate.'

'So it was never Robert Dudgeon that he meant to kill.'

338

'I'm not so sure,' I told him. 'Out in the street, it was certainly Bobby he had in his sights. When he went to the Rosebery Hall to poison the flask . . . he might have thought that "the Burry Man" – meaning Bobby – would be the one to drink it. But when he brought the bottle here he must have meant it for Robert. To punish him for harbouring his son.'

'*Here*?' said Alec looking around the dark woods.

'Yes,' I said. 'He brought it to the cottage and left it there on Burry Man's day. Of course, once Robert Dudgeon dropped dead at the greasy pole Brown knew that he had drunk the flask and the bottle here wasn't needed; more than that, he knew it would be dangerous to leave it here in case the police mounted an investigation. So he packed Joey off to get rid of it. That's why she was dug in like a dog in a foxhole. That's why she was so very unnerved when the sisters started offering Cad a drink of whisky and saying that they'd seen a bottle of malt, and *that* was what she'd been doing round the back of the cottage when I happened upon her.'

'What do you mean?' said Alec. 'What had she been doing?'

'She'd been pouring the poison away and putting the bottle on Donald's rubbish heap,' I said. 'I met her coming back.'

'So do you think it'll still be there?' said Alec, pressing down on the pedal and making the little motor car surge forward.

'No,' I said. 'I know it's not. It's buried in some undergrowth between the cottages and the castle. I know it is because I put it there myself. But Brown doesn't know that and, unless I'm mistaken, he'll be out the back at the cottages, searching for it, or waiting until everyone has gone to bed so that he can search for it then. Stop here, darling, and let's walk.'

We stepped down and made our way silently along the verge of the lane, slower and slower until we were only edging forward. In the dusk, the kitchen lights of the cottages were winking at us through the tree trunks and the outlines of the sheds and midden heaps at the bottom of the gardens stood out against the glow. We stopped as soon as we had a decent view of the whole scene.

'I don't think he's here,' said Alec. 'Where *is* he? If he didn't come to Mrs Dudgeon's and he's not at the castle what's he doing here at all?'

Before I could answer, there came a drumming of running footsteps, getting louder all the time, twigs snapping. I spun around on my heels, my heart hammering. It sounded like an army approaching us and both Alec and I took a couple of hesitant steps towards the lights of the cottages. Then we began to make out shapes, low and scurrying, and to hear the ragged panting and the high pitch of the hissing voices as they rushed towards us.

'We're nearly hame, Lila, come on!'

'We'll get Daddy tae go and catch 'im.'

And above the voices came Lila's whimpering and deep, revolting sniffs.

'Oh, God in heaven,' I said, stepping towards them, 'if he's hurt one of them . . . Donald? Randall? Can you see me?'

When they heard my voice they changed direction towards it like a flock of starlings on the wing and began shouting their news.

'He's back, missus. He's goin' to the holes.'

'The demon's back and he seen us and —'

'Hush now, hush now,' I said as they drew near. 'Is anyone hurt? Did he touch you?' They barely paused in their clamouring but amongst the shouts I could make out 'Naeb'dy got catched' and 'We're a' grand but —'

340

'Very well,' I said. 'Now listen. Where is he?'

'In the woods, missus.'

'He's goin' to the ghostie holes.'

I raised my voice to be heard above them. 'Randall,' I said to the tallest boy, 'can you find your way there and show us?' Randall's eyes flared with fear, but he nodded even before I had had the chance to reassure him: 'We'll both be with you. We won't let him lay a finger upon you. You other children go inside. Donald, tell your mummy and daddy –'

'I'll come with you, missus,' said Tommy.

'No!' I told him. 'Absolutely not. Donald, you are responsible for getting all these little ones safely inside, do you hear me?'

'Aye,' said Donald. 'Will I tell my daddy that the demon –'

'Tell him that Willie Brown killed your uncle Robert and he's trying to run away.' Donald nodded, already shepherding the smallest brothers and Lila before him.

'Come on then,' I said and, taking Randall's hand firmly in my own, I led him and Alec back into the trees.

'You're telling the truth about this?' said Alec to Randall.

'They always were,' I said. 'A demon, Randall, wasn't it? A bad man with a bottle of the demon drink went into Auntie Chrissie's house when no one was there?' Randall's head was nodding furiously.

'He shouted that he'd come back and kill us in oor beds if we telt on him,' said Randall in a voice struggling with the bravado of a ten-year-old boy who fears nothing and the horror of a small boy, only ten years old, who wants to run to his mother's knee. 'But Lila telt Daddy and Daddy said he was *real*.' I tightened my grip on his sweaty little hand.

'Monster,' Alec whispered.

'And the ghost of the soldier who was living in the den until Lila's accident there?' I said to Randall. 'He was real too.'

'Aye,' said Randall. 'But he wid nivver hurt us.' There was a pause. 'He's like a ghostie doon the shell holes.'

I felt a shiver run through me from head to toe and I was aware of Alec moving in a little closer towards me. If the demon and the soldier were flesh and blood, then what were we to make of these holes that we were heading straight towards, not to mention the ghosties that lived in them? We hurried on, silent except for the quick thump of our steps on the soft forest floor.

It almost beggars belief, but so intent were we on our progress, threading our way as quickly and quietly as possible through the trees, that we heard nothing and one can only assume that the same was true for him, for the first we knew of Shinie Brown was the sudden flash as he flitted across our path not twenty feet in front. Randall and I both shrieked and at that Brown broke into a run and began crashing forward, all thoughts of stealth abandoned. Alec took off after him like a hound. I hesitated for a second and looked at Randall, who looked back at me, then of one mind we plunged into the trees.

Covering the ground more rapidly than I could have believed – Randall was, of course, as fit as a flea and there was no way I could hold him back and no way on *earth* that I would let him go – we were at Alec's heels in an instant, Shinie Brown ten yards ahead of us and going strong. We were gaining on him all the time, though; *he* was struggling through thickets of bramble leaving it clear for us behind him. *He* was darting and twisting looking for a path and we could save seconds following. And as well, most curiously, he was not only running, but was also shrugging himself out of his jacket, ripping off his shirt, as he raced on. At first

I thought he was caught on thorns and would leave the things behind him, but he held on to them as he ran, and with his shirt off he began to struggle out of his braces too.

'What's he doing?' I panted.

Shinie threw a desperate glance over his shoulder at us. He stopped running. Then, just as suddenly, he was off again. He had changed direction. Now he was making his way to the right, to the west, out of the woods. We surged after him. It was easier going now, heading out of the trees, but all that meant was that Shinie started to pull away. We passed his coat on the ground and then his shirt and, unencumbered, arms pumping like pistons, he sprinted ahead. By the time we gained the edge of the park he was across the ha-ha and well on his way to the castle rise. I kicked off my shoes and, ignoring my burning lungs, trusting that the jellied muscles in my legs would keep working even though I could no longer feel them, I let Randall pull me along, concentrating hard on Alec's back and refusing to think. We saw Shinie Brown scale the slope, digging his hobnailed boots into the glossy grass, and then unbelievably we saw him wrench the door open and disappear.

'They didn't,' I managed to pant on one breath. I could not believe it, even of Buttercup and Cad. They had a door of oak so thick I could hardly move the thing on its hinges and yet, knowing there was a murderer on the loose, they had not locked it. And now he was in there with them.

Reaching the start of the slope, Alec dug into Brown's footsteps and, slipping a little in his light shoes, he scrambled up. Randall and I dropped to our hands and knees and crawled after him. At the top, Alec tugged on the iron handle of the door but could not budge it.

'He's locked them in with him,' I wailed and began to pound on the door. 'Buttercup! Buttercup, can you hear me?'

From deep inside the castle there was a shuddering clang. I clutched Alec's arm and pulled Randall in close behind me.

'Was that a shot?' Alec said, thundering his fists on the door.

At that moment, the sound of a police klaxon came clearly across the park from the woods and, as we turned to look for it, the iron bar scraped and the door swung open behind us. We reeled round again and gaped.

There was Cad, beaming from ear to ear, and twirling an enormous sword like a showman with a silver-topped cane.

'We got him,' he said. Alec and I rushed inside with Randall at our heels and made for the staircase.

'This way,' said Cad, at the kitchen doorway. 'In here, of course.'

In the kitchen, Buttercup and Mrs Murdoch stood arm-in-arm and panting, leaning on two more swords as though they were rolled umbrellas. From the doorway in the corner we could hear the faint scrabbling sounds of Shinie Brown trying in vain to climb the slick walls of the oubliette.

'We saw him coming,' said Cad. 'We were watching for him. Only he didn't see us through the arrow slits, of course.'

'And Mrs Murdoch was waiting in here,' said Buttercup. 'In there, you know, at the back, in the dark, with the grille open.'

'And when he got too close to see,' went on Cad, 'we stood in the Great Hall doorway and watched him through the murder hole.'

'To see if he would come up the stairs or go straight to the kitchen.'

'And he came up the stairs. So we hid.'

'In the fireplace, behind the fire. He couldn't see us, standing behind the light.'

'And we waited and waited and waited.'

'And then, when he went back downstairs at last . . .'

'We followed him, with our swords.'

'And he went into the kitchen and Mrs Murdoch made a little whimpering noise as we had agreed she would.'

'And he come right over like a salmon on hook,' said Mrs Murdoch. 'He lookit in and saw me, but he didnae look down. Well, you dinnae, dae ye?'

'He just stepped towards you, didn't he, Mrs Murdoch?' said Buttercup.

'And down he went,' said Cad. 'And then clang!'

'Yes,' I said. 'So we heard.'

'I think an apology is in order, Dandy,' said Buttercup.

'For what?' I asked.

'For telling us we were silly,' she said. 'Or at least for thinking it and for all the smirking. You said this castle was impractical. *Impractical*. Huh!'

'Is he all right?' said Alec, as the sound of the police motor car stopping and doors slamming shut came from outside.

'He's fine,' said Cad. 'Come and see.'

In the oubliette, with the grille firmly closed and a barrel resting on top of it just in case, Shinie Brown stood defiantly in his string vest with his braces hanging down and stared up at us.

'Ye're a very bad man,' shouted Randall, which pretty much summed things up for me.

Chapter Eighteen

There was close to a party atmosphere in Mrs Murdoch's kitchen once Brown had departed with a sergeant and two constables; except that Buttercup had only got as far as uncorking the cherry brandy when Flaming Donald Lamont arrived in search of his son. She finessed the bottle and corkscrew into a convenient breadbin with a sleight of hand born of many speak-easy raids and Mrs Murdoch put the kettle on instead. I noticed, nevertheless, that a good slop of something went into our cups which did not go into Donald's (Mrs Murdoch's broad back hiding the operation from all except me) and when I took a tentative sip I felt as though a hole had opened in the top of my head and let out a jet of steam.

'Ginger bun, madam?' said Mrs Murdoch, proffering a plate. 'They're ma own recipe too.' And she winked. I took a cake but set my cup down. Nothing would ever change this little burgh, clearly, but I was off moonshine for a while.

'What I still don't understand,' said the inspector, 'is his motive.'

Alec studied the floor. I glanced at Donald, unsure of how much he knew, but all his attention was taken up listening to Randall retelling the tale for the dozenth time. Cad and Buttercup stared at me, their meaning quite plain: I was on my own.

'Must you know his motive?' I said. 'There's more evidence than you will ever need. We have the flask he left in Dudgeon's pocket, and we have the bottle he took to the house in case the flask wasn't drunk, not to mention the still. So why worry about motive?'

'I'd be happier,' said the inspector. 'I know they were far from being pals, Willie and Rab, but it takes more than that.'

Inspiration struck me.

'It went further than not being pals,' I told him. 'Willie Brown blamed Bobby Dudgeon for his son joining up. Young Bobby was a heavy influence on his friend by all accounts and the feeling is, very much, that if Bobby hadn't volunteered, Billy wouldn't have either. And then added to that, Joey – Miss Brown, you know – had got engaged to Bobby Dudgeon against her father's wishes. And perhaps she's determined to honour his memory, not to marry at all now. So it's quite easy to see how, with enough brooding and enough grief clouding his mind, Brown could blame the Dudgeons for everything. Perhaps the Burry Man's day was just the last straw – everyone cheering Robert Dudgeon on as though he were some kind of hero.'

The inspector nodded, reluctantly.

'Be lucky to get murder on that, though,' said the remaining sergeant, lugubriously. 'It sounds . . . fevered like. The defence'll go for manslaughter, unbalanced mind, diminished responsibility.'

'You could be right,' said the inspector. 'And who's to say it's not true?'

The sergeant sighed.

'Mind you,' he added, 'it would be a lot worse if young Bobby Dudgeon had come home.'

I tried not to look too astonished at this and I could see Alec trying to do the same.

'How d'you mean, Sergeant?' Alec said. It was the inspector who answered.

'Well, if one son was lost and the other one was safe,' he said, 'a jury could easily understand the jealous grief of the one father making him hate the other. But seeing as Bobby Dudgeon fell too, you'd think Shinie could have found some compassion.'

'Aye, sir, let's look on the bright side,' said the sergeant. 'With both boys gone the same way, we might get murder and a hanging after all.'

The inspector looked suitably pained and Flaming Donald, catching these words as Randall paused for breath, seemed to decide that he had better get his boy out of earshot and home to his mother. The party, clearly, was breaking up.

I took no part in the general leave-taking, however, for the sergeant's words had hit me like a brick. I was dimly aware of the inspector talking to Cad and Buttercup about their formal statement; I knew that Mrs Murdoch was pressing a basket of treats on Donald to take back to Chrissie Dudgeon; I could hear the vague rumbling of the sergeant scratching his head over how to divide the departing bodies amongst the remaining police motor cars, but essentially I was alone, lost in the middle of a shifting cloud of impossible but irresistible new ideas.

'I tell you what, Sergeant,' I said suddenly, grabbing my chance, 'if it's all right with his father, I'll volunteer to take young Randall home. We couldn't have done it without you, you know, Randall, and you deserve a treat. How do you fancy driving my motor car across the park?'

Randall's eyes, naturally, lit up at the prospect and his father made no demur. Alec, I was aware, was watching me closely as I prepared to leave.

'Straight home?' he asked, with an unreadable look on his face.

'We might take a scenic route,' I said, and then I turned to Flaming Donald. 'If that's all right with you?'

'The laddie's as high as a kite anyway,' he said. 'It'll make no odds.'

'Splendid,' I said. 'I'll just fetch Bunty.'

'Is that your spotty dog?' said Randall, for whom the journey was getting steadily more enticing. 'It's a braw big dog, eh no? I've seen it.'

Bunty was indeed 'a braw big dog' and I trusted that in the dark where no one could see her polka-dots and her lolling grin she might pass for a guard-dog. But first we had to get there. I held my breath and gripped the edge of my seat as my precious little Cowley lurched and banged over the turf in Randall's eager but incompetent hands and I was heartily relieved when we arrived at the edge of the woods; it would have taken a much bigger idiot than me to let him steer it between the tree trunks, no matter the pleading.

'Randall,' I said, back in the driving seat, 'do you want to come on an adventure?' He nodded faintly, expecting a trick to cure him of his sulks, I think. 'And can you keep a secret?' He nodded with a little more enthusiasm. 'I mean it. You have to keep it secret from all the grown-ups and especially from your brothers and sisters. Can you promise?'

He was enchanted by the prospect, so I finalized the deal.

'Cross your heart and hope to die?' I said.

'An' devil find me where I lie.'

We spat and shook.

'Right then,' I said. 'Whereabouts are these holes?'

*   *   *

I drove under Randall's direction for a minute or so, through the woods and towards the riverbank, until he told me to stop.

'Ye cannae get any nearer in the car, missus, but I ken the way. Follow me.'

'You're not frightened, are you?' I asked him as we began walking. It was almost completely dark now, and my conscience was thrumming about mixing him up in this.

'Naw,' he said scornfully, and he certainly did not look perturbed, striding out with his head up, holding Bunty's lead proprietorially. 'I'm no' feart of the ghostie.'

'Splendid,' I said, wishing I could say as much for myself. I took a deep breath and put my shoulders back.

'Here,' said Randall, suddenly stopping. Either he had eyes like a cat from all the time he spent in these woods, or he knew the place by scent and sound like a Red Indian tracker, for it seemed pitch black around us now and yet he moved decisively and spoke with absolute conviction. There was a creak of wood and a cold draught which bore upon it the tarry smell of a coal hole.

'Doon here,' said Randall. 'There's a ladder, but it's fallin' to bits so ye'll need tae be right careful.' Although I could not see him I could hear that his voice was lowering towards my feet. I crouched and groped, finding the shoulder of his jersey before he disappeared completely.

'Stop,' I said. 'Get out. I'm going down on my own.'

'But there's miles of it,' he said. 'You'll nivver find him.'

'Miles of it?' I echoed. 'Miles of what?'

'Tunnels mostly,' he said simply, as though I should have known this. 'And some caves.'

Finally it fell into place: the 'shell' holes, the smell of coal, the little cart and the tiny pony, and Cad's description of the failed business ventures on his uncle's estate.

'Do you mean mines, Randall? Is that where we are? An old shale mine?'

'Aye,' said Randall, patiently. 'I telt you. It's supposed to be all blocked up but there's holes everywhere where it's collapsin'.'

I took a huge breath and let it out in a tune of little puffs.

'And there's miles of it?'

'Ye'll have to take me,' he said. 'Or ye'll get lost.' I think I must have relaxed my grip on him while I tussled with this because suddenly he ducked away from me and I heard his feet pattering lightly down the rungs of a ladder.

'Stop at the bottom and wait,' I ordered, fear making me harsh. I felt around for the edge of the hole and, finding it, began to search for the top of the ladder with a foot. It felt rather soft.

'Bunty, I can't carry you, darling,' I said. 'So you must decide for yourself whether you feel like jumping.'

The ladder was on its last legs and I slipped a couple of times at the start of my descent as the rungs gave way under my feet. Bunty was whining at the sound of me moving away from her and, as I looked up to speak some reassurance, I suddenly shot all the way down, scraping my chin against the rocky side of the shaft as the ladder disintegrated. There was a thump as I landed and I swore viciously, making Randall giggle.

Once I had righted myself he took my hand, squeezing it as though *he* were exhorting *me* to be brave, and we set off feeling the dank walls on either side of us as close as breath and the weight of the earth above us

351

lowering down. When we had gone no more than a yard, there was a slithering and yelping behind us, then the click of Bunty's toenails on the stone floor.

'Oh, good girl,' I said. 'She'll take care of both of us. Walk on, Bunty.'

'I dinnae need tooken care of,' said Randall, but his voice had a little lift as he grabbed Bunty's lead again and I thought I could hear a slightly more determined note as his feet struck along behind her.

It seemed hours that we tramped along like that, our feet ringing on stone or crunching in slivers of shale, our heads being dripped on from above and always with the fetid, filthy-smelling damp all around us. Once or twice a heap of earth and shale in our path cut us off and we had to retrace our steps and strike out in a different direction.

'It's like a maze,' I whispered.

'Aye,' Randall whispered back. 'They had tae make wee tunnels and leave bits in between so it didnae all jist collapse.'

I wished I had not spoken. Every so often, a faint breath of fresher air would tell us we were passing a ventilation shaft. At least that is what I told myself, preferring not to think that these were unofficial holes caused by subsidence. Randall was still fairly jaunty however, on his home ground, and Bunty seemed to view this new kind of walk with perfect equanimity. I could tell from the sound of her snuffling that she was pacing forward with her nose down. I wished Hugh could see her now.

After a while, although there was nothing new to be heard around us, and certainly nothing to be seen, Randall paused and hissed to me to be quiet. I reached forward and caught Bunty's muzzle in my hand, guiding her head and holding her face against my leg to keep her quiet too. Then I heard it. Breathing, and the slap of bare feet on the dank stone as someone not far from where we stood moved away. If this was a ghostie, it was a much more fleshly ghostie than any I had ever imagined.

'Stay here!' I said to Randall, holding him hard by both arms and shaking him in time with each word. 'No more nonsense. Do you promise?' Randall, ten years old again, the intrepid sherpa quite driven off by the sound of fear in my voice, trembled and nodded.

'I'll stand guard and keep an eye on Bunty,' he said, which was much better psychology, of course.

'Excellent,' I told him. 'Now point me in the right direction.' Randall stretched out his arm and I felt along it then, with some difficulty, I let go of him and walked away. It was a narrow passageway and I bumped against the walls a couple of times as it twisted around corners. It was lower too than the main corridor where I had left the boy and soon I was walking slightly hunched and wondering also if I was only imagining the downward slope under my feet. I could hear Randall murmuring words of encouragement to Bunty and could just about hear, if I strained, the sweep of her tail forward and back across the floor. It was while I was straining to hear that comforting sound that I became aware of the breathing again. I stopped, fumbled in my pocket and struck a match.

When it flared I caught sight of a face, deathly pale, or rather half a face above a beard, before a bare arm rose to shield its eyes from the light.

'Put it out,' said a cracked and muffled voice. I shook the match and pinched it carefully with wetted fingers before dropping it. 'Who are you?' said the voice. 'What do you want?'

'Billy?' I said. 'How long have you been down here?'

'You tell me,' said Billy Brown, in a lost voice. 'What date is it? You tell me.' He was shaking, but whether from fear or cold I could not say. I walked towards his voice with a hand outstretched but when I touched his flesh he flinched away.

'I'm sorry,' I said. 'I've only just worked it out, or I would have come sooner.'

I crouched down before him. 'Your father's been hiding you? Keeping you safe here?'

Billy gave a short sound that could have been a laugh.

'Safe?' he said. 'He's been keepin' me prisoner. But then, I'm a deserter, you know, so I deserve nothin' else.'

'But if he wanted to punish you –' I began.

'Why didn't he turn me in?' said Billy. 'Easy. Because if he'd turned me in everyone would ken and he'd nivver hold his head up again. This way I get what I deserve and none of it washes off on him.' I could tell that this was a litany he had rehearsed to himself many times down here in the dark.

'But why didn't you just run away?' I said.

Again he croaked a laugh and then I heard a dull knocking sound.

'What was that?' I asked.

'For a start, I'm naked,' said Billy. 'He took my clothes away. And then there's this.' Again there came the same dull sound.

'What is it?' I said, but I could guess. Only it was such a horrid, such a ludicrous, idea I could hardly believe it.

'It's a ball and chain,' said Billy. 'A good one too. A while back I tried tae smash it open and ended up smashin' my ankle instead. So now, even if I got the thing off me . . .' He had the offhand way of talking that one puts down to bravery, the just-a-broken-arm-old-chap air that I was used to hearing from officers in the rest home where I volunteered but which I never expected to find in a deserter, and this tone as much anything else was making the scene as unreal as a pantomime.

'Where on earth did your father get a ball and chain?'

Billy laughed. 'Ye'd be amazed what ye can find lying around,' he said. 'It was likely out of the old castle.'

'The *old* castle?' I said. I knew he must mean Cassilis and if Shinie Brown had raided the dungeons before Cad and Buttercup had arrived on the scene . . .

'Billy,' I said again. 'How long have you *been* here? It's August now. 1923. How long has it been?'

'August '23?' said Billy. 'Really? I was tryin' to keep track but it's hard, you know, in the dark. It was winter when he put me down.' I waited. I could not begin to imagine the journey he must have made, from France five years ago to here and I could not demand that he tell me, so I waited.

'The worst bit of all,' he said, 'is bein' on ma own. I wis nivver supposed to be all on ma own. Ma pal and me had a plan. I should say, ma pal and me had a new plan, after the old plan didnae work. An' that was after the *first* plan didnae work. At first, we were goin' south. Bobby said that would keep us safe. Everybody was on the watch for deserters headed north, so we went the other way. We were goin' to Spain, to Morocco, to live in the sunshine.' This time the laughter went on so long, ragged croak after ragged croak, that I feared he would never stop. 'Live in the sunshine,' he said at last. 'An' look where I ended up.'

'So what went wrong?' I prompted.

'I dinnae ken where tae start tae tell ye,' he said. 'I suppose, underneath it all we jist got so tired. We jist got so damn tired, strugglin' all the time for the next meal, the next couple o' days' work, a safe place to sleep. In the end, Bobby had had enough o' it and he said, "Come on, Billy. Do or die, pal, eh? Go for broke. Do or die."

'We would come back here and get Bobby's mammy and daddy tae set us up wi' papers and gie us enough money so's we could get right away oot o' it for good. America, Australia, New Zealand even and wi' papers, so that we would never look over wur shoulders again. So we struck oot. We kent we'd nivver keep together a' the way and the plan was that if Bobby got back first he'd go straight to his mammy, if I got back first I'd keep masel' goin' somehow, hide away in the woods and wait for him. We kent his mammy and daddy might no' feel the same way if it was jist me as if it was me and him together.'

'And your own father?'

'Aye,' said Billy. 'I telt myself over and over again that I kent my ain father too well to chance it. Bobby made me promise I'd nivver go near him. Bobby kent it would be the end o' it for both o' us if *my* father found oot. But when I got here and I'd been up there in the woods, in the winter, livin' on God knows what, scrapin' oot folks' bins at night, I just couldnae believe that he widnae . . . his ain son. I couldnae believe he widnae . . . So, at four o'clock one mornin' I walked doon the railway line a' the way doon intae the Ferry and chapped on his door. And – to cut a long story short for ye – here I am.

'God knows whit happened tae Bobby. If he made it, he'd ken I'd been here – I left the signal for him. So

356

he'd search for me, I'm sure, and he'd wait, but he widnae wait for ever. If he even made it.'

'He did,' I said. 'He made it, but – I'm sorry – you've missed him, he's gone.'

There was a long silence after I had spoken and I could almost smell, almost taste the defeat in him. Then he caught his breath.

'Whit d'you mean, I've missed him?' he said. 'I'm stuck doon here. He might well have been and gone but what do you mean to say I've *missed* him?' The hope in his voice was heartbreaking to hear and it occurred to me that what his voice had had before, what it had shared with all those shell-shocked officers in the nursing home, was not bravery after all, but resignation and defeat. Now that he thought he could sniff a chance, his voice strained with hope.

'It's over,' I told him. 'Your father has been arrested. He found out about Bobby and he killed Robert Dudgeon. Murdered him.'

'Aye,' said Billy. 'That sounds like my father. But what about you? Who are you? How did you find me?'

'I followed your father,' I said. 'When he knew the game was up he came straight to you.'

'I'm sure he did,' Billy said. 'To finish me off so's nobody ever found out.'

'No,' I said, suddenly remembering Shinie Brown struggling out of his shirt as he raced along. 'He was coming to set you free. He was going to give you clothes. He must have been going to unlock you. And when he realized that he was being followed he drew us away from you even though it meant giving himself up.'

'And what about you?' said Billy again. 'What are *you* goin' to do?' Without giving me time to answer he went on. 'I'll tell you one thing, missus, whoever you are. If you turn me in and they put me against the wall and shoot me I'll still be glad I ran away. At least it'll be quick and I'll ken for sure this time it's over. Just like when Billy and me turned north and headed fur home; we didnae care by then. You jist get so damn tired.' He did not speak defiantly, nor belligerently, but only as though he wanted to explain something I should never otherwise know. In this, of course, he was right. I never should. The closest I could ever get, if anything of the like happened again, was where Chrissie Dudgeon was, where Willie Brown was. I took a moment to examine my conscience, but it took no more than a moment and there was no doubt.

'Stay here tonight,' I said. 'I'll come back tomorrow to the hole with the broken ladder, with clothes and money, and an axe for your chain, but then you are on your own. I can't help you any more after that.'

'What will I do?' he said.

'I don't know,' I said. 'It's not my affair. I won't help you any more than that.'

'But I'm all on my own,' he said. 'I wis nivver supposed to be all on my own.'

I could feel the tears begin to gather in a spiky lump in the back of my throat. It was as plain as could be that Bobby Dudgeon was the leader and I did not give much for the chances of this boy all alone with no one to make the plans.

'I'll tell Joey,' I said at last.

Billy snorted. 'She'd turn me in quicker than you can blink,' he said. 'She's married to a soldier, a hero.'

'Did your father tell you that?' I said. 'It's not true. Of course, you must decide for yourself whether to believe the man who kept you prisoner or the woman who's setting you free, but I say go to Joey. Get as far away as you can. And take her with you.'

Billy lit a match to show me the start of my way and, knowing he was naked, I could not turn to bid him farewell and so I left without another look or word and began to feel my way back to where I had left Randall, in the dark. He had sunk down on to the stone floor of the passage and had fallen asleep; he woke with a gasp as Bunty barked at my footsteps.

'I telt ye he widnae hurt ye,' he said as I reached him.

'Come on,' I said. 'Time you were home.'

The hole we had come down was hopeless obviously, but Randall knew another escape route: a huge pile of earth, up which we crawled on our tummies, feeling it slide away beneath us, until it brought us within feet of a ragged hole amongst tree roots, a nice size for Randall and Bunty to pop through like rabbits and just big enough for me to squeeze through with much grunting and effort and leaving behind me of buttons and trim.

'God, no wonder you're all so filthy all the time,' I said, spitting out crumbs of dirt and trying to shake the worst off my hair and what was left of my dress. 'Now let's get you back to your mother.'

Inspector Cruickshank's motor car was still parked at the Dudgeons' gate when we drew up there minutes later. Randall jumped down and raced up his own path, turning back to face me halfway and drawing a cross over his heart. Then he opened the door and slipped inside to face, I expect, a scolding from his mother for being just slightly dirtier than usual. I, just slightly dirtier than him, was already dreading the scolding to come from Grant. I sat for a minute, wondering what was going on between Mrs Dudgeon and the inspector, hoping that the widow could get her story straight, or that the inspector might regale her with my version of Brown's motive and that she might only have to keep quiet and nod.

I was just about to restart the engine and leave, when

the passenger door opened. Bunty, asleep on the back seat, did not even stir.

'Alec?' I asked, as he climbed in. 'Have you been waiting here or did you . . . follow me?'

'I came here to meet up with you,' he said. 'I didn't work it out in time to follow you, unfortunately.'

I said nothing.

'Did you find him?' he asked at last.

'Yes,' I said. 'Naked, in chains, half-starved. I found him.'

Again we sat in silence, but this time it was me who broke it, just as Mrs Dudgeon's door opened.

'Here comes the inspector,' I said. 'So if you have anything you want to say to him, now's your chance.' Mrs Dudgeon, seeing me, waved sadly before she shut the door.

'No,' said Alec. 'But there is something I want to say to *you*. I have a few old clothes with me that I don't really need any more. If I were to look them out . . .' I could not speak; if I stopped biting down on my teeth I should sob.

'I'll get them in the morning,' I said at last. The inspector was walking towards us and I hoped the darkness would cover the worst of my dishevelment. 'I need to pop into the village to the bank,' I said, 'and then I thought I'd ask Mrs Murdoch for a picnic basket and come for a picnic in the woods.' Inspector Cruickshank drew up beside us.

'You're not too scared to be in these woods now?' he said, hearing me.

'Not at all,' I replied. 'In fact, I think I'd like to be alone tomorrow, Alec, if that's all right with you.'

'I think so too,' Alec said.

'What can I do for you?' said the inspector. 'You were waiting for me, I see.'

I was momentarily stumped, but Alec came to the rescue.

'Thinking things over, Inspector,' he said, 'it occurred to us that you can close another case you've got open on your books. A double murder, four or so years back?'

The inspector scratched his head for a moment and then whistled, impressed.

'By George, I think you're right,' he said. 'It was exactly the same. I'll get right on it, sir. First thing tomorrow.' He reached across me to shake Alec's hand and then took mine too. 'See and enjoy your picnic, madam. Or is it more than a picnic?' he went on, twinkling. Solving three murders in one night had put him in a tremendous good humour, it seemed. 'Are you bringing an offering to all these spirits and demons and beasties we hear so much about? Don't let the Turnbulls catch you at it.'

'No, not an offering,' I said. 'Just a picnic lunch. After all, it's the living we need to take care of, isn't it Alec, not the dead.'

Facts and Fictions

Most of the places here are real places, although Brown's Bar is fictitious, as is Cassilis Castle, which can be understood to lie somewhere between Scotstoun and Carlowrie. There was a short-lived shale mining enterprise on the spot where I imagine Dandy and Randall had their adventure, as well as the larger and longer-lasting Dalmeny Shale Oil Works, the entrance to which lay just behind the station.

Most of the minor characters in the book – the Turnbulls, the Lamonts, Father Cormack, The Rev. Dowd, The Rev. McAndrew, Inspector Cruickshank, Dr Rennick, Provost and Mrs Meiklejohn, and Pat Rearden – are entirely fictitious, as are all the principals: the de Cassilis family, the Dudgeons, and obviously the Browns. Folk like that could never belong in the Ferry.

Some of the others are real. The three families of Linlithgows, Roseberys and Stuart-Clarks did and still do live in three estates around Queensferry; I have stolen some land from the Dundas and Dalmeny estates to make way for Cadwallader's acres. Also, in 1923, Mr Faichen was the undertaker, Mr Fairlie was the grocer, Mr Mawdsley was the harbour master, and there were Quigleys, Marshalls, Christies and McPhersons in Queensferry as there are today. It should be noted too that Dandy was right about wee

Doreen Urquhart: she did grow up to be a beauty and she had a huge personality inside that tiny frame.

As far as I know, there never was a feud, a squabble, even a murmur, over the Burry Man or any other aspect of the Ferry Fair. Also, although Queensferry does have its fair share of ghostie stories and pubs, it is not *quite* as steeped in horrors as I have suggested here.

Finally, the Burry Man can still be seen walking the town on the second Friday in August. Hip, hip, hooray.

Acknowledgements

For invaluable help with historical detail I would like to thank: Jimmie Boner, Ranald Mackay, Sheena Mackay, Lyla Martin, Len Saunders, Jimmy Walker and the other members of the Queensferry History Group; Robin Chesters and Carol McDonald of the Almond Valley Heritage Centre; Nancy Balfour, Jim Hogg, Ann Morrison and the rest of the staff at the Edinburgh Room of the City Library; Jeff Balfour at Kirkliston Library; and Jim McPherson for patient recall of details of the old Ferry. Thanks too to Nancy Johnson for her Queensferry memories.

I would like to thank Lisa Moylett and Nathalie Sfakianos at the agency for wrapping up such professionalism in so much warmth and wit. I am greatly indebted to The Trinity: editor Krystyna Green, copy editor Imogen Olsen, and jacket designer Ken Leeder who remove howlers and add elegance. Thanks too to all the Constable staff, especially Bruce Connal and Haydn Jones.

Thanks again to Cathy Gilligan, ideal first reader.

I am grateful, as ever, to my parents Jim and Jean McPherson, and the rest of my family (here goes), Amy, Audrey, Callum, Claire, Fraser, Greig, Harris, Iain, Lewis, Mathew, Megan, Ross, Sheila, Tom and Wendy for many different kinds of enthusiasm from detailed critique to drooling on my shoulder.

Finally, to Neil McRoberts for financial backing, website management, editorial advice, advanced listening and ballroom dancing – endless thanks.

DATE DUE

MAY - 8 2015			
APR 0 ~ 2016			
			PRINTED IN U.S.A.